†HREADS

OF

Saint

AND

SEVER

A Novel

by

Zamantha Roberts

Threads of Saint and Sever

Contact Info: www.allhailasphodel.com
Cover Art: Rex Roberts
Editor: Caroline Knecht

ISBN: 979-8-9985698-0-7 (Paperback), 979-8-9985698-1-4 (Hardback), 979-8-9985698-2-1 (eBook)

Second Edition: February 2026
10 9 8 7 6 5 4 3 2

FIC027440 FICTION / Romance / Paranormal / Witches

To a warm, witty, and worthy partner. Allowing me the space and time to smooth away the rough edges that trauma leaves behind and the support to turn it into something beautiful.

It is often the ties meant to cradle us during those tender years that bind us to supposed truths. Knowledge can sever the threads, but they will always leave a scar.

PROLOGUE

Frost-soaked soil clung to her fingertips. The icy bite of winter nipped at her shivering flesh, and the billowing precipitation from her labored breaths was the only sign of life this morning. The sun was just cracking the darkness apart, and nightfall had yet to surrender to the warmth of the day ahead.

Like every morning, Selma wore her heavy pink wool coat and a scarf with baby sheep on it. She struggled with the harsh fibers as they poked at the sensitive skin around her neck. Her fingers were cracked and dry with nothing to protect them from the arid winter air. But she needed to be able to access them. To touch the soil. It would not work otherwise.

"Remember what we talked about," came a low, comforting voice near to where Selma knelt on the hard, frostbitten ground. "They will not hurt you if you respect their power. Once you feel it."

"I know," Selma snapped.

This morning was just like every other. Her tall, domineering father had forced her out of the comfort of her quilts and dragged her to the outskirts of the island to practice before school. She had heard all the lessons before. She knew them by heart. And still, her magic would not cooperate with her. Perspiration gathered on her brow as her threads fruitlessly drudged through the earth.

"You are holding on too tight, Selma. The energy will not trust you if you do not trust it back," he said.

Selma slumped in defeat. Her thin magic retreated once again into her trembling fingers. She could not look up at her father. His disappointment was too much to bear this morning. Instead, she focused on the earth, waiting for him to give in and finally take her home. A warm hand grabbed hers and lowered it to the ground. They were tattered and scarred, as if they were no stranger to a battlefield even though Selma had not so much as seen her father carve into the flesh of a cooked bird at dinner. His large palms cradled her fingers, and she watched as his iridescent red threads glided down his fingers and burrowed into the soil. Selma could feel a slight tingle from the power as it swept up the threads that now made an intricate web searching for energy. They pulsed as they came alive, converting energy into magic. Her timid violet threads intertwined with her father's magic, creating a web of color that reminded Selma of the candied rope she could buy at the beach sometimes.

"They are beautiful," Selma said, wide-eyed. The shining threads did not reflect in her eyes. She knew that she was the only one who could see them, but she never quite understood why. Her magic threads seem different than what was described to her.

Selma thought back to the stories her mother and aunts had shared with her, about shriveled witches with the mark of death

2

feeding on the souls of life forces to gain power. Images of tentacles of energy threads strangling small children and draining them of their magic carved onto the pages of books her mother read to her before bed. Those stories haunted her sleep.

"I don't want to be like them," Selma whimpered into her jacket collar, careful not to speak too loudly lest the witches hear her and come for her next. "What if the witches come and give me the mark of death or suck my soul out?"

Her father stood and stared at her as if he were looking for something or someone. For a moment, his eyes held sadness. But he shrugged it off and held out his hands as if he were carrying an invisible bowl. Then he poured the impalpable contents onto the forest floor. A beautiful garden of flowers rose from the dirt, splitting the frozen ground with fresh blooms. Jasmine vine sprouted and weaved around the trunk of a tree, letting its fragrance spill into the air.

"Trust your threads. They are a part of you and your magic. You have nothing to fear," her father assured her. "Only someone who is weak will tell you otherwise."

Selma's father plucked one bloom from the vine and placed it in her hair.

"But even the weakest among us can be dangerous. Your magic will not hide forever, Dove. It is in your blood," he said, and he turned to walk back toward their home. His dark frame walked away, silhouetted by the morning's first sun, and the blooms at his feet withered. Her father disappeared with them.

"Any magical beings that speak of or worship the false goddess will be punished."

—An excerpt from Edicts of The Order, property of the Master

CHAPTER
I

One foot stumbled out onto the scorched pavement, the thick rubber soles of her boots propping open a heavy metal door. Selma balanced the inky black plastic sack full of remnants of the day's workshops. Half-eaten sweet treats, disposable champagne flutes, phallic-shaped party decor in various shades of metallics and pinks. Heat radiated from the asphalt and left a haze in its wake. Only moments outside, and the strands of dark hair framing her face stuck to her skin. The malleable black material of the bag threatened to give way at any moment, and her knees shuddered under the weight of it.

The alley behind the shop, like most alleys, left little to be desired. It was a stain, hidden away from the main street, a trove of the lost or forgotten. She could not help but think that she belonged back here more than she belonged out there. Tucked away from view, while the city out front beat on to the sound of distant horns from a street band. Although it did offer her a reprieve from entertaining a group of intoxicated travelers during an instructor-led workshop that her boss had affectionately named "Witch Bitch," she felt too alone in the alley. Selma was rarely alone. Not truly. And her skin began to itch against the confinement.

The workshops were a big draw for tourists because of the region's believed magical history. They offered instruction on how to make a smudge stick or a witch's broom. People loved the workshops, and so did Selma's employer, Tandy, because they brought in substantial profits. This was no surprise, considering they were creating flammable trash out of dried tidbits that Tandy pulled from her garden. It was typically two hours of trying to wrangle enthusiastic but bemused attendees, all the while making them believe that they could harness the power of magic through their creation. Of course, Selma knew the profound results of fragrant smudge sticks. She had spent hours of her childhood tying sweetgrass together to bless the births of babies that neighbors hired her mother and aunts to oversee. However, without witch blood and the ceremonial offering to the Goddess, these smudge sticks were no more than overpriced incense.

Selma swung the cumbersome sack into the dumpster and immediately felt the cold embrace of solitude. As if the silence were lying in wait to take her prisoner.

The darkness, the darkness, it's here, in me, leave me alone, a crackled voice slipped into her mind.

A wave of unexpected relief washed over her, and Selma fluttered at the intrusion. It was not the first time an uninvited guest had gripped her mindful senses, but it was jarring when she did not see them coming.

Looking around for the host, she spotted a woman rummaging through another dumpster a few shops down.

"Stop it! Go away! I did not invite you for tea today," the woman bellowed as she swatted her hand at the invisible intruder.

Selma found herself privy to the inner emotions and thoughts of this peculiar interaction, but it had chased away the unnerving loneliness, and for that she was grateful. However, invading people's privacy felt dirty. Like stealing a piece of them. Their private thoughts.

"Damn," Selma cursed. She had never fully mastered how to keep from hearing other people's thoughts, and she had skipped her morning wellness routine, which usually helped her keep such interludes at bay. Selma fidgeted with the onyx-colored pendant around her neck. It was not humming on her skin. The bauble had been given to her as a child and was supposed to warn her of danger. Occasionally she would feel it hum, but she was never sure if it was her quickened pulse or the warded pendant that shook, tickling her skin. Either way, it was a comfort, and as she held the inactive charm in her slick palm, she knew that the woman was harmless. Still, breaching the woman's senses was exhausting.

"Be present and breathe," Selma recited, letting out a long-controlled breath.

Her therapist, an eternal optimist from Portland, had suggested a "grounding" exercise that he insisted would settle her emotions long enough to let her take in the world around her in a calm and controlled manner. Unfortunately, she could not share the true origin of her anxiety. But his technique did help her wrangle her gifts, or what Selma might argue were the annoyances of her circumstances.

Since starting her wellness journey, she had racked up a hefty therapy bill, a propensity to compartmentalize, anxiety, codependency, and surely an ADHD diagnosis. Selma was still waiting for the last one, but her rich history of jumping from task to task without following any to fruition made her think that it was basically on lock.

According to her therapist, her challenges may have been due to her "unconventional upbringing." If only he knew just how unconventional it was. But she had decided that even in therapy, some things are better left unsaid. Selma had not been entirely forthcoming with him, which she was sure would be frowned upon.

Selma stopped fiddling with the small obsidian gem and slammed down the wall in her mind that allowed her to keep the uninvited guests away. Her shoulders relaxed. Her thoughts were lighter and washed clean of trespassers. Walking back into the shop, she was happy to hear only the rumblings of the woman's outer monologue. To cleanse the space, a bell chimed overhead as the door opened and closed, yet still Selma sensed the thick crackle of energy in the room. The bitter smell cutting through the incense.

Magic.

She had never come across any genuine witches at the shop. Anyone with magic in their blood would know full well that the cauldrons and knickknacks sold there were merely trinkets to appease the occasional goth or witch-curious tourist. Selma did appreciate the animated clientele that frequented the store, who were keen to talk about their goddess groups or pagan celebrations. She recognized a piece of herself in them. Fervently wanting to be part of something bigger than themselves and never quite getting the results they hoped for.

But this was not that.

She looked around the busy shelves bursting with spell books, charms, and crystals, all constricting her view enough that she could not see anyone. The group she had been working with had gone on their way, and the street outside was calm. What could she be sensing? Her pendant began to pulse in time with her heartbeat. She froze.

Selma hadn't had much experience with the magically gifted outside of her mother and aunts, and the thought of coming face to face with another witch was exhilarating. Even if her pendant was forewarning her. Selma often wondered how her mother could possess power and not want to create a community of those who shared her gifts, but she supposed that her own propensity to fumble her power was a stain on the family name. No need to splash that news around.

The front bell chimed again, and Selma's breath caught, her nerves flashing with a momentary pang of pain. A woman carrying multiple shopping bags entered, and as quickly as the eerie feeling came, it was gone. The bitter scent was leached from the air, replaced with rosemary from the black and white candles burning next to the entrance, and Selma's charm grew subdued once more. She gathered herself as much as she could, knowing she was likely on edge after the workshop. She took a long, calming breath, letting her lungs enjoy a satisfying stretch.

Then she turned her attention to the new customers and cleared her throat. "Hello, can I help you find anything?" Her voice came out fractured.

The woman was wearing a theme park T-shirt and jeans with tan ankle boots. The man who accompanied her was tall and well-manicured. He was good-looking in a "maybe he used to model for some overpriced, overexposed clothing line" way. His silver hair gave the impression that there was a slight breeze, and his fingernails were perfectly groomed. Selma would not have been surprised if he had a standing manicure appointment. She gazed down at her crackled cuticles and made a quick mental note to get her nails done as soon as she could afford it.

"I should hope so," the woman drawled with the inflection of a southern belle. She wore a smile that was more armor than friendly gesture. "God knows I don't want to have to find another place like this." Her lips formed a tight line as her eyes roamed the shelves. "My stepdaughter is one of those 'alternative' kids." She lifted her fingers to make air quotes. Her pile of shopping bags shuffled in the process. "You know. Goth," she whispered, leaning toward Selma.

"Sure," Selma responded curtly. "And what can I help you find?"

"Well, my husband insists that we bring her something back, and my cousin said that y'all sell stuff for those types of people. Ah, but I do not want any devil worship nonsense or anything like that," she flapped.

The man stayed quiet, picking up a smudge stick next to him to smell. Selma hated the way magic was portrayed sometimes. It did not even work the way most people imagined it did. Magic was about energy and manipulating elements. She was not sure how the devil got wrapped into the whole concept, but the Goddesses were never mentioned.

While Selma had not met many other witches, she knew that witches born without threads were Common. So much so that they had a name. The Commons were witches with a drop of witch blood somewhere in their family line; they could not access magic through threads but could perform minor ceremonial spells, such as simple healings or hexes. Selma herself was not Common, but her mother had used the term to describe her many times, as she'd been born with pure witch blood but could never harness her threads.

Selma considered sending this couple home with a curse candle. Just in case the stepdaughter in question had witch blood and could tie her dear stepmother's stomach into knots for days. The couple seemed like the type of people who did not make you sad when you heard they had suffered a bout of food poisoning on their latest vacation.

The door chimed again. This time, a tall figure stepped past the threshold, his frame swallowing the light that attempted to sneak in from the outside. His features were striking, and Selma could not muster her regular greeting as his crystal eyes bored into her, scanning her figure for longer than she was comfortable with.

The woman waved her hands in front of Selma's face, snapping her fingers. "Hello! I don't want to be here all day."

Selma's cheeks flushed with heat. She did not know how long she had been staring at the stranger, but it was clearly longer than was appropriate. She cleared her throat.

"Um, yes, of course. Our anti-devil-worship crystals are over to the left. They will be easy to carry back home for your stepdaughter. But our devil-worship crystals are half off today, in case you reconsider," Selma added, plastering a tight smile onto her face and ushering the couple to the side wall where the glittering stones were displayed.

Her attention was then pulled back to the stranger. He was right where she had left him moments before, his eyes still glued to her. She managed, "Welcome, can I help you find something?"

His relaxed black T-shirt was pulled across his broad chest and rested just above the low-slung waistband of his jeans. He must have ridden here on a motorcycle, because his heavy leather boots would have been much too hot for casual wear on this muggy summer day. Tattoos swirled down both arms and up his neck, but she quickly looked away, not wanting to spend too much time taking them in and embarrassing herself.

"I'm just looking around." A gritty voice dripped from his lips.

His face was steely, and it gave Selma an uneasy feeling in the pit of her stomach. But her pendant was still at rest, showing no signs of danger.

"I'll take this one, I guess," said the woman, once again sliding in between the dark stranger and the counter. She placed a small, cerulean blue stone on the wooden counter.

Selma took one gulp of air and swallowed, picking up the small stone and examining it. "Ah, angelite. It can calm anxiety and stress."

It figured that these two would find the only stone that was believed to facilitate communication with the angelic realm. As if all the objects in the shop sensed the couple's repulsion and insisted on keeping them away from the craft. Selma wondered if angels were as arrogant and vain as her aunties proclaimed.

The woman gave Selma a satisfied smile, as if relieved to have found something that would not damn her to the gates of Hell. "You do not need to wrap it up. I will just throw it in my purse," she said, snatching the stone from Selma's grip.

As Selma turned to ring up the purchase, the tall, brooding man spoke up from behind them. His hands examined a terrarium of fox bones and dried florals.

"Angelite is also known to assist in speaking your truth," he murmured.

Annoyed, the woman glanced down at the blue stone and scoffed. "The truth is I wish this brat didn't exist and we didn't have to waste time rummaging through this rat hole to find her a stupid gift. I can't stand the little bitch." Her eyes went wide, and she slapped the palm of her hand to her mouth as if she had just registered the words. The father's jaw dropped.

"I...I didn't mean that," the woman stammered as the girl's father turned and stormed out of the store. The woman followed close behind, dropping the blue stone on the ground. At least he showed some resolve in the end.

Selma's brow furrowed as she glanced down at the stone. It now lay abandoned on the shop floor. It had to have been a coincidence, or had Selma awakened the stone's energy by mistake? No, she had never shown enough power to do that. Not without help. A large, callused hand gripped the smooth surface of the stone, plucked it from the ground, and placed it in front of Selma.

"The truth isn't always angelic, is it?" asked the dark stranger.

The air between them was tense. Selma's lips parted. She wanted to say something, but she was cut off by Tandy yelling out from the back.

"Selma, where did we put the extra feathers? We have a group from Florida coming in later, and they love feathers."

Selma turned to answer her. "They are in the basement. I'll grab them for you." But when she turned back around, the stranger was gone, and although she knew she should be relieved, her pendant hummed to life.

CHAPTER 2

"**H**ello, gorgeous," an inviting voice called from the front of the shop.

Selma must have been distracted counting candles. She had not noticed him come in. Hayden, her boyfriend for almost a year, was casually sauntering toward her carrying two iced coffees. His sandy blond hair was combed back, and his crisp, buttoned-up shirt was neatly tucked into a pair of well-fitted trousers. The only indication that he was relaxed was the unbuttoned collar. Hayden never left the house looking disheveled, even when he knew he would be on an airplane for hours. He was always prepared in case an opportunity to network presented itself. Selma admired how intentional Hayden always was. It was a stark contrast to her chaos.

"Oh! You are here. Why are you here? Not that I am complaining, but you were going to be in Houston for another week," said Selma.

His lips curled up. Hayden's sweeping smile was always the first thing people noticed about him. It was endearing.

"Nope. Some people stayed behind, but the city approved the plans, and I pay people to stick around and kiss ass. My best girl was back home. So, I jumped on the first plane I could and came straight here. I mentioned it in that email I sent you last week," he said.

Hayden did not grow up here in Crescent City, but he was great at adapting. He blended in flawlessly with the crowd and made friends easily. Not like Selma. People intuitively knew that she was not from around here. Oftentimes, they were as confused as Selma as to how she and Hayden had found themselves dating one another.

"Are you almost done? I will take you to lunch," he suggested, handing her one of the creamy caffeinated beverages.

She thanked him but hesitated. "Not exactly. I have another four hours left on my shift. The candles are not going to stack themselves," said Selma.

"Take off early," Hayden ordered. "Come on, I missed you."

It was flattering that someone wanted to spend time with her. In fact, the feeling was new, considering she had not spent much time with anyone growing up, let alone dating. But she hated being put on the spot. And Hayden, oozing with confidence, did not empathize with her doubt as she sat there wavering.

"What is the worst that could happen? They fire you," said Hayden, leaning in and grabbing her by the waist. His last words were more of a statement than a question.

"Yeah. Tandy fires me and I end up selling stems of roses on the corner." Selma scoffed, knowing full well how close to true that would be if she lost this job.

"If you moved in with me, you wouldn't have to worry about that," said Hayden. "In fact, I think you should take next week off and go away with me." There was that smile again. Selma could not help but think that he offered that same calculated smile to his clients. But it was mesmerizing nonetheless.

"An entire week? I cannot pull that off on short notice. Tandy would never let me, plus I cannot afford to go anywhere right now," Selma protested, even though she knew that Hayden would likely jet them off to someplace fabulous and she would love the time away.

"My treat," Hayden quickly added. "We'll call it your birthday present. Just you and I on a beach with cocktails. All you need to pack is a bikini and your passport."

There he went, putting her on the spot again. And her birthday was not for a couple of weeks. She lowered her lashes, trying to hide away her discomfort. Hayden smiled at her and pulled her closer.

She smiled back at him. He was not going to let this go. Once he got something in his head, there was no fighting it. Rather than going back and forth on a ceaseless path, she submitted to his request. Besides, she had already earned her tips for the day, and she could persuade Tandy to let her go.

"Give me a couple of minutes, and I'll meet you outside," said Selma. "We can start with lunch and go from there. And I think I'll need more than a bikini and a passport."

"Not if I have my way." Hayden winked and leaned in to give her a kiss on the cheek before he turned to leave. His eyes were already glued to his phone, no doubt booking whatever plans he had for the two of them.

She reached for her bag behind the counter and fumbled around inside for a small vial of oil and a knife. She wiggled the vial in front of her, and the contents of vetiver, clove, calamus, licorice, and tobacco, along with some other choice ingredients, gently swam around. She unscrewed the top and emptied a small amount onto the brass plate behind the counter. Careful to look around and make sure she was alone, Selma turned her palm upside down and gently blew on it, prompting a small flame to light.

As it hovered above her skin, she quietly recited her offering to the Goddess. "*Matri deae gratiam praebeo. Sit tua virtus influunt per me.*"

With that, she pricked her finger with the tip of her knife and let a drop of crimson blood drip into the plate of oil and herbs, staining the liquid. She then tipped her palm, and the small flare fell into the plate of oil and blood, igniting in a flash of black flame. As quickly as it blazed, the flame died, leaving an unassuming oil concoction in its wake. Selma picked up the plate and went back to talk to Tandy.

Her employer was on her computer, ordering what was sure to be more kitschy witch knickknacks. She turned to face Selma. "You should really be out front. What if someone comes in?" Her frizzy, dyed-black hair jolted away from her face and tangled with the elaborate Victorian collar that she was wearing tight around her neck.

Selma replied, "I wanted you to try this oil. It was included in the new shipment. Tell me what you think."

Tandy leaned in to take a whiff. "It is fine, I guess. Just put it with the rest."

"It smells better if you rub it on your wrists," said Selma as she offered up the brass plate one more time. Tandy rolled her eyes but obliged. Selma watched as she gently lathered the oil onto her bare skin, and then her pupils dilated.

Now was the time to ask. Selma was careful to craft a question disguised as a statement. "It is dead out there. You can handle the shop by yourself?"

Tandy replied quickly, "Oh, sure. I'll handle it from here."

Satisfied with herself, but trying not to let the guilt eat away at her, Selma turned to leave. It was the most manipulative of her lesser magic, but it did come in handy from time to time. She had never shown promise in the raw magic that her mother and aunts excelled in. In fact, she floundered. But her lesser magic always seemed to be extra potent.

‡

The taco truck was abuzz with the promise of a dazzling Friday afternoon. It was packed with a crowd who were eagerly discussing their weekend plans. Even though Hayden had wanted something more formal, she had insisted that they eat someplace that would be quick and fun. It also had the bonus of being loud, lessening the chance that Hayden would mention moving in together again.

Selma concentrated on blocking out the thoughts of people standing in line. She was so preoccupied with her task, she did not notice that Hayden had already picked up their plates of steaming tacos and chosen a picnic table.

"Selma, babe! Over here," Hayden yelled at her from across the patio. It was uncanny how Hayden could look posh and dignified no matter where he was. Even the weatherbeaten pink-painted picnic table bowed to his poise. It was like he was a robot sometimes. But that is what she liked about him. He was normal. Settled. Perfectly beige.

When she sat down, she barely had time to take one bite of the saucy taco before Hayden jumped in with his questioning. "So, what do you think?"

Hayden had the habit of assuming she was always thinking about the same thing he was. Probably because she could hear his thoughts a lot of the time. But he did not know that. He just assumed that they were perfect for each other and always on the same page. It was probably sweet. She had been concentrating on blocking out everyone's inner monologue, so she had not actually heard his thoughts. But this time, she did not need to invade his musings to know what he was talking about.

To avoid the subject and waste a bit of time, she played dumb, quietly asking, "About what?"

He took a bite of his taco and rolled his eyes at her. "About moving in," Hayden said in short, clipped tones.

"I think I have six months left in my place, and it's too early to be talking about this," Selma said, dismissing the question.

"I could cover the last six months of your lease," Hayden casually threw out, finishing the rest of his taco in one bite and wiping the escaping sauce with a napkin. "You want to live in a nicer place?"

She huffed, but he either did not notice or ignored her irritation. The question flew out of her mouth. "What is wrong with my place? I do not have a roommate, and if you ignore the catcalls from 2F, it is cute. And I just think we should be sure."

Hayden put down his taco and finished chewing while wiping peppery sauce off his freshly shaved chin. His expression had become more serious, and this was exactly what Selma had been trying to avoid.

"I thought you would be making progress with your therapist by now," said Hayden.

"I am. I did my grounding exercises this morning. However, I am not sure how that has anything to do with moving in with you," Selma retorted.

"You're still making this about your dad," Hayden proceeded. "Look, I know he left when you were young, but that does not mean everyone else will leave too."

Her nerves raced. She gleaned the same sensation when she found herself out of control. An anxious reaction that had stifled her confidence since she was a teenager. It felt like someone had walked into her body and turned on all the lights. Nothing seemed to help. It was best to simply wait for it to pass. She must have looked exactly how she felt, because Hayden said her name a bit too loudly, as if he were repeating himself and growing frustrated.

"Selma, do you think you can talk to them about this in your next session? I really think living together could be great," Hayden said. He was squeezing a lime on his next taco.

Selma nodded. It was all she could do.

"Oh, and we have that thing with our friends tonight," said Hayden.

Selma was grateful for the change in subject, but she quickly pivoted to confusion when she could not recall what inane social obligation she had agreed to.

"You really don't read your emails, do you? We are meeting up with our friends for drinks at Tully's." If he was annoyed at Selma's indifference, he did not show it.

"You mean *your* friends, and do we have to go?"

Hayden responded without missing a beat. "Yes. They will never let it go if we bail. And you said you loved Jemma."

"No. I said Jemma minded her own business. That is different," said Selma, stopping to give Hayden a look that meant she was trying to make a point.

"Whatever. You'll love her in no time," responded Hayden.

A low hum moved through her lips. "Maybe. I will think about it. The apartment and the party," said Selma.

This must have been enough to appease Hayden for the time being, because he smiled and nodded. Selma was quiet and continued to chew and stare at her plate. Deep down, she knew that he meant well, and that he was genuinely excited for them to live together. And he had the means to make it happen. The problem was that Selma was not as excited as he was. The thought of binding her life to someone else so fully made her tummy turn, and she instantly regretted taking such a large bite of taco.

Steadying her nerves, she inhaled through her nose in calm, calculated breaths, forcing her nerves and stomach to cooperate. The two finished their lunch and talked about their upcoming trip. Selma nodded back when appropriate, all the while thinking about keeping the contents of her stomach down. When they were done, she gave him a quick kiss goodbye and headed home, promising that she would be ready for drinks by 8:00 p.m. Later, as she got dressed, she knew that that was not their last conversation about moving in. She would not be surprised if, when she went over to his place later that evening, he had already cleared out space in the closet for her.

"The Brocken, the birthplace of our Goddess, is the only true source of magic."

—An excerpt from the Canon, as translated by Emery Kara, property of the Warriors of Sever

CHAPTER 3

The party was fine. She was exhausted from keeping her mental shields intact along with hours of mind-numbing small talk. After strategically trying to avoid future invitations to baby showers or kickball leagues, Selma and Hayden found themselves back at his apartment, entangled in linen sheets.

A slight breeze ran through his east-facing bedroom window, and the white curtains gently danced between the early rays of sunlight, changing from pale yellow and coral to bright ivory. She drank in the hazy light. Hayden wrapped his arm around her waist, pulling her close. One leg had made its way between hers and was pushed up against her backside, heating her core. She could feel his breath, warm on the back of her neck, as his fingers made lazy circles around her stomach. Hayden offered light kisses on her shoulder, and Selma took them greedily. She angled her neck, hoping that his mouth would find its way there. It did, indeed, find the spot she had been hoping it would. Hayden softly kissed the sensitive spot above her collarbone, and she was more than content to sit in his sweet embrace until he lifted his hands from her belly and gripped her chin, turning her head toward him and taking her mouth with his. Claiming what he had wanted all along. He tasted her. Starved for her body. Each flick of his tongue wanting more. Selma comforted in his touch. She took him in fully and effortlessly. Each movement was a beautifully versed song.

When they were finished, they lay side by side, their chests rising and falling in unison, and Selma relaxed. The unripe late summer air had a hint of jasmine in it. She closed her eyes to let her nose feast on the fragrance. It begged her senses to recall a memory, but she could not quite capture it. Although the scent was faint, it felt familiar and warm. The stifled sounds from the street below wafted in through the window bars, and she ruminated on her decisions. Selma watched the curtain ebb and flow in the breeze, giving short glimpses of the sky outside, allowing her thoughts to wander. She loved New Orleans and its blend of the old world with its perfectly simple modern amenities. It was tough to manage every day, but she loved being around the energy. It was a far cry from the small coastal hometown she had left behind. She had not yet made many friends except for the ones she had met through Hayden, but they were nice enough and made for fine happy-hour company.

Then there was Hayden. She certainly cared for him, and they paired nicely. He lit up any room that he walked into, and Selma knew that other women envied her on his arm. His friends had, not so subtly, asked about their intentions, and Selma would smile and wave them off politely. Not because she did not want to marry Hayden, but because she was not sure that anyone was meant for such permanence. Epic love stories were only meant for the pages of the books she pored over in her free time. She had learned early that grand gestures did not exist, and her knight in shining armor was not coming to save her. She equated weddings to fairy tales and reserved her unconditional love for her book husbands.

But she enjoyed the way Hayden looked at her. She knew, without a doubt, that he cared for her. There was no question in his embrace. No ransom for her love. As far as she had seen of relationships, which was not much, this was a good one, and she needed to do what she could to not mess it up. Which probably meant moving in with him.

Selma had relocated to New Orleans the day after her high school graduation, and aside from the occasional terse phone call with her mother, Selma's best friend, Millie Cooper, was her only real connection to her old existence. Millie was spirited and carefree in a way that Selma could not understand but had always envied. Millie seemed to float through her days high on confidence, and in turn found Selma's cynicism hilarious. They would sit in their fortress built of pillows and blankets or branches and rusted siding and talk about moving to the city. They conceived of a life of art and cocktails and interesting people. Those summer afternoons made everything seem possible, and they were a welcome distraction from Selma's conservative and guarded reality.

Their nights were filled with sketching clothing designs and giggling, counting down the days until they would bring their visions to life. Unfortunately, the girls' crayon dresses and glitter shoes stayed two-dimensional, and Millie still lived in Belhaven. She owned a vintage shop one block off Main Street that sold charming dresses and refurbished furniture from decades past. It was not the star-studded boutique they had envisioned, but it was cute, and Millie had built the business herself. She got married right out of high school to a boy they had known since he had cooties, and the two of them were the definition of hometown adorable.

Selma's brush with nostalgia had her gently searching through mental images of Millie, carefully turning over each memory in her mind. She frowned as she recalled that their conversations had been fewer and farther apart in recent years, and suddenly her heart ached for her friend. Just as her melancholy began to get the better of her, a cold tingle ran down her arms and legs. When the phone rang, she knew exactly who was on the other end of the line.

Selma tossed the linens aside and popped out of bed, quickly pulling her arms through Hayden's blue-striped button-down shirt, which covered just enough of her curves to not give the neighbors a show. Her phone had slipped under the black throw pillows on the sofa, dampening the sounds of the rings.

After fumbling awhile, she located the buzzing brick and gently swiped her finger across the screen, placing it to her ear. "Millie, are your ears burning?"

It was not an entirely ridiculous question. Selma knew full well what had prompted the call. Or at least, she thought she did.

There was hesitation from the other end of the phone. Selma repeated her friend's name, thinking there might be a bad connection. "Millie?"

"I'm here. Hey, girl," Millie said with a whimper.

Selma then heard a muffled cough. She asked with concern in her voice, "Are you alright? Are you sick?"

Again there was silence. And then the phone disconnected.

Selma's memories were instantly jolted back to her eighth summer. Back to their beginning.

They had gathered stems of flowers from the garden. One flower to represent each girl. Dahlias for Millie and her full heart, and sturdy stalks of wild strawflowers, which defied the odds of nature, for Selma. The girls hung them upside down, allowing the petals to dry out. Selma then ground the flowers into a fine powder using a mortar and pestle she had borrowed from Aunt Meriem's kitchen. The delicate powder from both flowers mingled and intertwined in a floral potpourri.

When the autumn solstice came around, Selma's mother and aunts were off to the Luminescence Ball. Selma had no idea what the annual witch gathering was for, and she was usually jealous that she was not permitted to attend, envying the beautiful gowns they wore. But not that year. That year, she would perform a spell. After her mother and aunts left for the evening, Selma and Millie left Selma's Victorian home. Toting a bag carrying two photographs, charcoal, a pocketknife, their flower concoction, and a jar of juice, they disappeared into the mossy woods. The two of them knelt in front of their favorite gnarled tree, their knees touching the damp forest earth. The girls' nightgowns reflected the lantern light as they piled sticks into a triangular shape toward the stars. Selma raised her palm and gently blew, as if sending a kiss, and slowly a small flame sparked to life above her flesh.

Millie gasped and looked at Selma with confusion. Selma met her gaze, holding her breath. Millie was the first person she had shared her gift with. And history had shown that people did not react kindly to that which was different. Moments seemed like years as Selma waited for Millie to react. She was prepared for the worst, but soon Millie's lips parted in a smile that grew from ear to ear.

"Wow. How long have you known how to do that?" Millie asked approvingly.

"A while," Selma lied. It actually had not been that long. When her father left, Selma's magic seemed to leave with him, along with a piece of her heart. She could no longer access the magic iridescent threads that he had spent so many hours coaxing out of her. In their absence, her Aunt Verda had taken to teaching her lesser magic.

"So you're, like, a witch?" asked Millie.

Selma nodded slowly, thinking that any moment Millie would let it sink in and start reaching for stones.

"But you really cannot tell anyone," said Selma, with vulnerability in her voice. "There are rules about sharing your powers and exposing your coven. I'm not exactly sure what would happen, but I know Uma would not be happy."

Both girls shuddered.

Selma held her breath until her chest hurt. "Do you promise?"

"Whoa! *Coven*?! Cool! I promise," said Millie, raising her hand as if she were taking an oath. "But can you make that boy in lab stop throwing frog legs at me?"

Selma smiled and nodded. She turned her attention back to the small flame in her palm, whispering, "*Matri deae gratiam praebeo. Sit tua virtus influunt per me.*"

She moved her hand above the sticks and flipped open the pocketknife, exposing the sharp edge. She dug the tip into her finger, letting the blood pool enough to drip out onto the branches.

Millie gasped. "What are you doing?"

Selma ignored her friend. She needed to concentrate.

She slowly tipped her hand toward the ground, and both girls watched the flame roll off Selma's fingers and onto the pile of sticks, coating them in a blazing fire.

Then Selma took the charcoal and drew a symbol on her photo, instructing Millie to do the same. They each took turns taking sips of the ripe pomegranate juice they had added to the flower powder to make it more palatable. They were careful not to spill, and once the juice was all gone, Selma tossed her picture into the flames, nodding at Millie to mimic her action. As the pictures began to char, their corners curling as bright embers crept inward, Selma grabbed Millie's hands and spoke into the night.

"Matri deae gratiam praebeo. Sit tua virtus influunt per me."

"Matri deae gratiam praebeo. Sit tua virtus influunt per me."

"Matri deae gratiam praebeo. Sit tua virtus influunt per me."

Both girls began to feel a tingle. It moved from their hearts down their arms, through their fingers, and into the other. The sensation was so strong that when they finally let go, they began giggling uncontrollably. Their bellies filled with laughter as they sat back on the forest floor. Now, no matter where life took them, when one was thinking of the other, they would each feel the warmth.

Over the years, despite their distance, whenever one woman felt the other thinking of them, it would prompt the other to pick up the phone or visit. Selma did not know if the spell had begun to wear off after all these years; they had been eight years old, after all. Or maybe they simply were not thinking about each other as often. But there was only one reason Selma's memories pulled at her so tightly in those moments. It was because someone was tugging on the other end of the bond.

Selma quickly pulled up her recent call list and tapped on Millie's number. When she heard a soft "hello" on the other end, relief settled in.

"Millie, you're scaring me a little. And spare me the overreacting lecture," she said, trying to remain calm though she was never any good at it. "What's going on?"

"You know, in civilized societies, people offer a welcoming greeting of some kind, like a 'hello' or a 'good morning.' You should try it sometime," taunted Millie.

With the little patience she had nearly gone, Selma's tone bordered on shrill. "Maybe someday I will. Not today. What is going on?"

"I'm fine…right now," Millie stuttered. "I have good energy today, but I am not feeling well. I haven't been well for a while, and the doctors are still looking at everything, trying to figure things out. David has been looking after the store, because my energy runs low these days."

"Why didn't you call me sooner?" Selma asked. "Maybe I can help."

"Because we don't have all the information yet, and you know I would never ask you to use your gifts to help me. Except with that asshole in third grade who kept throwing frog legs at me. Do you remember him? He works for a nonprofit that sends food and supplies to third world countries now," Millie said. This was her attempt to change the subject.

"No shit? Well, then we will consider his unfortunate skin condition that year a teaching moment," giggled Selma.

There was a deep-rooted pause between the two women.

"I helped you back then, and I'll help you now. I am on the next flight out, and give me the name of your doctor. I want to make sure I have all the information by the time I arrive. And Millie?" Selma asked.

"Yeah?" Millie replied.

"Everything is going to be fine," Selma said, because that was what she always said when she didn't actually know if it would be. "And besides, you cannot die now. You still have my Refused T-shirt," she joked.

Millie laughed out loud, clearly taken by surprise, but it trailed off with a cough. "It looks better on me anyway," she said.

Selma hung up the phone, stepped back, and took a deep breath as a tear began to fall. Her friend, her sister, was in trouble, and she had been oblivious to it.

Wiping the salty tears from under her eyes, she yelled out, "I'm going to have to go soon," into the other room, where Hayden was still sleeping. She heard him get out of bed with a grunt that she guessed was something along the lines of a protest.

"But I thought we would look at flights for your birthday trip," Hayden said as he walked into the living room. She took a moment to check out his shirtless body. The man was good-looking. There was no denying that. "I was thinking the Bahamas."

Selma cringed, scrunching her face up. "I am sorry. An emergency came up, and I have to go back home."

Concern washed over his features. "What's going on? How can I help?"

Selma let out a long breath, allowing the guilt of his complete understanding to wash over her. She did not want to take the time to explain everything. Plus, she did not want Hayden anywhere near her mother or aunts. Selma knew the moment Hayden was exposed to her family, it would be hard for him to justify staying with her, and she did not want him to leave. If she was going to screw up this relationship, she was going to do it the old-fashioned way. With passive aggression and jealousy

"At least have breakfast with me," Hayden said, pulling her in for a kiss. "I'll make you my famous eggs Benedict."

Selma gave him a tight smile. "That's alright. I really need to get going. Besides, you do not have any food here. You have been traveling, remember?"

"That's what makes it so famous. It is nothing like eggs Benedict and is only made with ingredients you have on hand," Hayden replied, opening the fridge and gazing into it with a quizzical look, as if he were solving a puzzle.

But she did not have time to gently spar back and forth with him. After a few short minutes and a quick glance in the mirror to clean herself up, she grabbed her purse and raced out the door.

"Creatures that exemplify magical gifts of our Goddess Saint must commit to her love, fully and wholly, by wearing her mark."

—An excerpt from Edicts of the Order, property of the Master

CHAPTER 4

She would need to grab the red-eye flight tonight and loiter at the harbor until the first ferry in the morning. Booking her flight was easy enough—except for the price. Her stomach clenched at the sight of the number that appeared after the dollar sign. She had pulled out her unused credit card from an envelope labeled "Plan B" and tried not to think about the fact that she did not have another envelope labeled "Plan C."

With a groan, Selma threw her luggage onto the bed and yanked her gaze over to the closet. Millie had mentioned her gifts, but Selma had not even considered using magic. She was not sure what Millie was thinking. What could Selma do that centuries of well-funded medical research could not? She only used her magic for a few small, convenient tricks once in a while. She glanced down at her fingers. Cracked cuticles and smooth skin. Nothing out of the ordinary about them. She kept staring, but her attention drew inward. Taking stock of her body. Her breath, her pulse. Her senses searched for any hiss of power. Where did it hide away? Or had she lost it completely? Perhaps it had escaped through the gaping hole in her heart, the one her father had left in his wake. Selma did not even know if it was possible to lose track of one's threads, but the slither of her magic strands was silent.

Her mother and aunts had all been born with substantial gifts. As pure-blooded Elemental witches, they had a keen sense of their threads. Her Aunt Verda had described it as plugging yourself into an energy source and feeling your magic come to life. Selma would watch as they moved the earth in the garden without lifting a finger or created a cool breeze on a hot summer day.

The neighbors noticed as well, which certainly made for an interesting childhood. Millie was the only person who did not treat her like a leper. But magic had never come easy for Selma, and after her father left, what little power she had learned to harness had fizzled. She could no longer access her threads, which fed on energy. Selma did not know if it was typical for gifts to flounder in pure lines. She had barely met any other witches, and those she had were Commons. She considered herself lucky to have any connection to magic at all. She knew that there had been a council, or somewhat of a "witch government," while she was growing up. But she had never seen these witches nor heard her family speak of them since she was small.

Elemental witches were certainly favored by the ruling class of the Order. Lesser magic was often considered embarrassing, and the Order did not take much interest in it. Selma assumed that was why her family had never brought her to Order events or ceremonies. But she did not mind it much. The witch society that she had seen her mother and aunts bend their lives around had always seemed outdated and staunch. Her family never spent much time attending events dedicated to worshiping the Goddess. For all she knew, magic was dying out, and small shops like the one she worked in would be the closest thing the world had to magic soon. Magic had seen its heyday, and now it was on the half-off shelf with the rest of last season's goods.

Selma sat quietly, thinking to herself for a few long moments. If she could help Millie, even just a little, then it would be worth a try. And having some magic at the ready around her aunts would not be the worst idea.

She marched over to the double folding closet doors and pulled on the small gold handles, releasing a gust of air. With both arms, she shifted the hanging clothes to the left. They let out a sharp squeak, then settled. Selma lifted a folded pile of blankets and tossed them to the side, letting them fall to the floor, revealing a black chest. It was dusty and scratched; the well-worn imperfections etched in the leather latch were like notes to a melody. Aunt Verda had gifted her this chest. She passed when Selma was a teenager. On that day, Selma felt as if she had lost her own mother. Aunt Verda did not have children of her own. None of her aunts did. For what reason, Selma was not sure, but she had always been the only child, growing up without cousins to get in trouble with. That was another reason Millie's friendship had been so special to her.

Selma unbuckled the leather latch and with both hands on either side of the chest opened the top, releasing a potent smell of dust, herbs, and something sour. Dozens of little bottles, each labeled with their contents, lined the inside of the chest. Some bottles were larger than others. Also among the vials of assorted sizes was a leather-bound book. The hide was black, with a smattering of tobacco-colored brown spots. Her pendant purred on her chest, the way it always did when she was around the book. Not the buzz she felt when she was nervous, but a gentle hum.

On the front of the book was a brilliant medallion made of

bone with the insignia of a skull and flowers growing upside down. It was connected to what seemed like a series of complicated locks that were wrapped around the side of the book to keep the discolored ivory pages safely inside. Cradled inside the carvings of flowers was a collection of markings. Selma knew that magic itself was thousands of years old, and that the language these symbols represented had been lost. It wasn't as though she could take the book to a museum and ask if they had any knowledge of ancient magic. She could not risk exposing herself and her family.

Selma had not learned how to open the locks, and she had never seen what was hidden away on the ancient pages. The tip of her finger grazed the soft leather, pushing the dust aside and letting the oils from her skin mark the hide. Even now, as she scrambled for memories, intentionally digging at the corners of her mind, the memories faded. Her father's sharp nose faded. Aunt Verda's cackling laugh muffled. Selma carefully placed the leather tome back in its place, its secrets locked away.

Selma looked down at the chest the same way Hayden looked at the contents of his fridge. She was solving a puzzle, but for what? She would need to bring all of it. She was certain that checking a hundred-year-old chest full of frog heads and snails would raise more than a few questions at the airport. She would need to create a phantasm charm, to make the chest look like any other piece of luggage and mask the peculiar items inside. That would take all her energy and focus—not to mention blood—before her plane departed.

‡

At the airport, people hustled back and forth on the concrete sidewalk. Families with mountains of luggage. Business travelers glued to screens, walking with a sense of urgency and a profound knowledge of their regular route. Cars were shoved into any vacant spot, careful not to block in any other chauffeurs for too long.

Selma's rideshare pulled up to the curb, and she hurriedly got out of the car. Her driver quickly met her behind the black SUV and opened the trunk, revealing a modern, compact gray suitcase nestled inside. He lifted the luggage by its handle, but to his chagrin, it did not budge.

Embarrassed, Selma quickly reached in to assist. "Sorry, let me help you. I am an over-packer," she said, offering him a shoulder shrug.

The driver nodded and smiled but thought nothing of it as he put his side of the gray rolling bag onto the luggage cart and got back in his car.

As the vehicle raced off, Selma wondered how much she was going to have to shell out for her heavy bag and gulped in a large breath. The scent of jasmine had been mightily replaced by the scent of exhaust.

She walked up to the check-in counter, trying to keep her face calm as she struggled with her luggage.

"Identification and boarding pass," the ticket agent groaned.

Selma wordlessly handed over the requested items and glanced down at her phone. She had forty-five minutes before the doors closed, and the thought of wasting even a minute away from Millie wrenched at her heart.

Selma's trance was broken by the gate agent asking her questions, which she must have repeated several times, judging by the annoyance plastered on her face.

"Uh, yes. Yes, I am checking a bag," said Selma.

She leaned down, placing her left hand just under the base of the rolling bag and her right hand along the top. With perfect form, bending at her knees, Selma looked as though she were competing in a weightlifting competition. The gate agent continued to type, looking up at her screen only every couple of seconds and paying no mind to Selma and her Olympic stance.

Selma dropped her luggage onto the stainless-steel weight with a sharp clunk. The ticket agent glanced down at the blue numbers, and her eyes flared. Her luggage weighed well over the recommended fifty-pound limit. Selma, pushing past the obvious judgment in the gate agent's expression, reached for her wallet and the "Plan B" envelope that was tucked carefully inside.

"Do you take credit cards?"

‡

Three hours and twelve minutes later, the sun had not yet started to rise over the horizon as her plane landed. The view out of Selma's window was still dark, hiding the inky water that she knew was nearby. She let out a breath. It was not relief flooding her thoughts, but something else. She was not sure. Either way, she was closer to Millie, and, barring a snafu with her luggage or an unfortunate ferry delay, she would be at Millie's side by lunch.

Selma made her way over the scuffed tile floors toward baggage claim. The metal slats of the whirling machine scraped and squeaked as it noisily spat out orphaned luggage, summoning each passenger to step up and check the identification tag. Everyone standing near the loud, circulating contraption was both bothered and ashamed when the chosen bag was not theirs and they had touched someone else's property in the meantime.

She had chosen gray for her phantasm charm. The color was dull enough that the bag would not draw more attention than it already did with its bloated weight, but it would stand out just enough in what seemed like an endless sea of black rolling bags.

Finally, the bag emerged, strangled by crimson tape. Large black letters spelled out "HEAVY" every few inches. If that were not enough to call attention to her, as she leaned down to pick it up, her cross-body bag fell off her shoulder and tumbled in front of her, allowing her rolling bag to escape down the conveyor belt past the other anxious passengers still waiting for their bags.

"Damn it," Selma growled.

She tossed her cross-body bag back over her shoulder, falling back half a step with the weight of it swinging behind her. She haphazardly chased after the charmed chest, pushing people aside and apologizing every few steps as she nudged past them.

"Excuse me. Sorry. Sorry. Excuse me. That one is mine. I'm so deeply sorry. I'm the worst." Selma expressed regret but paid no mind to the annoyed faces as she passed.

Having made a fool of herself among the sea of people who were looking at her, Selma decided that this attempt needed to be successful, or she would burrow through the ground back to New Orleans, shamed from ever returning. Selma reached for the bag, and before she could touch the handle, a large arm wearing an antique leather watch seized the suitcase and tugged it off the belt. Selma did not even need to look up to know who it was. She recognized the watch immediately. Millie had given it to her husband on his eighteenth birthday.

"Smooth," David chuckled.

"You know me," Selma returned.

David put the bag on the ground and pulled up the handle, clicking it into place. Selma was proud of that. For a phantasm charm to work, every element needed to be visualized clearly, down to the mechanics. Without focusing on the details, you could end up with a rolling bag that did not roll or a door that fell off its hinges.

"Thank you so much for coming, but you really didn't have to pick me up. I could have ridden the ferry," Selma offered, tilting her head in an apologetic nod.

David snorted. "Ha. Are you kidding me? Have you met Millie? She would never allow that. Besides, she probably knew that a drive would be good for me." He paused, looking down, fussing with his key ring. A tight smile formed on his face as he said, "It has been tough."

Selma did not need to reach out to his thoughts to know the pain and fear he was feeling. She was struggling with those herself.

"Well, we better hit the road. We do not want to get caught in morning rush hour," said David, reaching for the handle and turning the bag so that it would roll behind him. "Do I even want to know what you have in here?"

"Nope," replied Selma.

‡

On the road, Selma checked her email on her phone. Two down from the top was an email from Earl D. Fishbourne, M.D., and then a short response from her boss, Tandy, explaining that she would need to be back at work as soon as possible. Selma tapped on the message from the doctor. The glow from her phone illuminating her face.

Miss Plumey,

Unfortunately, I cannot discuss Mrs. Cooper's case with you, as she has not given me permission to speak to you, nor would doctor-patient confidentiality allow it, as you are not direct kin. However, Mrs. Cooper is welcome to request copies of her medical records for further outside treatment. She can simply give my receptionist a call.

Sincerely,

Dr. Fishbourne, M.D.

"Great," Selma scoffed. That was a waste of time. She knew it would be a long shot to get information from the hospital, but she figured that since she had known Dr. Fishbourne since she was smiling through braces, he might make an exception.

David must have noticed her displeasure. "What's wrong?"

"Oh, nothing. I am just trying to get some medical history for Millie, and the hospital is being difficult," Selma replied.

"Dr. Fishbourne? He is a good guy, but he has been around since the dinosaurs and will not budge an inch," said David, not waiting for confirmation. "But I can get the information for you."

"Thanks," Selma replied, and she let out a breath. "I just want to see if maybe we could find a second opinion," she explained, hoping that would be enough to keep David from asking questions about what she was going to do with the information.

David nodded, his eyes on the road. "It would be more like a third or fourth opinion by now," said David.

Guilt wrenched at Selma's gut. She had been absent and oblivious to the hell her dearest friends were going through, and now she had the nerve to waltz in and think she could fix everything.

"Look, Selma. I do not need to know what miracles need to happen to save my wife, but whatever it is, I am not going to stand in your way or judge," David whispered, still looking forward through the windshield.

Selma's lips parted, but she thought twice before saying anything. Did he know that she was a witch? Had Millie told him? Selma had made it clear to Millie that she was not to share anything about her family's gifts with anyone. But could she be upset with her sick friend for sharing something with not only her partner, but Selma's friend as well? This was a problem for another day. Whether David knew she was a witch or not, Selma suspected that he was being held together by sheer hope, and she figured silence was the best solution right now. Her eyelids fluttered shut, and a wave of exhaustion tumbled over her, the hum of the radio like a siren lulling her to sleep.

The trees outside her window became still, no longer a blur as they flew past them. She was no longer in the car but sitting cross-legged on a bed of moss. Her mind was jostling to make sense of the sudden change, but something inside her felt familiar and safe. A dark figure was walking away from her in the trees up ahead. David, possibly? She called after him, but he did not stop. The figure kept moving away from her. She pushed off the soft, cushioned ground and started after him, picking up her pace as she went. Why was he not stopping? She kept calling after him.

Then Selma saw him turn and gaze over his shoulder. Not David, but her father. What was he doing here? Was he still in Belhaven? Had he come to talk to her? Her stride quickened even more, but her legs felt heavy underneath her. With her every step, he took two more, adding to the vacant space between them, but she knew she could reach him. She needed to catch up.

Selma fought for every step, heaving for breath, but her leaden feet drudged beneath her. Vibrant flowers withered away in an instant as she watched her father walk into the distance. Just a dark figure. Soon the earth was blackened and dead, except for the crawling vine. Jasmine vine leaped up from the ground, pulling her father down into the dirt as he struggled to get free. Selma yelled for him, but no words came out. She watched in horror as the ground swallowed him whole.

The car came to a halt, and Selma jerked awake. A dream. It was a dream. Her mouth was dry, but her cheeks were flushed. She and David were parked in Millie's driveway, and the sun was finally rising above the sloping hills.

"I figured you would want to see Millie right away. I am also guessing you have not told your mother that you are in town yet, and this would give you a chance to call with a heads-up." David turned to Selma as he shifted into park.

"She already knows," Selma replied, looking up at the house. "Mother's intuition or whatever."

"Right," David retorted. "Are you alright? You were restless. I thought about waking you up."

"Yes, I'm fine. But you are right—I do want to see Millie." Selma smiled.

"Let's head in then. I will grab your bags," David offered as he stepped out of the truck and onto the gravel drive.

"Sentient beings deserve life above all else."

—An excerpt from the Axiom, as translated by Lilibet Lourdes, property of the Museum of the Academe Arts, current location unknown

CHAPTER 5

Crushed oyster shells crunched and settled as her soles met the driveway. The sea fog was still blanketing the coastline, and Selma took a deep breath, inhaling the damp air. She placed her hand on her heart, dulling the intangible ache. Even though she had just arrived, her pulse quickened as if she had been dumped in the middle of a story's tense climax. Her surroundings may have been home, but they felt foreign.

The accent lighting was still illuminated in the pale morning light, and it shone onto the boxwood bushes that lined the house's front. A gold Victorian lamp hung over the kelly-green front door. Millie had bought her parents' house from them after they retired to Florida. Aside from some lawn upkeep and the flower boxes under each front window, the property was the same. The flowers inside the planter boxes had long since dried and drooped, no doubt the first casualty of Millie's illness. The house was a beautiful 1920s Tudor-style home with a stone façade and a steeply pitched roof.

The two overlapping gables that sat atop the structure were tucked into the embrace of tall Douglas fir and cedar trees that protected the mossy grasses and ferns down below. It was a house from fairy tales, one that always made Selma feel warm and welcome. It beckoned guests to come in and make themselves at home.

Selma glanced around, taking in every inch. There were no doubt some curious woodland creatures looking out over the scene. They danced around the ground cover and perched on long, unsteady branches, taking in every movement, assessing it for danger. But as Selma stepped onto the stone walkway, an eerie silence choked the natural surroundings. She looked deeper, holding her breath as she did. There were undoubtedly two large, beady eyes staring through the pale darkness. They seemed to look right through her, unwavering. A shiver ran down her arm, and goose bumps tickled her skin inside her trench coat. Out of habit, she reached for her pendant, feeling its sharp edges cut into her skin, waiting for it to offer any sign of danger. But there was nothing from the black bauble. She had been in the city for far too long if she was this nervous. It was just a neighbor's cat or something.

David turned the brass doorknob and walked in, letting light spill out into the early morning air. Selma walked in, and more tiny goose bumps rushed over her skin. What was it that was so unfamiliar? Almost like the absence of something, or bare feet on concrete floors. The fire was crackling, but still it felt like all the air had been sucked out of the room.

"We're back," David declared, placing her luggage on the floor next to him with a strained look, puffing up his cheeks and slightly bending his knees to do so.

A shadow moved around the corner. Blue eyes that could cut right through you and long, unkempt silver locks. Selma scanned her friend as she surfaced. Slow and frail, Millie greeted David and then Selma. She was so small. Her cheeks were hollow and gaunt, and her fair skin was somehow paler, lacking the life that Millie had always exemplified. Selma smiled and tried to hide the worry on her face as she reached in for a hug. She could feel Millie's bones under her sweater.

"You look terrible," Millie declared, looking up at Selma, breaking open the silence in the room, and all three erupted in belly laughter.

Selma scoffed. "I have been traveling all day. What is your excuse?"

Millie gestured to David. "This asshole has me eating kale and lemon smoothies every fucking day. That, and what's her name and that famous football player broke up. How are we supposed to believe that love exists if they cannot make their third marriages work?"

"The one who sings?" Selma asked.

"I don't know if he sings," Millie scoffed.

"No, football— Never mind. Breakups are hard," Selma retorted.

Both women giggled as they made their way into the living room and sat down on the sofa.

Millie jumped in first. "So, how are you?"

"Peachy," Selma replied. "Let's talk about you. I heard back from your doctor, but he would not give me much because I am not family. How long has this been going on?"

Millie kept her eyes down while she fidgeted with the hem of her jeans. The denim was sitting too loosely on her waist.

"Millie," said Selma, staring straight into her friend's eyes. "I love you, and I know this is the fucking worst, but I'm here to help, and I cannot do that if you're deflecting the whole time."

"Such a way with words, this one," Millie said as she glanced up at David, readjusting herself as she reached for a pillow.

David rushed to her side, grabbing it before she could strain herself too much.

"About a year and a half," Millie whispered. "The symptoms were mild at first...headaches, dizziness. But pretty soon I was getting sick every morning. I thought I might be pregnant. Man, do I wish I could have just been pregnant," she finished, rolling her eyes and tossing her hands behind her head.

"We are going to figure this out," Selma said, leaning forward in her seat, placing her elbows on her knees, and threading her fingers together.

Millie nodded and gave her a half-hearted smile. "I'll make up a bed for you. Oh, unless you want a mimosa? David will not let me have alcohol, but since my bestie is in town, maybe the warden will make an exception," Millie declared, opening her lips into a sarcastic smile.

David scoffed. "Like I could make you do anything."

"I know, darling. This is just my loving way of maintaining the illusion that you are the head of the household," Millie said, leaning up to give David a kiss.

"Thanks, but I'm going to stay at my mom's and get out of your way. You all have a lot going on here, and I would not want to intrude," said Selma.

"Nonsense. Plus, that old hag will drive you crazy." Millie giggled. "Just joking. She actually looks phenomenal. Could you tell her to send over whatever dark magic herbs she is using to look so young? It is like she is cheating time over there on that island," she said, waving in the direction of Selma's childhood home.

"Will do," Selma replied as she stood up from her seat. "Now, why don't I make us all breakfast, and you can tell me all about the people from high school that got ugly."

"Do you want to give your mom a call first?" David asked.

"Trust me. She knows," Millie and Selma both replied in unison.

"One need not call on the false power of the mortals to end life. Death at the tip of a blade or at the helm of magic is the only honorable choice. Any other kind is strictly against the Canon."

—An excerpt from the Canon, as translated by Emery Kara, property of the Warriors of Sever

CHAPTER 6

The manor was just as towering as it was in her memories. The gargoyle weather vane scowled down at her from its perch high atop the turret. Its rotating gaze had kept watch over the Plumey witches for centuries. The house was primarily dim except for a light flickering behind the stained-glass window on the top floor, overlooking the widow's walk. Another light lit up the bay window just to the left and below it on the second floor. That glass had acted as Selma's porthole to the world when she was a child.

She had put this off long enough. While catching up with Millie all day, the idea that her mother and aunts were expecting her niggled at the back of her thoughts. The house had been warded generations ago to warn of impending visitors. And her aunts and mother would have known for hours, maybe days, that she was coming. She silently weighed the pros and cons of turning around and taking Millie up on her offer to stay with her. A headache anchored in her temples at the image of Uma's tightly pursed lips as Selma announced that she would be hosted by friends instead of family, and she thought better of it. Staying in her childhood home would be vexing but necessary. If only for a little while.

Selma gently bit her lip. Perhaps after so many years they had calmed down and settled into themselves.

The stained-glass window on the third floor was swallowed into darkness. A few moments later, three older women spilled out of the front door and stood completely still on the steps. Like predators assessing their prey. Her mother leaned against the porch column, one hand resting on her hip, while the others flanked her on either side. Selma could tell it was her mother even with her slim silhouette backlit. Uma's silver hair draped over her shoulders, her polished tresses yielding to the summer breeze along with her caftan. Selma could almost make out the shimmer when the gentle current swept up the fabric. She never disappointed when it came to her appearance.

Uma held a glass of red wine in one hand and a joint in the other. She took a long drag. Selma released a deep breath right as her mother blew out a puff, and any hope that they had settled over the years dissipated along with the swirls of smoke.

Selma walked up the perfectly manicured path and dropped her bags on the ground. Preparing for a verbal sparring match would be easier if her hands were free. There was no need to worry about hearing the women's thoughts. Selma's family was all too familiar with her ability, and they were adept at shielding themselves against it.

Uma's eyes assessed Selma as she sipped her wine. She asked Selma in a tone that held more reckoning than greeting as she shifted from one hip to the other, "To what do we owe this pleasure?"

Offering up too much information to Uma always backfired.

She'd only weaponize it later. It was best to give only the necessary details. "I came to see Millie," Selma responded. Factual and curt.

"Mm, I know. Poor dear," said Uma as she turned toward the house.

Selma's muscles tensed. "You knew? You knew that she was sick and did not think to tell me?"

Uma turned and looked at Selma for a few moments in silence. Her face showed nothing but boredom. "I'm a busy woman, dear. If you want to know what's going on here, then I suggest you look inward. Running off was not something you inherited from me," Uma said, and she turned around to amble inside.

And just like that, Selma's stomach hollowed out. Uma's words had cut through her so swiftly and deeply that it took a few moments to recover. Her mother never had to utter much to inflict maximum emotional damage. Selma's aunts offered apologetic smiles but did not say a word, they just turned to follow her mother.

Selma leaned down to pick up her bags, but they were already being lifted by a concentrated wave of air. Iridescent green threads flowed from the garden to her Aunt Meriem. They slithered and climbed over and around one another, mimicking vines growing on a trellis as they fed Meriem her magic. Elemental magic was particularly convenient for moving heavy objects, and Aunt Meriem had an affinity for the air element. The soft green light did not reflect off the house walls, and the women never seemed concerned that an onlooker might catch a glimpse of their delicate magic.

Selma's room was exactly how she left it. A layer of dust coated the bookshelves, and concert posters hung on the inside of her closet door. A wistful shiver swept over her as she meandered around the room, taking in the trinkets now thick with a speckled blanket of time. Dried flowers and torn magazine clippings littered the dresser's mirror. There was no sign that anyone had been in there besides the fresh linens folded on the mattress. Did they miss her?

Her unfocused gaze caught a glimpse of a long-forgotten Polaroid, now faded with time. It was her and Millie on the beach, wearing matching yellow sunglasses and wide, toothy smiles. Air stretched Selma's lungs as she peeled herself away from memories of the past.

She walked over to her chest, which was no longer charmed to look like basic luggage, and unlocked the ornate latch. The wood creaked as it opened, as if protesting being woken from slumber. She carefully moved bottles and pouches aside, quickly looking at the aged labels until she pulled out a small canvas bag labeled "vervain," along with a small black cauldron, a mortar and pestle, and a few other supplies. She placed them all on the desk by the window. She opened the pouch, added a pinch of vervain into the mortar and pestle, and crushed the delicate flesh of the dried plant. When she was satisfied with the consistency, she transferred the floral powder into the cauldron and mixed in a touch of cinnamon and slug mucus. This particular warding spell did not require a blood sacrifice, but she still offered her chant to the Goddess, striking a match on the side of the cauldron. She watched as fire ignited, heating the concoction inside the cauldron until it began to bubble and spit.

Selma spooned the mauve, milky substance into a bowl and made her way toward her door, letting the flames die on her desk. With her middle and index finger, Selma spread the slippery liquid around the threshold of her bed chambers, all the while focusing on the individuals who would be able to enter with her permission and repeating their names. With a dusting of her hands, Selma let out a quiet, sharp breath and stepped back to admire her work. Not that she had much to hide behind the door, but she really did not want prying eyes where they were not invited.

Selma let out a whispered affirmation. "How bad could it be?"

Her muscles ached with weariness as she settled into the billowing bed linens. She tried not to think about the unsettling vulnerability in Millie's voice earlier or the ache in the back of her throat at the thought of losing her.

✝

Selma's phone buzzed from the bedside table, waking her from a restless sleep. Her bags were neatly stacked in the corner. She had been too tired last night to unpack them into the wooden hutch. Besides, she did not know how long she would be here.

She had one missed call from Hayden and one text from Millie. Selma unlocked her screen and tapped Millie's text first.

Have you two murdered each other yet? If not, David made mushroom "coffee" and gluten free muffins if you want to come over and pretend to eat them with me

Selma looked at the time stamp and began tapping her thumbs on the screen.

Perfect timing. I will stop in town and grab muffins and coffee. We can swap them out without him noticing.

Three dots floated, and then a blue message swished on the screen.

You are evil, and I like it. See you soon.

A morning with Millie was just the motivation Selma needed to get out of bed and start her day. She wanted to find the underlying cause of Millie's illness. But first she would need to ask one of her aunts for help. She would never dare ask Uma, as she was sure it would come with a barrage of guilt for not being able to perform the spell on her own. She also, technically, under witch law, was not allowed to attempt a spell of this magnitude. Witches did not have many rules, but because Selma did have magic in her blood and minor power, she could still hurt someone or inadvertently spill carefully guarded secrets to humans. She was not exactly sure what could happen if she messed the spell up, but she was not in the mood to find out.

At the knock on the door, Selma sighed, knowing exactly who was standing outside. Reluctantly, she slunk out of bed and made her way over to the door. She was almost proud that her Aunt Meriem had not simply burst in without warning, putting her wards to the test.

When Selma opened her bedroom door, sure enough, there she was: Aunt Meriem, wiping her hands on her floral apron. She was a few inches shorter than Selma, and her silvery locks were always tied to the side in an intricate braid that now reached her hip. Her sage green linen shirt was wrinkled and splattered with stains from whatever she had been whipping up in the kitchen this morning.

She offered Selma a tight smile. "What is it that I can help you with?"

Typical. The women's threads had always crept around the house, seeking out energy. It had not given Selma an ounce of privacy growing up, but Aunt Meriem had always been more intuitive than the rest. Her elemental threads inevitably discerned any stress that Selma was feeling, sometimes before she even felt it herself. And although Selma regularly asked for help with magic growing up due to her lack of abilities, she was going to need to admit to Meriem that Millie not only knew that Selma's entire family were witches, but that Selma had been the one to tell her about their powers. Letting a non-gifted person in on the secret was highly prohibited in the witch community.

"I was hoping you could assist me with an energy scan." Selma hesitated. "On Millie."

Meriem stared at her, her lips downturned. Here it comes. The lecture that Selma had been dreading.

"Very well. I will meet you over there in an hour. Do not be late, and wash off that awful perfume. It will interfere with the process," said Meriem, walking away.

Selma blinked rapidly. "That's it? No lectures? No 'you know what happens to witches who don't follow the laws'?"

Meriem yelled back over her shoulder, "Why? You never listen anyway."

She mumbled something else as she made her way down the stairs, but Selma could not make it out. It did not matter. Meriem was going to help, and they did not have to go twelve rounds in order to make it happen. Selma let out a breath of relief.

"Much like the magic that had created them, the sisters absorbed and learned from the mortals. Embracing community and perseverance, love and lust. But they also adapted to their cruelness and cunning."

—An excerpt from the Axiom, as translated by Lilibet Lourdes, property of the Museum of the Academe Arts, current location unknown

CHAPTER 7

The Plumey manor was nestled on a small island not far outside of town. The commute would offer Selma time to ponder her plan for the day. She tried to relax and lose herself in the sounds of the birds chirping and the foliage brushing up against each other. But her brief reprieve was cut short by her hastened steps. Even in the seemingly tranquil surroundings, her worry sank in. Selma could taste the coppery tang of blood from chewing on her lip. Before long, she found herself on the steps of the Mud House, a local coffee shop. She opened the weathered red door, her pendant pulsing as she stepped inside. It had been unruly ever since she stepped off the plane. Her only explanation was her anxiety about coming home and who she might see.

Voices rushed into her thoughts. Cupping her temples with her fingers, she tried to drown out the intrusions as quickly as possible. She must have been tired from all the travel. Selma tried to focus on the warm smell of freshly baked scones and roasted coffee beans. Steam shot out from the espresso machine behind the counter, startling her and causing her to jump. She wiped her sweaty palms on her jeans as light chatter filled the space. Her attention was immediately pulled to the back corner, where a dark figure sat at a small table, his elbows pressed up against the feeble, mismatched furniture, reading a leather-bound book. Dark, wavy hair fell forward over his face as he read. She could not make out many of his features, but he seemed familiar somehow. Before she could manage to move around the table and try to get a closer look, her pendant went still.

"Selma? Selma Plumey, is that you?" A voice from the back of the room floated above the coffee shop chatter.

Selma paused and let out a breath. Whoever this was, there was a high likelihood that Selma would rather burrow through the floor than talk to them. But she turned, plastering a tight smile onto her face.

"It is! Oh my gawd! Selma Plumey," screeched a woman with golden brown hair tied back in a ponytail. She outstretched her arms, indicating that she wanted a hug, and barreled into Selma's chest, bringing her in tight for an embrace.

"I haven't seen you in, what? Maybe a decade. How are you? What are you doing in town? You know I see your mom all the time. She looks fabulous. I do not know what moisturizer she is using, but I need to get some. I usually just…"

Selma realized quickly that she did not need to be a part of this conversation, and she stopped listening. She continued to nod her head at the woman but desperately wanted to turn her gaze toward the man with the dark, windswept locks. After what seemed like several long minutes, Selma reached to touch the woman's elbow in hopes of stealing just a moment of quiet. Enough time to signal that she was going to make her exit.

"I have to run, but it was so good to see you. Take care," Selma said, and turned toward the counter to order, hopefully not running into anyone else in the process.

Unfortunately, Selma's gesture was not clear enough, and the woman popped up next to her in line.

"I could use a little decaf jolt myself—I cannot do caffeine. It makes my heart race something terrible. So, how have you been? You are in New Orleans, right? Or was it Hollywood? Do you know anyone famous? I do not think I would like it, with all the pollution and smog. And that traffic. Whoosh. I cannot imagine spending all day in my car." Selma tried to dust off any memory of this woman. Even as the barista asked Selma for her order and waited patiently for her to respond, the woman continued to talk.

In another attempt to stop the incessant questions, Selma turned to her and interrupted. "I'm so sorry, but I have to rush off. I have an important breakfast to get to, and I am already late. But we should totally get together and catch up," she added, knowing full well she was not going to follow through with that proposition.

"Yes! We should absolutely do that, and invite Millie. It will be like an Eagles reunion. Millie, that poor woman. How is she? I know things have been tough. I heard it's cancer. Some people think it has something to do with genetics. Didn't her parents die young? But if you ask me, it is all those herbs and things she takes. The body needs meat. People cannot survive solely on vegetables, you know? How horrible."

At that comment, heat began to build in Selma's chest, and her nerves were buzzing. She felt as if she could burst into flames at any moment.

Selma spat, "Millie is fine. And it's not really anyone's business. I'm sure Millie and her family would appreciate their privacy, especially on a matter that you know nothing about."

This shut her up. The woman's eyes widened, and she tilted her head. "Well, I see not much has changed," she hissed.

"What? You mean once a busybody, always a busybody?" With that, Selma turned to the barista to finally give her order. Perturbed silence radiated from the woman beside her.

Once Selma had her pastries and coffee in hand, she fixed her gaze on the back corner. The man was nowhere to be seen. Only an empty seat and an abandoned coffee mug lay in his wake. Her nerves and her pendant were now content and hushed.

‡

Selma strutted up Millie's walk carrying fresh pastries and three coffees. As she reached the stoop, the hard, heavy air hit her like a brick. There was a stench wafting through the air, one that smelled of copper and rot. She had not smelled this yesterday when she arrived. Perhaps there were decaying plants nearby, or animals that had not survived the night. Or maybe it was David's mushroom coffee. She would not be surprised if Millie had thrown it out the window when he wasn't looking.

A crack from the trees startled her, and Selma jerked her head in the direction of the sudden disturbance. Surveying the tree line, she spotted nothing out of the ordinary and relaxed, letting out a quick breath before turning toward the house. She looked up at the windows. Her eyes moved slowly over the ornate carpentry, taking in every inch. She was not sure what she was looking for, but something had to be causing this sickening feeling in her stomach.

The front door cracked open, and Millie filled a tiny corner of the empty space. Even with her diminished frame, her smile warmed the air, and just like that, the copper-tinged, weighted air whipped away, allowing Selma to take a deep breath and fill her lungs with morning air. Until then, she had not realized that she was taking shallow, short breaths. Still bemused with the energy shift, she returned Millie's smile and offered up the pastries and coffee.

"Hot buns, my favorite!" exclaimed Millie, reaching out for the pale pink box that Selma was holding.

"Well, I do work out," joked Selma.

Millie rolled her eyes and grabbed the box. "You obviously know that your tits are your best feature," she said.

Selma nodded her head at the compliment, raising her hands and shoulders up in agreement. "We all have our gifts," she said.

Millie set the box down on the kitchen table and opened the lid. She leaned down, closed her eyes, and breathed in the sugary pastries.

"Mmm. Oh, how I have missed you, old friend," said Millie.

"I'm going to guess you're not talking about me," said Selma.

Millie reached into the box, chose the pan au chocolat, and took a bite. Her eyes rolled back in her head, and she let out a hum of approval. Still chewing, she said, "Almost as good as sex."

"I disagree," said a voice from the other room.

Millie's eyes widened, and she tossed the half-eaten pastry at Selma, who was sitting at the kitchen table and luckily not sipping from her coffee. Selma anticipated the handoff beautifully, grasping the chewed croissant with one hand and taking a bite.

David walked through the arched entryway of the kitchen and looked at both women. "That better be flaxseed," he said, pointing at Millie.

Millie nodded her head, still chewing on her last bite.

"You're a terrible liar," said David. He walked over, wiped a stray bit of chocolate from his wife's lips with his thumb, and sampled it. "But you are *my* terrible liar." And he leaned in for a kiss.

Then he turned to Selma to greet her. "Hey, hot buns," said David. "I thought that was my title, but I guess I have been dethroned. I am headed out to check on the store. I'll be back this afternoon to take you to your appointment. Do you ladies need anything from me before I go?"

Both women shook their heads.

"Great," said David, and he was out of the kitchen as quickly as he had come. "At least drink the green juice with the coffee, will you?" he shouted from the front door.

Millie gave him a vulgar gesture followed by an air kiss, and the two smiled at one another as David closed the front door behind him.

"You two are disgusting," said Selma with a smile on her face.

Millie's eyes turned sad, highlighting the dark circles that were weighing them down. Selma could tell what Millie was feeling without reaching out for her thoughts. The sadness that came along with the question, "What if?" They might be happy now, but for how long?

Millie sat next to Selma and propped one elbow atop the vintage dinner table, letting her chin rest in her hand. She gazed at Selma for a long moment.

"I'm glad you're here. I missed you," said Millie.

Selma gave her a smile and threw the pastry back at her. "I saw someone from high school at the coffee shop this morning," she said.

Millie had already devoured her pastry and was leaning in to take another. "You are going to have to be more specific."

"Brown hair, busybody, does not know when to shut up." Selma offered up the description, certain that Millie would not know who it was. But it was not the woman that she wanted to talk about.

Millie tossed up her shoulders, not excited to talk about the woman either.

"There was someone else too. A man. Dark hair, tall. At least, I think he was. I did not get a chance to talk to him, but I had never seen him before, and he did not look like the caliber of man who usually frequents the Mud House," said Selma.

Millie gave Selma a vicious grin, still chewing on her pastry. "How's Hayden?"

Selma let out a sigh. "He's fine, why do you ask?"

Millie swallowed but continued smiling at Selma. "Because you're trawling for guys at the local coffee shop and digging for more info. I was just wondering how you two were doing."

Selma scoffed. "He's great. He is perfect, in fact. Just because I'm asking about someone doesn't mean I want to go to the bone zone."

Millie spit out her bite with a laugh. "Bone zone?"

Selma's cheeks heated. "Stop it. Change of subject. I would like to do some energy exploring if you're up for it."

Millie gathered herself and nodded in agreement. She let out a deep breath and shook her arms, like she was resetting and repelling all her sad thoughts away.

"Now, what the fuck is energy exploring?" asked Millie.

"It is a shame she will never know her true self. We do a disservice to ourselves as much as her by hiding the truth."

—Journal of Verda Plumey, property of Uma Plumey

CHAPTER 8

The three women sat on the ground in the garden, facing one another. Their legs were crossed, their palms facing upward, resting on their knees.

"Are we going to fucking meditate?" asked Millie?

"Would you just relax? No, we are not going to meditate, although it sounds like you could use it," Selma said.

Meriem clicked her tongue in Millie's direction as a warning. Selma knew that even though they were at Millie's house, they were still very much considered children to her aunt.

"Listen, girl." Meriem scowled in Millie's direction. "We are putting ourselves in a great deal of trouble here today. The fact that you know about us at all is in itself an atrocious violation of our sacred laws. You will forget everything you see and feel here today. You will keep your mouth shut. Do you understand me?"

Millie's shoulders tucked inward, and she looked up at Meriem from under downturned eyelashes. A child scolded for not obeying. Selma wanted to snap at her aunt, but Meriem was right. They needed to be careful. Selma would do anything to help her friend, but putting her family at risk was a high price.

She was not entirely sure how this was going to work, but the concept was simple enough. Energy exploring worked much like how her aunts' threads could detect her stress when she was inside their house. Elemental threads were sensitive to energy, along with any blockages of energy. With some work, they might be able to pinpoint where Millie's illness originated. At least, that was what Selma hoped they would do.

Sometimes, without prying eyes, Selma could heal small wounds or aches by using her lesser magic, but she had never seen magic used for something quite this complex. Which was why Aunt Meriem had been brought in. Her threads' intuition was unmatched. She would need to tap into Millie's energy to see if there was anything hidden away, anything that the doctors might have missed. The real question was, could Meriem do further damage while she was exploring? While Selma could not be sure, she didn't think so, simply because she herself could not alter people's thoughts when she was swimming through them. Therefore, she was more of an observer than a participant.

Selma's voice cracked. "Are we sure about this? We are not going to hurt her, are we?"

Meriem scoffed. "Of course not. I am not doing anything but looking around. Her eyes wandered over the rosemary, and she rolled her eyes. Selma had picked rosemary from Millie's garden and placed the stalks base to tip in a circle surrounding them, cleansing the space of negative energy. Selma always had more success with her magic when she was outside or near nature. She did not know why this was, but she loved the idea that even with Common magic, the earth supported her spells and made her feel more connected to the community. Her entire life, she had been considered less than because of her lack of magic, but when she was outdoors, she could almost feel the earth helping her along. Part of her believed that anyone could tap into magic if they believed enough, that she and her family were no more special than any other living creature on earth. It was never the magic that kept her from embracing the witch community; it was the witch community itself. Lesser magic had always been frowned upon in her house. If she could not summon her threads, then there was no point in doing it at all. But, eager to assist, she ignored her aunts' churlish disapproval.

Her phone buzzed, the way it had all morning. Another missed call from Hayden. She would have to manage that later.

Meriem huffed. "Are we ready to begin?"

Selma placed her fingertips on Millie's hands and took a long, loose breath. Millie giggled, and Selma looked at her with irritation.

"I'm sorry. I am sorry. But come on, we look ridiculous," said Millie with a laugh.

Her laughter hurt in a different way than an insult or a physical attack would have. The giggles came out barbed, each laugh reminding Selma of what she could lose. This sweet, incredible friend who she was sure had been put on this earth to make her a better person.

"Of course we look ridiculous. This whole thing is fucking ridiculous. But if conventional means do not give us the answers we need, we must use unconventional means. And if looking ridiculous is going to help you, then I will look like an idiot any day of the week," Selma said with a scowl.

She could feel Meriem's gaze burning into the side of her head, but she did not take the bait. They did not have time to argue. Jokes could no longer mask the desperation fighting to stay hidden behind her glossy eyes.

Millie and Selma looked at each other for a long moment until a breeze broke their stares, cleansing the tension and washing away the hurt that had sat between them—no doubt Meriem wielding her air element.

Meriem took the opportunity to move things along. "Now, I want you to think about your body from the top of your head to the tip of your toes. The more detail, the better. And go slow. You might feel my presence. It will be uncomfortable."

Selma added, "And if it gets to be too much, just tell us, and we can stop."

"No, we cannot," Meriem cut in. "Magic is not a boom box that you can just turn off at will. Once I'm in there, we must continue until we are done."

"Have you done this before?" Millie asked, not expecting the answer she was about to get.

"Don't ask stupid questions, girl. It will only delay us," said Meriem.

Millie nodded, feeling just as juvenile as Selma did in this moment.

Sensing her unease, Selma reached out for her. "The most likely thing that happens is nothing, and we just sit here. We are just going to look to see if any of your energy is stifled."

Millie said, "So, we *are* meditating."

Selma's eyes were pleading, and Millie nodded with understanding. She lay back in the grass and shut her tired eyelids. As the two women held one another's hands, Meriem placed her palms out, pointed up toward the sky.

For a moment, the stillness in the air was all that surrounded them. But Selma could feel the shift moments before Meriem's ethereal green threads reached out toward Millie's frail body. Even though it was an invasion of privacy, Selma silently reached out to hear Millie's thoughts. She needed to know if Millie was alright, or if the magic was hurting her. She heard the same calming sentence over and over again, softly swimming through Millie's consciousness:

Peace flows through me with every breath. Peace flows through me with every breath...

The affirmation helped keep Selma at ease as well. Like a lullaby, it relieved her tension and rocked her into a peaceful cocoon. She watched in awe as Meriem's threads paced around Millie, scouring her energy for anything out of the ordinary. Meriem remained silent, focusing fully on her task. The three women sat there, quiet and tranquil, for several minutes. Then Selma heard a still and almost incoherent whisper fill her ears. It was melodic, like a song. She jerked her head from side to side but did not see anyone. Even David had cleared out of the house.

But she saw dozens of thin strands emerging from Millie. Individually they were as thin as strands of hair, but flowing together they began to form stronger bonds, glowing with an iridescent silver color. No, violet. They were violet, and they were beautiful. The strands grew in length and ventured out and up until they created a perfect egg-shaped cage around Millie. Was it possible that Millie somehow had threads of her own, that she had forged a barrier between herself and Meriem?

Selma looked at her aunt, only to find her straining. Her fingers tensed, and her brow dripped with sweat. What was happening? Millie did not show any change, but Meriem was quickly losing strength. Selma felt a tug on the threads. Was it Millie pulling back? No, no, no. Time did not seem to matter as the violet threads surged toward Selma. She could feel a pulse of energy begin to grow and weave from her core down her arms, wrapping around her fingers. It was unlike anything she had felt before.

Selma was so caught up in the rush of energy, she had almost forgotten that Millie was on the other end. Her pendant began to pulse again. She needed more time. She wanted more time. This feeling was incredible. She had only just begun, and she still had no idea what it was that she was looking for.

The pull was stronger now. Something was tugging back, asking to be released. A voice in the distance called to her. It was unlike the song she had heard earlier. It was muffled but stern. Meriem's voice. Selma tried taking deep breaths to calm herself. She turned her focus to Millie once again. Selma stared harder, past the mass of weaving threads, watching them dive in and out of one another. She realized that it was not only her and Meriem's magic present, but something else. Something incorporeal, like her threads, that moved like smoke. Selma could feel the strain as it pulled away, each thread stretching and aching. Any more, and the threads would tear. Selma watched as the smokelike substance slithered toward her beautiful violet threads, as if it had just sensed her. As if it was hunting.

As Selma began to call her threads back, the magic raced toward her, quicker than before. This time, it latched on to Selma's violet threads, squeezing and hacking at them. Selma felt a rush of pain, and Millie tensed, pulling away. She needed to release herself but did not know how. She pulled her threads back harder, but the dark, inky fog grabbed hold of her and began tearing away at the iridescent strings. Pain shot through her body. Selma let out a scream, but no sound came out. Her pulse was quick, her heart pounding on her ribs when a burst of energy shot through her, pushing her away from Millie and tearing the gentle threads to pieces. All she could feel was searing pain through her limbs.

Selma lay on the ground, high-pitched tones ringing in her ears, her vision blurry. Every nerve in her body felt like it was on fire. Her hands fumbled through the dirt, reaching for anything that would settle her and keep her head from spinning. All she could feel was the grass and torn bits of rosemary stalks around her.

Selma called out for Millie, but she did not hear a response. Every nerve in her body begged her to stay put, but she needed to get to Millie. She needed to see if she was alright. Pulling her pounding head from the ground, Selma frantically looked around for her friend. There she was in the distance, lying on the grass with her knees pulled up to her chin. Selma crawled over to her and pulled Millie's hair from her face.

"Are you okay?" Selma did not know why she had asked that. Of course Millie was not okay. She had just used what little energy she had to let Selma blow her through the air with unruly magic.

Tears streamed down Millie's face as she looked up at Selma. She just nodded and released the grip on her legs.

"Meriem! Meriem!" Selma called, panic dripping from her voice.

Meriem was slowly getting up and brushing herself off.

"Are you alright?" Selma asked her aunt.

The woman did not look at her as she nodded. Her movements were tight and jerky.

Turning her attention back to Millie, Selma apologized. "I'm sorry, Millie. I never should have asked you to do this." But it was no use. Millie was not going to yell or get upset. She was simply going to get up with more grace than Selma had in one finger and dust herself off. Millie would never let Selma know if she was upset or hurt. Even her tears were a surprise.

Selma helped Millie into the house and made her some tea. Even though Millie would insist that she could do it herself, the action was more for Selma's sake. She felt terrible for what she had put Millie through, and if she couldn't make her tea in return, she was helpless.

Meriem had quickly gone back to the manor. After a long time sitting in silence and sipping on chamomile, Millie cleared her throat. "What did you see?"

Selma was startled by Millie's question. She thought they would let the entire experience disappear into the ocean, never to be talked about again. The truth was, she had thought about what she had seen every moment since walking Millie's fragile body back into the house. But she did not know how to describe it. She had never experienced anything like that, had never seen anything like the carnivorous black vapor that attacked her. So, instead of burdening her friend, she simply said, "You have a lovely light inside of you."

She was not sure if Millie believed her, but it was enough to have her sip her tea and settle back on the sofa until David got home.

"Fear is knowledge's greatest enemy. It is with this discourse that magic felt its most monumental loss."

—An excerpt from The Forgotten Goddesses by Tara Wallingford, property of the Massachusetts Public Library

CHAPTER 9

Still reeling and weak from her and Meriem's bizarre undertaking, Selma walked along the small road out of town. Her eyes followed the dancing cracks in the pavement along the forgotten path that had since been reclaimed by mother nature. Tall blooms of Queen Anne's lace framed each side of the pavement, beckoning travelers onward in their journeys. She continued walking down the path, lost in thought as the crunch of twigs and dead leaves under her shoes and the shuffle of wildlife created a cacophony of sound around her. She had more questions now than when she started. What was the dark, smokelike creature? Was it magical? It had felt predatory—she had sensed its hunger. She needed to get back to the manor and talk with Meriem, so she quickened her steps.

"I know you disagree, but maybe they could help."

Selma was so absorbed by her thoughts that the intrusion barely registered, and she crashed into a rigid form. A fury of limbs writhed in the air, and Selma looked up just in time to see the stranger's camera fall to the ground and hit the pavement with a heart-wrenching crack.

Selma immediately jumped back, hastily tossing apologies out in front of her, hoping to appease whomever she had just abruptly barreled into.

The woman, slightly taller than Selma but more athletic, turned to face her. To Selma's surprise, a smile formed on her face, and her large, bright, hazel eyes were warm and welcoming. But even more surprising was the enormous silver and black dog that sat next to her. Selma gasped and stepped back.

"I guess that's what I get for standing in the middle of the road," said the stranger.

"Oh no—it was my fault. I was not paying attention," stammered Selma, reaching down to pick up what she hoped was a still intact camera. She kept one eye on the dog, noticing that it was not on a leash. It looked like a husky or some other extra-large breed that was meant for the cold. It was the biggest dog Selma had ever seen up close. If he had not been sitting so near to the stranger, she would have sworn it was a wolf.

Selma's face scrunched up as she examined the camera, gently turning it this way and that. "I can pay for the damages," she said, not really knowing if that was true or not. She did not know much about cameras, but this one looked expensive. The lens protruded out several inches, and the multiple dials and buttons suggested that this camera was not for a novice photographer.

"No worries. I'm sure it's fine. It has been through worse," said the stranger as she reached for the camera in Selma's hands. "I was just taking pictures of those trees. I moved here months ago, but I still cannot get over them," she added.

Selma looked off in the direction of the trees. She supposed she had never noticed the grove of aspen trees nestled among the larger, more domineering ones. They were beautiful. It was always the redwood trees, whose branches spread wide over the road and forest floor, creating a dense canopy, that caught more attention. Growing up here, Selma had always resented their towering presence. Always looming over her and blocking her view of any life outside of this town. But the aspen trees were different. Some of their leaves danced in the breeze and flashed from gold to green.

"I love the way they touch, almost like they are reaching for one another," said the stranger. "I am Amalie, by the way."

The tall brunette slung her braid over her shoulder, holding her camera gingerly in one hand and reaching out with the other, indicating she wanted to shake Selma's hand.

"I'm Selma," she said, stumbling forward to returning the gesture. "Beautiful dog." Selma instinctually stepped back, noting its size and putting space between her and the animal with large teeth. "Where is your friend?"

"Friend?" Amalie's brows knitted.

"I thought you were talking to someone. It's nothing. Never mind." Selma had clearly been distracted, and now she probably sounded silly to a complete stranger.

She looked over at Amalie, noting her dark features. They contrasted with her bright eyes and smile. It seemed oddly familiar somehow, but Amalie mentioned that she had only moved here months prior. She could not have been an old classmate. But why would someone move here, of all places?

"This is Akia," Amalie said. She looked down at the dog and seemed to shush it even though it was not making a sound. "I love new friends. I feel like I never get to meet new people here. Do you live in the area?"

Selma let out a breath and suddenly realized that not only did she not have the energy to explain what she was doing here, but she really did not have the time to take on a new friend, especially in a town she was trying to exit as quickly as possible.

"Uh, yes. I mean, no—not really. Sorry again. I am glad the camera is not broken. I better be on my way," said Selma, gesturing up the road.

She took a few steps forward, adjusting her bag and brushing off some invisible dust on her clothing, when Amalie stepped to her right. She beamed at Selma and walked next to her, almost adding in a slight skip to her steps.

Selma glanced sideways, taking in Amalie's childlike gait.

"If you're worried about the camera—" Selma began, but Amalie cut her off.

"Not at all. I figured I would just walk with you; we can keep each other company," said Amalie in a high-pitched tone that made Selma tense.

"You really don't need to do that. I will be fine, and besides, I am headed away from town," said Selma, hoping her half-hearted attempt to shake Amalie would work and she could continue her quiet walk, sulking and trying to figure out her next move.

"I insist. Two wild women. In the wild," said Amalie. Her enthusiasm, taking up so much space, forced Selma back on her heels. "So, where are you from?" Amalie asked, still clutching her camera in one hand.

"Um, I grew up here, but I don't live here anymore," said Selma, looking forward up the road.

"Cool. Which house? I am fascinated by the homes here. They are so gorgeous, and I feel like each one is different," said Amalie.

Selma had never been comfortable giving out personal information. Living in the city, she was aware of the possible dangers lurking around every corner. Sometimes she felt as though she were playing some brutal first-person video game, where a monster could jump out of any dark alley, ending her life with a dramatic "KO" across the screen. Not to mention, growing up in the Plumey manor had elicited plenty of unwanted attention from neighbors and classmates over the years. But she knew that with a small amount of effort and her obvious charm, Amalie would find out soon enough. There was no use in being evasive now. Still, Selma could not bring herself to give a straight answer.

"North of town," said Selma, hoping that would be enough to quench Amalie's curiosity.

"On the beach, or in the north side neighborhood? Are you Beth's daughter? She is just so cute. I help her mow her lawn," said Amalie.

Selma could see that Amalie was not going to stop with the questions. She was better off getting it over with.

"I grew up in the Victorian overlooking the cove," said Selma.

Amalie stopped walking, and her lips parted slightly, forming a tentative half smile. But her dazed look was quickly replaced by a sweeping grin, and she jumped in step with Selma again. Selma assumed by Amalie's response that even in her brief time here, she had heard rumbling of her aunts' shenanigans.

"You are Uma's daughter," said Amalie in a much more reverent tone than she had been using.

Selma nodded in confirmation, and Amalie was silent for a few more paces.

"That is a beautiful house," she said eventually, breaking the silence. "One of the oldest on the coast."

"I know," said Selma. "It has been in my family forever."

"What was it like growing up there?" asked Amalie.

Selma let out a long breath, looking up at the tree canopy. She did not want to get into this right now. So, she did the only thing she could think of. She lied. "It was great. A dream. Really awesome."

She knew she had overdone it, but it was all she could do to get as far away from this conversation as possible.

The two women walked in silence. The dog trailed close behind. Selma could see Amalie peering down the gravel road and shuffling her feet. Her energy had plummeted, and Selma worried she had been too dismissive. Amalie was only trying to be nice and meet someone new, which was difficult to do in this town, especially in her age group. To make up for her rudeness, Selma turned toward her and asked a question.

"Why did you come to Belhaven?" Selma worried that her question sounded rude.

Amalie looked at her with a smile that did not reach her eyes. "I have family in town," she said.

"Who are they? I have not been home for a while, but nobody ever leaves. I bet I know them," said Selma.

"*You* left," responded Amalie.

"Well, yes. But I am the exception," said Selma.

"I better get going. It was nice to meet you, Selma," said Amalie, and with that she turned and jogged down the road, dog in tow.

Selma watched Amalie and Akia head toward the horizon and disappear over the hill. Then her phone began to buzz. "Boo," popped up on the screen over a picture of her and Hayden on their third date.

"Shit," Selma swore under her breath.

She slid her finger over the screen and placed the phone to her ear.

"I'm sorry," she said sheepishly.

"Hi, stranger," said the voice on the other end of the line. "You left so quickly the other day, and then I couldn't reach you. Is everything alright?"

Selma sighed. She should have been relieved that Hayden was not angry with her, but it pulled at her guilt. He was always so understanding. It made her feel like a derelict every time he just smiled and brushed off her terrible behavior.

"I'm alright," Selma responded. Even as she said the words, she knew they sounded like a lie. "I am sorry that I made you worry. It has just been crazy here."

"No worries. Listen, I have this thing for work tonight, and I would love for you to come. The dress code is cocktail attire. I can pick you up around six, and we can grab a drink before. I know these things make you nervous."

Selma quickly brought her palm to her forehead, creating a slapping sound. Her eyes scrunched closed, and her lips disappeared in a thin frown. She had not clarified that she was leaving town, not just his apartment. But she knew the minute she mentioned her hometown, he would have questions that she had zero desire to answer.

"I'm actually out of town," said Selma, hoping she sounded casual enough to avoid an argument. "I had to come back home for a friend. I thought I told you the other day. You must have been tired from your flight," she added, feeling the lie slip over her tongue.

"You sound stressed," Hayden said. "Why don't I fly over there? I've never met your mom, and we did want to go to a beach for your birthday."

"No," Selma blurted. Celebrating her birthday with people who loathed her existence seemed like a nightmare. "I mean, I don't think you need to do that. I will not be here long, and besides, you have only been back a short while. Enjoy being home, and I will see you soon."

There was a long pause, and then Hayden broke the silence. "Try not to let her get to you. She's just your mom."

"What is that supposed to mean?" Selma asked. The attitude switch happened smoothly, as if she were just waiting to be baited.

"It's just that usually after you talk to her you are not exactly yourself, and I can tell you have been spending time with her," said Hayden.

"Well then, I will not waste your time with my attitude, I guess," said Selma curtly. "I have to go be manipulated now. I'll talk to you later." She disconnected the call.

Heat rose in her chest as she stared at her phone. She hated that she was so transparent, and that he was right. Selma had always turned into an angrier, distorted version of herself around her mother. But most of all, she hated that she treated Hayden like that. She wanted to pick up the phone and immediately apologize, but she did not think it would come across as genuine so soon after she had weaponized his kindness. *Later*, she thought. She would apologize later, and she continued her walk toward the island that had been her family's keeper all of these years and the haunting Victorian manor that sat propped atop its bluffs. Seeing. Judging. Knowing.

"We honor our spent life forces by protecting the living."

—An excerpt from the Canon, as translated by Emery Kara, property of the Warriors of Sever

CHAPTER 10

Selma walked through the tall antique wooden doors that adorned the front of her childhood home. She might have wanted to get out of here as fast as possible when she was younger, but there was no denying that the house was beautiful. The massive doors opened to reveal an arched entryway with two hand-carved columns on each side. It made way for a beautifully curved staircase with a banister that culminated in detailed florals and Gothic gargoyles hewed into the wood. When she was small, she imagined them coming to life and playing with her.

To the right was the sitting room. A massive fireplace commanded the space and held a large mirror trimmed in gold. It leaned against the wall in an upward tilt, making the room appear even larger and gifting its viewer a striking physique. The top of the mirror almost touched the vaulted ceiling, leaving just enough room for the double crown molding to sneak by. The mirror was flanked by large black urns that held fresh cut flowers from the garden. Aunt Meriem had gathered them at their peak and carefully arranged the stems so that each bloom was displayed. The fresh flowers almost made a mockery of the rest of the room, which she had not been allowed to touch. They'd coax her in with promises of warmth and laughter, only to take it away at any sign of threat to the room's perfect decor. The sofa was a creamy white velvet, and it cozied up with the hand-stitched black and cream throw pillows that Aunt Meriem had given her mother. Selma remember Uma sneering at the tassels that swung from the corners and immediately taking scissors to them. Uma would not be caught dead owning pillows with tassels, and she would not be stuck looking at tassels every day. Not that she ever went in there. Nobody did unless they had company. Which they never did. The sofa mirrored a pair of French provincial high-backed chairs, and well-cared-for green and dark purple plants filled the empty spaces, contrasting with the deep blue walls.

Past the sitting room and through another arched entryway was a dining room. A large black iron-and-crystal chandelier hung from an ornate ceiling medallion in the center of the room. It overlooked a long wooden table that could seat a dinner party for sixteen people if necessary. Selma wondered if her grandparents or great-grandparents had hosted dinner parties. Large, lavish affairs with decadent dishes and boisterous conversation while smoke billowed from their long cigarette holders. The men would have dismissed themselves to the parlor for cigars and brandy while the woman gossiped about which neighbor's prize-winning orchids had "magically" withered away overnight. Selma had once read that it was customary for cigarettes to be passed around during the salad course, which was to be served after dinner. Tiny, useless bits of information like that fascinated her, and she would carefully file them away in her mind for safekeeping.

Her stomach grumbled. She strode past the dining table, careful not to make eye contact with any of the numerous portraits from generations past. She pushed against the swinging door and entered the butler's pantry. The room was filled from floor to ceiling with translucent glass jars, all home to various herbs, spices, and the occasional taxidermy wing. She glanced over the labels stuck to the jars, hoping to find one filled with cereal or oats. No luck. Her tummy groaned in response.

When she opened the swinging door, her nostrils were instantly hit with overwhelming delicious smells. Rosemary, sage, and lemon all wafted out from the room. Plates stacked high with lamb chops and potatoes. Fresh greens topped with goat cheese and heirloom cherry tomatoes. Freshly baked bread released steam from the top of the intricately scored designs.

She turned to sit at the kitchen island when she came face to face with Aunt Meriem and smiled at the silver-haired witch responsible for the harmonious smells. The older female said nothing at first, but her body language screamed disappointment. Her glare sat heavy on Selma, and the wrinkles around her lips were more pronounced than usual, as if she were holding back the words fighting to jump out of her mouth.

Meriem's eyes were irate. "Goddess help us, how long have you known? You have no business toying with magic, especially unsupervised." Each word she spat sounded like it had punctuation after it. Like she could not find a way to soften it.

With her tense phone call with Hayden still fresh in her mind, Selma snapped back, "Known about what?"

Meriem's nostrils flared. "About your magic. Someone could have been killed."

"I have no idea what you are talking about, but I did want to talk to you about what I saw," said Selma, trying to keep her voice even.

"You should not have seen anything!" Meriem screeched. "This was a terrible idea. I should have just left it alone. If anyone finds out, especially your mother, you are going to wish that the Order would come lock you away." She grabbed the gold pendant around her neck, which had the insignia of Saint, and wordlessly prayed. "If the Order were to find out," said Meriem, shaking her head in disgust.

"Nobody is going to find out. I barely even know what happened. I just felt something. It was similar to when my father showed me magic."

Meriem's lips sagged open. Her shoulders slumped. "He what?"

Selma cursed under her breath. She had never mentioned her early morning hikes with her father when she was small. He had told her it was their secret. But she supposed it was no longer a secret. And she needed answers.

"I used to go on walks with my father before he left, and he tried to get me to summon my threads. He had faith that my magic would show up, and sometimes it did. It felt a little like it did today, but not on that scale," Selma said. Her head lowered as a sheepish question slipped from her lips. "Do you think Millie has threads?"

"He should not have been doing that," said Meriem. "He had no right."

"He was my father, and you're being an alarmist. I'm just trying to grab some lunch before I pass out," said Selma. She pushed off the counter, intending to grab a snack.

Meriem's eyes tracked her movement. "What did he tell you?"

Selma sighed. "Nothing. He told me nothing. Just that my magic would come to me one day. And stories. He would tell me stories. What does that have to do with today?"

Meriem huffed. "What kind of stories?"

Selma rolled her eyes as she took in a large gulp of air. Scouring her memories, she tried to remember the tales that her father would weave on their walks. "He would tell me about the Goddesses and how they came to be. Something about a big tree and breaking magic apart."

Meriem stood still. "And your magic? How did he describe your magic?"

"He didn't." Selma attempted to fend off her aunt's questions. "He just said to trust my threads, and that my magic would not hide forever."

"Toying with magic is dangerous," Meriem spat. "If I had not practically sucked that garden up into a tornado and torn you away, you would have drained all of us."

"I don't know what you're talking about. I did not do anything. I cannot do anything. You and your flock of hateful biddies have made that abundantly clear!" Selma yelled.

Instantly, she regretted that statement. *Damn it*, she thought. This was exactly what she thought would happen. Yes, her Aunt Meriem was annoying, but she was not evil. She did not deserve to be spoken to like that. It was as if Selma's inner gremlin was turned all the way up when she was around these witches.

"What are you doing here?" Meriem asked without hesitation.

"Well, for starters, I always feel so welcome here," said Selma with a wry smile.

"Seriously, Dove. Everything is a joke with you," said Meriem. Selma had always hated her little pet name. A dove seemed harmless enough, until you considered that doves are typically used as ingredients in what might be called witch spell sacrifices.

"No, everything is a *deflection* with me," Selma responded. She waited a few moments to see if her aunt would send back another zinger, but the only response slung her way was a glare.

"I'm here because Millie called me. She is sick and—"

"Well, your interference is doing more harm than good. Your magic was chaotic and untamed. I had to pull you out of there before you hurt anyone," said Meriem.

"You said we couldn't hurt her. And I do not have magic. Whatever we saw was coming from Millie," Selma argued.

"It wasn't Millie. It was you. You were—" Meriem halted her speech.

Selma was not sure why she stopped But before she could ask, Meriem summoned a wind, and a plate appeared in front of her, piled high with a sandwich and a salad.

"Thank you," Selma said, startled but appreciative. She was famished. As soon as she sank her teeth into the crispy crust of the bread and tasted the fluffy inside, her eyes rolled back, and she let out a small moan. Satisfied with that response, her aunt's lips curled up at the corners, and she turned to work on something else at the counter. Meriem was a lot of things, but a bad cook was not one of them. Selma dug in, devouring the plate in front of her and wondering what her aunt was going to say. She watched Meriem's anxious dash around the kitchen.

Selma felt like she was dining inside of an old apothecary. The kitchen island was made up of a large workspace with countless drawers. Some of the drawers were half open, revealing containers with fresh herbs cut from the garden: sage, thyme, basil, mint. Selma loved the smell of mint. The entire fence along the back of the property was encased in mint bushes.

Selma sat in silence, hoping to get through the rest of her meal without questions, but that plan quickly diminished.

"Why do you insist on stressing out your mother?" Meriem asked matter-of-factly, placing her hands on her hips.

Selma let out a low laugh, almost choking on her forkful of salad. "My mother? I am not so sure I am putting her out much, considering I have seen her once since I arrived. Besides, why does it have to be about her?" Selma stopped as the door to the kitchen swung open.

Her mother passed over the threshold and sent a cold glare her way. Her dark eyes narrowed slightly, and her lips tightened and curled up on one side, giving the impression of a smile. Not a smile that had any intention of transforming into laughter, but the look that prey receives right before being devoured.

"I know our friendship, however strained by the depths of war, will never pay tribute to the greatest sacrifice I will ever ask of you."

—Recovered correspondence from Alister Lourdes to Uma Plumey, property of the Plumey Estate

CHAPTER 11

Selma swallowed hard. The bite she had been chewing felt more like a rock as it sank into her stomach. Her mother was silent as she held her gaze on Selma. Her slim figure crossed the room toward the refrigerator. She was dressed impeccably in a purple caftan. Her shoes had a symbol on the toes that Selma was sure warded off something, and her neck was decorated with a long chain that held a lock with the Goddesses' symbol and a tiger's eye.

Uma carried on with her task, grabbing a vintage crystal champagne flute and opening the wine hatch on the floor to find what Selma assumed were some midday bubbles. When Uma disappeared into the wine cellar, Selma looked over at Meriem to see if she, too, was holding her breath. The silence was palpable, even with the tinkling of wine bottles from below. When her mother emerged, she still had that smile on her face.

The silence was too much to take.

"Hi, Mom," said Selma, poking her fork at the plate and looking at her mother from under lowered eyelashes.

"Dove," Uma said, leaning heavily on the O. "Always a treat to have you home. I just love feeling like a guest in my own house." She stopped to open the champagne bottle, twisting the wire counterclockwise and removing the green and gold foil.

Pop! the cork sang out as it twisted from the top of the bottle.

"But I suppose a guest would not be gossiped about behind their back. Which makes me..." Uma stopped to tap on the side of the champagne bottle with her long fingernail. She turned her eyes up into the air, as if looking for a phrase that she had put away just for this occasion. "A fool," she said finally.

Selma knew she did not mean it. Uma would never consider herself a fool, but she never missed an opportunity to call attention to herself.

Selma remained silent. She was not going to take the bait. History would prove that there was no winning when her mother was involved. No matter how many complicated chess moves one might memorize and practice, the queen always wins.

Uma touched the flute stem, covering it in ice crystals. Uma's element was water, and she never wasted an opportunity to put it to clever use. She took a sip from her glass without lifting her brutal gaze from her daughter. Aunt Meriem jumped in and asked Uma if she would like something to eat.

"I have lost my appetite, but thank you," Uma explained, finally breaking eye contact with Selma. "My ears might be deceiving me, but I could have sworn I heard bits and pieces about a little spell that Meriem was helping you with." Her eyes darted to her sister.

Meriem dropped her gaze to an imaginary spot on the floor.

Selma rolled her eyes and put down her fork. She crossed her arms in front of her and leaned back on her stool. *Here it comes.*

Just then, the door swung open, and a swift, loud woman in red overalls came barreling into the room, halfway through a story and not caring who might be there to listen. In Selma's experience, her Aunt Gerta did not much care about her audience, just that she had one. All three women looked up at her as she entered the room.

"The old, wrinkled nag from across the street planted garlic and put up another Goddess-damned cross in her front yard. This one is six feet tall and pointed right at our front door. That ignorant doormat is convinced we are vampires. I say we play into it. Maybe then she will stop asking for donations for that fucking silent auction in the winter," said Gerta as she grabbed the champagne bottle and took a pull.

Selma giggled to herself. Aunt Gerta was a lot, but she was certainly entertaining. Selma could not help but think of the look on the neighbor's face when a truckload of coffins and old blood bags from the hospital were delivered to her doorstep. In fact, she might even come back for that show.

Selma broke from her reverie in time to see Uma whisper something to Gerta, something she assumed was about her "little spell casting" from earlier. Gerta shook her head in response and looked over at Selma, her eyes filled with shock and disappointment.

"All the cake and none of the veggies, huh?" said Gerta. "Figures. This generation knows nothing about hard work or sacrifice. Let me guess, you thought you could just call on whatever magic scraps happened to be lying around? Your unfortunate genetic circumstances are no excuse for poor behavior."

"It's not my fault I wasn't born able to wield threads with the energy of the elements," said Selma. "It has nothing to do with hard work."

Meriem chimed in, "It's the essence of Saint, young lady, and this isn't about wielding the elements."

Selma dropped her fork and shot back, "Then what is this about?"

"Pardon me," Uma drawled. Her face contorted so that any wrinkles she had were on full display. "You know very well what this is about. You put all of us in jeopardy when you shared our secret with a human. All we have tried to do is keep you safe. And this is the behavior we get in return?"

"It's fine. It is just Millie. She is not going to tell anyone, and Meriem pulled us out in time," Selma spat back.

Aunt Meriem's eyes darted to Selma, and she shook her head from side to side. All three women were now looking back at her from across the island. Selma instantly regretted trying to win this argument, and she realized what she had just exposed.

"I was quick. In and out," she said, hoping it would be enough to end this conversation.

Gerta and Uma turned to Meriem. Uma didn't hesitate for a second before asking, "What are you not telling me?"

Meriem shook her head at Selma quickly—too quickly for Selma to notice. The other women were silent and did not take their eyes off Meriem.

She answered in barely a whisper, "Selma may have manifested some of her magic today."

Great. Meriem could not keep it to herself.

Uma was calm. Too calm. As if she had been expecting this

news.

"What if the Order finds out?" Gerta cut in.

Selma did not understand the look of dread on their faces. If her magic was manifesting, then she wouldn't be any different from them. Yes, it would be chaotic for a while, but she could learn to control it, just like they had.

Uma gathered herself, clearing her throat. "Well, I suppose delayed magic is better than having a hiccup in the bloodline. Did anyone see you?"

It cut deep. No matter how many times she had heard that she was a mistake, that she was broken, it still felt like acid on a wound.

"We were discreet," said Meriem.

Uma nodded and turned to Selma. "I suggest that you do not use your magic again. It is also important that you keep your mouth shut—no matter how badly you feel the need to put everyone in their place."

Selma grabbed a lemon and thyme cookie off the plate and scooted off her stool. This conversation had already lasted much longer than she had patience for, and she had actual important things to worry about besides the Order finding out that she had told one person about her gifts.

Her pendant started to hum against her skin again. She reached up to hold it in her palm. Uma's gaze was unmistakable as her eyes flicked down to the pendant.

"We will just keep quiet about everything," Meriem said, her voice trembling.

"It's too late for that," said Uma in an ominous tone. "They are coming."

"Who?" All three women looked at Uma with questioning eyes.

"The Order," Uma replied. "I suggest you clean up. You don't have much time."

Selma took a bite of cookie, pushed on the door, and make her way outside.

"And I'm not removing the wards to my room, so deal with it!" she yelled back at the woman as she flung her hand in the air in an act of frustration and defiance.

Cookie crumbs fell from her lip onto her shirt as she twisted the front door handle to leave. The door swung open, and Selma was met with an imposing darkness blocking the door.

The same broad shoulders that had been huddled over a book this morning were now swallowing the daylight. He was dressed in all black, in a button-down shirt, black jeans that fit him snugly around the waist, and black boots that looked weathered but not scuffed beyond repair. They were more like well-kept vintage footwear. Selma remembered the inky swirls that threatened to escape his collar and cuffs. His eyes, once hidden below his lashes, were now piercing straight through her. Light blue swirled around his pupils. They swept over her body, taking in every inch as he leaned against the sacred wood.

Selma caught crumbs in her throat and coughed dry air to knock them loose. Her voice broke as she greeted the man. "Hello. Can I help you?"

Goddess, he was beautiful. But why was he here?

"Perhaps," said the tall, dark, gorgeous figure. "May I come in?"

Selma was not sure who this man was nor why he was here, but every fiber of her being wanted to be closer to him.

"Selma, stop being rude to our guest!" Meriem bellowed from behind her.

Selma tossed a glance behind her in confusion.

"He is a messenger from the Order," explained her aunt. "Please, come in."

Shit.

Selma moved aside to let him gently shove off the doorjamb and enter the house.

"We will not be long." His dark tone clattered deep in his chest.

Selma looked up at him, and then over at her aunts and mother. They were stiff. Silent. The towering man reached into his jacket and removed a rolled-up parchment held together with a wax seal. He handed it to Selma. She was still chewing on her cookie, as she had stuffed the whole thing into her mouth to dispose of it.

Her swollen mouth gargled out, "What is this?" She swallowed, carefully ripped the seal, and unrolled the paper.

"You are being summoned," said the dark man before her. "Now, why don't you be a good girl and come with me."

Every inch of Selma's body heated.

CHAPTER 12

Holding up the parchment for everyone to see, Selma asked, "What the hell is this?"

Uma cut in before anyone could answer. "What my animated daughter means to say is, though we are honored to have notice of the council, it would be helpful to know the purpose behind the summons."

"Everything will be explained, although I'm sure you can make a few guesses," he responded with a growl. "And we both know better, don't we?"

Fuck. Selma was not sure whom he had aimed that last dagger at, but it cut at all three women. Meriem meekly uttered, "Our apologies. She will be there."

"I know," he rumbled. "I will be taking her now."

Selma shuddered at his order. Her mom and aunts were not

going to let him take her, were they? They did not even know the brooding man, and he still had not mentioned where they were going. She reached out to hear his thoughts but was met with a dark wall. As if he had anticipated this and shielded himself against her.

He closed the distance to her in one hulking step and placed his rigid arm around her waist. She was pressed against him, her body bowed into his.

"Hold on," he ordered.

The air swirled and shifted. Her body did not feel like her own anymore. Their bodies floated in a sea of mist. Panic started to set in as she realized that she could not determine which way was up, and she held on tighter, breeding resentment toward the taut figure at her side. For making her feel powerless. Sick to her stomach. And for her feeling inexplicably roused by the places their bodies touched. It was as if her senses were dulled and any logical assessment of her surroundings was deprived of information. Before her panic could swallow her, her feet landed on dark marble slabs, and the tall stranger disappeared into the mist.

Selma retched onto the marble floor, every bit of her lunch coming back up. Breathless, she wiped the back of her hand across her mouth, cleaning off the evidence of her body's betrayal. Unfortunately, someone would have to deal with her lunch making an encore appearance. She gawked at the high-ceilinged room. The walls were made of stone and must have been built long before Selma was born. The artwork was dark, not just in tone but in its dark, moody scenes of beasts tearing at flesh as robed figures looked on in the background. One portrayed what looked like the two Goddesses rising over a tree, but the tree was unlike any that Selma had ever encountered.

The owner of this artwork must have had a fondness for lore. One painting portrayed the Goddess Saint hovering over a smattering of bodies that were covered in white robes, their faces shriveled and pale. She focused on a painting near the top, of a black dragon, the creature's gorgeous wings broken and burned, with what looked like intricate metallic purple veins woven in. Dragons were not real, of course, but this fairy-tale creature had long been a symbol of the dark Goddess Sever.

The most prominent painting was of another tree, a perfect match to its smaller counterpart nearby. The leaves were all distinct colors, and the tree's trunk was dark black. The bark contained purple eddies, much like the wings of the dragon that accompanied it. They were beautifully painted, but all of them held a sadness, as if the ornate gold frames were the only thing keeping the beasts and villains trapped inside.

She heard faint but quick footsteps making their way toward her. Each step matched her heartbeat, until a small woman in a beige cotton dress came into view. Her dark eyes gave nothing away, and her silver hair fell to the middle of her back. She stopped just inside the threshold and raised one arm in the direction of Selma. Palm up, she slowly curled her fingers, gesturing for Selma to come forward.

Although taken aback, Selma followed the tiny, mute witch. Her legs and belly were still unsteady. If this woman was part of the Order, it was even more reason to do what she wanted without causing too much of a scene. With any luck, they would realize that this was a small, inconsequential infraction, and the whole debacle would be over soon.

As Selma followed the petite witch, she tried to think about what she was going to say to the Order. She had barely had time to grasp her summons before she was whisked away without consent. *Bastard*. She was not sure by what law the Order passed down judgment. But without any real idea about what was waiting for her, preparing seemed to be a futile exercise.

One room led to another and to another and to another. The manor was endless. Selma had never laid eyes on a dwelling so grand and ornate. Long hallways dimly lit by flame connected the vast estate, and Selma could not help but think that they were in a castle. She was not aware of any castles on the coast, but then again, she was not sure what kind of magic had been used to get her here, nor how strong it was. She could have been anywhere, and that thought alone was unnerving. Panic threatened to stop her in her tracks. She started finding it hard to breathe, and each step became heavier.

Just as Selma was about to turn and run, not caring about the consequences, the small witch stopped in front of a set of double wooden doors. Now was the time. She could still run, but she was certain it would not solve anything. They had found her before. They would find her again. She could only face the Order and plead her case.

She had only told one person about her gifts—Millie. And for a good reason. They would have to see her argument. The woman just looked at Selma with a blank expression, but her eyes were gentler than they had been upon Selma's arrival.

Then a voice rang through her thoughts:

Be cooperative, but only answer what is asked of you.

Selma's eyes widened. The witch had spoken to her, mind to mind. How? Selma tried to ask, but the witch simply shook her head and placed her hand on Selma's shoulder. Selma could have sworn that the woman was giving her a few moments to gather herself. Right now, she could use all the allies she could get. And with that small kindness, Selma found the courage to stay. She took a deep breath, letting the air out slowly between two pursed lips, and straightened her posture. Then she gave the tiny witch a small nod.

The doors opened to a light, open space. Compared to the rest of the building, this room was far less intimidating. It did not house any oil paintings of ferocious beasts threatening to jump off the canvas and devour her in one bite. In fact, it was the exact opposite. Skylights let natural light pour into the room and drench the large garden pots that were overflowing with flowers and greenery. Plants hung from hooks, letting their leaves float through the air, no doubt fuel for her hosts. Several men and women fluttered around the room, holding teacups and small napkins with little sandwiches. None of them even looked in Selma's direction as she entered. She stood there holding her hands together in front of her, waiting for instructions.

While she waited, she took in everyone's faces. They were vacant, almost bored. Their clothing was high-end but not ostentatious. This was a crowd she would have expected to see at an East Coast country club, not a chilling mansion. In the same breath, she realized that not only were these witches and warlocks used to holding all the power, but they viewed her as nothing but a nuisance. She had been called away from Millie. Away from helping her friend get well just to show up in front of a group of puffed-up, privileged warlocks with nothing better to do than watch her squirm and dance.

Rage rose in her chest, and her arms began to tingle. The floor underneath her trembled. Perfect, an earthquake. Exactly what Selma needed right now—a natural disaster. The chatter came to an abrupt halt, and all heads turned toward Selma. Her charm was still humming on her chest, and she felt certain that it was simply responding to her emotions.

One man in the back corner finally spoke up. He was eerily

familiar, but she could not place him in her memory. He cautiously looked around the room and set his teacup down on a side table.

"I believe we should begin. Everyone, if you would not mind taking your seats, we can call this summons to order," said the rawboned man with a melodic accent.

Teacups tinkled as they were set down one by one, and people scurried around the room. Some gathered their belongings, while others exited through the back, the heavy door shutting with a thud. When the room was settled, Selma noticed that there were no longer any women besides herself and the small witch who had guided her here. Only five men remained poised in front of her. Selma stayed quiet. No need to give them any ammunition before they even began.

All five men stood or sat on one side of the room. If she did not know any better, she would have assumed that she had stumbled into a magazine cover shoot for *Rich and Wicked.* They all wore blank expressions, except for the man who had called the summons to order. He gave Selma a tight smile. She tried to hear any thoughts in the room but was met with a cold silence. In fact, she could not even feel the thrums of thought. It was as if there were a wall between her and them. If she had not been in this bizarre situation, she would have found the silence more peaceful. But the one time she needed her gift, it had been muzzled.

"Selma, welcome," said the smiling man. He walked toward her and gave her two quick kisses near each cheek.

The embrace was appropriate but jarring nonetheless. It took everything in her power not to react. She returned what seemed like an unflappable expression, hoping someone would offer more information.

He gestured to dismiss the small witch, and she turned to leave the room. The man walked over to a teapot and poured a fresh cup of tea, humming to himself as the hot liquid splashed into his cup. "Ah, la la la, *mon amie*, forgive my manners. Would you like a cup of tea?"

French. The man was French, or Canadian, Selma thought to herself. She knew some French. Her mother had insisted that she take classes in school, and Selma had hazy memories of hearing it as a child, but she did not know the dialect well enough to distinguish between countries.

"*Non, merci, je n'ai pas soif*," said Selma. The sentence came out smooth enough. She only hoped that she had politely turned down the hot beverage and not insulted her hosts.

A large smile formed from on the man's face as he clapped his hands together in delight. "Ah, *oui, c'est merveilleux*. It seems that your French is as rusty as your grasp on the law, but I do love a woman who is willing to throw herself on the coals."

Selma's stomach sank. She supposed she no longer had to guess whether or not they knew that she had told Millie about her family's magic.

"Now that most of us are here, let us begin," said the man. "Miss Plumey, do you know why you are here?"

Whether it was survival instinct or plain stupidity, Selma lied. "I do not, sir."

His eyes shone, as if he had seen right through her lie and sensed her weakness. "You may call me Olivier. I am of the Artigues bloodline." He turned to the other men in the room. "And we have representatives from the founding families Poueyferré, Julos, Omex, Lugagnan."

Olivier put his tea down and smiled wider now, showing off

a feline smirk. "You will have to excuse our absent guest. We do have one bloodline missing. Your presence has been requested here, before the Order today, because not only have you put all of us at risk by choosing to reveal your family's gifts to a human, but you have also chosen not to follow the path of commitment to our Goddess Saint."

The back door groaned open, interrupting Olivier's speech. The tall stranger that had taxied her here gracefully passed through the threshold. His features were brutal but gorgeous. His eyes were light, in stark contrast to his olive skin and severe demeanor. The man stalked to a chair near the back and settled in. He placed one leg over his other knee and rested his elbows on the armrests, revealing intricate black and gray tattoos that swirled over the top of his hands and fingers.

Her pendant was practically hovering off her skin now. The missing bloodline, perhaps?

Olivier shot him a look of annoyance but turned to carry on.

"If I may continue. We simply cannot have witches and warlocks wandering around casting on humans and sharing our secrets without oversight from the Order. Humans are dangerous when given too much information, and it is our job to ensure the safety of our world. There rules are in place for a reason, and without the proper training or supervision, you have irresponsibly put this Order and your magic brethren in danger." Olivier paused to take a sip of his tea. "Thankfully it has been brought to our attention. Otherwise, who knows what trouble you could have gotten us all into. As is customary in these situations, the accused is welcome to say a few words before we hand down our punishment."

"Punishment!" exclaimed Selma, finally saying something aloud—not that she had any control over it. The words had practically jumped out of her throat.

"Yes, Miss Plumey, there must be consequences for your neglect and reckless actions," said Olivier with a calmness that Selma did not return.

"There must be something I can do to fix this," pleaded Selma.

Olivier sent her a quizzical glance. "Are you insinuating, Miss Plumey, that you know better than the people in this room, who have dedicated their lives to keeping our kind safe?" He rested his chin on his fist and gave Selma a half smile.

Selma quickly looked around the room, eyeing the other members of the council. They only shook their heads in disapproval. "No, I…" she stumbled. "I'm just curious if there is something I can do in order to earn the opportunity to learn more about committing to the Goddess and the resources that the Order can offer young witches and warlocks. I can assure you that I meant no harm."

She released a subtle breath, hoping that the room would not notice her evasiveness. She stole a glance over at the dark man who had joined late and could not read him. His cold, calculated stare remained unwavering.

"I do not believe it's our duty to chase after you and implore you to live up to your responsibilities, Miss Plumey," said Olivier. His tone grew firm. "In fact, I don't even believe it's your family's job to contain your rebellious nature—although they certainly could have done a better job at preparing you for your calling despite your magical shortcomings. Even those of the Common have a responsibility to the craft, and to our Goddess."

The dark man in the corner spoke up for the first time. His voice was low and entrancing. He still sat lazily back in his chair, wearing a bored facial expression. "If I may. Why are we wasting our time on this? It is obvious that her power is minimal at best.

Making her serve in the covenant would be nothing more than a waste of resources."

Rage and embarrassment bubbled in Selma's chest. To insinuate that she was a drain on their resources without knowing anything about her...*Bastard.*

One of the council members chimed in from the side as he fidgeted with his pearl cufflinks. "On the contrary, the covenant is the perfect place for her. She can work off her crime and learn some manners. Servitude would do her some good."

Something snapped in Selma. "What? Servitude? What decade are we in? I do not know what kind of authority you think this club of yours has, but I have rights. You cannot just place me in 'servitude.'" Selma held up her fingers, giving air quotes.

Searing pain shot through her body in an instant. Her vision blurred, and her skin felt like it was on fire as she dropped to her knees. And as quickly as the pain had taken over, it was gone. Selma huffed for breath, looking over her skin for any injuries but finding none. There was only a cold sweat covering her flesh.

"I would suggest you keep your attitude at bay, Miss Plumey," said Olivier with a sneer. "You may not appreciate the power one can wield with the elements, but I assure you, being brought to your knees is just the beginning. And as for our 'club' that you refer to with such disrespect, it has far outreached your pitiful understanding. We have overseen the most prominent and influential magic-wielders for countless generations. We are the heart of the magic community, but I can see now that the apple does not fall far from the tree. If you don't keep quiet, we will not only be forced to place you in the covenant for mandatory volunteer service to the founding bloodlines, but I believe you will lose something far more valuable than your freedom."

Selma could not think of a single thing, besides her magic, that she would value more than her freedom. But they could not take her magic. It was a part of her. She sat in silence, looking at each member, hoping to gain empathy from the numerous onlookers. Then she lowered her head in submission.

Olivier's lips curled up, and there was another short silence as he took yet another sip of his tea. "Now that we have your attention, what do we do with you? Decisions, decisions," he said. His stare cut into Selma like a knife. "Marta, why don't we bring in our guest?"

"Our only obligation is to our greatest treasure."

—Recovered correspondence from Lilibet Lourdes to Alister Lourdes,
property of the Lourdes Estate

CHAPTER 13

Nothing could have prepared Selma for the gut-wrenching fear that crippled her senses when the door opened to reveal a delicate form being led into the room by a guard twice her size. The confusion on Millie's face eased a bit when her darting eyes landed on Selma. But they again lost their focus when she clearly registered Selma's dread.

Her mind was flooded with a stream of Millie's jumbled thoughts. One thought crashed into the next in a series of panicked questions. All Selma could do was smile at her friend and wordlessly mouth her reassurance: *Everything is going to be okay.*

But she did not know if everything was going to be okay. Why would they bring Millie into this? Why would they invite a human if they had intentions of letting both walk out of here?

"Ah, Mrs. Cooper. It's so nice of you to join us." Olivier smirked from the place where he had been sipping his tea. "I'm sorry for the sudden intrusion, but we had an important matter to discuss with you, and I'm afraid it could not wait. It seems that you have been entrusted with a rather large secret by our dear Selma here."

Millie looked over at Selma, needing some guidance. But Selma just sent her a quick shake of her head. The last thing Selma wanted to do was put her friend in danger, and admitting anything on Millie's end would do just that.

Millie responded, her eyes still darting between Olivier and Selma, "I do not know what you are talking about. Where have you brought me?"

Olivier clicked his tongue. "Tsk. Tsk. I'm afraid lying will not do either of you much good here, Mrs. Cooper."

He walked over to a large iron hutch on the opposite side of the room. Iridescent green threads grew from his form, reaching out from his back like wings and plunging into the floral pots, drinking in their energy. Once he stood in front of the ornate metal doors, the threads did something that Selma had never seen threads do before: they wrapped themselves in front of Olivier and encased the large hutch in their webbing.

What is happening? Why are we here?

Panic rose from Millie's thoughts, and Selma once again tried to think of anything that would calm her friend. After a few moments of slithering in and out of one another, Olivier's threads spelled out a symbol, its curves and lines bright and pulsing. It must have been a rune to ward off anyone from opening the hutch.

Millie's thoughts became more frantic. The rise and fall of her chest was deep with each labored breath. Selma did not take her eyes off Millie, trying to get her glassy eyes to look Selma's way and calm down. Instead, violet threads came into view. It was the same vibrant color that Selma had seen when she and Meriem performed

Millie's energy scan. Only they were not coming from Millie.

Selma followed the delicate strands, watching them weave and bend from their origin—Selma's own body. She was summoning threads. They grew outward toward a trembling Millie, cradling her in their embrace, growing brighter and stronger each second. A strange sensation fell over Selma's body, and she watched Millie's form calm and her breaths even out. Was Selma—or rather, her threads—manipulating Millie's emotions? Millie let out a breath, her shoulders rounding as her muscles relaxed.

Selma watched as her threads returned to her body. As the last one retracted, she lifted her gaze to find the dark stranger's ice-blue eyes boring into her. Had he noticed? Had he seen, or at least sensed, what she had done?

The two doors on the dark iron hutch finally opened. Selma held her breath as she waited to see what was locked away inside. Clearly, it was important enough to be warded. The doors slowly swung open to reveal a single vial of dark, swirling liquid. Olivier reached in carefully, picking up the small bottle and turning toward Selma.

"You know, Selma, our Goddess wielded the same magic that flows through us. It was her and her sister who gifted magic to those whom they felt deserved it. It is a great responsibility to bear, one that I fear not all appreciate," said Olivier. He stared into the glass vial. The dark purple swirls inside reflected in his pupils. "This container of Brocken bark is all we have left of the Goddesses' raw magic. It is from the very tree that sprouted from their blood. It is incredibly potent. A single sliver holds enough power to alter the DNA of any being. It has been said that not all survive its transformation."

Olivier put the small container back into the hutch and carefully closed its doors. He waited until his magic finished warding the vial's prison once more, then he turned to address Selma. "Now that the Goddesses sleep, it has fallen on this council to uphold the standards of magic that the Goddess Saint would wish us to. She is, after all, the one who gifted elemental magic, the one who wasn't deceived by greed."

Finally possessing the courage to speak, Selma asked, "Why are you telling me all of this?"

"Many years ago, this council was betrayed by one of our own. His very blood runs through you, and it is time for him to pay for his crimes," ordered Olivier. "I believe you can help us find him."

"What—" Her mouth made motion, but no words came out. Selma's throat and lips had gone dry. Her stomach turned, and she felt relief that she had already emptied its contents.

Olivier stalked over to her, leaning down to whisper and sending a cold shiver through her body. He was so close to Selma that she could smell the brandy on his breath. "And before you refuse," Olivier went on, "you should know that we have already fed a dose of the Brocken bark to your friend. She has not yet felt its full effects because of my kindness. I alone hold it frozen in place in her body, but one thought from me and it will attach to every fiber of her being, changing her forever. Whether or not she survives is up to the Goddess."

Olivier's look was cold, unyielding. Selma's eyes widened, and her jaw went slack. She did not dare look at Millie for fear of seeing her terror and breaking her heart wide open.

"You cannot do this," Selma murmured.

The room giggled as if she were throwing a temper tantrum. They knew that she was powerless to stop anything, and she was making herself look small in the process of trying.

Olivier sneered. "Of course we can, girl. Where do you think your powers came from in the first place? Magic does not simply exist. It is earned and bestowed upon you by the strongest among us. The Goddesses saw to that."

"There has to be something I can do." Selma's tone came dangerously close to desperate.

Olivier's eyes pulled to the side as his shoulders shrugged. "There is. Tell us the location of your father, and you and your friend are free to go."

Selma's breath caught. Silence filled the room. Even though Selma felt no allegiance to her father, she still did not know where he was.

"I cannot help you," Selma offered in a whisper.

Olivier's jaw ticked. But the dark stranger showed no reaction. His gaze remained steadfast. Questioning looks and whispers cried out in unison, threatening to crack the room in half. Olivier waited, it seemed, for those in the room to collect themselves and give him their undivided attention once again.

"I don't know where he is," Selma responded. "I have not seen him in years."

Olivier plastered a sinister smile onto his lips. "Then perhaps you are in need of some additional motivation." He turned to Millie.

Selma pleaded, "I don't understand. What does my father have to do with any of this?"

His eyes continued to bore into her. "As you are now aware, your father is a known enemy of the Order. He has committed heresy against the Goddess Saint and evaded our efforts in bringing him to justice. However, if you cooperate, we are willing to forgive your own indiscretions. Surely you would not feel the need to protect a man who not only committed crimes against the Goddess but ran away from his family…if turning him over will keep your friend from harm."

Selma stayed quiet. Heat rose from her toes up through her body. She sensed the awkward shifting of bodies once more. She debated running. But they would come after her, and running from an entire magical council was not something she had the capacity for right now. So, she closed her eyes and reached inside for something, anything, that would help her right now. But all she could think about was burning this castle to the ground.

She thought of Millie, so small and fragile with sickness; she thought of her Aunt Verda and how disappointed she would be. Selma reached for anything useful in her sad, dark thoughts, but her mind was blank. The rage took over everything else in her head. What little she knew about this world was now going to be her downfall.

Selma held back the tears. She would not cry in front of them. She would not let them see how much they were getting to her.

Olivier's sneer turned into a scowl. "Very well. Someone will pay for his crimes. Bring her to me." Two large warlocks grabbed Millie by her wrists and dragged her over to Olivier, throwing her to her knees in front of him. His emerald threads snaked out of his fingers and wrapped around her throat.

"Did you know that the body is over fifty percent water? Fascinating, isn't it? I do wonder how much it takes to fill the lungs," he said. His threads made their way into Millie's mouth and down her throat.

Millie choked on the bitter tang of magic, tears running down her cheeks.

"Stop!" Selma pleaded. "I do not know where my father is, but I will help you find him. Just please stop."

Olivier's threads retracted, and he let Millie fall to the floor, coughing.

"You have three months to deliver his location to us, or you and your family will pay for his crimes in servitude. To ensure that you are taking this seriously, you can save your friend by participating in a series of trials assigned by the Order. All will be completed to our liking and display your commitment to our Goddess. If you are genuinely interested in committing to our Goddess Saint, then I am sure you will have no trouble with them. Deliver your father to us and complete the trials. You and your family may then maintain your freedom, and your friend her life," said Olivier.

Selma blew out a breath of relief, but her rage still bubbled just underneath her skin.

Olivier called her attention once more. "That isn't all, Miss Plumey. Razon will watch over you and assist in your mission." His gaze fell to the dark stranger in the back of the room.

A shudder wracked Selma's body. "And if I refuse?"

"Then we will see how strong your friend truly is when the liquid makes its way into her system. It is a gruesome process. I do hope she survives it," said Olivier.

"I don't understand why you are doing this. I am a witch." Confusion and hurt tugged at her gut.

Olivier whispered in a shrill tone that made her muscles tense, "Even witches bleed."

Selma's breath caught in her throat. "How long will you keep the poison in her blood?"

"For as long as you are useful," Olivier replied.

Reluctance dripped from her nod, but what other choice did she have?

"C'est magnifique!" He sauntered back over to Selma. "If I find out that you know the whereabouts of your father and don't comply with this council, rest assured that your punishment will be much more severe. I don't take being played for a fool lightly."

Everyone rose from their seats and began to shuffle out the back. Selma took a step toward Millie, who was still lying on the ground with tear-soaked cheeks. She did not dare look at Razon.

"Selma," Olivier called out with a snarl. "I am only generous once. Your friend will remain safe as long as I am happy." He tilted his head. "It's a shame how frail the human body can be."

Selma gently picked up Millie and ushered her out of the room as quickly as possible, trying desperately to keep the bile from rising to her throat. When she looked back over her shoulder, Razon had risen to his feet and was closing the distance between them. Dizziness hit her as arms wrapped around her waist. The room went dark.

"The title of warrior is not simply given but earned."

—An excerpt from the Canon, as translated by Leven Kara, property of the Warriors of Sever

CHAPTER 14

The darkness enveloped her. Selma blinked back the fog, and panic raced through her veins as she recalled her last memory before passing out. Millie on the ground, gasping for a sip of air. Selma's hands fumbling around her, trying to get a grasp of where she was.

She was back at the manor. But where was Millie? Whispers danced through the crack in the doorframe. Someone was still up.

Selma got out of bed and stumbled across the hardwood floor. She was still in the clothes she'd worn to the summons. She needed to find Millie and see if she was alright. Whispers stopped her in her tracks and battled each other for dominance. Three voices, but Selma could not make out what they were saying. She gingerly moved along the hallway. Peeking her head around the banister, she could see that the door to the library was cracked open, letting a ray of light slice through the dark hallway.

"Do you not feel that she deserves to know?"

"Know what? It will not change anything. She will still be in this mess."

The voices were barbed, tussling with one another to gain ground.

"But if she knew more about her mother's magic, she might be better prepared."

Her mother and aunts. What was her mother not telling her about her magic?

"And if—"

"Enough. Selma has already been burdened with enough. We remain steadfast."

Selma leaned in closer, eliciting a high-pitched creak from the stairs. She mouthed a curse and shot up so she would not get caught crawling on the floor and eavesdropping.

The group of women shuffled out of the library one after the other.

"You look like hell, but at least you're awake," said Gerta. "Millie is at home with her family. Razon took her right after he dropped you off here."

"Razon!" Selma exclaimed. "And you trusted him with her? She could be hurt or scared. I have to go see her."

Selma turned to leave, but her mother caught her by the elbow. "She is fine. Startled, but not any more harmed than she was when she arrived. We gave her a sedative, and she is resting. You should allow her to rest."

Selma pulled her arm away but did not carry on down the hall.

"You know? You know what happened at the council summons? Is that what you expected when you turned me in? That they would threaten Millie?"

Meriem placed her hand on her chest. "You think *we* did this?"

Selma spat back, "Didn't you? How else would anyone know about Millie? Now she's in danger, and it's your fault."

"Oh, don't be daft, girl. We had nothing to do with it. Besides, laying all the blame on us is childish. You are the one who told her about us in the first place. You should start with shouldering at least some of the responsibility, however hard that might be for you," snapped Uma. "The Order has been looking for your father for a while now. They had someone watching you, waiting for you to do anything that would justify bringing you in."

Selma kept her eyes on the floor, like the solution to the whole mess would be carved into the wood grain. She thought back to the dark stranger she had seen in the shop, and then again at the Mud House. It was him. Razon had been watching her.

"They think they can use me to pry my father out of hiding. Why have they not tried this anytime in the last twenty years?"

Uma's eyes flicked up at her. "Because they did not know about you. We did our best to not draw attention to you. Because of your father."

Selma's eyes narrowed on Uma. "What did he do that was so horrible?" Selma fought every syllable out of her mouth. "Did it have something to do with him leaving? Or my magic?"

Uma's eyes widened, panic ebbing in her pupils. "They didn't see you use magic, did they?"

Selma scoffed. "No. I was too busy figuring out how to keep them from killing my friend right in front of me." In truth, she could not be certain that the council did not see her use magic. But if they could keep secrets, then so could she.

Uma let out a sigh. "At least you got out of there relatively unscathed." The words dripped from her mother's lips like acid.

"Yes, but for how long? Unless *you* know where my father is?" Selma let the questions hang in the air.

"Always so dramatic," Uma hissed. "We will figure something out."

"Ah, yes. I did get the impression that they were understanding when they were trying to drown Millie with water from her own body. We will just explain to them that my deadbeat dad did not leave a return address, and everything will be fine," said Selma.

Her eyes narrowed on her mother again. Leaving her aunts staring at her in the hallway, she stomped back to her room, slamming the bedroom door and releasing a cloud of dust and a loud cracking sound.

The women got there mere moments later, practically slamming into the door as they came to a crashing halt. Knocks thundered through the wood, along with their shrill voices calling her name. Selma had little desire to hear anything from them at this moment. The years. All the years she had put up with their snide comments and disapproval, believing it was all just a part of family dynamics, now seemed so trivial compared to this ultimate betrayal. She did not care what they had to say nor where they thought she should go from here. The more she marinated in the betrayal, the more heat rose through her body, and she let out a boisterous curse into the universe, feeling all her energy trail down her nerves in a hectic wave of power.

She looked down at the tops of her hands and watched as sparks of violet threads webbed and crackled. All at once, a sharp, stinging sensation overwhelmed her senses. It felt as if magic had just exploded inside of her skin and poured out of her. Before she could control them, her violet threads were racing toward the door. They were stronger and faster than they had been before. She had never felt her magic do this. It was as if they were just as pissed as she was and wanted to scream just as loudly. Her family stopped yelling through the door. But Selma heard their footsteps as they moved down the hallway.

Bringing her hands to her face, Selma made herself small. Perhaps if she made herself small enough, she could disappear and not deal with this. All she had ever wanted was to summon threads and be like the rest of her family, but now magic was raging inside of her, burning under her skin, and she could do nothing about it. It only caused trouble for her. For Millie. Selma looked toward her bedroom window and abruptly knew what she had to do.

She got up, kicking the candles aside, and reached for the glass of the large bay window. She used all the force she could muster, with both hands pushed up on the frame. It did not budge, but she was running on adrenaline and wrath, and she needed to get out of this house and check on Millie.

Selma looked around her room for any tool that might help her pry the window open. Frantically pacing around the room, opening drawers and hutch cabinets, Selma came across a candle snuff that was shaped like scissors. It was not ideal, but it might just do the trick. Using the sharp end of the candle snuff, she scraped paint off the windowsill, slowly peeling away small shards. After a few minutes of sheer determination, Selma tried again. At last, the window conceded defeat, and Selma slid the glass up, letting a waft of fresh air into her bedroom.

Placing one leg after the other, Selma ducked her head and kept her balance on the short awning. The branches of the tree outside her window were much closer than they had been when she was younger, and she was relieved to see that she could climb onto them easily enough. Quickly but cautiously, Selma made her way down the branches and jumped, stumbling just a bit as she hit the soft ground cover. She dusted off her jeans and removed a stray leaf from her hair, turning to move down the driveway. She needed a strong cocktail, and even though she doubted that any bars would be open, she did know of a liquor store on the way to Millie's house. There, she could pick up enough libations to forget that this day had ever happened.

A deep voice caught Selma off guard. "Going somewhere?"

"A child's heart is fragile but finds itself on the most dangerous of paths."

—A recovered journal entry, journal of Verda Plumey, property of the Plumey Estate

CHAPTER 15

Selma quickly turned to see Razon standing there, towering over her. And he was even more stunning in the moonlight. The ink that clung to his carved arms seemed to somehow move in the dim light, and the silver flecks floating in his deep blue eyes were mesmerizing. So much so that she did not realize she had been staring. Was that pulsing beat from her pendant or her heart?

His lips parted, and he spoke in a melodic accent. "See something you like, love?"

That did it. *Bastard.* Selma shook her head to clear the fog that had taken over, swapping out her gaping mouth with a scowl. His composed nature and polished guise made her blood boil. He likely spent more time pressing his boxer shorts than he spent doing anything else. And he had been the one who brought her to the Order. He had surely been the one to bring Millie to them as well. The overreaching conservative collective that had threatened not just her, but Millie, to within an inch of her life and was still clutching her delicate existence in their hands. Razon's smug presence only reminded her of his cruelty.

She reached out with her gift to try again with his thoughts, in case there had been a ward on the castle to keep her from using her magic. She quieted her nerves and reached toward his mind.

But Selma heard only the first inkling of his mental musings.

Tsk, tsk. None of that now. You will need to try much harder to get in here. He lifted one finger to the side of his head and tapped.

Selma gasped and pulled back.

Razon responded by tilting up the corner of his lips ever so slightly. *I think the far more important question would be, why would you assume I wear boxers?*

He smiled. The kind that said he knew he was getting under her skin. *You were going somewhere. I have been tasked with looking after you.*

"Stop it!" Selma yelled. "I didn't think the Order would send their errand boy today. Not that it's any of your business, but I'm going out. And you will not be joining. You may have been assigned to watch me, but stalking is still a crime. Who are you, anyway?"

"Do not ask questions you already know the answer to. It wastes my time." He spoke aloud this time. His voice was deep and rich, like velvet. She had heard it at the summons, but hearing it here and now sent a chill down Selma's spine.

Selma froze. Heat bubbled up in her chest. *Bastard.* "Whether or not you want to answer my questions does not change the fact that you cannot follow me."

"You only have three days before your first trial." Razon prowled toward her, each step unveiling a new breathtaking detail of his formidable body. He moved flawlessly around Selma, so close she hoped he would not feel her body tremble. His breath tickled her ear. "Don't bother hiding. I know what you are thinking. What you are feeling." His eyes flicked downward, and a strange sensation rolled down Selma's spine, heating her core. "I can smell you. Every time you look over your shoulder, I will be there. I suggest you take the time to prepare," he added.

Her breath quickened. She only had three days. That was not much time. She knew nothing about the trials nor how to prepare for them, but she was not going to let that weakness show. For now, she straightened her back and shrugged. "And what, exactly, do you suggest I do to prepare?"

Razon tilted his head in amusement. "There are only a few details that they wish for me to share with you. The Order likes their prey to be weak."

Selma scoffed. "Cute. You have club rules. Is there a secret handshake, too?"

Razon began to walk away, but Selma yelled after him, "Typical for men to like their prey weak."

"Some men, perhaps. I prefer mine to have a bit of fire. It makes the catch sweeter," said Razon. He turned to face her, and his eyes licked up every detail of her body. He ran his thumb over his bottom lip. She knew he was trying to get a rise out of her. But she still wished she could bite his lip, right where his thumb had stroked.

"Blood, flesh, and fire," said Razon. "Those are the themes of the Goddess's trials. You will need to complete all three of them."

Selma placed her hands on her hips. "And if I do not?"

"If you care about your friend, then you will," he said.

"You will keep your hands off her," Selma spat.

The blue in his eyes lightened. "I will never lay a hand on her. I made sure she returned home safely. But the council is not known for their restraint. I suggest you find a way out of this. And soon."

Selma threw Razon a nasty gesture as he walked away. She could hear his deep-throated laugh, even as his words scraped against the corners of her mind.

See you soon, princess.

‡

On Millie's stoop, Selma clutched a dark bottle in her fist and brought it to her lips. The bitter liquid washed over her tongue with a promise to dull her senses. The air was still heavy with summer, but a breeze promised autumn soon. She had checked on Millie earlier, who was still foggy from whatever they had given her to settle her. Selma wanted to wait until she was rested to talk to her. Hopefully that would be before she reached the bottom of the bottle.

David arrived and pulled out two grocery bags full of food. He greeted Selma with a smile, no doubt in the dark about Millie's unexpected kidnapping.

"Here for dinner? If so, you're in luck. I found a recipe for plant-based ribs," said David. "How's our girl?"

Selma put the glass bottle on the ground and reached up to take one of the bags. She did not know how to answer that question.

"She is just fine," Millie answered from behind them. David greeted her with a smile and a kiss. But Selma just stared at her.

"Straight from the bottle—classy. I suppose you won't be needing a glass with dinner," Millie chimed as she stood in the threshold, pointing at the partially empty bottle of wine.

Selma sluggishly walked up the stairs to the front door; her shoulders were hunched, and while clutching a wine bottle in each hand she put her arms around her fragile friend. She could not bring it up now, in front of David, but she hoped her embrace would lessen just a little of the day's trauma.

"Nope. It would just mean more dishes to clean up later," Selma responded. Then she whispered, "I am so sorry. They are the worst. I wish I had been adopted." Selma said into Millie's shoulder, "Do you think it's possible for your parents to retroactively adopt me?"

Millie let go of Selma and sighed. "I think if they were to come back from the dead, that would certainly be the first task they would take on."

Selma appreciated the sarcasm. Sometimes it was the only way she realized that she had said something insensitive.

"Come on inside." Millie gestured for Selma to enter. "But you're sharing that wine."

Selma smiled, knowing her friend had already forgiven her for her comment. "Why do you think I bought two bottles?"

Hours passed as the two chatted. David went upstairs to sleep. The two women relocated to the outside patio, which was connected to Millie's she-shed that David had built for her on one of their anniversaries. It housed all of Millie's dark romance novels, along with her vintage home decor and plenty of large, fluffy pillows and blankets. But even the wine could not distract them any longer.

"I just wish, you know, that I could have been different," slurred Selma.

"Different how?" Millie had a better hold of her speech but was not far behind.

"You know. Without Uma and her ancient biddies. Without constant judgment. And Hayden…I don't know what to do about Hayden. He keeps calling and calling and calling. He asked me to move in with him, said he would pay the extra months on my lease, like I am a fifties homemaker," rambled Selma.

"I'm not sure that's what he meant, and every family has their shortcomings," said Millie with a shrug.

"Yours didn't have shortcomings. Yours was a damn Rockwell painting. Mine was more like the Addams family without Gomez," said Selma.

"The Addams family was actually pretty healthy. I wish I had Gomez and Morticia's sex life," responded Millie.

"You're missing the point," blurted Selma.

"No, *you* are missing the point. So your dad left. You were raised by a host of women who were not perfect. They might have even fumbled it royally, but you turned out fine," said Millie in a tone that was suddenly serious.

"Fine, sure. But I could have been—"

"Been what? Cancer-free with a loving boyfriend? Forgive me, but I really do not have the energy to dive into your daddy issues right now. I was just kidnapped from my home and threatened by some evil witch cult because of you, and we are sitting here pretending that it did not happen because we would not want to stress you out too much," said Millie. "Do you not see how twisted that is? Your dad left, and my dad had an affair with the neighbor for twenty-five years, but we got over it. You have to learn to not make everything about you, Sel."

Selma was silent. The air around them had become stifled. She knew that Millie was struggling with her illness, that she did not know it was the council that had poisoned her.

Finally, Selma broke the silence. "We don't know that it's cancer."

Tears were welling up in Millie's eyes. Selma saw the deep, dark circles underneath them more clearly now.

"We don't know if it's *not* cancer," responded Millie. "And I love you, Sel. You know I do, but I am exhausted, and I cannot keep taking care of you emotionally. Today, I was kidnapped because you chose to tell me about your magic. I did not ask for that. I did not ask for any of this. And you just sit across from me drinking wine like it's any other day, and you want to talk about your boyfriend. Where have you been?"

"The phone works both ways," uttered Selma. Her tone had more venom in it than usual, and she knew at once that it was the wrong thing to say. But the wine had made her fuzzy and combative. She knew she should be groveling. All of this was her fault, but she had no idea how to fix it.

Selma looked at the empty bottle of wine. "I should go. Do not worry—they will not bother you again. I'll make sure of it."

Selma was not sure if her words were a lie, but they were all she could come up with. Millie did not say anything as Selma got up from the pillows. She just nodded and wiped her eyes.

Selma walked back to the island with Millie's words still burning in her mind. She was too tired to bathe, but she washed her face in the sink, noting the dark circles under her eyes, and sank into bed. Not wanting to think about the trial or her aunts, her mind wandered, dredging up thoughts that she was not sure were promising and letting them lull her to sleep.

"Wargraves shall contribute, to the extent of our abilities, to promote equitable relationships between all sentient beings and to support the education of the ignorant, the healing of the sick, the protection of the weak, and the advancement of the downtrodden."

—An excerpt from the Canon, as translated by Leven Kara, property of the Warriors of Sever

CHAPTER 16

Morning came quickly. Selma's head throbbed, as if tiny jackhammers were doing construction on her brain. And with strained effort, she labored to open one eye and retreat from the bright sun pulsing through her window. Her wrinkled clothing from the day prior was still wrapped around her body.

"Argh!" Selma managed to let out a groan. "I feel like a garbage can."

"And you smell like one as well—or at least the recycling bin at a pub," came a voice from the corner.

Selma startled and popped up, instantly regretting her swift movements.

"You," she drawled.

"Yes, princess, me. It is morning. At least for those of us who do not smell like they fell asleep in a bar last night," said Razon as he nonchalantly turned the pages of an outdated magazine. "It seems that someone has been trying hard to get ahold of you. Your phone has been vibrating incessantly for the last hour."

Selma thought about the night before and her fight with Millie. Hopefully it was Millie calling to give her a chance to make things right. She clumsily reached for her phone.

"You have been here for an hour, just watching me sleep? Is that not a violation of my privacy? And speaking of privacy, stop looking through my phone," said Selma. Her voice sounded like it had been through a cheese grater. She took in Razon, who was sitting casually in the chair. The muscles in his arms tensed with every page he turned, and he looked perfectly delicious. *Stop it. Stop look-ing at your captor like a snack.*

"I didn't look through your phone; I said it was vibrating. That is different," said Razon.

Selma reluctantly looked at her screen. No calls from Millie. Selma could not blame her. The four missed calls were from Hayden. She could not blame him either. She had not talked to him since their last phone conversation ended abruptly. But that was a problem for another time. Right now, she had a monster headache to suffer through as a punishment.

Selma sat up and wiped her hair from her face. "I do not snore," she said with confidence. "Wait, how did you get in here?" Selma frantically looked from Razon to the door, which she was certain she had warded. No matter how tempting he looked sitting in her chair, nobody was supposed to enter or exit without her permission. So, how was he in her bedroom?

Razon let out a low chuckle.

"Your wards? For all the good they were, you might as well have written 'KEEP OUT' on a piece of paper with a crayon," he said.

Razon kept perusing the magazine as he spoke to Selma, like he was too bored with the subject matter to carry on a debate. He closed the magazine, dropped it on the floor, and got up from his seat in one fluid movement.

"Time to get moving, princess. We have a lot to do in a small amount of time, and we cannot waste any of it sitting here debating your bodily functions," said Razon.

"Ugh, don't say 'bodily functions' unless you want to witness another one on the floor next to you," said Selma, holding her closed fist to her lips.

"Delightful." Razon rolled his eyes.

"Just go downstairs. I will come down when I am ready," Selma said, gesturing wildly toward the door.

His stare was intoxicating. She felt like she could dive into the deep blue waters of his eyes.

Razon sauntered to the door with one hand in his pocket. "I'll have Meriem make you some fried toast. It will soak up whatever demons you battled last night," he said, and Selma almost sensed empathy behind his words.

"Burrito!" she tried to shout through her gurgling throat. It was the only word that Selma could manage to get out while keeping her stomach contents at bay.

"Toast will be better. Trust me," said Razon, nodding his head in a way that made Selma think that he believed this conversation was over.

"I loathe you," she murmured, burying her face in her pillow.

"Ah, no you don't. You think I am *tempting*," said Razon as he disappeared behind the door.

‡

Thirty minutes later, Selma slowly slunk down the stairs, wearing denim cutoffs, an oversized sweater, and sunglasses. She had managed to comb her hair, but the imprint of wrinkled sheets was still stamped onto her left cheek. She shuffled to the kitchen and began crashing through the cupboards, looking for the makings of a strong cup of coffee.

Meriem was fussing with the tea kettle while a pile of toasted rye bread lay stacked next to a jam jar on the island. Razon sat propped on the island, silent.

"Would you like some help, dear?" Meriem offered, but it was laced with sarcasm.

Selma slammed a bag of roasted coffee beans down on the counter and fussed with the dials of the grinder, refusing to utter one word to the witch and warlock.

Meriem spoke up again. "If you're going to ignore me, would you mind keeping it down just a touch?"

Selma gently placed her hands down on the counter and looked straight up into the air. She counted backwards from ten, all the while thinking of all the places she would rather be in this moment. Her head still ached, and she knew that Meriem or Gerta would have potent hangover cures, but that would mean accepting help from them, which was out of the question.

"What was that? Are you saying something? You need to speak up. I have always said that you mumble too much," said Meriem.

Selma did not turn to face her onlooker as her words blundered from her lips. "I don't want anything from you."

Razon remained steadfast as Aunt Meriem let out an offended huff before wiping her hands on her apron and stomping out of the room.

"And you. Why the fuck are you here in my kitchen? In my room? Barking orders at me and drinking my tea? I have already told the council that I do not know where my father is. I cannot hide anything from them if I do not even know what it is I would be hiding," said Selma, looking over at Razon with distaste.

"Such a foul mouth," Razon protested. "Well, I believe that this kitchen actually belongs to your family, and the other little bit has already been explained to you."

Selma sent him a look of both confusion and disdain. "That does not explain why you broke through my wards, trespassed into my room, violated my privacy, and proclaimed that we have a lot to do. What do *we* have to do? You said my trial was in three days, and *you* are not the one being tested," said Selma.

Razon looked up at Selma from under his long eyelashes, almost beckoning her. Goddess, he was gorgeous. He sent her a feral smile, and Selma returned his look with wide eyes. In her foggy state, she had yet again forgotten that he knew her thoughts.

Selma bit back, "Get out of my head!"

"But you make it so easy," said Razon with a shake of his head. "Plus, you cannot tell me that you have not tried the same trick. I have felt you trying to root around in my mind. Discover my secrets."

"Why would I do that? I doubt you have anything interesting happening up there. Brawns for brains rarely do," said Selma. "Could you go drool somewhere else? If I decide to have daddy-daughter day, I will be sure to tell you."

That got his attention. His eyes glued to her like he was looking for something. "What do you know about your father?"

"About as much as you do, so leave me alone about it," Selma snapped.

She poured her coffee and focused on the word "about." She let the steam lift from the rim of the cup up toward her nostrils. She took a sip of the hot, bitter liquid and let it wash over her tongue and throat. If only it could wash away last night completely. She thought of Millie and the way she had looked laying out all her emotions for Selma to drudge through. Her heart cracked, and in an attempt to think about anything else, anything at all, she surrendered to Razon's presence.

"How is it that you can read my thoughts? I have never come across anyone else with that ability," Selma asked, knowing that with each question, the thin veil that protected her from Razon was at risk of tearing apart completely. But she had no choice. She did not know where her father was. Her family certainly was not going to be of any help, and if she had any chance of getting through the trials and getting Millie out of this mess, she needed information.

Razon relaxed his shoulders. "How do you know that you have not met anyone with that ability?"

The thought that she may have come across someone who could read her thoughts seized her breath. Now she understood what Millie must have felt the first time she found out about Selma's gifts.

Razon carried on, "With your limited view of the world, it is not likely that you have. It's a rare gift."

Selma's muscles surrendered slightly. "And yet you have it."

"Not in the same way you do," he said.

"Then explain it to me."

"First you want me to leave you alone, and now you want something from me? It does not work that way," he said.

Selma's chest heated. "Are you going to be like this the entire time you are stalking me? If I have to put up with your presence this whole time, then you might as well be useful."

The side of his mouth tilted up in a taunting smirk. "Say please."

Bastard. Selma wondered how the smallest tilt of his lips could both infuriate her and cause the heat in her chest to move down her body. His posture straightened as he stalked over to her. Selma shifted her weight from one foot to the other but did not budge. She would not be intimidated by the Order's grunt man.

Razon moved like a wolf, his movements graceful and quiet. It was not until Selma felt the warmth of his body that she was startled by his closeness.

"Say please," he snarled.

Selma swallowed, her heartbeat once again matching the pulse of her pendant. "No," she finally uttered.

He smiled, releasing whatever hold he had on her, and stepped back. "Nice necklace."

He exited through the back of the room as Selma let out a breath.

"I'll be in the library," he shouted from down the hall.

Selma wrapped her fingers around the delicate chain on her neck. The thrumming of the pendant was undeniable at this point. But she was beginning to suspect that the unique charm held more magic than a simple protection ward.

She made her way to the library after two cups of coffee and fried toast. Her dry heaving had subsided, and the brain fog had almost lifted. She pulled out her phone and sent a message to Hayden.

Super busy with Millie and the doctor today. Call you later.

She did not exactly know why she was lying to him. But that text sounded better than, "On witch probation. Prepping for ancient torture trials with sexy warlock. Call you later."

In the library, she sat down on the cozy chair across from Razon, who had spread out multiple large scrolls across the worktable in the middle of the room. They looked and smelled as if he had dug them out of the catacombs. Mold and decay filled her nostrils. He had also stacked several books on the table. Selma slumped in her chair, still giving her best impression of a swamp monster, and watched Razon move around the room pointing to dusty leather books, his movements like liquid. She could not stand that he was the first person she had seen this morning. She loathed that he was barking orders at her, but she could not take her eyes away from his lips.

"I have chosen some readings that may be helpful for you. The ones over there are from my personal collection. I suggest you start there. Pay attention to the illustrations. You may find them helpful if you are asked about runes. Then move on to the scrolls," said Razon matter-of-factly.

"Why are you doing this? I do not remember anyone at the summons telling me that I would have a dictator tutor along for the trials," she asked, looking up at him with furrowed brows. Not that she was in a place to refuse help.

"I'm not in the habit of sitting around. Besides, your hangover is not my concern. If I am stuck here, I might as well help you not make a fool of yourself in front of the Order," said Razon with a bite in his tone. "Unless, of course, you have something else that you would like to talk about." His eyelashes tilted up to reveal pools of blue.

Selma straightened at the insinuation. "I told you, I do not know where my father is. And my Aunt Verda taught me about my lesser magic until she died, so I'm not completely without knowledge." Selma neglected to mention that her threads had emerged not once, but twice now. She tried to bury the thought deep in her mind, so that Razon would not stumble upon it as he rummaged through her head.

He stayed quiet. Assessing her response. Selma fidgeted under his gaze.

"I'm not always hungover," said Selma. It came out as defensive as it had sounded in her head, but it did succeed in breaking the awkward silence.

Razon revisited the books. He flipped through the pages of a leather-bound tome, finally stopping on one page and examining its contents. He ran his index finger down the weathered paper and asked, "Are these all the books your family has?"

Selma rose from her seat and yanked the book from Razon. Its pages were open to Goddess lore. She rolled her eyes.

"Fairy tales? I just watched Olivier almost drown Millie in her own body fluids, and you want me to read stories about two imaginary witches? What is next? You want me to light a candle? I knew how to do that before I could ride a bike."

Razon returned a blank stare and asked in confusion, "Is it customary for children to learn to ride a bike while simultaneously learning the history of magic?"

Selma could not tell if he was being a prick or if he genuinely did not know that riding a bike was a rite of passage for children.

"What I mean is, it's a simple thing that children do," she stammered. "Do kids not learn how to ride bicycles in France?"

Razon's brow furrowed. "What makes you think I'm from France?"

"Your accent, for one. Your arrogance for another," Selma shot back at him.

Razon smiled, revealing one dimple, then turned his attention back to the book. "I only want you to light a candle if you can access the fire element. Can you?"

Selma took a breath. "Lighting one candle has nothing to do with the fire element. It is simply lesser magic. Any witch could do it, with a blood sacrifice."

"Is that so?" Razon studied her. "Very well. I want to evaluate where we are starting from. Please, dazzle me."

Despite wanting to throw that book at his head, she stepped back and took a deep breath. Selma grabbed a letter opener that lay on the table next to them and dug the sharp end into the palm of her hand until blood pooled. Holding that palm up, as if she were waiting for someone to hand her an object, she whispered a few words into the air.

"Matri deae gratiam praebeo. Sit tua virtus influunt per me."

The small, familiar flame darted up from her palm. She concentrated on keeping it there as sweat formed on her brow.

Razon's face was unreadable. "Good. Can you summon?"

Summoning was always harder for Selma, especially indoors. But a few minutes later, as if out of thin air, a long, skinny stick appeared in her hand.

His eyes looked bored and confused. "A branch? That is what you chose to summon? A dirty piece of wood one can find anywhere?"

"Yes, for you. In case that stick in your ass ever falls out and you need to replace it," Selma huffed back and handed him the stick.

Razon tilted his head in amusement and threw the stick into the trash bin.

"Somewhat rudimentary, but I suppose it will do. Have you attempted to summon objects without your blood sacrifice? That magic is hardly used among the Elementals."

"Well, as we have already established, I'm not an Elemental," Selma said. Her eyes focused on the table in the middle of the room that currently held the scrolls.

Razon raised one eyebrow, but Selma ignored him and pointed to the table.

"What are all these?" She was genuinely curious about the weathered pages. She had never seen anything like them in person.

"Those are scrolls from the library of the Order," he responded. "I want you to start reading them, and we will talk about them when I return. Start with the ones near the top. Those are your history. And I would like for you to try your summoning spell without the blood sacrifice. The last thing we need you to do is pass out at the trial," he barked.

Anger and embarrassment bubbled in Selma's stomach. She thought of Olivier's words as the summons was concluding. He would not be generous moving forward.

"You're right. He will not be generous, and without arming

yourself with every possible bit of knowledge between now and then, you will fail. And I do not believe you are willing to make that sacrifice," said Razon.

"I didn't ask you," Selma responded. Her thoughts went straight to Millie. Razon was right. If she did not comply with the Order, then Olivier would sacrifice Millie, and she could not live with that.

"No. But until you stop keeping things from me and learn how to shut me out of your thoughts, I will already know," he said quickly.

"What did I say about staying out of my mind?" Selma shot back with a glare.

"Stop keeping secrets from me and I will not have to go in. Practice. I will be back," Razon said, waving a hand in the air.

"Ass," Selma whispered.

"Maybe. But it is a sculpted ass, if your stares are any indication," he growled back.

"Two children, said to be born of the earth and of no flesh and bone, harnessed the magic in their blood, making them immortal. The two sisters mimicked those of the mortal world, but they were more powerful, the only tangible beings known to wield the magic in any way they saw fit."

—An excerpt from the Axiom, as translated by Lilibet Lourdes, property of the Museum of the Academe Arts, current location unknown

CHAPTER 17

By lunch, Selma was a heap of exhaustion. She had tried to summon hundreds of objects without a blood sacrifice. She failed every time. She had even started choosing lighter objects in the room to make it easier. To her dismay, it had not helped.

Stagnant air brewed with the sour, earthy fumes of the scrolls, making her insides turn brackish. Remembering that she'd only had toast and coffee that morning, lunch was a necessary respite, especially if the early hours were any indication of what this afternoon would be. The sandwich shop in town was perfect. It had been open for as long as she could remember. The clientele consisted mostly of blue-collar heroes and the three heckling older men who sat outside in folding chairs they brought from home. It was not going to make any best-of dining lists, but they made a scrumptious Italian sandwich. Pair that with salt and vinegar chips, and her hangover would be history. Plus, a walk to take in the cool air would be helpful.

Razon's voice echoed in her mind. *Learned all you need to?*

"I'm going into town for lunch. I will be back for more of your warlock torture in an hour," said Selma, fluttering her fingers toward Razon and adding in her trademark rolling eyes.

Only a few paces out the door did she feel the heat of his presence behind her. Looking over her shoulder, she could see his black hair reflect off the hazy sunlight peeking through the gray clouds. Selma rubbed the visible goose bumps on her arms as her skin prickled.

"Why are you following me?" Her voice took on a hideous high pitch that was more akin to a squawk.

"I'm famished," he replied

"Great, the kitchen is right back there," she said as she pointed behind her.

"I have not had a chance to see your humble little town," Razon said, placing one hand in his pocket and examining the fingernails of his other. His sly smile said everything. He was not going to let her out of his sight.

They walked down the crushed gravel path toward town. Selma could hear the crash of hushed waves in the distance and smell the salty sea air rushing up the cliffs and over the grassy barrier. This place was beautiful. Green and lush. While most people enjoyed the open skies, Selma particularly loved the sea fog that blanketed everything. It had been painted over with a dark gray sheen in her mind for so long that she had forgotten how beautiful it was.

She looked over at Razon. The breeze was pushing his hair back from his face, creating a perfectly tousled coif. They had mostly been walking in silence since leaving the house. He was calm, taking in their surroundings. With his head turned, she noticed a mark peeking out of his collar. A scar. It was not like the other ink markings that covered his sun-kissed skin—at least, the parts of his body she had seen. Her thoughts wandered, and she pondered how covered in tattoos he was. She began to blush and quickly looked away, hoping he would not notice. He must not have been swimming through her mind. If he were, he would have had something to say about it.

Satisfied that she had dodged embarrassment, she broke the silence. "So, are you an elemental?"

He turned, startled. His eyes were glossed over, like he had been somewhere distant in his mind. He shook his head, clearing the haze. "No," he responded curtly.

Selma pushed on. "Does the Order use your ability to read thoughts?"

It would make sense. Selma had heard they were not too keen on witches who only possessed lesser magic. But the ability to read thoughts was a rare gift among the elementals.

"It's called being an empath, and the Order does not know I have that particular ability. I would suggest, for both of our sakes, that you do not tell them," said Razon.

"Oh, now you want something from me," scoffed Selma.

It did not make sense why he would share something so vulnerable. If he was keeping anything from the council members, then she had leverage over him.

She went on, "Say please."

He stopped walking and turned to her, wetting his lips. "Please." There was a genuine softness in his eyes. They were a shade lighter than they normally were.

Selma could not help but ask, "Why?"

"Sometimes secrets are the only thing we can hold on to," said Razon.

Not an answer. But she supposed she had not exactly been forthcoming either, so she could not blame him for his evasiveness. She nodded.

"Are you in the Order?" Selma asked, hoping to gain more information about the entity she was up against.

"No," Razon responded.

His lack of engagement was infuriating. This morning she had wanted nothing more than for him to be silent and let her be. But now, his brash, acute answers were worse.

"Well, you are clearly associated with them, or you would not be gracing me with your cheerful presence," Selma sneered.

Razon was looking off into the distance, either bothered by Selma's questioning or contemplating his answer. "What do you know of the Order?"

Selma had thought she'd made her lack of knowledge clear, but she must had done a better job than she thought of keeping it from him. "I know that the Order is made up of a member of each of the eldest families of magic," responded Selma with confidence. Her Aunt Verda had taught her that before she died.

"Not quite," responded Razon. "Yes, they are some of the eldest families of magic, but they are not the *only* founding families."

Annoyed by his willingness to correct her, she asked a question anyway, wondering if he would deliver a straight answer. "What do you mean? Who are the other families?"

"Magic is much more entrenched in the fabric of the world than you may realize," responded Razon.

Not a straight answer, then.

By this point they had made it to the sandwich shop, and it was in their best interest to cease this conversation until there were fewer prying eyes and ears around. Selma ordered an Italian sandwich, and Razon opted for the vegetarian option. His charms must have worked on the girl at the counter. She giggled as he leaned in with a playful grin. Selma's teeth clenched as the girl handed Razon free chips and soda. Well, he was not afraid to mix a little business with pleasure.

The men outside who usually had plenty to say to the clientele were, for once, silent. And Selma could feel eyes boring into them from the other tables. Newcomers were usually the center of conversation in Belhaven, but this seemed different somehow.

Selma reached out with her gift. Her magic came a bit easier when she was outside. The onlookers expressed fear along with lust. Razon's tall physique and piercing eyes were enough to turn heads, but the overwhelming unease of the people around them prompted Selma to suggest they finish their lunch back at the house.

"I suppose we have become a distraction," Razon agreed.

"I don't think I'm contributing to that," Selma added.

"The women sitting to the right seem to enjoy your striking features," Razon smirked, revealing that dimple once more.

Selma looked over at the table of women, each with a copy of the same book. They were giggling into their coffee and sharing whispers.

"I think they are more interested in your chiseled chest than me." Selma rolled her eyes.

"Have you reached out for their thoughts?" Razon asked, licking his fingers clean.

"They are too far away," Selma said sheepishly.

Razon cocked his head to the side. "It is not my chest they are interested in, but it is interesting to know that *you* are," Razon replied.

Selma blushed and gathered her belongings. If only there was a way for her magic to make her invisible right now.

"There is, but we will get to that," Razon answered.

She would never get used to him hearing her thoughts. For the first time, she understood what it felt like to be utterly vulnerable.

The fresh air was healing, and Selma's hangover was all but gone. She was still sluggish, but her headache had subsided, and her nausea had passed.

They passed old barns and cottages nestled on fenced properties along the cape. Some had been modernized, but all maintained the charm that the Puritans had brought over long ago.

"Where are you from? You have said you are not French, but you never told me where you were actually from." Selma wanted to know more about her dark stranger.

"Does it matter?" Razon responded in a cold, hushed tone.

"I suppose not. But since you and the council have insisted on invading my life and making a feast out of my choices, I believe it's only fair to offer some information about yourself," Selma huffed.

"Alright. If you are so eager to talk, then let's talk about how you summoned threads," said Razon. His serious tone carried weight with it.

Selma grew quiet. She had not talked about her threads with anyone, and the way that Meriem had reacted that day with Millie was off-putting. Selma honestly did not know how she had summoned them, or if she could do it again on purpose.

"That is what I thought. If you spend more time strengthening your mental walls and honing your magic than you do thinking about the trifling details of my upbringing, we will be out of this mess, and I can go about my business," added Razon.

"But then how would you be able to make a spectacle of what a prick you are?" Selma responded.

"I suppose I'm a bellwether and do not need your prompting," Razon responded with a wry smile.

The two stopped and sneered at one another for a moment, until their attention was called to the sounds of whimpering in the distance. Without questioning one another, they moved in the direction of the sounds, which were coming from the trees.

Selma pushed aside branches and tramped across the mossy forest floor, deeper into the woods, leading the way toward the yelps. It was clear that the cries were coming from an injured animal, and eventually she caught a glimpse of a furry silver hide. She hesitated. It was a dog—no, a wolf. She thought back to her walk, to Amalie's companion. Amalie had a pet wolf. No wonder Selma had been taken back by the animal. This wolf was similar, but the markings around its eyes were different.

Selma's heartbeat quickened at the sight of the apex predator in front of her. She let out slow, controlled breaths as she moved closer to the wolf, careful not to make too much sound and startle the injured creature. The mossy floor shifted under her feet as the wolf screeched in pain. The moans became sharper and more frequent. Selma leaned down and stroked the silver fur, raking over its pelt for any sign of injury. There was no blood, no wounds. But its breathing was shallow. The sight tore at her heart. She needed to do something.

"There is a vet in town. He can help," Selma offered. There was urgency in her tone. Without knowing what was wrong with the animal, she did not know how much time she had.

Razon stared back down at her. His gaze was cold. "I'm not going anywhere."

"He needs help. Please, go get the vet," Selma begged.

"We both know that this creature does not need a vet," Razon countered.

Selma's voice cracked. "What do you mean? Of course he does. Can't you see how much pain he is in?"

"I can," Razon answered.

"How did you summon your threads, Selma? Tell me." Razon's tone was cold and calculating.

Why was he questioning her about this now? They did not have time for this. She looked inside for her power, but she could not feel it. She moved her fingers to the ground. Her fingertips shook, seeking any trace of her threads.

"Tell me." Razon's voice was harsher and louder now.

She needed to ignore him. She needed to focus. Still, nothing. She cursed. Her power was nowhere to be found. Not even a spark. Only a pit of emptiness lay where her magic should be.

"I don't know!" Selma exclaimed. Tears began to fall down her cheeks. "I don't know how to summon them. I do not know where they come from or how I summoned them before. I only want to help. Please help me. Help *him*." Selma could hear her desperation in her tone.

Razon stayed still. The wolf's howls grew more frequent, mixing with snarls.

Selma's tears fell onto his silver fur. An arm nudged against her own. Razon was kneeling next to her. He put his hand on hers, and she could feel his warmth. Then tiny, iridescent red threads slithered down his palms and around their fingers. Selma stopped trembling. She looked over at him, but he was focused on the wolf.

"You're scared. Let go of your fear. Take down the wall you have built around it and let it go." His words were calmer now. Comforting. "It will tell you when it's too much, but you have to listen."

"I don't know how," Selma responded. "I…" She hesitated.

"Yes, you do. You have already done it," Razon reassured her. "It's already in you."

Selma reached out and into his mind. The dark wall that had been there had disappeared. She felt herself walk right through, into his mind. Bitterness, anger, and fear coated his thoughts. She could see his threads protecting them.

Selma reached back to that place in her mind where she could feel her magic when it ignited.

Razon whispered, "I know you can see your threads. Connect with them and hold on. Then tell me what else you see."

It was a small, dark hole. She pulled closer to it. There were jasmine vines. She could have sworn she smelled them. But that did not make sense. This was all in her mind.

Selma pulled back the vines, revealing an iron gate.

"It's a gate. A heavy iron gate," she said.

Razon nudged her. "Good. Reach out and open it slightly."

Selma pulled on the gate with her mind, content to see it slide open without much effort. Violet threads poked through the thin opening, and she could feel their warmth.

"I can see them," Selma said with a smile.

"Good. Now let them follow mine," Razon said.

Selma opened her eyes to watch her threads pair with Razon's. Together, they danced into the soil, scooping up pockets of energy. She could feel the familiar tickle, but this time it was much more powerful than usual. She could feel her heartbeat in her ears. The threads doubled back and surrounded the pup.

Razon closed his eyes. "Do you feel that?" he asked, looking up at Selma. His eyes were like ice chips.

"Feel what?" Selma asked, not sure what he was referring to.

"Open yourself up and feel the energy," Razon responded, looking straight at the wolf. Selma could have sworn his eyes had changed color. They were a deeper, swirling blue, and for a moment they flashed something unworldly.

Selma followed his command.

"Take a breath, and relax your hold on the threads. Trust them," said Razon. His tone was soft and reassuring.

As best she could, Selma relaxed her hold, though she was afraid that the threads would retract. The moment her breath left her lips, the threads glowed even brighter and tapped into the pocket of energy, sending warm waves of power back into Selma's body.

"Once you feel your power coming back to you, guide the threads toward the creature and perform the same search you did for your friend. Tell me what you see," Razon said.

She could sense the poison flowing through the wolf's blood. He must have eaten something. She needed to remove the poison, but how? Then, without warning, her threads went to work. They twisted and slithered through the wolf's every artery and vein, soaking up the toxins. The wolf's breathing balanced out, calmer than it was before. Selma's threads pulsed.

"Easy," Razon whispered. "You need to listen to your power. It is becoming too much. Pull them back." His words came out faster now, in short, clipped tones.

Selma's hand began to tremble again, and her threads became more frantic.

"Do not pull back too quickly," Razon coaxed. His eyes were now wholly focused on Selma. "Quietly go back to your gate and gently start to shut it. Your threads will follow."

Selma walked her mind back to her gate and gently pulled on the iron. Her threads followed her like a happy puppy. When the gate was fully closed, she no longer felt the heat of her magic. She relaxed her muscles, then gulped in air. She sat up only enough to watch Razon finish what he was doing. The wolf was no longer howling. His pain had subsided. He got up onto his paws, legs uncertain but unharmed. With a sniff, he was off. Hopefully to join his pack.

Selma's shoulders slumped. Razon looked equally exhausted, his skin paler now.

"Will he be alright?" Her words were shaky.

"I think we intervened in time," said Razon. Concern tainted his words.

Selma knew there was something he was not sharing with her.

She looked over at Razon. "Is something wrong?"

"Few witches can see their threads. Even those who have been accessing them for a while," he said. "I think it is time you start telling me about your magic and stop being an observer to your own life."

"One's own life never outweighs that of the greater good."

—An excerpt from the Axiom, as translated by Lilibet Lourdes, property of
the Museum of the Academe Arts, current location unknown

CHAPTER 18

Dark, frantic thoughts swirled through Selma's mind as she lay awake, staring at her bedroom ceiling. The scene from yesterday played out repeatedly before her. The yelps from the wolf were as loud and as real as if the poor creature were lying limp on her bedroom floor.

With her first trial mere hours away, she trembled with anticipation. But it was not even her imminent judgment that weighed down her thoughts. It was what Razon had said to her. He had called her an observer. It was not a vulgar name or a particularly ugly word, but it cut just the same. An observer devoid of passion. As if in his eyes she was stumbling through the wind like a discarded candy wrapper. An observer. A person in the background who was not supposed to stand out or draw attention to themselves in any way. A judgment from a newcomer who had barely entered her life and would hopefully exit just as quickly, but it had clung to her and not let go.

She had spent the last couple of days reading the scrolls and spells that Razon had brought over, but they were mostly fairy tales. Witch lore that talked about the Goddesses and the tree that grew from their blood, how they had broken magic apart to protect it from humans. The Goddess Saint, the goddess of light, life, spring, and summer, had collected the leaves. All shimmered with the assorted colors of the elements: air, earth, fire, and water. She would bestow those gifts only to humans she felt were worthy, thus creating the elemental witches. The other Goddess. The Goddess Sever, of darkness—death, winter, and autumn collected from the bark. The bark fed off the magic of the elements, draining all others of power. Selma had never heard anyone speak of the Goddess Sever. She assumed she was a myth to scare small witches and ensure that they used their magic responsibly. The stories frightened her as a child. Witches with the death mark that worshiped the Goddess Sever and fed off innocence. She was not sure how that information was meant to help her.

Judging by the rays of sunshine cutting through the curtain, she had a few more hours to try and sleep before her trial. In true witch tradition, trials were completed by the light of the moon. Or at least, she had heard that somewhere. She should have asked more questions about the rules. She was sure she could have pulled a bit more information out of Razon.

Selma tossed and turned for a couple of minutes, trying to get comfortable, but it was no use. She was not going back to sleep. She threw her quilt off and tossed her feet over the side of her bed. She could go try to talk to Millie, but she should do more research first. Maybe she would find something in the books that Razon brought over. She took a couple of breaths to try and convince herself that she was putting off talking to Millie because she would have more information tomorrow, not because she was avoiding her after their argument the other night. Besides, it was better to keep her distance. If she complied with the Order, Millie would be safe.

Selma went straight to the library and sat among the worn pages. The theme for this trial was "blood." If she could just figure out what that meant, she would have a better chance of passing the trial. Was she supposed to offer her own blood? That did not seem right, as it was not much of a test. But perhaps trials were not like tests at all. Perhaps they were proof of your commitment to the Order. Selma's stomach turned at the thought. She had never so much as joined a sports team, let alone pledged allegiance to some magical faction whose beliefs and actions were unknown to most of the world.

She took a breath and reminded herself that this was necessary to protect herself and her family. And since she still did not know where her father was, or even where to start looking for him, the trials were her only option. Now that the Order knew about her and her magic, she doubted they would forget about her.

Selma looked through the book titles on the desk in search of anything that would be helpful. But she had been looking at these titles for days—why would anything stick out now if it had not already? Selma tossed them aside, revealing untied scrolls underneath. There were elaborate illustrations and runes that Selma could not read. Drawings of witches with silver-tinted locks dressed in black robes. The scroll's border was a beautiful, purplish design of intertwining lines. Selma removed the rest of the books to get a better look. She traced the border with her finger, but the border continued farther down the page. Her eyes followed the pattern only to find it connected to the drawings of witches. The lines were not just a border. Were they violet threads? Selma had never seen anything referring to violet threads before. Because her mother and aunts could not see their threads, the topic had always been swiftly shut down.

Minutes ticked by, surrendering to hours, and eventually the sun sank below the trees. Selma spent the rest of her time trying to find books that would help her translate the runes, but she came up short. It was only a matter of time. She had not uncovered anything that she thought might help her, and the only real information she needed was the location of her father. Then they would all be out of this mess. But she did not even know where to start with finding him.

She let out a sigh and rolled up the scroll. She would investigate the purple pattern later. For now, she placed the scroll next to the other vials and baubles in her chest.

Selma stood in the entrance to her home, waiting for any instructions. But there was nothing. No witch council, no Razon. Not even her aunts were there. The house was completely silent except for the creak of the windows in the old house. Then a small spark ignited in front of her. It was floating like a firefly before her face. It grew larger, expanding with her every breath. Soon it was a spherical orb, its nucleus flickering and popping. Selma waited, not taking her eyes off of it as it beckoned her out into the night air, its masterful energy commanding everything around it, including the house. Selma watched, absorbed in the orb as the front door creaked open. Without hesitation, Selma followed the flame, not fully understanding why, but her magic was pulled toward the floating globe.

The orb continued deep into the woods. Selma stumbled several times, struggling to see the path in front of her. Fallen branches scratched and nipped at her legs and arms as she made her way through the trees. She moved closer to the flame burning inside, hoping that the light would assist her on their journey.

They came to a clearing in the woods, and the orb stopped in the center. Selma looked around but did not see anyone else. There was no sign that anyone had been there, no setup for any test. Her heart started to race. Was this some sort of trap? She was alone in the woods in the middle of the night. She could hear the wolves howling in the near distance. Just when Selma was about to turn and run back home, the orb burgeoned and burst, shooting light through the trees and blinding Selma. She quickly shut her eyes and put her arms up in front of her, protecting herself from any danger that might be coming her way. But when the light dissipated, five cloaked figures stood before her where the orb had been. The Order.

The dark, hooded figures stood arm-to-arm. The member in the center stepped forward, pulling back his hood. It was Olivier. She could barely make out his features, but his sharp nose was enough to distinguish him from the others.

Olivier spoke. "Have you come to your senses and decided to hand over your father's whereabouts?"

Selma was already bored with this question. But if she was going to stay alive, she had to keep answering it. "I cannot tell you where he is."

Olivier's brow furrowed. "Are you ready to be recognized by the Order and begin proving your commitment?"

All arms rose from the Order's sides in unison.

"I am," Selma reluctantly declared. This all seemed unnecessary. The ceremony, the pomp and circumstance, simply to make themselves and the entire movement of Saintism relevant.

Olivier turned to face the other members of the Order and raised his voice. "For thousands of years, Saint, the Goddess of life, light, and magic, has bestowed upon us the privilege of her gifts. Her power flows through our blood, as she is our creator and mother. The Goddess Saint looks down upon you with open arms, hoping to bring home another one of her children."

Selma rolled her eyes.

"Be wary, child, for Saint can sense your true intentions. Only those who are worthy and pledge their undying love will have her gifts bestowed upon them," said Olivier in a somber tone. He shot Selma a look that made her spine snap straight. He continued, "In order to show your full sacrifice to our Goddess, she asks for a piece of yourself in return. Just as you will hold a part of her in you, she shall keep a fraction of your very essence."

Confusion flooded Selma's thoughts. What were they asking of her?

Olivier stopped and placed his hand palm down in front of him, touching his index fingers and thumbs to form a triangle. The other cloaked figures began moving around the clearing, surrounding her, spreading out across the vast field. A stone bowl appeared on a pedestal alongside a dagger with an ornate silver hilt.

"Come, my child," Olivier said to Selma, motioning for her to step up to the bowl. She hesitated, then took a deep breath and walked toward the lanky robe.

"Goddess Saint requests a piece of your heart so that she may hold it," sneered Olivier.

Selma's mouth went dry. Her lips parted, but nothing came out. Surely they were speaking metaphorically, because it would be impossible to give a piece of her actual heart without dying.

"Is something wrong, child? Are you doubting Mother Saint?"

"How?" The desperate, broken sound was all she could muster.

Olivier gave Selma a smile that was as wicked as it was dangerous. "You may complete the trial by cutting into your heart with this dagger."

He turned to join the others at the edge of the field, dragging his cloak along the grass and mud as he went.

Selma looked down at the stone bowl. Her eyes darted between the deep, cold basin and the glistening dagger. This could not be her only option. This had to be a metaphor of some sort. She could not cut out a piece of her heart. She would die. Nobody could survive that kind of trial.

Unless she was forgetting something. Some tiny bit of information that Aunt Verda had mentioned once, something Razon had buried in a sarcastic rebuttal. There had to be some magic that she was overlooking. She frantically searched her memory. Perhaps if she presented a portion of her magic and verbally offered her allegiance to the Goddess Saint, it would be enough.

She looked around the field at the dark faces, each one unwavering as the seconds ticked by.

This was getting ridiculous. It had turned into the creepiest staring contest Selma had ever participated in. She thought back to what Razon had said about her being an observer. As if she were waiting to be invited into her own life. She was standing in front of a group of men who saw her as nothing. That idea infuriated her, and she decided that she was not going to be the one to walk away. They were a group of old, overprivileged, out of touch warlocks, and she was not going to balk. This had to be a strategy. They were trying to scare her away by insisting she tear a piece of her heart out of her own chest.

Her breath faltered as she thought about the hot, sharp metal cutting into her skin. But it was magic, after all. Perhaps the dagger was meant to be a symbol. Perhaps it would hurt but not kill. It could not be their objective to kill her, could it?

Selma walked up to the stand and closed her eyes. If they were putting her through this, she was going to make them wait. She took a deep breath in and counted as the breath left her. She picked up the dagger, taking in its rich, beautiful details. She had never seen a dagger like this. Then again, she had not seen any daggers, let alone held one in her hands. It was heavier than she would have guessed, and the hilt was much larger than her palm. Her hand looked small and fragile holding it. A small symbol was etched into the metal. It was similar to the symbol on the book her father had given her. It must have been equally old if it held reminiscences of a dead language. The blade certainly felt real enough.

She could have sworn she heard one of the Order members shuffle in place, likely perturbed by being made to wait. She turned the dagger over in her hands. It was carefully crafted with the finest details, down to the carved bone handle. It was beautiful.

She raised the dagger up above her head, the blade aimed right at her heart. She was not going to back down. In one fluid motion, she pulled the dagger down toward her heart and heard a scream in the distance. It sounded so familiar, but it could not have come from the Order. They had not moved. Just as the tip plunged into her flesh, Selma felt a heart-wrenching pain shoot through her. Her skin ripped apart as thick red blood spilled out of her and onto the grass. Her vision became fuzzy, and she could taste a copper tang on her tongue. Her head began to spin, and just when she could no longer decipher which direction the sky was, she collapsed onto the muddy ground. Her breathing slowed, and all she could feel was the cold.

"Out of the ground a great tree grew, its trunk made of dark adamant. Cool to the touch, it held a fire of violet flames within. Its branches donned leaves of aqua, green, crystal, and crimson, each shimmering with the movement of the elements in which they were born. Water, earth, air, and fire."

—An excerpt from the Axiom, as translated by Lilibet Lourdes, property of the Museum of the Academe Arts, current location unknown

CHAPTER 19

Heavy. She felt so heavy. Selma woke up with a dull ache in her chest. Her body was worn out and tired. She could barely hold open her eyelids as she took in the room. A fuzzy figure sat in the chair next to her. She was not alone.

Adrenaline pulsed through her veins as she fought to open her eyes wider and sit up, but the dull ache instantly turned into a sharp pain that shot to all her extremities. She let out a painful moan as her body writhed in agony. Visions of the night before rushed into her mind. The Order, the dagger. She took in an acute breath. Again, pain raced down her spine.

"You need to lie down and rest," came a voice from the chair. Deep and velvet. Razon.

"I can't. I think I am dying. I need to get to a hospital," Selma said frantically, using all the strength she could muster.

"It looks like you already tried that. Fortunately for you, you will not be meeting the Goddess today," said Razon as he gently placed one hand on her shoulder and one in her hand. "You are already healing. But it will all be for nothing if you do not rest. If you are careful, you should be back to normal in a few days."

Selma looked up at him. She could have sworn she saw concern in his face, but that could have been the pain talking. "What happened? All I remember is the dagger, and then hot, searing pain. And then nothing. I woke up here. How did I get here?"

"What does it matter? You completed the trial, and hopefully you will have weeks before your next one. The council has the Luminescence Ball to plan, and that should take their focus off of you for a while," said Razon without an ounce of hesitation. "Which is good, because you're in no shape to be doing anything but lying here."

"But I could have died," Selma said with a scowl, and she instantly regretted even that small movement.

"I wasn't going to let that happen," said Razon. There was that concern again.

"What do you mean? You were not even there," said Selma.

"I am everywhere," Razon said with a smile. He handed her a glass of water.

"Prick," Selma whispered.

"Prick I may be, but I'm a prick who was able to get you back here quickly so that you didn't bleed out in a field. That would have been unfortunate," said Razon. "Your Aunt Meriem has left you something for the pain, but it will make you drowsy. I suggest you listen to your body and succumb to the medicine's power." He handed her a cup of tea with a concoction of herbs. Selma knew better than to question her Aunt Meriem when it came to the contents of her recipes.

She rested her head back on the pillow, taking stock of her body. Her muscles ached, and her chest felt raw and exposed. Razon was right. She needed to rest. With that, she took a few sips of her tea and focused on the comfort of her bed. And without another word, she slipped into sleep. Her questions could wait. And any concerns about Razon being in her room or the dagger or the Order dissolved into dreams.

‡

Selma continued to slip in and out of sleep for days. A couple of times, in the brief moments in which she was lucid and strong enough to sit up, she would sip on broth that Razon brought up. Voices occasionally chimed from the hall, but Razon was always there when she opened her eyes. Even though he was her council-appointed captor, his presence was comforting. Not that she would ever admit that aloud.

Days later, Selma awoke to the sound of Razon speaking to someone. But she could not hear the person's response. They were speaking too quietly for Selma to decipher their conversation. She opened one eye slowly, and then the other. Her body was healing well. The ache she had been feeling was all but gone.

Razon was turned away from Selma's bed, facing the door. He was dressed in all black again, but his shirt looked crumpled and stretched out, as if he had been wearing the same one for days, and he was not wearing any shoes. She could only see the back of his hair as he used one hand to run his fingers through it. Her eyes settled on his backside. Even with the loose, wrinkled shirt, his muscles prickled with the slightest movement of his tall, solid frame. Each muscle that peeked out was polished, no doubt from years of being honed. She was so entranced by his backside that she had not noticed he was talking on the phone—her phone.

"Yeah, thanks, mate. And look, Hayden, she is going to be fine. She just needs some rest. I will be sure to tell her you called," said Razon, his demeanor much calmer than usual.

He passed along farewells and tapped the screen, ending the call. He turned around to see Selma glaring at him.

"Princess, you're awake. Good morning," Razon said smoothly. Selma could see the dark circles under his eyes.

She hissed, "What the fuck was that?"

"That was a greeting. Customary after periods of time away from one another," Razon offered with a blank expression.

"Not that. The phone call. Why are you using my phone, and please do not tell me that was *my* Hayden." Selma was hoping she was mistaken, that the hot warlock who had been, by the looks of it, sleeping in her room at night was not having a conversation with the boyfriend she had been ignoring.

"Well, I'm not sure if he was *your* Hayden or someone else's, but he did seem to be rather concerned for you," responded Razon.

Selma shrieked in an octave that was higher than she had anticipated. "Why would you call him? You had no right—"

Razon cut her off. "I did not call him. He kept calling you, and rather than having him show up here so I could explain that you tried to stab yourself to death, I thought it would be better to ease his mind a bit."

Selma asked, slightly panicked, "Who did you say you were?"

Razon tilted his head and gave her a half smile. "Well, I said I was me, of course. Who else would I be?"

"I mean, did you say you were a friend, a cousin, a—" Selma stopped. Silence hung in the air for a moment.

"A what?" Razon asked, still smiling at her.

"Nothing. You are nothing." She clenched her hands into fists beside her and felt her nails dig into her palms.

Razon dropped his smile and put his hands in his pockets. "If I am nothing, then don't worry about who I told him I was. I did tell him that you were going to be fine, and that we had it handled. I am, indeed, sorry about your little boy toy, but I did what I needed to do to get rid of him for the time being. We have more important things to worry about, and we do not need Harris sniffing around." Razon's tone suggested he was losing his patience.

"Hayden," Selma snapped back. "His name is Hayden."

"Whatever. His interfering might prove inconvenient," Razon said, staring back at her. His demeanor was serious once again, and his eyes were unwavering.

Selma did not back down. "*Your* interference is inconvenient, and I cannot get rid of *you*."

Razon turned toward the door.

"Where are you going? We are not done here. You cannot just use my phone!" shouted Selma.

"Understood." Razon nodded and continued moving toward the door. "I'm going downstairs to get you some food. Since you are feeling well enough to shout at me, you are well enough to get out of this room. Pull yourself together. We are leaving in an hour."

And then he was gone. Down the stairs before Selma could speak another word. She looked at her phone and contemplated calling Hayden back. But that would only elicit more questions. Questions she was not in the mood to answer. Razon had told him she was fine. That was good enough. Hayden had not noticed his seductive accent. He definitely could not smell his aroma of leather and cedar. Choosing to place this in a box in her mind, weigh it down with rocks, throw some packing tape around it, and throw it deep within the ocean of her thoughts, she shook her head, as if that would delete the last few minutes.

She tossed her bedcovers to the side and looked down at her pajamas—or lack thereof. She was wearing only panties that said "babe" on the front and a bralette. Which meant someone had undressed her. She gritted her teeth. Had Razon seen her naked? Or almost naked? First her phone, and now this. Her hand flew to her neck. Her pendant was gone. Rage pulsated through her veins. Her anger was so palpable she felt like she could pick it up and throw it at the wall.

She got out of bed and went over to the bathroom. She desperately needed a bath. Her hair was in knots, and if that stench was coming from her, a warm soak was more than necessary.

She started the warm water and stripped down. No need to be shy now. If Razon walked in, he would just get another show.

The water felt good against her skin. It relaxed her muscles, and she let the steam cradle her face. It was only then that she realized her nails were filthy. They were covered in a dark crust, like dirt. Selma gasped. Blood. There was blood under her fingernails. It must have gotten there when she stabbed herself. The very thought sent her mind reeling once more. Why did she stab herself? Although she could not remember stabbing herself. She only remembered the pain.

She placed both hands over her chest, over the mostly unblemished skin above her heart. She had never stabbed anyone, but she imagined it would leave behind more than the tiny mark that was on her. She traced the thin line with her index finger, feeling the slightly raised skin and taking in every detail of the imperfection.

Selma stayed in the bath until the water had gone cold and the suds had retreated to the sides of the tub. She still did not want to face Hayden or Razon, or her mother and aunts, but her pruned fingertips begged to get out of the water. She toweled off and got dressed in a pair of leggings and a sports bra. Her body was still too tender to wear anything too cumbersome. She hoped that being stabbed three days ago would mean she would be spared too much physical exertion, but she tied her sneakers and pulled her hair into a loose, low braid over her left shoulder anyway. She gingerly made her way to the hallway and down the stairs, still not knowing what her body would allow her to do.

Razon was waiting for her in the kitchen with a plate of food, but there was no sign of her mother or her aunts. Greens, corn, red onions, tomatoes, and grilled chicken with dressing filled a small salad bowl next to a glass of green juice. Selma could only imagine what they had put in there, but she was starving. A block of tofu would have looked good to her right now.

"Do I dare ask?" said Selma, holding up the jar of green liquid.

"It's good for your injury," said Razon.

"My pierced heart, you mean?" Selma snapped back.

Razon remained quiet.

Selma sniffed the juice and immediately regretted it. She turned to Razon. "Did you get a look at the goods?"

Razon flashed her a look of confusion. "I'm not entirely sure what you mean."

Selma scoffed. "I was basically naked when I woke up this morning. Is that typical in France, to look at women when they are unconscious? And where is my necklace?"

Razon sighed. "Once again, I am not French, but your necklace is safe. I will give it back to you when you are ready. And as for your clothing, I did not remove your clothing nor see any part of your body, other than the area around your scar. And even then, your aunt was in the room when I inspected it. Meriem was the one who changed you out of your clothing." He leaned up against the wall with one hand in his pocket. "You seem obsessed with me seeing you naked. That can be arranged, princess."

Selma snapped back, "You're vile."

Razon put down his tea and stood up taller. She barely reached his chest as he leaned in closer. "Maybe, but I've also been known to be generous."

For just a moment, Selma's mind wandered to all the ways those full lips could be generous. Her cheeks flushed, and she cleared her throat. "Where is everyone? I have not seen any of my meddling family this morning."

"They left," he offered.

Selma let out a small laugh. "They left."

He nodded. "They thought they had a lead on your father and assumed they would be more useful looking for him. They made sure you were going to be alright, and then they left early this morning."

Selma scoffed. "And you just let them?"

"They will not find him. Of that I am almost sure. But they will be out of the watchful eye of the Order. It is for the best," Razon responded.

Her blood boiled. "What would you know about what is best for us?"

Razon bit down on a smile. "More than you may know, princess."

"Stop calling me that," she said.

Selma was both embarrassed and angry. She picked up her plate and stormed outside to the porch. She had no intention of spending any more time talking about this. But when she reached the porch, there was Razon, leaning against a tree on the lawn, his arms crossed across his chest.

"Prick," whispered Selma.

"Ask me," he said, putting one hand in his pocket.

She scowled. "Ask you what?"

"Why the wards you placed on your room were pitiful rubbish," he responded.

"I have no intention of being schooled by an errand boy," she shot back.

"Maybe not, but this errand boy can help make you stronger. You could learn more about your gifts," said Razon.

Selma stood still for a moment. Was he genuinely offering her his help? "You left the other night without a word. Did you go to the Order? Is that why the trial was so gruesome?" She hesitated and looked around, checking to make sure there were no meddling ears. "Do they know about what I did in the woods, with the wolf?" She needed to know why he had offered to help. She needed to piece together why he had stayed with her, even when back in the summons he had basically referred to her as trash.

"If they did, you would be dead," said Razon.

Selma shot back, "I almost was."

"Good point," said Razon as he kicked off the tree trunk. *The dagger you used was charmed with a rune that was only meant to cut surface deep and collect a bit of your blood for the Order to keep for themselves. It was never meant to kill you. Only cause pain. Unfortunately, the magic did not work, and you were bleeding out. I stepped in to heal you. And while there was no sense of urgency on the Order's part, they did not stop me. If they had, you would be dead,* he said. But his mouth never moved. He was speaking to her mind to mind. He either wanted to piss her off or keep what he had to say private.

Selma kept her eyes locked on Razon. "And why did you heal me?"

"Because I am not your enemy," said Razon. "I think you have been hiding away for far too long, and it is time you start showing up."

"Stop doing that," Selma huffed.

Razon looked almost intrigued by the command. "Doing what?"

"Telling me I'm scared or not enough," she whimpered.

"I don't think you're scared, and I know that you are enough. A person who is scared would not plunge a dagger into their heart. You have a unique set of abilities, and I think you have been held back from seeing what your power can do. All you need to do is say the word," Razon said.

He was now inches away from her. She could taste his scent. It was delicious.

"Alright. Show me," Selma agreed, nodding her head in confirmation.

"We will start by strengthening your walls. If you don't want me in that pretty little head of yours, you will need to kick me out," said Razon. "I will not be able to teach you if I can't concentrate." His eyes darted down to her lips.

"Fine," Selma said reluctantly. "Anything to get you out of my head. Where do we start?"

Razon shot her a smile that would have made her knees wobble if she had not been working so hard to not flip him off.

"Follow me," he said. "I have just the place."

"It is a beautiful sight to behold. Like a grove of aspen trees all connected to one another through magic."

—Recovered correspondence to Olivier Artigues from Alister Lourdes, property of the Order

CHAPTER 20

Razon waited not so patiently while Selma finished her breakfast. The mysterious green juice was disgusting, but she was so hungry that she plugged her nose and chugged.

"Ladylike," said Razon.

"Fuck you. Is that ladylike enough for you?" She stared him down, ready for his retort.

Razon laughed. A deep, barreling laugh that she had not heard before. Since the moment she spotted him in that room with the Order, he had been so serious. Even his half smile felt heavy and half-hearted. But this was a laugh he could not control. His whole body moved with it, and his head tilted up to let the laughter pour out more easily.

When Selma was finished, she put her glass down and took a deep breath, relishing the warm feeling of a full stomach and letting the heat of the morning sun warm her cheeks. She looked over at Razon, who was staring back at her.

"I suppose you're not going to let me brush my teeth," she said.

"You have magic. Use it to clean your teeth, and let us start our day," hissed Razon.

Selma looked to the side, a little embarrassed that she had never thought to use her magic to brush her teeth. It was such a menial task.

"I don't know how to cast a 'teeth brushing' spell," she said, using her fingers to give air quotes.

Razon's lips parted, as if he were going to say something. But then he just lifted his hand toward Selma. Suddenly, she tasted a minty tingle in her mouth. She rolled her tongue over her front teeth, no longer feeling the grimy aftermath of breakfast.

"Huh," she said as she popped up from the ledge of the porch.

He rolled his eyes. "You're welcome, princess."

First clapping her hands together and then reaching one arm over the other and pulling it toward her body to stretch, she asked, "Alright, where are we going?"

Razon grabbed her by the wrist, and in an instant, they were swirling through the air. Selma could have sworn she was scream-ing, but there was no sound. Her words were swallowed up as soon as they left her lips. A hazy mist hovered over her body like steam over hot coals, and colors were muted. She instantly regretted eat-ing a full breakfast, as her stomach turned and stretched the longer they whirled around.

In a mere moment, they stopped. Selma's feet hit the ground, but the gut-wrenching feeling in her stomach did not abate. She turned, ran for the first bush she could see, and emptied the contents of her breakfast onto the ground. The green juice tasted the same coming up as it did going down, and she knew immediately that she would never drink anything green ever again.

Mortified, Selma wiped her mouth and turned to face Razon.

"See, this is why you need the 'tooth brushing' spell," Razon said, using air quotes.

She was still shaky from throwing up, and she wanted to flip him off, but instead she steadied herself. "I'm ready. What do you want me to do?"

Razon lifted his arms, and Selma could feel a pulse of magic race through her body. For the first time, she focused on his eyes when he cast, watching in awe as his normally bright blue eyes flooded with black from corner to corner. They were beautiful and haunting.

Not knowing if she wanted the answer, she asked, "What was that?"

"Wards. Now, how much do you know about your magic?" asked Razon.

"No, not that. Your eyes. Why do they do that when you cast? And how have I not seen it until now?"

"I guess you were just not looking hard enough," said Razon.

But Selma was not going to settle for a nonanswer. Not this time. She stared at him, waiting.

He smirked. "It happens when I reach into my reserve. I'm able to store magic until I need it."

Selma's brow furrowed. "But how is that possible? And wouldn't that be dangerous?"

"It can be, but I have been trained to hold a substantial amount of magic without harming myself. Plus, if you listen hard enough, your magic will tell you when it needs to be released. It comes in handy when my threads cannot feed. It has even saved my life."

His eyes pulled away, and Selma wished she knew where they had run off to.

As quickly as he had gotten lost in thought, he was back. "Now, how much do you know about your magic?"

Selma let out a loud sigh and thought about her Aunt Verda sitting her down for lessons. Always rewarding her with extra chocolate chip cookies after their lesson was complete.

"I know that magic comes from each of the elements, earth, air, water, and fire, and that if you use too much you could hurt yourself," Selma responded, feeling good about her quick response.

"Some magic is strengthened by the elements, but it's not born of them. And, yes, if you were to channel too much of that power, it could be catastrophic," Razon corrected her. He went silent, ushering Selma to continue.

"And I know that some can wield more powerful magic by using their threads to feed off raw energy from the elements. Some, through their threads, will have a more skilled use of one element or the other," she added.

"And...?" said Razon, pressuring her for more.

"And there are stories of Goddesses. The Goddess of light and love, spring and summer. The one responsible for gifting us our power—and who the Order is obsessed with," Selma joked.

"That is an oversimplified version of it, but I suppose it will work," Razon responded. He went on. "Magic was born in the earth—"

Selma interrupted him. "Spare me the fairy tale. I know you don't know me all that well, but I'm not going to be swayed by whatever cult-promoting gibberish you plan on spewing today."

Razon's head fell toward the ground. But there was a smile on his face as he asked, "If you don't believe, then why do you use magic at all?"

"Because. I just do. It is something I was born with. I am not going to get talked into worshiping some Goddess because you say I owe my power to her," she said. Selma knew that her rebuttal lacked a certain grace, but it was true. She did not believe that some celestial being had bestowed powers upon her.

"I didn't say anything about worshiping. But knowing more about your threads will help you better harness your power. Just like a family passes down blue eyes, dark hair, or even stubbornness…" Razon paused for a moment, narrowing his eyes at Selma. "Just like those traits, your magic was passed down to you."

"Then why can't I control it? Both of my parents are elemental witches, and yet my magic is broken," she said, feeling the sting of the words the moment they left her lips. The trauma of her shortcomings brought to life with just a few simple words.

Razon was still as stone as he looked at her. "Because you have not been given the opportunity to know your magic, and you have been too timid to claim it for yourself."

He went on, "Over centuries, some of the factions began to not trust one another. Differences scare people, and ultimately, the struggle for power and dominance can bring out the worst version of anyone. But whether you believe that there were Goddesses or not, your ability to wield magic does exist in your blood. And knowing which faction your magic hails from will be vital in controlling it."

Selma contemplated those words. *And knowing which faction your magic hails from will be vital in controlling it.* Her mind wandered to the illustrations she had seen in her family library. She was born from Elemental witches, so obviously those gifts would be the only option besides being born of the Common.

"Why have I not been able to manage my threads until now?"

"I think it's more important to focus on what you can do with them now," Razon answered.

"And you think I can learn how to control them?" Selma asked.

"Yes, and I can teach you how," Razon said. His eyes were darker today. Even in the sun, the black seemed to swallow up the light that hit them.

"Because I would not think you dragged me all the way out here to have me practice my lesser magic," said Selma.

"You're right. I do want you to practice summoning your threads." Razon paused. "But elemental magic isn't the only way to manipulate magic."

Selma's eyes narrow. Was this a trick? "What other option was there?"

Razon coolly reached into his pocket and pulled out her pendant, the dark charm dangling from its delicate silver chain.

Razon asked, "Do you know what this is?"

Selma nodded. "Yes, it is a protection stone. It warns me of any danger. It was a gift."

Razon still dangled the necklace. "From your father?"

Selma nodded again. "Yes. May I have it back?"

"This isn't a stone; it's an ancient element. Not much remains of it, and whatever was left of it was stolen," said Razon. His eyes lowered to the charm. "It's the same magic that can be used to fortify threads and make the magic more powerful. This is why they say the Goddesses gifted us magic. It was created by them and as far as we know, the touch of a Goddess is the only way. Our Goddess Sever gifted if to a few choice warriors to protect all of those with magic blood."

"What did I say about fairytales? And that nugget of information is a bit revisionist. The Wargraves were a brutal race of witches what mutilated their magic to gain more power. I read the books too." Selma shivered remembering the nightmares that would follow her aunt's bedtime stories. But she was an adult now. An adult that did not have time for this. She straightened her spine and focused her attention on the charm still dangling from Razon's fingers. "I'll take my necklace back now."

Razon's jaw went taught. His muscles flexed as he fisted the silver chain. His knuckles turned white with the strain. "Why are you so quick to dismiss that possibility?"

Selma swallowed trying to keep her breathing even. Something about his stare was putting her on edge. "What are you trying to say?" But Razon remained still. His gaze was unwavering. His words sinking into her skull again. But this time they sang to a different tune. *And knowing which faction your magic hails from will be vital in controlling it.*

"I don't know what you are suggesting, but my father was an Elemental. He would have never been in possession of forbidden magic." She scowled.

Razon stalked forward. Cutting the distance between them in half with two strides. "He wouldn't?"

Selma shook her head. "No." She swallowed again to keep the

burn of acid from rising in her throat. "Death-mark witches are from stories parents tell their kids to keep them in line. They use dark magic to drain life and hurt people. They worship the Goddess of death," Selma said with disgust.

"I believe your references are a bit outdated. And they are a faction of magic, not Krampus or the plaque," Razon responded. "Do you know why witches and warlocks had the death mark? They were not born with it. It was burned into them when they were marked for death."

Selma shivered at the thought. "My father might have left me, but he would never—"

Razon cut her speech short. "Your father gave you this for a reason. But no, I do not think he intended for you to use it. And 'the Goddess Sever' rolls off the tongue a little easier than 'Goddess of death' don't you think?" Razon moved closer now. His movements smooth like a predator after prey. "Does your necklace not react when I am around you? You speak of death and draining life. Aren't the elements alive as well?" Razon gave her a half smile, showing that dimple that Selma had started to become fond of, but now forced a shiver down her spine. "Because it's drawn to the very substance that is in my blood."

Selma eyes went wide. "Elements are different from a soul or a spent life."

"Everything has a soul, princess. Just like everything has a price. Including magic." Razon's pupils were indistinguishable. Lost in the swirling darkness of his gaze.

"Why would you tell me all this? Why are you telling me about the pendant?" Her voice shook, struggling to keep her words from retreating.

Razon was silent for a moment. Closing his eyes and filling his lungs with crisp air. Selma could not remember the last time she had taken a breath. Razon's muscles relaxed as if whatever had been just under the surface ready to pounce recoiled. "Because I think the council may have been mistaken about your power. If that is the case, you may be in danger," he said, his speech slow and calculated. He wanted Selma to absorb every word.

"What? Why?" Selma's voice was laced with panic.

"Nothing makes the Order happier than when the factions are at war. And if anyone has seen what I see, then your power may be considered a threat," Razon said, looking down at the ground.

Selma gulped down air. "What exactly is it that you see?"

"Your threads do not react the way people expect," he responded.

Selma put her arms over her head and tried to take in what she had just heard. *'Because it's drawn to the very substance that is in my blood.'* She paused, her eyes growing wide with realization. There was only one reason Razon would be able to see his threads and heal her and communicate through thoughts. He was siphoning her magic.

You don't need to fear me, Razon said quietly in her mind.

"Do you worship the Goddess of death?" Selma asked, her hands now trembling.

Razon's body relaxed, as if he had been waiting this entire time for her to ask. "Yes, and before you go on another marathon of questioning, yes. I am a Wargrave."

"Mortals and immortals alike have spent lifetimes searching for shards of the original magic, at no avail."

—An excerpt from The Forgotten Goddesses, by Tara Wallingford, property of the Massachusetts Public Library

CHAPTER 21

"A Wargrave? But they don't exist. They were—" Selma stopped short and gulped down the lump in her throat.

"Go ahead. Say what you were going to say." Razon's voice was low as his eyes zeroed in on her. She did not move. The words rattled around in her chest alongside shaky breaths.

"The word you were looking for is 'exterminated,' like pests. But I can assure you, princess, Wargraves do exist. There are few of us, but as sure as the blood beats through my veins, we do exist," Razon said. A guttural roar pulsed through him and darkened his eyes. The flecks of silver were no longer visible. Selma watched his muscles strain against his skin, and fear froze her in place. Everything she had heard about Wargraves was objectionable, or even beastly.

Selma's hand flew to her neck where her pendant once fell. It had been trying to warn her. Razon knew what was running through her mind.

"I figured your necklace was warded to sense my kind. You reached for it every time I was around. I am able to shield against it now. Thank you."

Selma's heart raced. Something between fear and rage rose in her chest. "You have been siphoning my power." Her fingers balled up into white-knuckled fists. She backed up a step.

"That isn't how it works," Razon said. He matched her step for step, his towering body a potent weapon in this secluded area.

Selma scoffed. "It's not? Then please. Enlighten me."

She needed more time. If he was who he said he was, then he was strong, and who knew what kind of power rippled beneath his skin.

"Wargrave threads run parallel to yours, matching them in every way. We can match your powers; we do not take them from you. We simply sense your magic and mimic it. It takes years of training," said Razon.

Selma's mind lurched. The Order had sent a Wargrave to slowly drain her power. She backed up again. How ignorant she was. Thinking all this time that she was going to make it out of this when her very downfall had been sitting across from her on the kitchen island.

"Why? Why would you heal me after the first trial if you knew you were just going to take my powers anyway?"

"I told you, it's not like that. I am not taking anything from you, and watching you die is different than stripping your powers," said Razon.

"Not by much," Selma retorted. She was now several feet away from Razon.

His hands dropped to his sides. "I know. I know it's not." His body relaxed, but that did nothing to ease her.

"Then why? Why heal me?" Selma yelled.

"I never said I healed you." Razon's jaw ticked, and his eyes narrowed on Selma.

"What do you mean? Then who did?"

Razon stalked toward her. His pace was calm as he moved behind her. Her breath quickened as he stood there. His fingers moved up to gently push strands of stray hair off her neck. Selma shivered. He carefully positioned the necklace in front of her, clasped it behind her neck, and then let it settle.

"For the last time, I am not your enemy. I am not pillaging your power. Don't believe me? Look in that book I know you have hidden away."

Selma's eyes widened. There was only one book he could have been talking about. The book her father had given her before he left. The one with the intricate locks.

She checked to make sure her mental iron gate was closed. The cold, heavy metal was solidly locked.

"I don't know what you are talking about." Selma forced out the words through a shuddering breath.

"Yes, you do. The book with the runes etched into the leather. I know you have it. What I do not understand is why you have not bothered to open it."

Selma tried to steady her breath. "How do you know about that?"

"It's called the Canon, and it's the Wargraves' oldest existing account of our history," Razon said. His serious tone had turned pleading. He was telling the truth, but could she trust him?

Razon cursed under his breath. "You need to let me help you, and this is the only way."

There was no reason to trust him. She had only just met him. But something in her gut told her to let go. Some small whimper of hope pleaded with her to let Razon help her.

Selma guided her mind to her iron gate. Her thoughts trembled. Reaching out, she unlocked the latch and invited Razon's iridescent red threads to follow her own through the crack. Razon held on to her as his threads followed Selma's, each movement of the silver strands matched by his.

Selma picked up a memory of the book, careful not to reveal where it was. She carefully examined it. The intricate locks, the etched runes, the fur-bound leather worn down after what must have been centuries. The unkempt ivory paper bound and hidden inside. Razon's threads did not touch it. They only swam around it, cradling the memory in a delicate cage. Then his threads retreated, working their way out of her mind. Selma followed. Once they were both out, she shut the gate behind her, locking it in place.

His face changed in an instant, the wrath taking hold once more. "I suppose it would be easier to stay ignorant. Why learn something when you could blindly follow what you have heard and paint me as a villain?" Razon held on tighter now.

They were still locked in a controlled hold when she asked again, "Who healed me?"

When he finally spoke, his gaze showed no negotiation, and his grip was unrelenting. "You did. Now, where is it?"

"We are stronger together. It is in our shared power that the Goddess is most proud of her children."

—An excerpt from the Axiom, as translated by Lilibet Lourdes, property of the Museum of the Academe Arts, current location unknown

CHAPTER 22

His fingers slid down her hips, his calluses scratching at her skin and leaving her wanting more with each delicious inch. She could feel his warm breath on her neck as he leaned down to gently place his full lips just above her collarbone. There was no space between them, and she could feel him hard against her. He whispered something, but she could not make it out. Leaning closer, she bit his lower lip and let her tongue dance along the sensitive skin there.

He moaned, "I want you," caressing her thoughts with his dark, velvety voice.

"It's time," Razon said, dropping his hands to her backside.

"Yes, now. Please," Selma pleaded. But Razon backed away, and she almost whimpered at the space between them.

"It's time to wake up," Razon said.

Clothing plopped onto the bed, jerking Selma from her slumber. Bike shorts and sneakers lay haphazardly on the bedsheets. She frantically popped up, grasping at the chain around her neck. It must have been noon.

Days had gone by, and Selma had still not shared the whereabouts of the book. She kept the gate in her mind locked tight, with extra chains as a precaution. She did not want Razon to slip in when she was not paying attention. Although some part of him must have.

Her cheeks blushed. It was a dream. She must have finally dozed off. The extra effort it took to keep her walls up was exhausting. It had made her even more torpid than she had been before. In fact, she could not remember the last time she had a restful sleep. Between her shields and her fight with Millie, not to mention Millie's well-being, midnight restlessness had become her routine.

"Why are you here?" she asked, still trying to rub the fuzzy morning haze from her eyes.

More clothing flew onto the bed. This time, a sports bra and a tank top.

"Excuse me!" yelled Selma. "What do you think you are doing? Those are my personal things."

Selma was still learning to trust Razon after he'd admitted to worshiping a death goddess and being a member of a long-extinct and forbidden group of hellish warriors.

"Oh, please. I hardly think these are private items. It is not like I went through your skivvies," said Razon in a bored tone. "Your underwear is the last thing on my mind."

"I didn't take you for a prude," Selma mocked.

"Hardly. Besides, I prefer to use my imagination." He gave her a wink. "Get dressed. We are going for a run."

"Ugh," Selma groaned. "Why? Is the next trial a marathon?"

"In more ways than one," he responded, and he was out the door.

Selma reluctantly tossed her blankets aside and got dressed. The last time she went for a run, she had ended up walking most of the time and had stopped for a coffee midway. This was not going to end well.

She switched out the bike shorts for leggings and added an old sweater, a hat, and some gloves she found in the closet. She knew she would be cold this time of year.

Twenty minutes later, she was out the door.

Razon was waiting for her, glancing at his watch. "How is it that everything takes you ten minutes longer than I would like?"

"I'm like a fine wine," she responded.

"I prefer scotch," Razon scowled.

An hour later, they were running through the woods. Selma had shed her sweater, gloves, and hat. She regretted not opting for the shorts, as the excess sweat that was running down her body was not just from physical exertion. She had been concentrating on keeping her mental walls closed. The iron gate that she had been mentally protecting was shuddering now. Her mind felt like a puddle, sloshing back and forth with each step. She stopped near a fallen log and put her hands on her knees, gasping for breath.

"It's better if you stretch your hands over your head. It will give your lungs the chance to catch up without restricting them," barked Razon. He had stopped a few feet ahead of Selma but was still running in place.

If she could catch her breath she would have shared some

choice words, but for now the only thing she could manage were exasperated breathing sounds. She shot him a vulgar gesture instead.

"Fair enough. You did not ask," said Razon through a muffled laugh.

"I'm a witch; can't you just teach me that transfer spell you do?" Selma knew her question sounded more like a spoiled demand.

"It's not a transfer spell, and no. As a witch, your mind and body are your best tools. The more you harness all your strengths, the stronger your gifts will be," he said.

She pictured throwing a rock at his head.

"If you are going to try to best me with a rock, I would suggest you put a shield around your mind beforehand. So as not to give me the upper hand. The element of surprise is always best," Razon said with a half smile. "I suppose here is as good a place as any for some practice."

Selma checked her iron gate and noticed a slight opening. Her mind trudged over to latch it back in place again.

Razon took in their surroundings. He lifted his hands, and a breeze jetted out from under him in all directions. This time, his eyes did not flood with black, but his threads shot out and burrowed into the ground. The thought that they were feeding off the energy of the dead sent a shiver down Selma's spine. The breeze settled everything, much like the darkness that spreads from a solar eclipse. Every natural element the breeze touched was quieted.

Selma stepped forward, crossing her arms. "Does that not bother you?"

Razon looked confused. "Does what not bother me?"

Selma rolled her eyes. "Using death threads to fuel your magic."

"Magic was born of the earth, Selma. Just as we were. We are honoring the dead by converting their energy," said Razon.

Goose bumps formed on her arms. She had never heard him say her name before.

"Now we are warded," he said, taking a few steps toward her. "We can practice away from the prying eyes of the outside world."

This frightened her a bit. The wards might mean that nobody would be able to reach her if she were in trouble. Selma had not seen much of Razon's powers since they met, but she knew now that he was sitting on a trove of power, and she still did not believe that he was not siphoning from her. Her face must have shown her hesitance.

"I told you that you can trust me," Razon said. "And the wards protect you as well. I have gone ahead and done the same for your room. Now nobody can enter without your permission."

Genuinely curious, she asked, "How does that work?"

"We are shielding ourselves from strangers passing by. They will not be able to see or hear us. They can still walk through the wards, however. So, if you see anyone, I would suggest getting out of their way," he said with a smirk.

She stayed quiet, contemplating being alone with him, so far from anything.

"Now, give me a fighting stance," said Razon. He was a few feet away from her, waiting for her to respond. When she did not, he tilted his head back, probably in annoyance.

He said again, "A fighting stance. What would you do if I came after you?"

"I would…" Selma hesitated. She did not exactly know what she would do. She always assumed that the right call to action would come to her in a dangerous situation, but one had never arisen. She gingerly lifted her hands in front of her and curled them into fists. Spreading her legs wide and bending at the knee a touch, she did her best impression of a boxer getting ready to strike.

Before her heart could beat against her chest, Razon spun and swiped one leg behind her, knocking her on her ass. She winced at the sudden pain emanating from her tailbone as it hit the ground hard, and she knew there would be a bruise later. Tears welled in her eyes as the pain shot up her spine.

"The fuck?" said Selma, winded from the blow.

"You're going to have to do better than that," Razon said, his voice low and guttural.

Selma slowly pushed herself off the ground and brushed off her legs. "I don't have to do anything," she spat back.

"You're right. You can sit on your ass and do nothing. Do not train, do not learn about your magic, do not call your friend and apologize. Just ignore it all. Because that is working so well for you," said Razon.

She took deep, plodding breaths. In through her nose and out through her mouth. Razon did not know her. He had no right to make sweeping judgments. Calm, intentional breaths.

"Try again," said Razon.

"Go to Hell," Selma responded.

"No, thank you. I have been there," said Razon, lunging toward her once more. This time he was slower, and Selma managed to get out of the way before he could knock her down.

"Good. Now put your hands up near your sides. You will want to be ready to either block or reach for a weapon," Razon instructed.

Selma had had enough. "I am not doing this with you. I do not need to fight anyone. I just…"

"Just what? Need to do the bare minimum so you feel like you tried?"

"Fuck you," Selma hissed, heat rising in her chest.

"Maybe later," said Razon, and the corner of his mouth tilted up.

Selma slapped him. His head flashed to the side. His cheek reddened. He lifted his thumb to the corner of his mouth, checking to see if his teeth had done any damage to his lip. All the while, he kept a wicked smile. "Is that all you've got?"

Selma let out a bellowing scream and lunged at him, but she was not quick enough. Razon lifted her up in the air. With one hand on each of her hips, he flipped her onto the ground. He slid one hand under her head, cradling it before contact.

Selma's breathing was even more erratic now. The pounding in her ears matched the strikes of her heart against her ribs. He was so close to her. His hips dangerously near the hot feeling that coiled in her core. His breath tickled the sensitive skin behind her ear.

"Push me off," he whispered.

Selma pushed against his hard body, but he did not budge. She let out a gasp of frustration at her failure to shift even an inch.

"If you want to help your friend, you have to open up to me. You must start trusting me, and you have to stop hiding," said

Razon. His low, deep tone rattled down her spine, making her skin prickle.

"I'm not hiding," Selma said, her voice cracking and barely audible.

"Yes, you are," he responded.

Selma pushed on his chest, and this time he moved, turning to the side to release her.

She was on her feet in an instant, her back to the man who had just overtaken her without breaking a sweat. Maybe he was right, but she certainly was not going to tell him that. She checked to make sure her walls were up. Luckily, her iron gate was squarely in place. At least she was getting better at something.

Selma turned to face him. "I don't understand how this is going to help me save Millie." She let out a labored breath.

"Because the poison used on Millie is the exact substance used by elementals in their transition to Wargrave. The transition is brutal on even the strongest warrior, and the smallest amount can be lethal to anyone without witch blood. The book will tell us how to save her," he said.

That was it. That was all Selma needed to hear. If there was any chance she could save Millie, then she was going to take it.

Razon broke the silence. "Where is the Canon?"

"Even if I were to show you, you wouldn't be able to open it. It is locked, and I have not been able to figure out how to open it," she said.

Razon stared down at the ground, his arms crossed across his chest.

"It's the only part of him that I have left," Selma sniffled.

"I won't take it from you. At least, not until you are ready," Razon promised. "I know where to find a key. But I'm going to need your help."

Selma thought about the years she had spent looking at that book, wondering if the answers to why her father left were inside. Wondering if she would ever know why he had left her to be raised by a mother who could barely look at her sometimes.

Taking a breath, she gathered herself enough to look up at Razon and ask, "What do you need me to do?"

"In one week, the Order is hosting the annual Luminescence Ball at their headquarters. As far as we know, the Canon and the key disappeared almost thirty years ago. You just confirmed you have the book, and I suspect that the council has the key. I do not know where exactly, but they will all be gathered in Lourdes at the ball. If we are going to find anything out, that will be the best place to start."

Selma hesitated. "I don't know if it's a good idea to see the council. I am not even invited to the ball. Olivier might see me coming as trespassing, or treason. I cannot risk putting Millie in that kind of danger."

"I was tasked with watching you, and they expect me to be there. It will be viewed as nothing but babysitting duty," said Razon. "While we are there, you can use your necklace to see if you can find anything. Everyone will be drunk and distracted. It's the best time to look."

Selma nodded in agreement. "I still do not understand why you want to help me or Millie."

"Because I understand what it feels like to be powerless to save the people you love," Razon said, his gaze softer now. "I do not need to see your thoughts to know that you do not see yourself the way you should. You are stronger than you know. And you cannot be strong for someone else until you can be strong for yourself."

She thought about the last time she had spoken to Millie or Hayden. It had been days, maybe even a week. She had come all this way and had not spoken a word to Millie since their argument. The argument in which her dearest friend had said she felt neglected. And Selma had treated Hayden so poorly, and for what? So, she could come to Belhaven and treat Millie just as horribly and be no help whatsoever? If Millie did not make it through this...If Selma lost her soul sister, she would be damaged beyond repair. It would be the blow that ended her. What would be the harm in trusting Razon with the only item she had of her father's?

Closing her eyes, she saw Millie and Hayden, Uma and her aunts. Her emotions ran wild as she took stock of each of those relationships. Everything. She could lose everything if she did not trust him with this.

She let out a tortured breath and opened her eyes. Her violet threads were wrapped around Razon, swirling and intertwined along his skin. Panic rushed through her as she took in the sight of him.

"I'm okay. You are not doing anything wrong, and they are not hurting me," said Razon. His voice was even. "Take a breath and call them back."

Selma did just that. She carefully called her threads back behind her.

"I feel something, like my skin is heating," said Selma.

"Good. That is the energy they have collected," Razon responded. "I think there is a chance they have been collecting energy for a while, but they have been weak. Too weak for you to see them clearly."

Selma started shaking. "What do I do with the energy? I cannot maintain it. It will burn through me."

Razon's voice remained calm. "Then use your magic. Cast."

Selma thought back to that day with her father, when he had made the flowers grow for her. She concentrated on the velvety petals and the thin veins in their leaves. She concentrated on their buds and how the intoxicating fragrance of the jasmine vine made her feel safe. The warmth in her body dissipated, and her breath evened out. When she looked down, the forest floor was covered in an array of flora. All assorted colors. Selma could not help but smile at what she had created with her own magic. A laugh filled her lungs and spilled out.

"Let's do this," she proclaimed.

Razon returned her smile. "You will need a dress, and I know exactly where to get one." He scooped her up into his arms, and they were whisked away on a sea of mist.

"Any and all members of the Order may claim exception."

—An excerpt from Edicts of the Order, property of the Master

CHAPTER 23

There feet landed on grass, the familiar shed just behind them. There was only one place they could be.

Shit.

Razon glanced over at her, an unyielding request in his eyes. With a deep breath, Selma turned toward the house, ready to swallow her pride and apologize to the one person she cared for most in the world.

As she stepped up to the back screen door, she was met by a scowling David.

"I told you to do whatever you needed to do to make her better. I wasn't expecting a miracle, but I definitely wasn't expecting you to make her cry. What the fuck, Sel?"

His words stung. Selma had not thought about the collateral damage of her acting like a spoiled child. David had been her friend for almost as long as Millie had, and the daggers he sent her way were enough to make her breath die in her chest.

"I'm so sorry, David. I know I have been an asshole, and I am here to try to make it right," Selma pleaded.

David looked up at Razon with hesitation. Selma remembered quickly that the two men had not yet met.

"David, this is Razon. He is a..." She hesitated, then said, "Friend of mine. But he can wait out here." She turned to Razon for confirmation. He nodded in response, but then a faint call came from the house. It was Millie.

"David, it's alright. I should try to walk around anyway," she said as she shuffled toward the back door. Both Selma and Razon's eyes went wide. Millie was even smaller than the last time Selma had seen her. The bruises under her eyes were dark and pronounced, a stark contrast to the ghostly pale tone of her skin. Sharp angles cut through the collar of her shirt as it hung from her tiny frame, swallowing her whole.

"That bad, huh? Way to make a girl feel sexy," Millie joked, a cough chasing after her giggle.

As she stepped onto the patio, David offered his hands to guide her. Her bones looked as though they might snap at any moment.

David helped her into a chair. "I'll go grab you a blanket," he said, but Razon was already racing toward the door.

"I'll get it," he said as he disappeared over the threshold.

David yelled over his shoulder, "Thanks. There should be one on the sofa."

Selma wondered if the couple would be stressed about an uninvited stranger in their house, but it did not seem to faze them at all as Millie settled into her seat. Razon was back quickly with a knitted blanket he placed gingerly on her lap.

Millie looked up at him, smiling. "Thank you. That is very sweet of you." She raised one eyebrow at Selma, no doubt noticing the unnaturally good looks of the kind stranger. Leave it to Millie to be on the brink of death and still able to appreciate the view.

Razon smiled back at Millie. His charm was undeniable. As if he had more practice flirting than the rest of them. How many people had he practiced on? The thought made her shudder with jealousy.

Stop it. He is a death warrior.

"I'll leave you two," said Razon.

David quickly spoke up. "Would you like some mushroom coffee?"

Razon politely accepted, and the two men disappeared inside, leaving Selma and Millie on the back patio.

Selma pulled up an Adirondack chair next to her friend, setting it down carefully in case the slightest jostle caused more harm. She focused on a knot in the wood on the deck below her, the imperfection easing her tension ever so slightly. Why were the words so difficult to get out? She knew exactly how she had let Millie down. She knew more than Millie did. Selma's flaws could be followed like a broken road pitted with neglect.

She looked up to find Millie leaning back in her chair, eyes closed, lips curled up at the ends. She was drinking in the sun like this were any other day. Her labored breaths and tattered, dry skin were the only indication that anything was wrong. But then a tear slowly fell down Millie's cheek, and both women cried. No words were needed. At least, not yet. Selma reached out and grasped Millie's hand in hers, and they shared a few uninterrupted moments together. It was not until Selma's eyes felt the hard grit of dry air that her apology slipped from her lips.

"I'm so sorry, Millie, that I have not been here for you. You deserve more, and I promise that I will try to be better. I want to be here for all of you, and my own selfishness has kept me from doing just that," Selma said.

Finally, Millie opened her eyes and took in her friend. She gently squeezed Selma's hand. The weak gesture barely registered.

"You didn't make me sick, Sel. But I did miss you," Millie said, wiping her cheeks with the back of her free hand. Selma's heart sank. But she *had* made Millie sick. She might not have given her the poison, but she was the reason the council had taken interest in Millie and used her as a tool.

Millie went on, "I shouldn't have said those things. You were dealt a shitty hand, and we are all just doing our best, damn it. You might be a selfish asshole, but you're our selfish asshole."

They both giggled, but their laughs drowned in muffled tears.

"I'm just scared," Millie whispered, her eyelashes lowering under the weight of her confession. "I thought I would have more time."

Before Selma could say anything more, her pendant began to pulse, and Razon and David opened the screen door, each carrying two mugs of steaming mushroom coffee. The feeling of concern still radiated off Razon.

David jumped in. "We heard giggling. Have you two kissed and made up?"

Selma and Millie stuck out their tongues at one another and broke out in a fit of giggles.

David rolled his eyes but smiled back at them and offered them both mugs filled with mushroom coffee. "I'll take that as a yes."

Millie broke the silence. "So, who is the smoke show?"

Selma's cheeks blushed, and she could have sworn Razon's did as well.

Through a laugh, Selma answered, "Um, Millie, Razon. Razon, Millie."

Millie eyed him, drinking in all the details. "And what are your intentions with our saucy Selma?"

"Millie!" Selma protested.

Razon offered a smile that Selma had never seen before. It was wide and welcoming.

"Well, I plan on escorting her to a ball," he offered. Hopefully, that would not lead to too many embarrassing questions.

Millie's face scrunched. "A ball? What are you, a duke or something?"

"Or something," Selma added.

Millie's eyes lit up. "Please tell me I get to dress you. I have the perfect dress."

Selma opened her mouth to protest, but Millie was already up and headed into the house to grab a dress for the Luminescence Ball. Selma watched her friend's pale frame make its way inside and tried to push down the guilt she felt for putting Millie in this situation in the first place. She would find the key.

She would fix this.

CHAPTER 24

Selma sat staring at the box on her bed. Her mind reeled with the events of the last week. Hopefully, tonight would get her closer to answers. She would find the key that would finally open the book she both cherished and resented.

She gently lifted the dress up out of the box. It was breathtaking. A vintage cream, backless, full-length gown with a high neck. The bottom flared out just a touch below the knees and pooled along the floor. She took in the thousands of individual pearl-colored beads that had been sewn into the fabric to give the dress a subtle metallic shine. The dress fell perfectly at her sides, cradling her breasts and exposing her back and collarbones. It was a little too long for her, but she could wear heels to make up for it.

She turned it around and held it up to herself in the mirror, noticing that the back dipped low, to just above her backside. It tapered in at the sides with delicate lace, creating a deep V shape.

It was stunning. Her cheeks started to blush as she wondered if Razon would like it. Selma shook her head to clear out those ridiculous thoughts. She should not care if he liked the dress, only if he could help her find the key.

She looked down at the box and pulled out a note written on pale blue linen paper.

It is not your vintage T-shirt, but I hoped it might do the trick. Thank you for your friendship, and sorry for being an asshole. Maybe now we can call it even. Be careful with the old girl. She is vintage, like you. Happy birthday.

Love,

Millie

Selma let out her breath and felt strength return to her body. She was ready to face them, the Order.

She sat down at her vanity and began to paint her face. She had never been one for too much glamour, but this was more than rosy cheeks and long eyelashes. This was war paint. She needed to walk into that ball and show the Order she was not scared of them.

She pulled her brush down the center of her head to part her hair. She brushed out the knots and waves that she was accustomed to and slicked it back behind her ears. She used hair cream to make her locks glisten as they hit the small of her back. It was a harder, sharper look than she was used to seeing reflected in the mirror, but it was the perfect armor for a den of beasts.

Selma slipped on the dress, admiring herself in the mirror.

Despite the weight of the beads, she was pleased with how it hugged her curves and made her look tall and lean. It fit her perfectly, even the length, and the small, metallic pearls glistened when she moved.

And then she felt it. The thrum.

"It's missing something," came a deep, smooth voice. Razon was leaning against the doorframe, looking annoyingly flawless. His black tuxedo was cut specifically to his tall frame. It was classic black (not that she would have expected anything less), but instead of the black lapels that would have usually been sewn into a high-end designer suit, his lapels were a cream-colored velvet fabric that matched her dress perfectly. His only accessory was a gold pin on his left lapel. Topping off his look was his intoxicating smile. Selma did not mind watching him stand there and rake his eyes up and down her body.

Eventually he extended his hand and bowed his head. "May I come in?"

"What is the use in asking? You have barged in before," said Selma.

He stayed silent and gave her a sharp glance. Goddess, those eyes. If he had been sent here to destroy her, she might let him.

Selma gently responded, "Yes, you can come in."

Razon gracefully kicked off the doorframe and pulled a box from his pocket. It was dark blue with a gold latch. Something was etched on the top, but Selma could not make it out.

Still looking down at the box in his hand, she asked, "What is this?"

"I told you I thought the dress was missing something," Razon responded.

Selma looked up at him from under her lashes. She could smell him. Cedar and leather.

Razon opened the top of the box with one hand, holding the bottom with the other. A pair of earrings sat atop a blue velvet cushion. Black pearls nestled in the center of a platinum poppy flower. They were stunning. Selma could not take her eyes off them.

Razon asked, "Do you like them?" Selma could sense a vulnerability in his voice.

"They are gorgeous," she said. Then she asked, "What are they for?"

Razon gave her his patented sideways smile. "They're for you, princess."

Selma did not know what to say. This was a gesture she had not prepared for. He was her captor. A burden put upon her by the council to restrict her privacy and freedom until she had successfully complied with their demands. And yet, he did not feel like either of those in this moment.

"I don't think so. I will lose one, and the owner will be livid. I do not want to worry about that tonight," Selma said, shaking her head.

Razon grasped her by the wrist. "They are for you. I am giving them to you. So you can throw them in the river if you like. Although I do believe they go perfectly with that dress, so it would be a shame," he said with a smile.

"What did I do to deserve this?" Selma's confusion was evident in her tone.

"Every princess needs jewels," Razon responded.

Selma let out a small laugh, and Razon gave her a look she had not seen before. His face lit up, and he looked more alive than she had ever seen him.

She removed the pearls from their velvet box and gently adorned each ear. She took a moment to look at herself in the mirror. He was right. They were exceptional with the dress.

Razon did not take his eyes off of her as his voice purred in her thoughts. *You are gorgeous.*

Selma's throat went dry. She wanted to get lost in his eyes and let those flecks of silver hold her suspended in time. But then she blinked rapidly, as if to wipe those feelings from existence.

"We had better get going," she said quickly.

Razon's gaze was still locked on her neck, where her pendant sat atop her neckline. "There may not be a lot of us, but there are others. And it is best if you do not let your guard down around the council. I can shield myself while I am fully corporeal. But others will not know what your pendant does. Keep it on you."

"It's odd that you don't trust the men you work for," Selma jabbed.

Razon's jaw ticked, and his muscles tensed, but only for a moment. Then he reached out for Selma, offering his hand, and Selma tilted her head in resistance. She remembered the last time Razon had offered to evanesce them. It had ended with her breakfast in a bush.

"Trust me, it's much better the second time around," he said.

He never took his eyes off her, and Selma held his gaze. She grabbed the small pearl clutch that had accompanied the dress and put her phone and a small lip gloss inside. She stepped closer, and their fingertips touched, sending a bolt of nerves down her spine, lighting her core. She could have sworn there was a vibration, but without any time to think about it she was whirled away.

The world faded. Her bedroom walls became the dark night sky. She held on tight to Razon as she felt her body tingle. She did not think about his violent past or her trials. His chest was hard against her touch, and even though she could not tell which way was up or down, she felt safe.

What seemed like only seconds later, her feet hit the marble floor. She instinctively pushed away from Razon and tried to adjust her dress and hair, as it felt like both had been whipped around. She furiously looked around for a mirror and was relieved to find one nearby. When she trotted over to it, confusion hit her. Not a single hair was out of place, nor was her dress wrinkled. It felt as if she had stepped out of a tornado, but there was no sign of it.

"I'm good at a lot of things. Evanescing is one of them," said Razon as he leaned into her and gave her a wink. He offered his hand again. "Shall we?"

Selma's heartbeat sped up. She wanted to lean into him even more and see what those lips could do. What was wrong with her? She was in the belly of the beast, in the same building as the people who were threatening her, the same people who had poisoned Millie. And all she could think about were Razon's lips and where she wanted them.

Selma smiled at him, and for the second time that night, against her better judgment, she took his hand.

She could not believe she was back in this castle. But this time it seemed different. Maybe it was because she was not on trial, or maybe she simply felt more confident. Her dress swished and folded around her as she walked. Several heads turned as they made their way through the lavish hallways. There was a herd of people walking up the giant staircase. Selma had not been up the stairs the last time she was here. She suddenly realized how vast the castle was. The key could be anywhere. She may never find it.

As Razon and Selma reached the base of the stairs, they were greeted by servers with silver trays balancing crystal flutes of champagne. Razon took two and offered one to Selma.

"You will want some, trust me. The speeches can be rather dull," said Razon.

Giving him a demure smile, she accepted the glass. But she did not take a sip. She needed to have her wits about her around this group. This could all be a trap. And even if it wasn't, she would still need to find the key.

The group of people moved like a current, swaying and twisting. She did not understand where they were going. The women were all dressed in full-length gowns. Some, Selma could tell, were couture. The men wore gorgeous suits, silk ties, and handcrafted shoes. Selma could have spent the entire evening relishing the outfits. They were like art come to life.

Razon must have noticed her fixation. "What has you so enthralled?"

"I feel like I'm in a painting," she responded. She turned to assess his expression. To her surprise, he was smiling at her.

Selma looked down at herself, examining the dress and wondering what he found funny. "What? Is my dress not zipped up or something?"

"No, you look lovely. I was just reminded that there are people out there who can look at something and see the beauty. No matter how tarnished or outdated it may be," said Razon.

He smiled and placed his empty hand on the small of her back.

His thumb just barely touched the bare skin above the lace, sending goose bumps racing over her. Selma looked at him blankly. Did he just give her another compliment? He must have realized his intrusion, because he quickly removed his hand. Selma was relieved that she did not have to say anything to him, but she simultaneously missed his touch.

The crowd moved down a long hallway, chatter and laughter filling the air. Selma could hear a faint melody in the distance. What was noticeably absent from this scene was any sign of green elemental threads. As they moved farther along, the light dimmed, finally surrendering to candlelight from ornate gold sconces hung on the walls on either side of the crowd. The flames flickered, as if responding to the collective energy. Finally, the swarm of people veered left.

"But also, your dress is unzipped," he said.

Selma looked back so quickly she startled the people behind them. Razon laughed and reached out to calm her, this time placing his hand on her elbow. Then he leaned into Selma. His mouth was so close to her ear, she could feel his breath.

"Pardon my mistake. Your dress is perfect. It may have only been unzipped in my mind," he whispered.

Selma caught her breath. This was not what she had expected. She suddenly felt woozy, like she had consumed too much champagne, but her glass was still full of bubbles.

"The body of a Maven holds the blood of our Goddess and therefore is sacred, bearing nay a mark."

—An excerpt from the Axiom, as translated by Lilibet Lourdes, property of the Museum of the Academe Arts, current location unknown

CHAPTER 25

Selma and Razon stood looking at one another for a few moments. It was as if she could not tear herself away. Her threads threatened to burst from her and pull him closer. But a bump from another guest in the crowd ripped her from her trance.

"Shall we?" Razon gestured in the direction that the crowd was flowing. Selma nodded in agreement.

They both turned to join the horde of witches and warlocks moving through the large archway. The marble columns on either side of the entrance must have been twenty feet high, and past them was the most magnificent room that Selma had ever laid her eyes on. A grand ballroom filled wall-to-wall with witches and warlocks opened to a ceiling that had been enchanted to look like the night sky. Immense black chandeliers, all adorned with glittering crystals, seemed to float in the sky. Giant trees with leaves in colors of aqua, green, crimson, and crystal filled the space, creating a brilliant sea of color. The ancient branches spanned as high as she could see. The canopy of foliage blanketed the entire room, and small leaves rained down on the guests but never hit the floor. Selma now noticed the green threads dancing in and out of the trees in every direction. A stage was in the back, large enough for a full orchestra, and the air smelled of cinnamon and rain.

In the middle of the room was a champagne tower as high as the ceiling. Hundreds of glistening champagne flutes held the dancing bubbles. A woman in a full-length silk gown and a shawl that was made of what Selma assumed was a fox walked up to the tower and reached for a glass in the middle, plucking it out from the enormous stack and cackling at the person behind her. Selma gasped and braced herself for an epic crash of crystal and liquor. But the crash never came. The glass was simply replaced by one from the top. The movement was instantaneous and fluid. Magic. Of course, the champagne tower was dripping with magic. She looked around the room and wondered what other surprises were in store for her tonight.

Razon was still holding on to Selma. She could feel him looking at her. Probably because she was gawking and making a fool of herself.

A few moments later, Olivier emerged from the chaos. The crowd easily parted for him as he stepped onto the stage. It was then she saw the witches lined up against the wall. All of them were dressed in red robes. Their large hoods shielded their faces from view, but not from scrutiny. Party guests scowled in their direction. Nobody interacted with them at all as the hooded figures hung their heads low. Witches destined for servitude by the council's judgment. The fate Selma might have undergone, the fate she still might if she failed to complete the trials or supply the location of her father. She wondered how the council had so much power over them. Even if the Order was the ruling body of the Elemental witches, there was still the human community to deal with. It was illegal to enslave someone, at least here.

Selma turned to Razon. "Why don't those witches and warlocks just leave? Does their piety reach so far that they would freely relinquish their freedom to the council and the founding families?"

Razon frowned. "The council drugs them. Even if they were to be reported, the Order has powerful friends who do not wish to make them the enemy."

Selma was speechless. She had no idea how powerful this community was, and she clearly had more to learn. "Drugs? What do the drugs do?"

Razon lowered his head and spoke low through his teeth. "Their magic is dulled, and they are more compliant." His jaw ticked. "They cannot speak."

"What?" Selma's volume caught the attention of a few partygoers, and she quickly settled herself and pasted on a tight smile. She grimaced over at the red-robed figures, knowing she should turn away, but her heart sank. "And what of their families?"

Razon swallowed and turned his gaze away from the group standing against the wall. "It is typically women who are sentenced to servitude, and they can choose to take their children with them. But it is a difficult choice, placing your children in servitude or leaving them behind."

Bile rose in Selma's throat. "We have to do something."

Razon was stone-still. His eyes searched Selma's. "Yes."

Selma was staring back at Razon, trying to decipher what his curt answer meant, when the crowd rustled behind her. Selma turned toward Olivier on the stage.

He was wearing a flawless, rust-colored designer suit. It was not a color she would have chosen for the villainous council member. It was too whimsical for what she knew of Olivier. It made him seem approachable, and threatening to take someone's powers from them made a person anything but approachable. But even the jovial seasonal color could not temper the twinge of sinister energy that pulsed from him. Selma was curious if anyone else could feel it. If anyone else had sensed that his smile was more of a mask than a welcoming gesture. Maybe that was why the witches and warlocks had given him a wide berth as he passed.

When he spoke, his voice boomed from him, as if he were holding a microphone. The entire room, including the few who had not noticed him climb onto the stage, too involved in their own conversations, turned to look at him. He now had the room's undivided attention. Selma looked over at Razon, curious about his reaction to the man who was threatening to take everything from her. His face held a look of boredom.

"Welcome to our annual Luminescence Ball, when we come together to honor our Goddess Saint and her gifts to us, her children, as well as celebrate the autumnal equinox. There was a time when we were vulnerable to the dangers and darkness that our enemies threatened. But this celebration is in remembrance of our triumph over the false goddess. It is where we come together and remind ourselves of our strength in numbers, our strength as a community, and our strength as a family. Together, we can protect one another from the darkness," Olivier boasted.

A low, polite clap scattered across the crowd. "Hail Saint!" came a voice from the back.

Olivier continued, "Yes, let us relish in Saint's light." He paused, taking in the crowd, drinking in each set of eyes as if taking a metal tally of who had attended tonight's festivities. "And may those who threaten to dim that light have the power of Saint brought down upon them."

Selma stood frozen as he uttered those last few words.

"Now, dance and celebrate, and may the Goddess Saint shine her light upon you!" Olivier ended with his hands clasped together as the crowd cheered and clapped.

A full orchestra appeared behind the grand host. The music began, and Olivier was off the stage before Selma could blink.

"I told you the speeches were dull," said Razon. "Would you like to dance with me?"

Her fickle body ached from miles of morning runs and training, but Selma cleared her throat. "Why don't you just ask the council for the key? Aren't they the ones looking for the book?"

The words seemed strained coming out of her mouth. They were distant, as if they had come from someone else. Razon tensed and looked around the room. He leaned in close and whispered, "It would be best to keep this between us for now. We should wait until people have a decent amount of liquor in them before we leave."

She had never been adept at dancing, and making a fool of herself in front of witch society was not something she wished to experience. But if she denied his invitation, he would undoubtedly find another partner and leave her alone to fend for herself.

Just as smoothly as he took their glasses and surrendered them to a server, he grabbed her hand and guided her to the middle of the floor. Razon bowed to her. She was surprised by this. It was not something she had seen before, and it felt old-world.

Razon moved to put his hands on her. "May I?"

"Oh, sure. Yes, I mean," Selma stumbled.

He took her right hand in his and placed his left hand on the small of her back, just as he had done earlier, in the hallway, but this time he was sure and confident. He took one step and guided them. Selma slid backwards and followed. She had never been formally taught how to dance, but she did not need to know. He was lifting and steering her. Her feet were light as they turned and stepped to the rhythm of the music. The notes fluttered off the bows and keys of the musicians, making their way around the room like a migration of butterflies and emblazing the room with a flurry of dancers. The melody felt familiar, and her body moved to the music as if she had known it all her life.

They were silent for long moments, and Selma closed her eyes and let Razon twirl her around the dance floor. For a moment, just a moment, she thought she could let everything fall away and just be. She did not know why she felt so comfortable letting her guard down, especially in a room where she was the prey, but she let her armor fall to the ground around her. Still, she was careful to keep her mental gate in place. Just because it felt good to have Razon hold her did not mean she needed him to know that.

When she opened her eyes, she found him staring back at her. Silver flecks floated in his blue eyes. They must have been making wide circles or become a spectacle, because the crowd had moved to the edges of the dance floor, allowing Selma and Razon space to move and turn.

"For someone who ran from witch society, you do seem to be fitting in nicely," Razon commented as they swirled around the room.

"A shower and nice dress can hardly count as fitting in. And I didn't run away. I just didn't know the rules." said Selma.

Razon mused. "Hmmm, and counting oneself out before the game even begins? What is that?"

Ignoring his jab, Selma pivoted. She was curious to know more about her captor. "Have you always relied on your magical gifts?" Razon furrowed his brow, looking down at her with confusion. "What do you mean?"

"I feel more relaxed than I should at this party, and dancing has never been my strong suit, so I assumed you're using your magic to calm me," Selma explained, letting her theory sink into her dance partner.

A deep sound left his throat as he exhaled and straightened his shoulders. "I'm not sure I have uncovered your strong suit yet." Razon dipped his eyes low, taking in her body once more. "What would you say it is?"

Selma scowled up at him. At his full height, he towered over her. "I would say it's my uncanny ability to assess risk," she added. "Even when there are wolves dressed in sheep's clothing."

Razon tilted his head to the side and sent her a feral smile. "Indeed," he whispered. "And where do you think you inherited those impeccable instincts?"

Selma shrugged. "From years of watching the wolf."

They were silent for several moments, letting the dance take over as the room around them filled with swirling witches.

"How is it that your kind still exists? I was told you all died out hundreds of years ago. I thought Wargraves were a myth." Selma dug in using hushed tones. "Immortals that were vicious and power hungry. And obviously that is not true, so tell me, how is it that the Wargraves have continued to recruit warriors and I had no idea?"

Razon's jaw ticked, and he straightened a bit. "Many did perish, or 'die out,' as you put it. Survival was not without cost. And unlike you, princess, most are not allotted the freedom of choice or the luxury of ignorance."

"So, you didn't choose to become a vicious soldier? Let me guess, your family made you train, and you obeyed out of a sense of duty," Selma mocked, giving her best impression of a large male soldier.

Razon was silent for a few moments, and part of Selma felt victorious for having gotten to him.

"My family were not Wargraves. They never pressured me into service," Razon said in a reserved tone. His face was neutral except for the dark smokiness flooding his eyes. "But they did die because of it."

Selma lowered her eyes to his chest. "I'm sorry."

"Thank you. But it was a long time ago," Razon added, "and not a topic of conversation for the current festivities."

And just like that, his eyes cleared, nearly too quick for her to notice anything at all. Razon brought his gaze back to her and lifted one side of his lips into a smile.

"I'm not enchanting you with my gifts, princess. You are relaxing all on your own."

Selma was not sure she believed him. She never relaxed. Not like this. But she was melting into him.

"Hayden is a lucky man," Razon said.

And just as quickly as she had been swept up in it, the night cracked before her. Hayden. What was she doing? Hayden was kind and supportive and real, and here she was dancing with another man while he sat back at home worrying about her. She looked down at her dress and felt wretched. She was not worthy of its beauty.

Razon stopped moving and looked at her with concern. "I'm sorry. I should not have—"

Selma cut him off. "No, you are right. He is a lucky man, and I think we should do what we came here to do."

"Of course. I need to greet a few people, then I will meet you at the refreshments table," he said blankly.

He gathered himself, straightening his lapels and picking a fleck of dust off his jacket. Then he left the floor. Selma turned in the opposite direction, ripping herself from the feelings that had engrossed her. Instead of making her way around the room to greet people she had no desire to meet nor earn the approval of, she headed to the restroom to freshen up. Razon would be much better at charming them anyway. She stole a glance at him across the room. He was already locked in an alluring conversation with two witches and a warlock whose attire could have financed a cruise down the Seine.

Making her way to the restroom, she passed a group of people who were overindulging in the party's offerings. A blend of slurred speech and boisterous laughter fill the hallway. When she finally reached the alcove that led to the powder room, she was overtaken by a swift urge to keep going. As if an invisible rope were tugging her down the hall. But there were no people that way, and it was dimly lit. It was clearly off limits to partygoers, so why did she perceive a strong sensation to carry on in that direction?

A prickle called attention to her fingers, where she could see her threads peeking out from her fingertips. The key. Razon was right. It was here. But her pendant was still against her skin. Selma looked behind her, checking that the hordes of witches and war-locks were still too wrapped up in themselves to notice her. This was what they came here to do, right? She would find the key, and they could get out of here. She tapped into that energy that was beckoning her and proceeded down the long hallway.

The orchestra's melody was but a murmur now. Barely louder than her heartbeat. She could only see a few feet in front of her with the dim light, but the tug at her threads was stronger with every quiet step.

Her feet were throbbing. She regretted the tall heels she had worn. Every step had to be exacting to keep them hushed. Doors lined the dark hallway on either side of her, but still the invisible tug lurched her forward. It was not until they led her to a circular stairway leading down that she began to doubt her choice to go about looking for the key on her own.

Her heartbeat raced faster. She could go back and fetch Ra-zon, but that would take time, and she did not know who might be roaming the halls when they returned. She had come this far. Letting out a breath, Selma traversed the first step and was instant-ly rewarded with the thrumming of power pulsing through her threads.

Around and around, Selma journeyed downward through the dizzying stairwell, losing count of the endless turns. Just as she was beginning to doubt this entire endeavor, the steps ended in front of a small, unassuming wooden door. This had to be where the key was hidden. Her nerves were humming. She doubted that the door would be unlocked, and she figured she would need to use her magic somehow. But with all the stone surrounding her, she was not sure how much power she could harness nor how reliable her threads would be.

Walking closer to the wood, she noticed it was inscribed with runes. The door was locked by magic. That made sense. There was no noticeable deadbolt or latch keeping the door sealed. She put her hand on the distressed wood, looking for any markings or hint of entry. Then her threads encased the door, and it crept open, letting out a high-pitched whimper of relief. Her blood pumped faster as she gently pressed her hands against the wood, throwing the weight of her body into the movement.

The room was small and circular, which seemed odd. Without warning, her threads scattered in every direction, the violet strands weaving over the abiding stones that had been stacked to create a small chamber. There was a wooden desk in the middle with piles of parchment, scrolls, and quills. A thick layer of dust coated every surface. The room looked as though it had been plucked from history. A rogue outlier lost in modern times.

Making her way around the desk, her eyes took in every object, her hands pulling open every drawer. Nothing. Was she mistaken? Were her threads simply drawn to this trove, to the ancient magic that must have been imbued within the walls?

The walls.

Her threads were still caressing the stones along the outside of the chamber. She turned to take them in. Some were crumbling from time, crushed under the weight of the castle, and she reached out and touched one. There had to be something, a secret latch or another hidden room. The idea made her laugh aloud. Two weeks ago, she was teaching tourists how to make fake smudge sticks, and now she was fondling ancient stone walls, hoping to find a secret passageway. This situation was ludicrous but also thrilling.

She released her grip and beat her palms against each other, knocking dust and silt free from her skin. When she looked down, she noticed that her violet threads were glowing brighter than before. She held up her hands to examine the strands more closely when they slithered to a stone just in front of her. Her pendant vibrated off her skin, and Selma watched in amazement as the stone was released from the wall, sliding just an inch out of place. Pulling on the brick with all her strength, she managed to unwedge it a few more inches. Selma stood on the tips of her toes to look over the top. The stone had been carved out in the middle, creating a small compartment, and sitting inside was a small gold key. Selma reached in, plucked it from its home, and admired the entangled detailing. It was like no other key she had ever seen.

She opened her small pearl clutch and tugged at the silk lining inside. A heart-wrenching rip tore through the damp air, and Selma slipped the key inside the silk lining. Millie would have to forgive her for that.

As she turned to make her exit, an arm swung around her body, pinning her arms in place, and she felt the distinct, cold burn of sharp metal against her throat.

A voice hissed in her ear, "Is this the after party?"

Before Selma could breathe, she was enveloped in a swirling cloud of dark mist.

"The most well-known Goddesses are the Goddess of Life and the Goddess of Death."

—An excerpt from The Forgotten Goddesses by Tara Wallingford, property of the Massachusetts Public Library

CHAPTER 26

Drip. Drip. Drip.

Selma felt the cold hard ground beneath her. Moisture dripped down from the ceiling and soaked through the fabric of her dress, pairing with the goose bumps forming on her skin. It was pitch dark, and she could smell the sweet, earthy smell of soil and decay. As her thoughts began to hurtle back to earth, she felt the tightness of rope cut into her wrists. She was bound. Her hands tied behind her back and to a chair that she was sitting in.

One eyelid slid open, and then the other. Though heavy in her skull, she fought them to obey. Muddled figures filled her blurry vision. She could hear her heartbeat in her ears. She could only make out dark, blurry shapes as watery tears fell down her cheeks. Sounds began to pile up around her, inciting anxiety within her, as she did not have enough of her faculties to summon a fight-or-flight response. The whispers jumped from one corner to the other like bolts of electricity, too fast for Selma to catch, until she felt a hand touch her shoulder and gently nudge her. With all the strength and adrenaline, she could muster, Selma jerked her head up. Her eyelashes fluttered, trying to clear away the murkiness. Slowly, her surroundings sharpened. She was no longer in the circular stone room, but was she still in the castle?

Instinctively, she reached for her threads, but she could not feel them. She could not feel any of her power. She blinked the tears from her eyes and took in the scene around her. Confusion threatened to crush her as the first vision came to life. It was Amalie, the woman she had met near the island on her walk, staring back at her. She held her hands up in front of her in surrender. She was not moving and was gulping deep, calm breaths.

"Selma, you are alright. Everything is alright," Amalie muttered. Her hushed tones were clearly a tool to create some calmness, but her efforts were falling flat. Without her magic or free use of her arms, Selma's anxiety was at full magnitude.

"What are you doing here? Where are we?" Selma asked as she craned her neck to take in the rest of her surroundings. Her voice was like a whisper struggling to get through a fog.

Selma breathed deep to try and calm her nerves. Had the Order sent Amalie? If she needed to defend herself, she would need to get out of these restraints, but whatever had incapacitated her had made her threads sluggish. Without a clear idea of what was happening or what kind of threat Amalie posed, she did not want to make any rash decisions. But one thing was certain: She needed to get out of this room.

"I know what this looks like, but it really isn't as bad as that," Amalie added, noting Selma's panic. "I used a simple incapacitation spell. You should be alright, but you may feel a little woozy. I just needed to talk to you, and I couldn't risk you running off."

A simple conversation did not usually include kidnapping. But Selma remained quiet and focused on Amalie. She also slammed her gate closed to protect her mind. Her necklace was still pulsing on her skin. Selma looked around the room, trying to see anything through the darkness. "You are not the one who attacked me. Where did they go?"

A dark figure broke through the darkness. Selma did not recognize him. He was long and lanky. His pocked skin almost hid the scar that slashed across his left eye. He was not armed, as far as Selma could tell, but he had magic, which was more deadly.

"I'm right here. Glad to see you missed me," he hissed.

Selma scoffed. "How could I miss that face?"

Before Selma could breathe, the lanky newcomer closed the distance between them and struck her across the face. Her cheek exploded with pain.

Amalie shouted, "Stop! Harwick, you said you were not going to hurt her."

Selma fought against her restraints.

"Do not bother, girl." Harwick scowled. "You would not be able to get out of those even if you could summon threads. The stone in the tombs is thick and laced with iron. There is no way to cast, with or without threads. So you might as well play nice and answer some questions," said Harwick, his words sodden with violence.

Selma cut in. "What am I doing here?"

"Don't—" Amalie began.

"Answer me!" Selma insisted.

Amalie blinked and dropped her arms to her sides. "What were you doing down in the chamber? Were you not enjoying the party?"

"Not particularly, no," responded Selma.

Harwick's face twisted. "What were you looking for?"

Selma stayed silent. They knew she had been looking for the key. A moment of panic ran up her spine as she thought about her purse. Had she dropped it when they took her?

"The restroom. I was looking for the restroom," Selma answered.

"You missed it," Harwick scoffed. "Where is it?"

"The restroom? I do not know. I still have not found it, and I really need to pee," Selma said. Her cheek screamed in pain as she spoke, but she tried not to let it show.

"You know what I'm talking about. And you know that nobody knows where you are right now. We could be here all night if we need to. I am in no rush," said Harwick, leaning in so close to Selma that she could smell the sweet stench of alcohol on his breath.

"Alright, alright," Amalie cut in. "Selma, they just want to know if you took anything."

"No," Selma said. The lie slipped off her tongue without remorse. "Please let me go. I did not take any of your precious trinkets. I was just looking for the restroom and got lost."

Amalie turned to Harwick. "Can we have a moment alone?"

"No. Once Olivier finds out she has stolen something, she will be at their mercy. Until then, she does not leave my sight," he said.

Amalie's eyes were pleading. She whispered to Harwick, "You can stand right outside the door. I will only need a minute."

Harwick scowled. "One minute." He stormed through the darkness, and Selma could hear a door shut behind him.

Liquid started to puddle in Amalie's eyes, and she let out a long, drawn-out breath. "I knew you were out there somewhere, but that day we ran into each other, and you mentioned where you lived…I was not prepared," said Amalie.

"Prepared for what?" Selma asked, keeping her guard up.

"I know who you are," Amalie said, not answering Selma's question.

"And who am I?" Selma responded, still not wanting to give too much away.

Silence fell between the two women as they shared glances. Only the sound of moisture dripping from the ceiling and scattering on the floor drifted over to them.

Amalie broke the silence. "I know what you're thinking."

"Oh, I bet you don't," spat Selma.

Amalie looked toward the ceiling, either out of frustration or in search of the words she needed to calm Selma down.

"I know about your family and what you can do," Amalie finally said.

This was feeling increasingly like a threat. How much did Amalie really know? She had kidnapped a witch and pissed her off in the process. Amalie was either sick, naive, or powerful, and without that information, Selma was not going to make any moves. But she did need to find out what Amalie knew and buy herself some time to form a plan of escape. She tugged at the bindings on her wrists.

"Win a blue ribbon every year? I know my mother's orchids are stunning," Selma snickered.

"Don't do that. Do not mock me. You have been an impatient asshole since I first ran into you. Other people have problems too, you know. And I know you're thinking I'm some sort of crazy person, but news flash—you weren't what I was expecting either."

"Expecting?" Selma said.

"I know who you are because I'm your sister. I know you and your family are witches because I am a witch, and I know you are an asshole because you *are* an asshole," said Amalie in frustrated tones.

Selma let her calm mask slump to the floor. There was no keeping the surprise from her face after that.

"My sister? I think you may be mistaken. I am an only child," said Selma, letting out a small chuckle. She could not exactly defend the witch accusation, seeing as they were at a gathering of witches and warlocks without a single non-magic-wielder in sight. But even if Amalie did know that Selma was a witch, there was no way she was going to get her to admit it aloud.

Amalie scoffed. "Oh, bullshit. I know it, and you know it, so let us just know it together."

"How is it that you're upset with me right now?" asked Selma, now more annoyed than scared. Selma was the one who had been taken against her will. She was the only one who had the right to be pissed. But provoking her captor was a terrible plan, so she quickly recovered. At least Amalie was not asking about the key. Although, she had no idea where the key was now.

"Alright," Selma said. "If you are my sister, then how old are you, and how did you find me?"

"I'm five years younger than you. I know that because I have been scouring the world trying to find information about my family. I did not have much to go on." She paused briefly. "My mother died shortly after I was born, and there are not many records in foster care. But I was finally able to find my father's name after a lead brought me to Belhaven. An old picture of him was all I had when I entered the system. It was difficult, and I almost gave up plenty of times, but finally I found a name. His name is Alister Lourdes. After running a background check, I discovered that he had been married before. I have been watching your mother and aunts ever since, and if they are not witches then they are aliens—which I would not put past them at this point. The last few years of my life have been strange, to say the least."

Selma felt a sadness spill over her. She knew what it was like to feel that something was missing. The feeling that if she had known more about her father, maybe she could understand herself just a bit more, or at least understand why he left. And even after being treated like a prisoner, a small part of her wanted this woman to be right. Selma wanted to help her fit at least one piece of her puzzle together, but she could not.

"I'm so sorry, but I'm not your sister. My father's name was Alister, and I know that is not a common name, so I understand the confusion. But my last name is Plumey, not Lourdes," Selma said with empathy in her eyes.

"I might not be what you pictured, but it is what it is," Amalie added.

"I didn't picture you, because you never existed," said Selma, stumbling through her sentence. The words seemed to shoot out of her mouth without her approval.

Amalie sighed and knelt on the ground before Selma. They were eye to eye, and it was then that Selma saw it. Amalie's undeniable and familiar determination. They were the same eyes Selma had thought about every day since he left. Was Amalie telling the truth? Selma's mind felt addled with whatever poison or magic that they had used against her. Could she trust this woman?

"The Order can help us find our father. They said they can." Amalie's tone was almost pleading. "Just give them back whatever it was you found, and they will help us."

There it was. Even if her father had sired another child after he left, Selma would never trust the council. They were never going to help her with anything. And even if they did, to what end? What was in it for them? No, she was not going to fall for this.

Selma was losing hold of her cool façade when the door burst open. Harwick's figure sailed past and hit the hard ground with a crunch. Amalie screamed and put herself between Selma and whatever was coming for them. Boots stomped on the ground. Selma's heart pounded as she desperately fought to release the bindings on her wrists. Harwick stumbled up and lunged forward through the darkness again, leaving Selma and Amalie in the chamber, listening to the clashing of bodies through the shadows.

Calm. Selma needed to be calm. Think. Focus on getting out of these restraints. With the door open, she could coerce her threads out. Letting out a breath, she closed her eyes and searched for energy around the room. She could sense bodies, but they would not do. She needed some element to feed her magic.

The fighting continued, and its violent sounds came closer. If she did not get out of her binds, she would surely be next.

"Please, please, please," Selma begged.

There, an energy source. She was not sure what it was, but she could feel her threads emerging. Feeding off the energy source, drinking it in. She opened her eyes and saw purple threads swirling around her. Not silver or violet like before, but deep purple. Power tingled under her skin as she pictured red-hot fire around her wrists. The bindings lit aflame, burning her skin and reducing the rope to ash. She was free.

Amalie was kneeling on the ground, trembling. Selma picked her up off the floor just in time to see Harwick stagger back. He was walking backwards, retreating from something. Moments later, Razon emerged, his vast figure towering over Harwick. He was no longer in a tuxedo but equipped in black fighting leathers from the nape of his neck down to his boots. Daggers were sheathed along his abdomen, and his face was carved into a pledge of merciless-ness both brutal and gorgeous.

"The dark adamant of the violet flame forms to our threads, forever changing them."

—An excerpt from the Canon, as translated by Leven Kara, property of the Warriors of Sever

CHAPTER 27

There was a kick to Harwick's chest, and Selma could hear the bloodcurdling crunch from across the chamber. Razon cut the distance between the two warlocks in two strides. His inked arms crossed his chest to unsheathe two daggers, one on either side. Selma barely blinked. Her eyes were wide, taking in the sight of a Razon she had never seen. His muscles tightened with every swift movement. He leaned over Harwick, who was now bleeding. A stream of crimson was streaming out of his mouth.

"You were never worth the title," Razon thundered. "You have the blood of countless innocents on your hands, and now you will die in a pool of your own."

Razon lifted his dagger into the air as Amalie shouted. "Don't, please! We only wanted to get the key back. Please don't kill anyone." Her voice cracked with desperation.

Razon looked back at Selma, dagger still at the ready. "Do you have the key?"

Selma shook her head. The fog was finally lifting. It was not a lie. She did not have the key.

Just then, Harwick reached for one of the other daggers sheathed in Razon's leathers and pulled back to strike, aiming for Razon's heart. Selma's purple threads shot forward, claiming the dagger and tossing it across the chamber.

Harwick's eyes widened. "How? Who? This room is full of iron; there is no way you could summon magic threads." He paused, his face contorting. "Unless...Unless you are one of the depraved," he stammered. "Do you bear the death mark?"

Harwick was staring straight at Selma, but Razon did not give her the chance to answer. He plunged his dagger straight into Harwick's heart and watched as the light left his eyes. Razon plucked his dagger out of the body now lying lifeless on the stone floor and wiped it on his leathers. He stalked toward the two women now, dagger still in hand. His eyes were darker than she had ever seen them. Not even a faint hint of blue.

Razon greeted Selma with dark, guttural words. "Why can't you simply do what I ask?"

His gaze now fell to Amalie. His eyes narrowed on the small, trembling figure cowering before him.

Selma cut in, "She didn't hurt me."

This did not seem to quell Razon's rage. Ire leaked out of him.

"She seems to think she knows something about my father," Selma said.

Razon's eyes sliced over to Selma.

"I would like to talk to her more," she pressed.

"If the Order finds out what happened here, they will come after both of us," Razon said to Selma. He grabbed both women, leading them out of the room and leaving Harwick's body in the iron torture chamber.

Once they were far enough from the room, Selma could feel a familiar power coursing through her threads. Razon stood silent, taking in the trembling Amelie, no doubt reading her thoughts for ill intentions. Selma spotted the familiar pearl clutch lying abandoned on the stone floor and leaned down to pick it up. Unclasping the gold enclosure, she poked her finger into the torn silk lining and felt the gold key.

"Very well. She will remain alive, but if she disappears, the Order will come looking for us. She must stay here," said Razon. He leaned in close to Amalie, his voice still quiet. "If you tell anyone what happened here tonight, I will come for you, and you will end exactly as Harwick did. There are too many lives at stake. Do you understand?"

Amalie nodded, tears falling down her cheeks. It must have been enough, as Razon held both women and whisked them away into darkness and mist.

Amalie clung to Selma as they evanesced to an alcove in the castle. The party still raged in the distance. Razon's eyes filled with a pearl and ivory hue as his red threads circled Amalie. The dark mascara running down her cheeks was cleaned up, along with her hair and gown. She looked as fresh as she had when Selma awoke in the iron chamber.

"Now, rejoin the party, and if anyone asks, you have not seen me or Selma all night, but you did see Harwick leaving the party alone," Razon instructed.

Amalie gave Selma one last look—the kind of look you would

give someone you were never going to see again—and turned to join the party.

As Selma watched her walk away, she asked, "What if she talks?"

"She won't. I cast a memory-blocker on her just in case," said Razon. "We have to get out of here," said Razon.

He reached for her waist, and they evanesced out of the castle and onto familiar mossy ground. Selma's eyes focused on her family home in the distance, and then on Razon. He was still holding on to her.

He gently ran his callused thumbs down her arms. "Are you okay?"

Selma looked down at her dress and took stock of her body. Her mind was finally clear of whatever spellcasting Harwick and Amalie had used. Her thoughts were no longer muddied. The flesh around her wrists was no longer red with burns. But, she made a mental note to ask about defensive magic. That seemed like a tool she was going to need and soon. Her arms were sore, and small cuts riddled her exposed flesh, but the crimson blood had clotted and dried. Her eye and cheek no longer throbbed where Harwick had stuck her.

"I'll be fine," she managed to get out.

"I knew you were strong, princess," Razon said with a wry smile.

Selma lifted her head and looked at the sky above them. There were so many stars, and if she had not just been kidnapped and been so close to a dead body, she would have been able to enjoy them more. Harwick's dead body. She had never been so close to one, had never seen the life leave someone's eyes. She started shaking, and Razon took her in his arms, rubbing his hands up and down her back and resting his head on top of hers. Her body was swallowed up by his considerable frame. Leviathan in size. It was calming. She pulled away just enough to look up at him, and he stared back at her. His eyes lightened just a touch. It was not the dregs of magic that were making her cheeks flush and her stomach tickle.

"I almost lost you tonight," he said. "And if it hadn't been for your magic, I would be lying lifeless on that stone floor instead."

"You were the one who saved me," she responded.

"And if I hadn't been there, you would have figured it out, because you're incredible. I don't think the Order knows what they are up against," said Razon. He smiled at her, revealing that dimple.

Selma took in his smile, his lips. Those lips again. She could not take her eyes off them. Razon leaned in closer, sharing her breath. The reddish tint of the blood moon cast a warm light on his face. He cupped her cheek with one hand, his eyes glassy. They stood there for a moment. And she did not know if it was the adrenaline pumping through her veins or the silver flecks swimming in his dark gaze, but she leaned in and kissed him. Her body relaxed as his muscles tensed around her, hard against her body. His lips were soft and welcoming, and she let his scent waft around her. He held on to her tight as his lips parted, making way for his tongue as he tasted her. It was tender and yearning all at once, everything she needed right now. The Order was a blur in the distance, and whatever consequences came from indulging in this moment, she would bear in the light of the morning.

CHAPTER 28

It had been a long, exhausting night. Razon had changed back into his tuxedo. Selma was not sure which one she preferred more, the precise cut of his tuxedo or the hardened leathers that sat so snugly along the curves of his backside. With a snap of his fingers, he had also cleaned up her dress. Her wounds were all healed now, and he had insisted on making sure she was safe behind her wards before he left.

Walking up the bifurcated stairs inside the front door, Razon at her back, Selma was too tired and flushed to notice the figure waiting outside her bedroom door.

"Hayden." Her voice cracked. "What are you doing here?"

Hayden gave her a half-hearted laugh but did not answer her question. Instead, he looked down the hallway, gesturing to something or someone. "When I couldn't get a hold of you, I decided to come out here. It was not that hard to find your mother's house," he said.

His tone was laced with uncertainty and something else that Selma could not identify. Was it anger?

"I hadn't heard from you in a while. The last time I knew anything, you were sick, and some friend of yours was answering your phone," Hayden said, emphasizing the word *friend*. "Is this him?" Hayden pointed to Razon. Razon's expression was a mask of boredom.

With that, Selma grasped Hayden by the wrist and led him away from the prying eyes of Razon.

"What's going on?" Hayden was clearly looking for answers, as his tone suggested he was not leaving until he found out why she had been ignoring him.

"Nothing. I am fine, and you really should not have come," said Selma. She intuitively knew it was the wrong thing to say. Hayden's eyes were both hurt and furious as they looked her over.

"What I mean is, I know that I haven't been calling, but is it really necessary for you to come all the way up here unannounced to check on me?" Oh, Goddess, that was not it either. It just kept getting worse.

"What would make it necessary?" Hayden spit his words out as if they held venom. "Your best friend almost dying? You never introducing me to your family? An undisclosed sickness that kept you from returning my calls for over a week? Oh, right—those did happen."

In yet another blow to Hayden's ego, Razon walked up. "Is everything alright here, mate?"

Hayden fumed as Razon leaned against the door like he belonged there.

"Yes. Everything is fine. Thank you for walking me home," said

Selma. She was giving Razon a look that hopefully said, *I am sorry, but please do not make this worse.*

"I'll see you tomorrow, princess," said Razon with a wicked smile on his face.

He'd made things worse. Selma wanted to burst into flames and take Razon with her. He knew calling her "princess" would make Hayden jealous. Razon was always one step ahead of everyone. Why had he chosen to make this more difficult than it needed to be? But, of course, recklessly toying with people was in his nature. The kiss was probably some sort of manipulation.

Selma knew this was not leading anywhere good. She walked to the door, pushing Razon in the chest. She not only hated that she enjoyed the touch, but that she was thinking about enjoying the touch in this tense moment. Razon still wore his wicked smile as he easily stepped back, letting Selma move him out of the room. One final shove sent him into the hallway, and she slammed the door.

Selma pushed her hair from her face, running her fingers through the stands. When her attention turned back to Hayden, his expression was cold. Selma would have reached out with her gift, but there was no need to. She knew what would be waiting for her under the surface. Hurt. Betrayal. Anger.

"Look, I have had an intense evening," Selma said in a calm tone, trying to ease Hayden's mind. "Why don't we get some sleep, and we can talk tomorrow."

Hayden's eyes flashed with anger. "Tomorrow? You want to blow me off again?"

"No, I don't want to blow you off. I just do not want either of us to say anything we might regret. And you must be tired," said Selma. She walked up and put her arms around him. She could feel his heart beating quickly in his chest. "I'm sorry. I'm glad you're here." It was not a lie. His embrace felt comforting.

He kissed the top of her head. "I want to be here for you. Let me be here for you," said Hayden. "Tell me what you need."

Selma let out a sigh and buried her face in his chest. "Right now, I need some sleep."

Hayden shook his head. Selma could see anger rise again in his expression. "Where were you tonight?"

Quickly, she attempted to ease his mind. "I was at an event for a group that my mother and aunts are a part of." Not a complete lie.

Hayden nodded. "And him?"

Razon. Hayden wanted to know about Razon. What could she say that would not ignite the situation further?

"He is a friend of the family," she said, giving him a half smile that she hoped communicated that she was apologetic.

He leaned down and kissed her. A loving, delicate kiss. His embrace was warm, his touch welcoming. She fell into him and hoped that he could not taste Razon on her lips.

When he pulled back, Selma could no longer feel his anger. "Happy birthday, Sel."

She took his hand and pulled him inside. Selma's heart ached from how she had treated Hayden, and she knew that the hurt and rage in his eyes when she had shown up with Razon would feed her guilt for a long time to come. But she could not repair the damage now. There was too much at stake to worry about repairing her relationship. In the morning, she would find a way to make him go back home. She would have to find a way to make him understand later, a way that didn't involve telling him the truth about Razon. Because if Selma was being completely honest with herself, then

Razon's kiss would blow up everything, and she did not have time to deal with the wreckage. Compartmentalization had always been her best tool. She wanted to rush upstairs and open the book her father had left her, but she knew if she did, she would only fall asleep on its open pages. For tonight, Hayden was here with her, and she needed to rest.

Selma's body ached. Her arms felt like liquid when she tried to raise them.

She recalled the events of the night and tried to make sense of them. She desperately needed to talk to someone. She wanted to check on Millie and tell her all about Razon and the kiss. She had been a trash friend and a trash girlfriend—she should have just let Harwick tear her to ribbons. For now, she would crawl into bed with Hayden and let his steady heartbeat lull her to sleep.

‡

The following morning, Hayden's arms were still wrapped around Selma when she felt her pendant hum awake. Razon's threads caught her attention first. The red strands made their way into her room and stopped at the foot of the bed. Razon entered and stopped abruptly, his gaze resting on Selma's topless body wrapped in sheets. She popped up quickly, waking Hayden in the process. Hayden's sleep-drenched eyes found her first. He kissed her on her shoulder and then turned to see Razon. His gaze darkened.

"Oh. Hey, mate," said Hayden.

Selma had never heard him use that term of endearment before. It was most definitely meant as a jab. Razon's jaw ticked.

Hayden got up and adjusted his boxers, his well-toned body on display. Years of gym time and golf had sculpted his body.

Selma scurried out of bed and carefully wrapped the sheet arounder her. "I'll be right down. Just wait for me in the kitchen," she said.

Razon growled, "We have work to do."

"Yes, absolutely. I will be right down," said Selma. Her stomach dropped in embarrassment. She knew exactly how this looked. Just a few hours prior, she had kissed each man, and now she was on display for both.

Hayden put his body between Razon and Selma. "She will be down when she is ready. Or are you hard of hearing?"

Razon smiled but did not say a word as he turned and left.

"What do you need to work on, and why is he here again? You and I have to work through whatever you think this is," said Hayden, his finger jolting back and forth between the two of them.

"Hayden, I have not been completely honest with you," said Selma.

"No shit," responded Hayden.

Selma sighed. "I want to tell you, but there are some truths that are simply not mine to tell. Millie and my family are in the middle of—"

"Of what? What are you in the middle of? Is it illegal? Because if you are caught up in some kind of legal battle, I can help," said Hayden.

"No, it's nothing like that." Selma responded quickly. "I can't explain why right now, but I need you to go home. I have some things that I need to take care of, and it will be better if you aren't here."

Hayden's brows knit together. "If I go home alone, do not expect me to be there when you get back. I love you, Selma. Let me in."

Her chest tightened, and tears filled her eyes. "Understood. And I love you too. But it's better this way."

Hayden scoffed and dropped his head. His breathing was labored as he took her in for the last time. "Good luck with whatever it is you're doing. I hope it's worth it."

He gathered up his clothing and was out the door before Selma could let her wet misery dribble down her cheeks. She knew that Hayden would be safer back home, and she cared for him enough to want to repay some of the kindness that he had shown her. If the Order was targeting her loved ones, it was better if they did not know about him.

CHAPTER 29

The key sat in the palm of her hand. It took everything she had inside her to keep her threads at bay. Over the last few weeks, her magic had sprung to life, making it difficult to control. It was particularly taxing to harness her threads when she was emotionally exhausted. Hayden leaving had not helped. But at least she knew he was safe.

Her skin felt like fire and ice were battling for dominance underneath. Her threads wanted to be free to feed. But she still did not fully understand them, nor how to release her magic once they had fed. They had only become stronger these last few weeks, engrossed in the key and the book that rested on the hardwood floor in front of her. The key was like no other key she had ever seen. Instead of one bit and one bow like traditional keys, this one had four bits all facing different directions, situated in a circular pattern. The bow, an intricate pattern of interlocking lines, sat in the middle. And the notches along the end of the bits, which were usually jagged, were straight instead, like the crenel of a castle.

The key sat next to the leather- and fur-bound book. The last piece of her father. The Canon.

"I know where we can take it," said Razon.

Selma's head whipped up, and she met Razon's eyes. "Why are you here? And why were you so adamant on the day of the summons to say that my powers were worthless? We both know there is something brewing inside of me that I cannot explain."

Razon said nothing.

Her lips hardened into a thin line, and her words strained to get out. "You have been helping me since the moment I got back from the council meeting, and I do not understand why. Are you or are you not part of the Order?"

Razon's eyes were chips of ice as he entered the room and shut the door.

"I was sent here by the Order," Razon said calmly. "But I was also sent here to look after you by someone else."

Selma's blood boiled as her threads moved out from her fingers and around her body, shielding her from any threat. "Then why were you there with the council that day? Who is it that wants to keep an eye on me? And remember that I have access to my power now, and my threads seem to have a mind of their own," Selma said, her tone promising violence.

Razon settled into a chair on the other side of the room. The same chair he had watched over her from when she was fighting for her life. "What more do you know about our history beyond what we touched on that day in the forest? We talked about the Wargraves, but did your Aunt Verda ever tell you of the Goddesses or the others?"

"Enlighten me," Selma spat.

Razon gulped down a breath. "The Order killed my family."

The tension in Selma's shoulders eased, and they slumped forward. Her threads retreated inside her body.

Razon continued, "The Order has ruled over Elemental witches for nearly five hundred years. Several decades ago, they had a substantial following who believed that Elemental witches should have ultimate power over all other factions of magic. They preached that the Elementals were the purest form of magic and that all others, the Wargraves included, were unnaturally using energy. They argued that feeding on living or once-living beings was an abomination. Commons were spared, probably because the council didn't feel that they were much of a threat. But everyone else was a target of hate."

Selma's brow furrowed with confusion. "Aren't Wargraves just Elementals who have undergone the change?"

"Most are, but you don't need to be an Elemental to turn Wargrave. There were others, although few," Razon answered. "And once we take the bark of the Brocken, the same substance in your necklace, our threads need to feed from spent life forces—beings who were once living but no longer are."

Selma waited for him to go on. When he did not, she asked, "Who were the others? The other factions?"

Razon's voice was barely a whisper. "The Mavens. They were powerful."

Selma had never heard of the Mavens. "Were?"

Razon went on, "Yes. Mavens were immortal, like Wargraves, but destructible. Their lifespans where far greater than Elemental witches. Mavens were born with the same substance in their blood that Wargraves used to transform their threads. It is the same substance that allows them the ability to feed on the rawest form of energy to fuel their magic. It made them powerful." Razon paused, letting his gaze fall to the floor. "But not powerful enough. The council, led by Olivier, spread lies to make people believe that they were dangerous. That the Mavens and Wargraves were siphoning power and feeding off other witches. Those who were captured were marked for death. It was a war."

Selma thought back to the scroll she had found. The witches in white robes wielding violet threads. Her thoughts swirled. "I thought those were just stories. Witches with death marks who drained life and power from other witches?"

"They are stories, but they are tales of history, not lore. And Mavens were marked, but they heal quickly. The mark never stuck around for long. Wargraves, however, still bear the mark," said Razon. He pulled down his shirt collar, revealing a scar. The raised edges of his skin knit together to portray the Goddess Saint's symbol. "Olivier and the others felt threatened by the Mavens, and eventually they had enough support to attack. The Mavens were all killed. The council found a way to use their own threads against them and burn them out. It wasn't long before Wargraves jumped sides to help the council gather them."

"But why would the Wargraves help the council after they spread such terrible lies?"

"They had their reasons." Rage rose in Razon's words. "They threatened our families if we did not comply."

An entire group of witches eradicated. The thought made bile rise in Selma's throat. And then the information sank like a brick in her mind.

Immortal. Wargraves were immortal.

Selma turned to Razon, her hands shaking. "How— How old are you?"

Blue eddies swirled in Razon's eyes. His face was calm and relaxed, like a weight had been lifted off his shoulders. "I was born just before the council was formed. Once we make the change, our aging slows. I was in my twenties when I decided to join the Wargraves. It took me a decade to train."

Selma gulped down air. Razon had been alive for over five hundred years. She knew that witches had extended lifespans. Her grandmother, Uma's mother, had lived to be one hundred and thirty. But Selma had never heard of anyone living to be over five hundred. The sheer weight of that number was immense.

Razon studied her. She could feel his gaze.

"Mavens believed in community and love above all else. Think of the Mavens like a grove of aspen trees, all sharing the same root system. They would band together to protect one another by sharing their magic and feeding off of emotion. The magic they were able to wield was incredible, but they used it responsibly, always careful not to interfere with humans, and never against others," said Razon. "There is something else that I think you should know—"

Selma interrupted him. She turned to Razon, who was slumped over. "And you?"

His furrowed brow suggested that he did not know what she was asking. "What about me?"

"What do you believe?" she asked.

He let the question marinate. "I think everyone should have access to their magic, and no faction should be discriminated against. We were all born of this earth, just as magic was."

Selma stood up tall. "So you don't stand for the same atrocities that the Order stands for?"

"I do what I can to make the council feel that I'm loyal, but I also work with a small rebellion tasked with tearing the Order apart," Razon answered.

Selma picked up the book. "And do you think this can help us? Help Millie?"

"It's a start," said Razon.

Selma took in everything she had just heard. Everything that had been kept from her, or that she had insisted on not learning. Had she been sheltered from this? Or had her selfishness kept her flush with ignorance?

"You said you wouldn't take the book from me until I was ready," argued Selma.

Razon tilted his head. "I would not be taking it. I would be protecting it."

"That is the same thing," said Selma. "Where would you be taking it?"

"Someplace safe," he assured her.

Selma wrestled with the idea of giving up something so important and entrusting it into the hands of someone she barely even knew.

"No," Selma pronounced.

Razon's jaw ticked. Clearly, he was not expecting that response.

"It's not safe here," he gritted through his teeth.

Selma rolled her eyes and uttered, "I've had it for over twenty years and nothing has happened to it. What's a few more hours?"

"The Order could come looking for it. Plus, it does not belong to you," said Razon. The words sliced at her like the daggers that she now knew he could wield not just proficiently, but prolifically.

"Excuse me. My father gave—"

"It wasn't your father's to give," Razon countered. His sober tone washed over Selma.

Sadness settled over her. Her heart ached as she peered at the book. Such a small token of hope to hold on to. She had not even set her eyes upon the pages, and yet it held all the credence that her father did love her. But what if there was no sign of his affection for her in it?

It was not just a book she was losing today. She felt like she was losing her father again.

"I'm coming with you," Selma ordered. "We will open the book here. Then you can take it wherever you need to take it, but I'm coming with you."

Razon nodded in agreement. "But we do it here, behind your wards," he said.

Razon took the key from Selma and observed the gold detailing. His thumb skimmed the cold metal.

"This symbol is a protection rune. It was used on all the War-graves' armor," said Razon, his voice soft, like his thoughts were far away.

Selma let that fact burn into her. "What is the other thing you wanted to tell me?"

All she could see were his lashes as he peered down at the key. He was pensive, rolling Selma's question over in his mind.

Selma knew. She knew what he was going to say. "You think that my father was a Wargrave, don't you?"

"Yes, I do," Razon finally responded.

Even still, his answer took her breath from her lungs.

"Here, open it," Razon said, handing Selma back the gold key.

As she took it, her breaths slowed, and she closed her eyes. She felt her power waiting for her in her bones. It had settled inside her, no longer screaming to get out. Now it felt more like another limb than something she needed to control.

Without a word, Selma summoned her threads, and they wrapped their delicate strands around the book, bending and slithering around the ornate brass locks. She paired one side of the key with what looked like its match and turned it counterclockwise. Immediately, the book obeyed, submitting to Selma with a soft click.

The binding released like it had been waiting for the day to tell its secrets. Selma gently stroked the ancient texts, careful not to damage the fragile woven vellum. She took in the foreign words and symbols that graced the pages. They were complex and beautiful, but she did not know if they held the secret she so desperately needed to know. Somewhere in this book was to answer to saving Millie from the Brocken poisoning. But its contents were vast and foreign. It could take years to translate, navigating the fragile pages for answers.

"This is incredible," Razon mused. "So many years of history locked away."

Selma turned a page, and two small sheets of paper floated loose along the binding. The coloring was different from the other pages, and the texture was thicker. One sheet was a letter adorned with a crest on the top, a skull with flowers growing upside down.

The letter was not in English, but she could make out the name signed on the bottom.

Alister Lourdes.

"A group of magical beings charged with keeping peace among the factions."

—An excerpt from The Forgotten Goddesses by Tara Wallingford, property
of the Massachusetts Public Library

CHAPTER 30

Selma held up the paper for Razon to see. "Do you know what this crest means?"

He was holding up the other sheet of paper that had fallen from the book, examining it closely. "I think you need to see this," said Razon, handing her the aged paper.

It looked like an official document of some kind. A stamp inked the paper haphazardly in the margin. It contained words and numbers, but they were all in French.

She looked up to find Razon staring at her.

Her voice was reserved as she said, "Back in the chamber, with Amalie. Do you remember that I told you that she knew something about my father?"

Razon nodded curtly.

"She said that her father's name was Alister Lourdes, and…and she said that I was her sister." She paused, fighting for the words to ask the question. "Do you think that my name is not actually Plumey, but Lourdes, and that she may be right?"

Razon's shoulders were tense. His gaze was unwavering.

Selma's cheeks bloomed with redness. It was a ridiculous question. Of course Amalie was mistaken. The idea that she had a secret sister was absurd.

Selma comfortably settled back into reality and turned her attention back to the book, sliding her finger down the sheet. Her heartbeat froze.

Selma Lourdes.

No, that could not be right. It was a mistake. Selma closed her eyes tight and shook her head, resetting her eyesight. She had seen it wrong. Her tired mind was playing a trick on her. But there it was, etched in black ink on the paper. *Selma Lourdes.* Amalie was telling the truth. She had a sister. Why had her last name changed?

Selma backtracked, observing the piece of paper in a whole new light. Her birthday was listed, along with a location. "Alister Lourdes" was listed under *père* and under *mère*…

Selma's heart sank. How? How could she not have known?

"Maybe I can help," a small voice came from behind them.

Selma stood quickly, shutting the book with more force than she should have. It was Meriem, standing at the door looking up at them both. Her shoulders were pressed back, her spine stiff. Razon had moved to put himself between the two women.

Selma steadied her breath, but she could not keep the anger out of her voice. "Help with what? Explaining why you have been lying to me all this time?"

Meriem's expression softened. She looked down at the hardwood floor in defeat. "You were so young, and children with magic blood are so rare and precious. When Alister came to us and asked for help, we were all in shock."

"I don't understand," Selma whispered.

Meriem continued, "Your father and your...Uma were childhood friends. They lost touch when your father left to seek out the Wargraves. She was devastated. But then he showed up here with a baby. You were so small and could not even speak yet. He asked for you to stay, for us to keep you out of the prying eyes of the Order. Uma objected at first, but she always had a weakness for Alister."

Meriem delivered that last piece of news disapprovingly. Tears began to well in Selma's eyes.

"Your father soon caught wind that the Order was seeking him out for crimes of heresy. He made us promise to keep caring for you. And then he was gone. We have not heard from him since," said Meriem. "And we felt it would be best if you did not use your magic and call attention to yourself. We didn't want to lose you."

Selma's chest rose and fell with her heavy breaths. She could feel Razon's presence, but he did not dare touch her.

"The Order showed up here after he left. They did not know that Alister had sired a child, and they wanted to know where he was. We were terrified to lose you, so we lied and hid you away," Meriem bit out, her voice cracking. "We told them you were Uma's child, and we hid your powers and kept the truth from you. Gerta and I were too scared to confront Uma, but Verda was always the bravest of us. She wanted you to have tools to learn some magic. She ignored Uma and started giving you lessons in lesser magic.

The council must have found out the truth somehow."

Selma's heart hit the floor. Verda. Even Verda had kept this from her.

Her stare burned into the older witch standing before her. How dare they keep the truth from her? All she had ever wanted was to feel comfortable in her own skin, and the people entrusted with helping her find her way, her magic, had kept her from it. Her family, her own…"mother" had been complacent in her pain and anguish for years.

"We made what we thought was the right decision," said Meriem, defending herself. "Magic outside that of the Goddess Saint is un-natural. The Order is only bringing balance by protecting what is rightfully ours."

"Stop. Just stop. Nothing is *rightfully yours*. The Order does not bring balance to magic," Selma said through a tight throat. "And all this, lying to me for all these years, it was not your decision to make."

"Perhaps," Meriem carried on. "But either way, we were charged with your well-being, and we did what we thought was right."

"What you thought was bullshit!" Selma cried. Her tears were flowing freely now. "Who is my real mother?"

"We don't know," said Uma as she and Gerta came into view. "Your father never said."

Selma's gaze jerked to the women.

"Whether or not you agree with how we endured these many years does not matter now. You are entitled to make your own decisions about your magic," said Uma, her demeanor solemn.

Selma could not help it. She reached out her threads toward

the three women. She needed to know, after all this time, if they held one droplet of love for her. But she could not hear their thoughts—her own were too loud. But she could sense a tinge of sadness among them.

They were silent for several minutes until Razon interrupted. He put his hand on her lower back and rubbed gently, soothing her. Her thoughts quieted.

We should go, Razon said. His voice stroking her thoughts and calming her nerves.

Selma wiped the wet, salty drops from her cheeks as Razon packed up the book and key.

Do you still want to come with me? Razon's question was quiet and kind. Full of more empathy than she deserved.

No. I need to check on Millie, and I need to be alone right now, she responded.

Razon nodded in agreement. *I understand. I'll be back tomorrow.* He turned to her aunts. "Did you find him?"

They all shook their heads in unison. They had come back empty-handed, without her father, which meant that Selma still needed to complete the trials. She slumped in defeat. The trials. How could she think about the trials right now?

In a blink, Razon was gone. And so was the book. The four women stood in silence, until Selma pushed through them and, without a word, left for Millie's.

‡

The tan kraft paper crinkled as Selma carried a bouquet of autumn flowers tied with a burgundy velvet ribbon. Selma had carefully picked out Millie's favorite flowers, and David had accepted them on Millie's behalf as she slumbered. Selma desperately wanted to fall apart in her friend's arms, but she knew that Millie was too weak. Selma needed to be the strong one right now, even if she felt she could crumble at any moment. She needed to find a way to get the poison out of Millie. But the weight of the task threatened to crush her.

"Love never seems to bend or break as you wish it to."

—Journal of Uma Plumey, property of the Plumey Estate

CHAPTER 31

Flesh. The second trial.

Razon returned the following night, as promised. He slept in the chair in her room, as he had so many nights, when she was recovering from a self-inflicted stab wound. The second trial was mere hours away. Ironic, as Selma did not feel as though her own flesh belonged to her. Not since hearing the news that her family was not as she had thought. Every fiber of her being felt foreign to her.

She did not know what the Order had in store for her this evening, but she and Razon had spent the last two weeks training. Her muscles ached from their early-morning runs. They had practiced some simple fighting techniques that Razon felt might be necessary. She had never used her body this way, and it felt good to start thinking of it as a tool. She had begun to notice how Razon used his body like a perfectly honed battle machine, no doubt from years of intense Wargrave training. She was not anywhere near his skill level, and she would never tell him this, but she had started to look forward to their training sessions. They were a bright spot in a long tunnel of darkness.

Razon had brought the Canon somewhere safe where it could be translated. He assured Selma that it was with someone whom he would entrust his life to.

"Can I ask you a question?" Selma asked, looking over at Razon, who was staring out the window of her bedroom.

"If I refuse to answer, would you leave it alone?" he asked, not tearing his gaze from the window.

"Doubtful," she said.

"Very well," he responded.

She went on to ask, "If Saint is the Goddess of light and life, why are the trials held at night, by the light of the moon? Would it not make more sense to complete the trials during the day?"

"Because the Order are showy bastards with matching egos," Razon responded.

Selma stared at him, one hand on her hip. She was not going to let him get out of answering this question. He might have been in a prickly mood tonight, but she needed answers.

Razon turned, sensing her intention of standing there until he gave a genuine answer. He let out a breath.

"It's a show of power. To complete the trials when Sever is watching means they can boast about the addition of another committed witch to the Goddess Saint," said Razon.

"Do the followers of Sever have trials?" she asked, wondering why she had not asked before.

"No. Sever does not need recognition. She only asks that we respect our gifts as she does," he said in a serious tone.

Selma opened her mouth to continue, but Razon cut her off. "That was three questions, not one."

She thought back to the woods, to the color of his eyes when he cast. She tried not to look too long into them now. She did not want to get distracted.

"Why did your eyes turn black when you warded the woods that first day?"

Razon stayed quiet for a few long minutes. Long enough that she assumed he was not going to answer the question. But Selma waited, not taking her eyes off him.

"The training to become a Wargrave is..." He paused. "Intense. Sacrifices are made. You should be getting ready for your trial."

Selma wanted to go on, but the finality in his tone suggested that he was not going to indulge her questioning any longer.

"I've been called back to the council. I leave as soon as the trial has concluded," Razon said.

Selma looked up at him with fear in her eyes. "Why? You don't think Amalie said something about the key, do you?"

Razon contemplated her theory for a moment. "No, I don't think that is it. Even if the Order knows that the key is gone, I used magic to block her memory."

Selma thought through the elements, considering which one would have made it possible to block a memory, but none seemed right. A memory was not like blood, not a liquid that could freeze. Fire would burn the flesh along with the memory.

As if he knew exactly what she was thinking about, Razon cut in, "As an empath, you can hear thoughts, but you can also manipulate them. I was able to mimic your magic. It is powerful enough that I am sure they do not know about Amalie and the key."

Selma shuddered at the fact that Razon could mimic her magic and hear her thoughts. The vulnerability that came with him having that much access to her was like nothing she had felt before.

"Then why do they want you back?" she asked.

"It could just be a check-in, or they want me to work on something else congruently. Either way, I do not know how long I will be gone. And it is important that you maintain your training while I am away. You are stronger now, and I believe you can control your gifts. Just be careful to not let anyone see you. I have warded the field in the woods. You can go there," he said matter-of-factly.

Selma did not know what to say. The light tonight was just as it had been the night of the Luminescence Ball. They sat there in silence as her memories turned to the kiss in the courtyard. He had not mentioned it since that night. Maybe it was merely adrenaline and nothing more that had brought them together under the night sky. She knew how much he had tried to help her over these last weeks. Bringing up the kiss and making him feel bad about it was the last thing she wanted to do. It was a lovely memory to end a terrible night, that was all.

"I'll be fine," she said, with no emotion behind her words. "I have to be, for Millie."

"I know you will," he said quickly. "It's almost time. You should get going. Remember about the field."

And Selma turned to see the floating orb summoning her once again.

The flame was easier to follow this time. The path was familiar, and Selma summoned fire to help her maneuver the path in the dark. The crackling flame in her palm lit her way.

The orb floated through the night. It led her to the same field where she had collapsed in heart-wrenching pain weeks prior. The same place where Razon had helped by carrying her home to heal. She realized just then, in that moment, that she had not thanked him for his kindness. She had been so caught up in her pain and problems that she had not extended her gratitude. Her eyes sank, and she regretted every moment they had spent together in which she had not thanked him. Knowing that he likely thought of her as selfish made her cringe.

When she finally arrived at the field, the flame in the orb's core burst, and she found the men of the council lined up arm to arm, wearing the same familiar cloaks. She could not make out their faces, but she knew where Olivier was. In the center, looking straight at her.

His all too familiar question danced off his lips as if he knew the answer and delighted in it. "Have you come to your senses and decided to give up the location of your criminal father?"

Selma's face hardened, and she wordlessly shook her head.

Olivier clicked his tongue, then walked forward past the other men. "As I suspected. Once again, we find ourselves before the Goddess Saint as one of her children wishes to commit to her love and light. The trial today is more than a symbol. It is an everlasting sign of our devotion and gratitude for being allowed to feed from the mother's powers and use them as our own. Step forth, child," Olivier requested.

Selma looked for anything that would give her a hint of what was to come, but there was nothing besides the pedestal and bowl that had been placed in the grass during the previous trial. Surely they were not going to ask for another piece of her heart.

"Tonight, beneath the light of the moon, the goddess Saint asks that you show your support and appreciation and mastery of the powers bestowed upon you. This evening, in defiance of the false Goddess, the Goddess Saint wishes for you to bear her mark."

Selma's breath caught in her throat. Permanently brand herself? Olivier must have been able to read her face, because his sneer lifted at the corners.

The Order dispersed as it had before, standing at the tips of what would be a pentagram in the field. The pedestal filled with blue flames.

Selma had no choice. If she needed to etch a scar into her body to get through this and keep her powers, then so be it. She had a tattoo of a dolphin on her ass from spring break first year of college, and that did not mean anything. A quick burn was better than piercing her own heart.

Olivier picked up a tool from the flames. A branding iron.

"Come now, and kneel before the Goddess Saint," Olivier instructed.

Selma hesitated as she thought about taking his head off instead.

"If you're stalling, child, please know that we are busy men with little patience for laziness," snarled Olivier. "We are running low on time. Do you wish to commit to the Goddess Saint? I am sure you remember the consequences if you do not," he said, annoyance growing in his voice with every punctuated word.

She knew she had no choice. Selma walked the few paces to the pedestal, and Olivier moved his finger in a circular motion, silently instructing her to turn before kneeling. Having her enemy at her back was terrifying. But the sooner she got this done, the sooner she could forget this entire night and wash the rotten feeling of Olivier's presence from her mind.

His cold finger grazed the back of her neck, feeling foul on her skin. And then, a scorching pain. The smell of burnt flesh made her eyes water and her stomach churn. Selma wanted to scream, but she would not give them the satisfaction. Instead, she let her whimpers die in her throat. She was certain that Olivier held the burning brand to her skin longer than was necessary, soaking in every last moment of her pain. When he finally lifted the iron, she felt instant relief, even though sweat was pouring from her brow as her body shook.

Selma waited for instructions, but nothing came. What were they waiting for? Minutes ticked by. As did the pain on her skin. But it was soon replaced by shivers. Goose bumps prickled her skin, and the chill in the air settled in her bones before she dared to move and look over her shoulder.

When she did, there was no one there. The pedestal with the stone bowl had also vanished. She was alone.

"The Goddess Sever, of death, dark, winter, and autumn, valued magic above all else."

—An excerpt from The Forgotten Goddesses by Tara Wallingford, property of the Massachusetts Public Library

CHAPTER 32

She spent what felt like hours in the cold mossy grass. Shivering, Selma made her way back to town, but the island and her mother's house were the last places she wanted to be right now. The only place that felt remotely like home was Millie's.

Her tired body carried her toward her friend as she wondered why the trial had ended so quickly and why the council had left without saying a word. All she had been asked to do was endure a marking. Sure, the pain was excruciating. It had hurt deeply, but it was only a burn. She was not in any mortal danger. Was it simply to humiliate her?

She stopped when she could make out a dark figure up ahead. She knew that frame. It had raced through her mind and dreams all too often lately.

Razon met her stare from Millie's patio. He leaned forward. His legs were sprawled out in front of him, and his fingers were plunged into his hair. He must have known she would not want to see Uma or her aunts after hearing the truth about her biological mother. When she got closer, she could make out the concern in his gaze. Twin bruises nested under his eyes, and his disheveled waves fell to the side. Goddess, even unkempt he was beautiful.

Razon got up from the chair and walked up to her, putting his hand in his pockets. His hair uncharacteristically fell into his eyes, and his worried features hid away, making way for a mask of calm. Whatever he had been doing while he was away had worn on him.

"We need to talk," said Razon. His tone matched his raggedy appearance.

"Is this about the trial? Because I thought it went rather well—aside from the searing pain," she added.

"Yes and no, but I heard it was quite the show," said Razon, rubbing his chin with his thumb and forefinger. "Olivier was not happy when he returned. What happened?"

"Nothing. They branded me with the symbol of the Goddess, and then they left," Selma said in a bored tone. She flung out her arms in frustration. "That was it."

His eyes narrowed. "They marked you. Where?"

Her fingers instinctively moved to the back of her neck and rubbed the spot where Olivier had held the hot brand.

Razon's eyes followed her movements. "May I?"

She nodded, and a moment later was caressing the spot on her neck that held her new mark. Heat flooded her low in her belly.

He spoke in a low, guttural tone that dampened her core. "Have you seen this?"

"No, I have not had a chance to look in a mirror," she responded. She reached back to feel the scar but felt nothing. The skin of her neck was smooth.

Razon summoned his threads. They worked quickly weaving together, creating a circular shape in front of her. Each thread was so close together, they created a mirror-like shield. "Turn around, and look over your shoulder. What do you see?"

Selma obliged. She could see her reflection in the opulent red light as she turned to look at the burn mark in the echo of his threads. But she saw nothing. Not even a red mark. There was no way the wound had healed fully in such a short time. Even if the brand had barely bitten the skin, there would at least be a burn mark.

"I don't understand," Selma stated, examining the place where inflamed skin should have been.

"The council has asked me to keep a close eye on you until your last trial," said Razon. "They have also asked me to watch your friend." Razon turned his eyes toward the house.

"Millie," she whispered. "I don't understand. Didn't I do exactly what they asked me to do? I let them burn their ridiculous Goddess symbol into my skin."

"You did. So much so that I suspect they may not have any intention of letting you walk away from your final trial," he continued. "I think there is more to your past than even your mother and aunts know," Razon said, his body tensing.

"Don't call them that," Selma snapped. "They aren't my family. Millie is. I need to see her. I need to get her out of here," she said, still trying to keep her insides down. Her entire body was overheating. Nausea threatened to take over. Panic hit as she thought about Millie. Beautiful, kind Millie…those monsters were taking everything from her.

Razon narrowed his eyes and took two steps, moving behind her. Her defenselessness startled her, but she held her ground. If she needed to use her powers, she still had enough room to turn and run. But his presence pulled her toward him. It was not threatening or violent. It was almost calming as he shadowed her small figure under his all-encompassing one.

"The best thing you can do for her now is to stay calm, but if we don't act soon, you're going to lose her. As for you…" Razon was calmer, looking at her like she was going to burst into flames right there in front of him.

Selma's heartbeat seemed to slow. She could hear it pounding in her ears.

"I don't care about me," Selma said. The declaration made heat rise in her chest. The Order had come after Millie. Her anger was buzzing through her threads. She had to get Millie out of here.

Razon's eyes filled with sadness. "But I do. And it has become clear that the Order has made you and the people who you care about targets. If we move Millie now, they will get suspicious. We are going to need help."

"Okay…b-but who?" Selma stammered through her response.

Razon answered quickly, "We leave tonight."

After everything that had happened today, Selma could not bring herself to ask where they were traveling to. Her entire world kept imploding in her face, one blow at a time. She felt dizzy and nauseous, but there was no time to rest. She needed to focus on harnessing her magic while trying not to think about her family's betrayal or the Order. What had Razon meant when he said there was more to her past? What was she missing? He said they needed help. But who was powerful enough to take on hundreds of years of warlock power? The thought made her feel utterly exhausted, and they had not even started their mysterious journey.

Turning to Razon, Selma put her hand over her chest where the scar from the dagger blade should have been. "Razon." He looked at her over his shoulder. "Thank you for healing me. I want you to know that I appreciate your help."

He lifted the corner of his mouth just a touch and nodded.

"The northern camp remains hidden, though we still remain cautious."

—Recovered correspondence from Warrior Leclerc to Warrior Lourdes,
property of the Warriors of Sever

CHAPTER 33

Mist and darkness cradled them as they evanesced, coming to a stop surrounded by vast walls and towering plants. The room was beautiful, with soaring ceilings and large windows. Flowers and plants spilled out of beautiful handmade pottery, and the artwork consisted of wide, sweeping landscapes or colorful abstracts. It was not at all like the castle she had visited when she first met the council. It was light and welcoming, decorated with slick modern touches.

Selma's eyes could not absorb it all fast enough. She asked Razon, only half listening to the answer, "What is this place?"

"This is Tullamore Castle, and I have a feeling they were expecting us. Follow me," Razon instructed.

He was racing away before Selma could get her footing. His pace was so brisk that when he stopped and turned and talked to her, she slammed into his unbuttoned, open chest. Razon put up his arms to brace her. And she stood there for a moment longer than she would have deemed appropriate.

Razon dipped his head to look her over. "Are you alright?"

Selma stepped back, creating a gap between them, and pulled her hair behind her ear. Her cheeks were flushed, and she hoped he would not hear her racing heartbeat.

"Yes, of course. I-I just need to…pay b-better attention," Selma stammered.

Razon must not have noticed her awkward giggle, or at least did not care to comment, because his head lifted and turned to the door behind them. Two tall figures draped head to toe in couture had entered the room. Their faces wore smiles, but their body language was stiff. Selma did not know how to react to the strangers, so she stayed still, her eyes darting back and forth between them and Razon.

Just when Selma was getting ready to summon her magic, the woman held out her arms and relaxed her shoulders.

"Hello, darling," she said in a sultry tone.

She walked over and leaned into Razon for a hug. He had since dropped his grasp on Selma's arms, and she realized at that moment that she missed it.

The woman was tall and beautiful. As tall as Razon, even without heels, with a pale complexion that beautifully complemented her long, golden-rod hair, which was tied back in intricate braids. Selma had always wished that her dark black hair and pale skin did not look so sickly. She envied the woman's bright locks.

The man stepped forward, equally as beautiful. He matched Razon in height but was slightly smaller in width. Although his muscles were toned, they were not as pronounced as Razon's. Both strangers shared the same green eyes, and Selma wondered if they were related. The woman still held on to Razon's arm and leaned her head on his shoulder. Selma felt her stomach tighten. Was she jealous? That could not have been it. Besides, this woman, whoever she was, seemed like a perfect fit for the carefully calculated confidence of Razon.

The man beside them spoke up. "To what do we owe this unexpected visit?" His voice was full of joy and comfort, like a warm toddy on a frigid day. "You must introduce us to your lovely friend," he said as he turned toward Selma.

Razon turned his attention toward Selma as well but did not let go of the woman. She stared at Selma, looking her up and down. "This is Selma Plumey, and I hope you will enjoy her company as well as I have these last weeks."

The man reached out his hands to greet her, but the woman narrowed her eyes, carefully calculating each inch of Selma. Knowing that the woman was a witch, Selma was quick to check on her mental walls.

"Welcome, Selma. Any friend of Razon's is a friend of ours," he said, taking her hands in his. "I am Leven, and this is my sister, Emery."

Selma nodded at both, her tired, sleep-starved body trying to conserve as much energy as possible. He continued, "I am sure you are both exhausted. I assume you will be staying with us? I am sure Emery will insist. Let us show you to your room so you can settle in and change. We can meet back up for supper later. Will we be needing one or two rooms?"

"Two!" Selma shouted at a volume that took both Leven and Emery by surprise. Razon just gave her a wry smile and turned to talk to Emery. They chatted through the hallways as two others carried their bags behind them. Selma wondered if they were serving punishment from the council, just as some of the council members had wanted Selma to do. But she could not picture Razon condoning such an archaic chastisement. Not after getting to know him better. But Leven and Emery were strangers to her, and so were their beliefs. If they were keeping servants from the Common, then Selma would find a way to free them.

Leven walked with Selma, pointing out various artworks and spewing stories along the way. Selma took in every word. This was the most amazing home and incredible art collection she had ever seen in person. She even spotted an original Berthe Morisot.

They arrived at the first bedroom, and Emery showed Selma in. It was absolutely stunning. A large bed with iron posts sat on one side of the room, and she could not help but think about how inviting it looked. It was barely late morning, but she was so drained from the night before that all she wanted to do was sleep forever. There were gold sconces with taper candles along the wall and a large, carved fireplace opposite the bed.

"Please make yourself at home, and if you need anything, just ask. We have plenty of people around who can help with whatever you need," Emery said. "Someone will come get you when supper is ready," she cooed. She moved as gracefully as a gazelle. "Oh." She turned. "And the room is stocked so you can pull energy for your magic. You will not need to strain yourself through the stone walls," she said, pointing at the various brass pots around the room. "Though I have heard that will not be a problem for you."

Selma nodded. "Death threads?"

Emery's eyes narrowed, and she saw Leven shift on his heels. "We do not call them that. But yes. Your threads can feed with the assistance of the containers."

Selma winced at her own thoughtlessness. "Death threads" was certainly a term the Order used to scar other magic brethren. She had since learned that the threads that fueled non-Elemental witches were feeding on the energy of the earth or emotion and not draining power from others. "Death threads" was the only way she had been taught to refer to threads that were powered by death or souls, but she needed to be more mindful. Especially around present company. Razon noticed her embarrassment and smiled at her in comfort and understanding.

The three closed the door behind them, and finally she was alone. She climbed into the bed and did not bother to remove her clothing or get under the covers. And just like that, sleep took her.

‡

She must have slept for several hours, because the sun had dipped below the tree line, and Selma's room was mostly dark when she finally managed to open her heavy eyes. Leaning toward the table near the side of the bed, she stretched her fingers to flick on the lamp, letting light spill into the room and chase away the shadows. Her stomach made it known that it had been neglected with a loud growl, and she hoped she had not slept through dinner.

Selma rolled off the side of the large bed, needing to hop down a little to reach the floor, and felt her muscles ache as she did so. She must have been so tense these last few days. She turned the ornate brass door handle and peeked her head outside. There were plenty of people hustling down the hallways, and one stopped in front of her door.

"Yes, ma'am, can I get anything for you?" Her accent had a touch of islander in it.

"Um, maybe. Do you know what time it is, and have you seen Razon?" Selma did not know if this person even knew who Razon was. She had managed to ask zero questions before she fell asleep.

"Yes, ma'am. It is half past six, and Razon is in his room, washing up for supper. I can tell him and the mistress you are awake if you would like?"

"That won't be necessary," Selma responded. Especially if Emery was "the mistress." Selma still did not know who she could trust. "Could you show me to Razon's room, please?"

The woman's eyes went wide at the request, and she hesitated but turned and motioned for Selma to follow her. They walked just a few doors down and stopped. The woman went to knock, but Selma put up a hand to stop her.

"Thank you. I can take it from here," said Selma.

The woman nodded once and carried on down the hall, looking back once to check on something.

Selma gently knocked on the door. She had no idea what she was going to ask when she got into the room, but she needed some explanation as to why they were here and who these people were.

When she did not get a response, she checked to see if the door was locked. To her delight, it was not, which either meant that Razon trusted these people and felt safe here, or his door was warded. She tried her luck with the wards and slipped inside with no problem, but the room was vacant. It was similar to hers, but she noticed plenty of clothing hanging in the closet—all black, of course. A desk was piled with paperwork, books, and a map.

She was leaning down to look at the map when Razon sauntered out from the suite's adjacent room. Water dripped from his hair onto the floor, and his inked skin glistened with the last remnants of a bath. He was wearing nothing but a bleached white towel around his hips, slung just low enough she could make out the indentations below his belly button. His soaked black locks fell into his face. She must have been staring, because when she lifted her gaze to his face, he tilted his head and tossed her a wicked, dimpled smile. Dammit, that dimple! She did not want to acknowledge that she had been drooling over his chiseled abdomen, so she quickly straightened and put on her cool, collected mask.

"What time is dinner?" Selma asked in an even tone, hoping her traitorous eyes were not giving her away.

Razon called her bluff. He turned away from her and pulled the towel up to his head, drying off his hair and exposing his backside in the process. His tattoos wrapped all the way around his thighs, and Selma's lips parted, letting out a small gasp. She turned away from his naked body, feeling her cheeks blush with heat. She was sure they were a dark shade of crimson by the time he answered her.

"Well, now that you're up, princess, I'm sure someone has already let Emery know and they are preparing it right now. We should be eating within the hour."

Selma thought back to the woman in the hallway. Even though Selma had told her not to mention anything to Emery, she was sure the woman had scurried off to do just that.

"Is there a reason you're so exposed?" Selma wondered aloud. She quickly checked her periphery to see if he had made himself decent yet. The towel was now back hanging around his hips.

"You came into my room, princess—unannounced, may I add." Razon took a sip of liquid that most definitely was not water. "I suggest you freshen up, and I will escort you down to dinner when you're ready. There will be some clothing in your closet if you would prefer something other than what you wore. Emery likes to make a show of things, so I'm sure she will be overdressed for the occasion."

Selma tried not to take offense to the slight suggestion that whatever clothing she brought was not good enough for the occasion. She had more to worry about than dinner etiquette, and her multitude of questions were brimming on the edge of her brain.

"What are we doing here, and how do you know Leven and Emery? And—"

Razon interrupted her. "They are friends, and there will be plenty of time to discuss that at dinner. "For now, get washed up," said Razon, without an ounce of compromise in his voice. He took another sip from his glass and pointed toward the door.

Irritation rose in her gut. She was once again being denied details. But without arguing, Selma turned and went back to her room. Besides, she was hungry, and nobody ever did anything well on an empty stomach.

Selma looked down at her faded denim jeans and clogs. Embarrassment turned in her gut thinking about eating dinner in front of Emery and Leven, who would no doubt be dressed impeccably at dinner.

"A wrinkled sweater probably isn't going to cut it," Selma huffed out to her empty room.

Reluctantly, she walked over to the hutch and opened both doors, revealing gorgeous, flowing gowns and cloaks in every color. Every garment was freshly steamed and in her size. She cringed at the fact that someone might have come in here and stocked the closet while she was asleep. The same way they had snuck in here while she was in Razon's room and lit all the candles. But the dresses were here now, and there was no reason to let them go to waste.

She decided on a simple frock, a black slip gown and slippers. As she was sitting at the vanity, brushing out her tangled mess of hair, her eyes caught a glimpse of the brass containers Emery had pointed out earlier. They were filled with sand and dirt. Selma contemplated what Emery had said about them, and it hit her—ashes. They were ashes from spent life forces. That would mean that Emery and Leven were also Wargraves. She wondered how old they were and how long Razon had known them.

Right on cue, a knock sounded at the door. She added the freshwater pearl earrings that Razon had given her. Those and her pendant had been the only personal possessions she had grabbed before leaving. She tied her hair back in a sleek, low bun and took one last look at herself in the mirror. Satisfied with her reflection she reached out her threads to the brass containers around the room, feeling them braid together and pulse with power. She still had not gotten used to the idea of knowingly summoning her magic with what she could only imagine were the ashes of dead bunny rabbits, but she could not deny that her magic responded much more willingly than before. She used some of the power to ward the door, weaving her threads together to create a net and then gently severing them so they'd still protect the entryway. It was something Razon had taught her to do during one of their training sessions. At first it was painful to sever the threads. But with practice, her magic seemed to listen and trust her more.

When she opened the door, Razon was smiling back at her.

"Nice. You have been practicing, I see," he said.

"Thank you," said Selma, returning a slight smile. She was slightly disappointed, but also proud, that he had commented on her magic rather than her appearance. "Nice to see you with clothes on."

She was lying, but she was not going to let him know that she preferred her earlier unfettered look at his naked body.

"You clean up nicely as well, princess." Razon offered his arm. "Shall we?"

CHAPTER 34

Razon guided Selma down the long hallways to the ground floor, where there was a dining room tucked away. It, too, had tall ceilings made of glass and dozens of hanging plants floating above the table, the leaves dripping down in various hues of green. Lights twinkled between the foliage, and Selma could not tell if it was electricity or magic that illuminated them. The table was stunning. Low-sitting blush roses, scotch thistle, and jasmine shot up from the table at various heights, giving the illusion that they were growing right out of the center of the table. Each arrangement was paired with small terra-cotta pots filled with flowering heather. The dishware and wine goblets were a deep teal, pairing beautifully with the vines that danced in and out of each place setting. Low, melodic music played in the background. Bagpipes, if she was not mistaken.

Razon pulled out a chair and ushered Selma to sit.

She looked around the table, noticing several vacant place settings. "Where is everyone?"

"They should be joining us shortly. I am sure Emery is fussing over a few final details in the kitchen," said Razon, eyeing the last place setting at the end of the table.

He took his seat beside Selma, and they sat in silence, waiting not so patiently for their hosts as staff nudged up against the walls around the table. Selma recognized the woman from before. She was dressed in the same white cotton gown but wore an apron now.

Selma had to ask, "Do they serve in the covenant?"

Razon frowned. "No. Emery and Leven have taken them in to keep them safe. They do not ask for anything in return, but most of those seeking refuge here wanted to pitch in to show their gratitude. Emery and Leven help them piece their lives back together. Once they feel safe and their homes are rebuilt, they will usually move on. But some have been here for years."

"Safe? I did not realize they were running from something," Selma added, taking in the men and women around the room. Some had vicious scars.

"The Goddess Saint is not very forgiving, especially with Olivier at the helm," Razon added quietly.

The Order. The council had done this. Hurt other witches and warlocks. The thought almost put off her appetite, only to be rebuffed by a stomach growl.

Finally, Emery entered the room. Razon was right—she was overdressed for the occasion. She wore a red velvet gown that reached the ground. The train pooled at her feet, but the center had a slit in front that reached several inches above her knees. The dress was fitted along her hips, and the top dipped low, revealing her cleavage and ink. It was similar to Razon's and sat just below her sternum. She was stunning. And Selma was grateful that she had opted for the black dress rather than the sweater and leggings she had arrived in.

"Hello, you two. I apologize for our late arrival. We do not make a habit of keeping our guests waiting, but the delay was unavoidable. I trust you rested well?" Emery asked the question, but Selma sensed that she was not listening for a response.

Razon looked worried. "What intrusion? Is everything alright?"

Emery shared the same worried expression. She lifted her gaze toward Razon as she fussed with her silverware, adjusting and readjusting them to line up perfectly.

"Em, who is the last place setting for?" Razon's expression had turned cold.

Emery inhaled a deep breath and let it out with a disingenuous smile.

"We have a last-minute visitor, and we never turn away guests. As you can imagine, surprise drop-ins happen from time to time," she said, her focus solely on Razon. It was surely a plea for Razon to understand, as they, too, had arrived unannounced.

Razon's tone was more serious than Selma had ever heard it. "Who is it?" He did not wait long before repeating, "Who?"

Emery's expression turned from concern to outright worry. Her eyes darted between Selma and Razon as she took a few moments to gather herself.

"You know who," she eventually said in a whisper.

"Damn it." Razon put his forehead between his palms. "A little notice would have been great, Em."

Emery rushed to defend herself. "I understand, and I tried to tell him that this wasn't a good time."

"No shit," snapped Razon. He was furious now.

Selma sat watching the two spar. She was just as confused as she had been all day and was wondering when she should jump in with questions.

"I was right down the damned hallway, Em. Could you not be bothered to come see me, or send a message? We cannot do this right now. She is not ready." Razon was not yelling, but his tone was resolute.

"She may not be, but she is not the only one here who will be asked to make sacrifices," Emery declared. She was standing taller now. "If the Order catches on to any—"

"Enough," Razon declared. He got up from his chair and turned to Selma. She reached out with her threads, feeling empathy and sadness…and something else. Was it guilt?

"If at any point you want to go up to your room, we can always send food up for you," said Razon.

"She cannot go now. We need to hear what he has to say—and she *definitely* does." Emery's eyes turned to Selma.

Her heartbeat was quick now. What did she need to hear, and who was this person Razon clearly did not want her to meet?

He leaned over, placing his hand on the table to brace himself. "I'm so sorry. I was really hoping to give you more time to process this," said Razon. There was genuine hurt and fear in his eyes.

"Sorry for what? I do not understand what is going on," said Selma with panic in her voice.

Just then, Leven walked into the room with another man. He was as tall and alluring as Leven, with dark hair and high-cut cheekbones, but it was not his towering figure that took Selma by surprise. It was that she saw her own eyes staring back at her.

"Wargraves are a conduit through which the threads may serve all."

—An excerpt from the Canon, as translated by Leven Kara, property of the
Warriors of Sever

CHAPTER 35

Selma's jaw dropped, and her eyes widened. It was as if she were staring at a ghost. Words turned to ash in her mouth as she stood like a statue in front of the man who had held his hand on hers in those cold gray mornings. He was older now, but if you missed the tiny strands of silver in his beard, you would not know. She could not say that his hair had not been silver before. It had been so long, she could not trust her mind's chronicles. Memories have the habit of tarnishing over time.

She could not move. Her breaths were long and deep but did not seem to supply her body with the oxygen her lungs desperately craved. What was he doing here? Did he know she was going to be here? But more than anything, more than wondering why her father stood before her, she wondered how long Razon had known her father. The weight of it squeezed her lungs tight. All these weeks they had spent together training, and Razon had never mentioned anything about her father. He had not even asked. And now she realized he did not ask because he already knew.

"Razon." The familiar but extrinsic voice rattled through Selma's brain as her father nodded at the man sitting next to her.

"Alister." Razon returned the gesture. "I thought you were up north."

Alister. Razon had called him by his first name. Like they were old friends catching up.

How could she have been so clueless for so long? Razon had known where Alister was this entire time, and instead of turning him over and saving her from the trials, he had remained silent. Selma's brain struggled to catch up. She thought back to the chamber with Amalie, trying to remember anything Amalie said. Clawing at anything that would help her piece this all together.

Selma leaned against the table for support as her hands began to tremble. Not knowing where to look, she turned to Razon. He did not return her gaze. Instead, he gestured to the empty seat and invited Alister to sit down.

Within moments, everyone, including Selma's father, was settling in their seats. Selma remained standing. She stared at the table settings and the flickering tea lights, wondering how all the delicate details that had warmed this beautiful space just moments ago had turned dark and predatory. Wondering how she could be only few feet away from the man who had walked out on her as quickly as he had walked into this room.

She felt a hand graze her arm. Looking down, she saw Razon's tattooed fingers gently touching her, and she lifted her lashes to meet his gaze. His eyes were filled with empathy, but all she could feel was betrayal. Everything in her begged her to turn around and walk away. That was what she had always done. Whenever anything in her life had felt hard, she walked away and found a simpler path.

Low stakes had been her currency since the day she watched his silhouette vanish.

Suddenly, the idea of sitting back and waiting for an invitation to her own life made the bile in her stomach begin to rise. Had she been any better than the man who sat across from her at this table? Maybe not, but it was time to stand up for herself even if the idea tore at her chest and threatened to swallow her whole. Whatever she had been tossed into weeks ago was no longer about her. There were more lives at risk and an entire world that seemed to have been unchecked for too long. She did not know if she could trust the people sitting among her, or if they could help, but there was a reason Razon had brought her here. For better or worse, she was going to find out why, and with or without them she was going to fix this.

Selma brushed off Razon's touch and took her seat. She took one fortifying breath and lifted her hardened gaze at her father. She was not sure what her eyes were saying, but they must have been doing their job, because Alister's broad shoulders stiffened, and his chin lifted ever so slightly, as if preparing for battle.

Leven was the first to break the silence. "Well, let us eat, shall we? Emery has prepared a mountain of food."

"Selma, you grew up." Alister spoke softly, but with authority.

Selma remained silent, still staring at her estranged father.

"Wine," Leven declared, clapping his hands together and attempting to cut the tension in the room. He whispered something to one of the men closest to him, and a few moments later, music boomed from an adjacent room. It was a lively cacophony of horns and ivory keys that did not match its audience's mood. The clinking of cutlery joined in on the symphony, and Selma could make out soft whispers from down the table.

Razon cut in, "Why have you come, Alister?"

Silverware clinked, and Alister shot Razon a narrowed gaze.

"I was unaware that I needed permission to visit my own home," he said.

"Not at all," Leven offered. "What he means is that we were just not expecting you. Of course you're always welcome, by invitation or not."

"The northern camp is settled, and I felt that my presence would be more productive here," Alister said.

Emery watched him intently from her end of the table. It was not clear whether she was as happy to see Alister as Leven seemed to be. "We have not received an update in a while. How is construction going?"

"As one would expect," said Alister, paying more attention to his plate than to Emery.

"Well, I suppose without an update, I would not know what to expect," said Emery. Her words were laced with venom, and she drank from her wineglass. The bitter liquid matched her shade of lipstick. "But I suppose one of the men at the table would be happy to hear your answer if you're more comfortable releasing such sensitive information to them. My female head gets so full sometimes."

Selma supposed she was not the only one in line to put her father in his place.

Alister placed both of his fists on either side of his plate. "If you would like, I can have a full report delivered to you by morning. Although, I'm not sure I answer to you or anyone at this table."

Selma had waited long enough.

"Where have you been?" Her voice carried above the clatter.

She was still staring at her father. He held on to his fork and finished chewing his bite of roast before wiping his mouth and beard with one hand stroke.

"Pardon?" Alister inquired.

"Well, here you are. It has been twenty years. I can assume you did not come for a family reunion and that all this"—Selma opened her arms out to her sides—"is not some frivolous dinner party, despite how people are acting. I would like to move on from this ridiculous display of niceties. So, where have you been?"

Alister cleared his throat. "It seems that Uma did not teach you how to be a gracious dinner guest," Alister huffed.

"Leave Uma out of this. That is a demon for another day," scoffed Selma.

"Except it seems that all of our demons have come to dinner," Alister responded quickly. "She is part of the reason we are all here now."

"What do you mean?" Selma was confused by his response but worked to keep her face steady.

"I tasked Uma and those sisters of hers to manage you and keep you out of the path of the Order. But they failed. Uma and her tedious sisters have always been too sympathetic to the Order," announced Alister. "I know why you made the journey. You want help to rise against them, but I am here to tell you that is not an option. At least, not now. Our numbers are not strong enough."

Razon's voice rose next to Selma. "Who are you to speak for them?"

Alister turned to Razon with fire in his eyes. Something Razon said had struck a nerve.

"I needn't remind you, boy, that the blood of the Wargraves runs through me," Alister cut back.

"Half," Razon responded curtly.

Alister's face turned dark red as Razon gently drummed his fingers on the table.

Razon curled his lip, his teeth showing. "*Half* of your blood runs Wargrave, while the other half apparently runs scared. Wargraves are protectors and peacekeepers among the factions, and we are calling upon them to do their solemn duty. Or have you forgotten that part?"

Alister stood from his seat as Leven and Emery sat dead still at the other end of the table. "I have been fighting this fight for a good long time, and I know what is at stake. I have made sacrifices to protect our world, and I would make them again if it meant preserving our kind."

Selma chimed in, "You mean like walking away from your family?"

Alister didn't look away from Razon. "Yes, like walking away from my daughter and the Order, and I would do it again if necessary." He looked like he was going to continue, still pointing his finger at Razon, but he was interrupted.

"*Daughters,*" Selma added. Her expression was pure ice.

Silence fell upon the room once more. The first side of the record had long concluded, and the only sound was the scraping of the needle on plastic grooves.

Selma found temporary relief in the confusion written on her father's brow. But the moment was as fleeting as the steam coming off the roast as she thought of Amalie and how alone she had been all those years.

"You left another daughter behind. But I guess leaving trauma in your wake is typical for you. At least I do not have to take anything personally," Selma scoffed.

Everyone's eyes widened. For a moment, Selma felt a tinge of regret for airing out her family drama among strangers, but there was nothing she could do about it now. So, she carried on.

"You know what? I do not actually care where you have been. Let me be clear: I do not give a shit about what you think you know or who you think you speak for. People's lives are at risk. People I love. I am done letting people make decisions for me and the people I care about. I need you to confront the Order. If you cannot do that, I need you to find another way to get my friend out of danger. It is because of you that they hold her life in their hands," Selma declared.

"I'm sorry for your friend. Many have suffered by the hands of the Order, but this is bigger than just her. Or me," Alister resolutely offered.

Selma glared across the table. Rage sparked in her bones as her lips pulled back and she bared her teeth. "If you are not here to move forward with a plan to make everything right again, then step aside, and I will search to the ends of the earth for someone who will. Now, if you will excuse me, it turns out I have lost my appetite."

Selma turned and walked out of the room without looking back. Her pulse pounded as she quickened her steps. She heard Razon call after her, but she did not acknowledge it. She did not know how she felt about him or his lies, and she needed time to sort it out before he tried to sway her with his sil-ver-speckled eyes.

"Soul threads are the most powerful and the most volatile, as they pull from the depth of one's emotions."

—An excerpt from the Axiom, as translated by Lilibet Lourdes, property of the Museum of the Academe Arts, current location unknown

CHAPTER 36

Brisk air burned her lungs in an instant. She had kept walking away from the dinner table until she found herself striding through a giant door and into an ornate, unkempt garden. Her eyes made their way up to the sky, which was peppered with an array of varying stars. All of them flickered as if vying for her attention. Turning slowly in a circle, still looking upward, she took in the massive stone wall with overhanging bartizans. It was otherworldly.

It suddenly dawned on her that she had no idea where she was, and panic replaced her awe and anger. She reached for her phone, but her dress did not have pockets. It was still sitting on the bedside table. Damn it! Had she really been so willing to let others guide her, trusting anyone, that she allowed herself to be trapped in an unknown mansion with no way of communicating?

Selma considered returning to her room when she noticed

Emery. She was wearing a long red coat with a matching fur collar. The soft hair framed her angled chin. She held a similar coat in one hand, holding it out to Selma as a gesture. But Selma stayed put, hoping that her goose bumps were not noticeable in the shaded light of the night sky.

"Freezing to death will not help anyone," Emery said in a low tone.

Selma crossed her arms over her chest, protecting her exposed skin.

"It's only a jacket. If you like, you can take it, and I will turn right back around and leave you be," Emery offered.

Selma thought for a moment. She did not want to go back into that house even though her only way of communicating with the outside world was inside its vulturous walls. But she would surely freeze to death out here without a jacket, so she reluctantly accepted Emery's help. Emery nodded and turned to go back inside.

"Where are we?" Selma asked.

Emery turned to face Selma and tilted her head to the side. "Razon did not tell you?" Her question hit more like an insult than curiosity. Selma stayed quiet.

"You're on the Isle of Skye," Emery answered.

Selma needed confirmation. "As in Scotland?"

Emery nodded with a half smile. "Many of those who survived fled here. Now it is home. It can be quite beautiful in the daylight."

"Did you know? When you met me, did you know that I was his daughter?" Selma did not know what response she wanted to hear.

"Yes, I did," Emery offered with no sign of remorse.

Selma let out a quick breath of air.

"Anyone can see that you have some feelings you need to work out. But if I were you, I would view this as an opportunity rather than…" Emery paused.

Selma looked up. "Rather than what?"

"Rather than validation of the victim card you seem so adamant to play," said Emery.

"You don't know anything—"

"Stop right there." Emery scowled. "If you're suggesting that I don't understand being misunderstood and screwed over by people who were supposed to be my allies, then you're more ignorant than I thought. Sorry, princess, but it's time to get a clue."

The nickname was getting out of control.

"Yes, Alister left you. He has always been a self-righteous bastard, not to mention a rake. You were brought up not knowing the full potential of your abilities, and you feel like a punchline right now. So what? If Razon is right about you and you have even one-tenth of the power that is rightfully yours, then you could effect real change. You could protect those people you care for so deeply. But if you want to sit here and sniffle about your daddy issues, then so be it." Emery tossed out the last words like they were trash.

Tears fell down Selma's cheeks, and her breaths were shaky. "Why does everyone keep calling me 'princess'? Surely you are more creative than that?"

"I suggest you speak to Alister. Knowledge is our greatest strength," said Emery. And with that, she turned and walked away, her heels clicking with every step, leaving Selma to sit in her words. Selma let them wash over her.

✝

The sound of dishes clinking together and muffled footsteps sang down the hall. Dinner must have concluded early, and Selma wondered if her early exit had anything to do with that, or if the meal had been full of more fireworks. She sauntered through hall-ways, looking for her room. The castle was daunting, and for the first time since she had arrived, there was nobody scurrying about. Selma wished she had taken better note of how she had gotten to the dining room.

Turning around for the twelfth time, she noticed a light flicker to life from a doorway down the hall. Maybe it was someone who could point her in the right direction.

Quickly, she made her way toward the light and turned the corner so swiftly that she barreled into the room and made immediate notice of herself. Standing there by the fireplace holding a glass of brown liquid was her father.

He was backlit by the flames, and the scene was eerily familiar. Selma could not make out all his features, but his body language was drawn, and his shoulders slumped. He did not say anything. He just took a sip of his drink. Emery's words rang in her ears, and she walked further into the room.

"I remember you," Selma whispered into the firelit room.

With that, he turned to look at her.

"I don't remember much, but I remember you taking me to the market in town. It was cold, and there was snow on the ground. I remember eating a waffle. At least, I think it was you," Selma said, looking down at her hands.

"It was the Christmas market, and it was in France," Alister responded softly.

Selma's brow furrowed. "France?" Her response was more question than observation. She had no memory of traveling as a child.

"Yes. I took you with me when I visited my home. Your mother was with us, but she had other business, so I took you myself. You ate crepes with caramel sauce until you were sick. Your mother was furious with me," Alister said. His eyes were far away in the memory.

Selma walked over to the decanter that hosted the same brown liquid that Alister was indulging in. She poured a healthy serving, put the crystal glass to her lips, and took a sip. The liquid burned on the way down, but it was oddly comforting.

"That sounds like Uma," Selma added.

Alister looked up at her. His face was drawn and wistful. "I'm not talking about Uma."

Selma's breath caught in her lungs. This entire time, she had focused her attention and rage on Alister, Uma, and her aunts. She had not taken a moment to think about her biological mother. Who was she? What was she like? And why was she not around anymore?

Alister crossed the room and poured himself another two fingers of the amber liquor.

"I need to know more. I need to know where I come from and why you are here. I grew up thinking that your last name was Plumey and that I was born Common. But there is an entire realm that I neither understand nor feel like I belong to," said Selma, shaking her head and looking down at her drink. "Part of it is my fault. I never pushed myself to know more. I was content to go along with the small bits that people offered me, but I don't think I have the luxury of turning away from it anymore."

Alister stared at the fire. His eyes reflected the flames dancing in the hearth.

"At least make me understand why you won't step in to help," she added.

This got his attention, and he quickly looked up at her. His eyes were still aflame, but not with those from the fireplace.

"What you may not care to understand is that I *am* helping. I am helping to keep the few we have left safe from slaughter," he boomed.

Alister downed his drink and went to sit in the leather chair. He rested his head on his hand and gently rubbed his forehead. A moment later, his threads reached out and grabbed the decanter, floating it over to his glass and pouring another heavy amount.

"My family has long been aligned with the Order. My ancestors pulled their magic from the elements and passed it down to every generation. They settled in the area where all the founding families now reside," said Alister.

Selma leaned in closer, making sure not to miss a word. She was finally going to get some answers.

"The Lourdes have always been a strong magic line, but your grandmother was a force." Alister looked up for a moment and laughed at some thought that was tugging at him. "We may not have agreed on much, but did she demand respect. And as Master of the Order, it was nearly impossible to get her to bend. She honed her powers, and she and your grandfather made it their life mission to teach me every magical skill they could so that I might become too powerful to quell," said Alister.

"Master of the Order." Selma had never heard of that title. Alister must have noted her confusion, because he tilted his head to the side in response, his eyes widening as he did so. The small gesture suggested that he was dumbfounded to discover that she did not already have this information.

"What do you know of the Order? Has your mother and gaggle of gossiping aunts carried on your studies in my absence?" Alister asked in a condescending tone.

Selma responded quickly, "I do believe that what my aunts have or have not taught me stopped being your concern the moment you left."

Alister let out a long sigh. "Yes, I left you with Uma. But that is no excuse."

Selma's cheeks heated. She was tired of people pointing out her ignorance but not offering any information in return. "No, it may not be an excuse, but here we are, an uninformed witch and her deadbeat dad. Why don't you do us both a favor and clue me in so we can move past this, because I am tired of people looking at me like I am the punchline. I may be misinformed, but I am not as naive as you might think. There are profound consequences for people if we don't help, and if you sit there insulting my family and intelligence instead of sharing anything useful, then you are no better than the people you're so adamant about looking down on."

Alister looked pensive for a moment and stroked his beard with his fingers, an action that Selma quickly realized was a stress response. Finally, he spoke, motioning for Selma to sit in the worn leather chair across from him.

"The Master of the Order is the leading role of all the council members. It is a highly coveted position that our family has held our place as Master of the Order since the council's inception. The only way to unseat the Master of the Order is death," Alister responded.

Selma chose her words carefully hoping to find out that her grandmother was still alive. "And what happens after they are unseated?"

"If there is an heir then it passes to them," Alister responded.

"So, you?" The words fell from her lips before she could process them.

Alister nodded, "I am the reining Master of the Order. And then to you. Unless, of course, you are challenged and fail."

Selma's heart sank at the news of her grandmother. "And by fail, you mean-"

"Death," Alister responded curtly.

Selma was taken aback by the admission of violence. "That seems crude and unnecessarily aggressive."

"Perhaps, but it as it has always been. Power shows no mercy," Alister said. His eyes dropping to his glass. "When the Order rose to power, they were like any other leadership, finding a community and protecting them. It was not until the last couple of generations that it began to sway more toward exclusivity. Certain members of the Order found a following among a niche group of extremists who believed in the binding. These witches wanted to find a way to bring magic back together again. They wanted to abolish the separation of power so that magic could once again roam unchecked. It was a romantic way of looking at our world, back to a time when no one faction had more power than the other. It was especially appealing among witches who had been denied powers from birth. The Order promised equality and strength for the weak, when what they really wanted was to combine magic so they could claim it for themselves."

Selma shuddered at the thought of Olivier having more power than he already did.

"The most efficient way to control any group and take power for yourself is to deny them knowledge and then plant fear in them. Dissent is the most efficient way to win a war," said Alister. "The Order has successfully erased all factions of magic to hoard power. And the ones they could not silence, they spread lies about."

Selma's mind was slowly piecing her fractured world together. Even with the new and terrifying information, the knowledge was healing. She took in her first full breath since entering this room.

"The Wargraves adamantly opposed," Alister went on. "They argued that while magic began as one entity, with the unruly nature of unchecked power it would have burned out and ultimately destroyed us. They believe that separation of magic is what allows us to carry on, and that is why they have dedicated themselves to protecting the separate factions. It is why I left my home to become one of them. I trained for many years, and when my mother and father were killed, I refused to take my place on the council."

Killed. Did that mean her grandfather and grandmother were murdered?

Alister went on, "But the Order was gaining more and more support. They sought out members of other factions like the Wargraves and tried to turn them. If they refused, their families would be targeted. This is how I met Razon. He had tried to hide his family, and he asked me for help, but we were too late. They were all killed. Razon is an incredibly skilled warrior, but it did not prove to be enough against the Order. It was then that Razon decided to offer his service to the council and report back to us."

For a while, only the crackle of the flames filled the space. Both were silent until Selma spoke up. "And when did you meet my mother?"

"She was beautiful, like you. Fierce and brutal," Alister said. Selma could hear his heartbreak in his words. "She would have been proud of you at dinner, putting your old man in his place."

This made Selma smile even though she felt a great sadness, as she would never know that for herself.

"I met your mother while she was healing at one of the Wargrave training camps. We keep them hidden underground and warded so that humans do not detect them. The change can be unmerciful. She was there to monitor us," said Alister, his memories lost in a different time. His eyes made their way to the silver chain and dark pendant hanging around her neck. She had almost become used to the soft thrum of the bauble while in the presence of so many Wargraves.

"That was hers." Alister pointed at Selma's neck. "She gave it to you right before she died."

Selma hesitated. She was terrified to hear the truth, but she needed to know. "And what happened to her?"

It was like Selma was watching his heart splinter into shards of glass. A darkness swirled in his eyes, one that had not been there before.

Alister spoke in dark, punctuated tones. "The Order killed her and any like her. Except for one. One who was shielded by the purest form of magic. A piece of the Brocken gifted to us by the Goddess Sever. You, my daughter, are the last of her kind. A Maven.

You are the rarest of witches, able to access all threads of magic, and perhaps our greatest hope for saving our kind."

"The balance of power is a lie."

—An excerpt from the Manifesto of the Order, International League of the
True Goddess

CHAPTER 37

Thick fibers from the lush carpet cradled her feet as Selma paced back and forth in her room. Though her eyes had adjusted hours ago, the room still fell in darkness as sleep escaped her. A lifetime of ignorance and her rage from the day before had simmered into sadness. She wrestled with the idea that the people around her may have put her in the dark, but she had been the one to embrace the shadows.

Just after dawn, Selma's attention was pulled to her door as shuffling steps came closer. She stilled as a shadow crept in from under the threshold. A paper, no larger than a postcard, slid through the crack. Selma waited for the steps to disappear into the distance before she raced over to pick it up. Elegant, sweeping handwriting filled the margins. Emery's handwriting, she assumed. The note requested that she be in the East Room after breakfast. That was still hours away. Selma went back to pacing alongside her bed.

‡

When Selma could not possibly wait any longer, she made her way to the East Room, her pulse quickening with each step. With her stomach still in knots, she had skipped breakfast and opted to wait in her room instead. Roaming the hallways meant too many opportunities to run into Razon, and she was not ready for that conversation. She had made good strides with Alister, but there were still so many unknowns. Without the Wargraves' help, she did not see much hope for their cause. And if her father would not return with her to confront the council, then she would need to pass her third and final trial alone and hope that that would be enough for Olivier to remove the poison from Millie before it claimed her. She may have been part Maven, whatever that meant, but she was still no match for the Order.

Her pace quickened, as she could hear voices nearby. Everyone else had already gathered, and she was the last to arrive. As she entered the East Room, she locked eyes with Alister. His face was drawn, and she could see bruises under his eyes, no doubt from lack of sleep. Emery was perched on the arm of a velvet sofa, her shoulders poised, as statuesque as she had been last night in the garden. Leven stood in the corner, his smile light and welcoming. Despite the complex decisions that were about to be made, he remained amiable and calm. Razon, however, held stiff. His face showed no kindness or warmth. This must be the warrior she had heard about. He was no longer the flirtatious, bored Wargrave he had been all these weeks. Now, he was a hardened strategist. His silver flecks were all but invisible, and his dark gaze offered no comfort.

Alister cleared his throat. "I have decided that it would be best if the Wargraves stayed hidden until we are more prepared."

Leven spoke up from the corner. "What if the Order is planning something? They have been after you for years, but they have never gone to such lengths to get your attention. Why now? What if they go after the mortals?"

"That may be possible, but right now we will use our time to translate the Canon and learn. Perhaps the answer is there," Alister responded.

Selma cut in, "What are we looking for in the Canon that we do not already know?"

Razon finally spoke. "When the Order massacred the Mavens, they were able to nullify their defenses and connect their powers together by somehow using Brocken powder. They took control of all the Mavens' power and used it against them. The strain of magic burning them from the inside out. They had the stock that they confiscated from the Wargraves during the war. But the council has been using the Brocken powder for experiments—like poisoning Millie. Olivier has now lived much longer than he should, but their supply is dwindling. We think they might be trying to find more of the Brocken substance. If they have an unlimited supply, who knows what they would do with it."

Alister's voice broke through. "We don't want to start a war before we are ready."

Selma's lips parted, and she gawked at her father. She looked over at Razon, but his face had not changed. In fact, not a single person in the room seemed fazed by this news.

"Whether or not you care to admit it, we are in a war. They have already started poisoning innocent people, and they are going to kill Selma," Razon huffed. "If you do not turn yourself over to the Order, or do something to stop them, they will kill her."

Alister's jaw ticked. "They still need the Canon. They will not kill her and risk its being lost. I cannot endanger the lives of many for the possibility that the Order will carry out such an ignominious act."

Razon turned to Alister. "And the innocents who will suffer? What will come of them?"

The room was heavy with silence. Selma thought about Millie and the poison ravaging her blood. Had Razon seen more people suffering the same fate?

"Their sacrifice will be mourned, and we will pray that the Goddess Sever will soften their passing," said Alister.

Selma knew in her heart that his decision was made, that he was not going to say any more about the matter.

Razon spoke up. "We are on our own."

Disappointment washed over Leven's face, but he did not say anything. Razon was right; they were on their own.

The thought sank into Selma's gut. She supposed they had always been on their own, but the little hope she had felt coming here and finding out that there were others, that there were friends of Razon's who could help, made her disappointment all the more sour.

Razon stormed out first, Emery and Leven quick to follow. Leven shot Selma an empathetic nod before turning to leave.

Alister was silent for so long that Selma did not believe he would say anything at all. It was not until she got up from her chair to walk away that he finally spoke.

"Not returning was one of the hardest decisions I have ever made. But, as Wargrave runs through my blood, I have a sworn duty to protect the factions of magic, even in the wake of such failure," said Alister. "It's why I cannot condone sending more witches to die in crusades for change."

Selma stared into the fire for a few moments, taking in the information that was just bestowed onto her. She thought about Leven, Emery, and Razon. They had lost so much already.

"But if the Order is as tainted as you say, if they have unlawfully taken so much, shouldn't they be punished? Shouldn't they be stopped before they hurt more people?" Her voice cracked. "Hurting innocent people while simultaneously preaching the value of life. And for what? For unbridled power? We cannot simply stand by. I am not asking you to turn yourself in. I am asking you to fight. You say that I am the last Maven and the daughter of Lourdes. That must come with some responsibility?"

"It's not that simple, Selma," Alister objected.

"It is. It is that simple," retorted Selma. "I may be naive, and I may not have had the training that equips me to carry the Lourdes name. But if the power of Sever runs through me, and if I descend from two of the most powerful bloodlines, then I can learn to stop them. If you have the resources, please help us. If not for me, then for all the witches who have lost so much. Please," Selma pleaded. Tears were streaming down her cheeks now. Still, Alister stayed silent.

There was nothing left to do but leave. Selma may not have been through a war, and she may not have been able wield her power as gracefully as the rest of them, but she knew how to read a room, and Alister had declared his intentions with certitude.

"She may be the answer, but the sacrifice is too great."

—Recovered correspondence to Warrior Lourdes from Warrior Leclerc,
property of the Warriors of Sever

CHAPTER 38

A knock at her door startled the deafening silence. The sweater she was trying to fold using elemental magic slunk to the floor from where it had been hovering in front of her. A small magic, but still elusive to Selma. Being a Maven was supposed to mean she would have access to several types of magic, including all the elements. It meant she could wield all the threads in theory. But she still struggled with her elemental threads. Maybe her mother had not passed down all her magic after all. But some was better than nothing. Weeks ago, she was simply writing on bay leaves to state intentions. Folding laundry by manipulating air was certainly an improvement. That is what Selma kept telling herself after hours of failing to conjure even a breeze.

"Come in," Selma replied.

The door slowly creaked open, revealing Leven. Selma was surprised to see him. Given their shared disappointment downstairs, she would have suspected he was sulking alone somewhere.

"Thank you for allowing us to stay here. I am sure we will be gone just as soon as we can gather our luggage," Selma politely offered.

"Razon and his friends are always welcome here," Leven offered with a half-hearted smile.

Selma let out a small laugh. "I'm not sure Razon and I are friends, but thank you anyway for your hospitality."

"Call it what you will, but I have not seen Razon look at anyone the way he looks at you. In fact, he almost seems like he was before," said Leven.

Selma stayed silent while she thought about that. She thought about everything Razon had kept from her and all the lies he told. She wanted to ask more. What was it that Emery had said? *Knowledge is our greatest strength.* This was Selma's opportunity to step into that power. But asking about Razon made her feel too exposed. Instead, she focused on the man in front of her.

"Did you lose anyone?"

Leven nodded. "And I am not the only one. It was a difficult and bloody time for everyone."

Selma did not need to reach out to feel his sadness. She wondered if Leven knew about her ability to hear thoughts, or if she should tell him.

Already knowing what she was thinking, he smiled. "I don't have anything to hide, and I trust that you know when and when not to look."

Trust. He had only just met her, and he was already bestowing faith in her. Selma returned his smile and felt how easy it would be to be friends with Leven. She wondered who he may have lost and hoped that she could pay them respect by measuring up to his elevated expectations of her.

"Do you miss them?" Selma felt silly the moment the words left her lips. It felt too intimate a question.

"I do, but some days are easier than others. It was a long time ago. They would have liked you." He kicked off the threshold and walked further into the room.

With that, her armor dented.

"What was Razon like? Before he lost his family?" A lump formed in the back of her throat. Selma knew she was entering treacherous ground, but she wanted to know more about the person she could not stop thinking about.

Leven's eyes seemed to retreat into another time. "He was a delight. Or at least, as much a delight as a seminal warrior can be. Still poised, and as damned good-looking as he is now."

"And besides his family…" Selma paused. "Did he lose anyone else?"

Leven knew what she was asking. "Razon has never been one to give his heart away easily. I will tell you one thing, though." Leven's voice got louder than before, almost like he was going to try and make a joke. But then another, deeper voice answered.

"Tell her what?"

Selma's skin prickled.

Leven turned to look at Razon. "I was going to tell her that she commands a room."

"She does," added Razon, his eyes fixed on Selma's mouth. And her thoughts wandered to all the things she wanted to do with her mouth. Damn it! She needed to shove her traitorous feelings aside. She had just learned that everything she thought she knew about her world was wrong, and yet she was studying the curve of his lips and perfect angle of his chin.

Leven's gaze darted between Razon and Selma. "We are going to help you."

Relief washed over her expression as warmth filled her eyes.

"You are? Why would you do that?" Selma was not sure questioning his kindness was a clever idea, but the words seemed to have dripped from her lips before she could stop them.

"Because it's the right thing to do," said Emery from the doorway. She did not stride into the room to join them. "We can worry about taking the Order down later, but you need to make it through your trial if we have any chance of helping your friend," she added, her face steady and resolved. "Plus, if they try and kill you, Razon will be unbearable."

If the Order tried to kill her. Only weeks prior, her most worrisome fight was whether or not to move in with her boyfriend, and now she was being hunted. The entire situation was surreal, and her heart cracked thinking of Hayden, but there was no time to wallow.

"When do we get started?" Selma asked.

"There she is," said Razon. He sent Selma a tantalizingly seductive wink that would have sent her to her knees if not for the additional company. "Bring your A game, princess."

Alister met them at the end of the long, outstretched black staircase that would lead them to the courtyard. He was still dressed in armor, and Selma wondered if he had ever changed out of it. Did he ever drop the mask of a warrior?

Leven, Emery, and Razon must have understood that he wanted a moment alone with Selma. They all nodded and carried on outside, leaving Alister and Selma alone.

"I know that I have to live with my choices, and that you may never understand," said Alister.

"I understand," said Selma. "That does not mean I agree. I forgive you. I have spent too long thinking that there was an easy answer as to why you left and why you did not love me enough to stay. I know now that everything is more complicated than that."

Alister stood still, staring at his daughter. Selma wondered if he saw any of her mother in her.

"Razon is a good man," said Alister. "I do not know how much weight that carries coming from me, but he protects what he loves. I am flawed, but I can say with certainty that I recognize verity when I see it. If he didn't share everything with you, it was with pure intentions."

Selma inhaled sharply. "And perhaps I am done letting people protect me." She had work to do, and she was done waiting for someone else to do it for her.

Selma took the last step of the staircase and moved toward the courtyard to join the others.

Alister spoke out behind her. "I've always loved you, Dove."

She paused and looked over her shoulder. Selma took one more look at her father, knowing that this might be the last time she would ever see him. She took in his beard and the white hairs that framed his face and realized that he looked so much smaller than in her memory. She nodded and disappeared into the courtyard.

‡

Selma, Razon, Leven, and Emery stood equidistant in the courtyard. Selma was in her leggings and a hoodie, which seemed drastically underdressed for the occasion, especially considering her company. Emery had shed her glamorous attire and now wore leathers, the same leathers that Razon had worn the night he killed Harwick. Leven's armor was more relaxed, but he still wore protective gear. All the leathers were adorned with the protective rune that had been on the key. Selma looked at her counterparts, taking in the brutality of the armor that made them all look merciless. Even Leven, with his blithe nature, looked barbarous.

Selma yelled out, "When do I get some of those?"

"When you earn them," Emery shot back. She had daggers strapped to every inch of her body, it seemed, and a small crossbow attached to her thigh.

Razon walked over to Selma, his demeanor calm but alert. Stopping a few feet away, his hand rested on the pommel of a short sword.

"Not that I'm complaining, but why don't Wargraves use guns? You look like you are about to ride into battle to save the damsel in distress," Selma asked, still staring at his sword and the tightness of the leathers around his waist.

"Isn't that exactly what I'm doing?" Razon said, winking at her.

Selma rolled her eyes and let out a long sigh. "No, thank you. This damsel will knee you in your balls. I don't care how tight your leathers are."

Razon briefly looked down, assessing her threat. "We do not use guns because they are a coward's weapon. It is part of our code.

The Wargraves have been living by a code laid out in the Canon for centuries. Do not worry, princess. I can do just as much damage with a blade as a bullet."

Selma had no doubt that this was true. Even through the leathers she could make out the cords of his muscles. His tattoos peeked out over the tops of his hands. Gorgeous.

"You know, even with your shields up, I can tell when you're eye-fucking me," Razon said, tilting up the corner of his lips to cradle that dimple of his.

Selma returned his smug smirk. "I was only assessing the best spot to sink a dagger into you."

Amused, Razon asked, "Do you remember what color your threads were when you looked into Millie for the first time?"

"Violet," she responded.

Razon nodded. "And with the wolf?"

Selma thought back. "They were violet. Unless those were yours?"

"They weren't," Razon responded curtly. "And in the chamber?"

"Silver." Selma cringed when she remembered Harwick's dead body lying limp on the stone floor. "Harwick had called me one of the 'depraved.'"

Had Harwick known that day that she was a Maven? Is that what he meant by "depraved"?

Razon did not take his eyes off her. "Right. That is because your threads were feeding off of his emotions. Have you ever cast your elemental magic?"

Selma's chin lowered, and she deflated. "Not that I can remember, why?"

"Elemental witches, as you know, cannot see their threads. I, too, could not see mine until my training to be a Wargrave was complete. Now I can not only feel my magic, but I can see it," said Razon. "Green threads are sourced from the elements: earth, wind, water, fire. They are how the Order and most of our kind summon their threads. When we take the Brocken liquid and go through the change, the threads we were born with morph. They are more powerful than elemental threads, but they do not exist congruently. They replace our old threads. You, however, can access all the threads."

"But I can't—" Selma started.

"You can. You have just not been given the right motivation. You have summoned all the threads except those of the elements. If your biological mother was a Maven, then you have more power than you know. It was why the rune did not nullify the dagger and keep it from piercing your heart during your trial. It's why the Order could not burn you with the mark of Saint, and it's how you were able to summon soul threads in the tombs."

Selma thought back to all those moments. All those moments when fear collided with necessity. She had no idea what to make of them at the time.

"My mother's magic," Selma whispered.

"*Your* magic," Razon corrected her. "You have a block, cutting you off mentally from the elements. But I think you can open up that part of you."

Selma hiked one eyebrow up. "If my magic is as powerful as you say, then getting stabbed by a dagger does not seem like the best reward."

Razon smiled back at her. "You are not susceptible to runes. It is unfortunate that you found out that way, but knowing that you cannot be manipulated by magic is powerful. Besides, your advanced healing got you out of that scrape." He winked at her again.

Leven and Emery joined them.

Selma quietly asked, "And if I can't access my elemental threads?"

"Then you don't, and you nurture the threads you can access and make them your own. But I would like you to try," Razon said.

Emery grabbed Selma's hand and gestured for her to sit on the grass. It was golden, with only hints of green still grasping hold of the summer.

"Lie back and feel the ground," Emery said. Her words were velvet off her tongue. "Take in the sounds and the feel of the earth."

Fuck, they were doing a grounding exercise? Were they serious? Thousands of years of magic, and they were using a cheap therapy tool to unclog her magical potential?

"I can feel you resisting," Emery said pointedly.

Selma scoffed. "I am not resisting; I just do not see the validity of this. If therapy did not help me ground, then how can this?"

"You're right, that doesn't seem like resisting at all," Leven deadpanned.

"Shut up, Leven," said Selma.

"Yes, ma'am," Leven returned.

Emery ignored them. "You are not trusting your threads. You must show them the way and teach them what to seek out. Nurture them. Now, what do you feel?"

"Cold grass," Selma said with a raised eyebrow.

"Good," responded Emery. "What else? Describe it to us."

"Cold skin," Selma added, now shaking her head.

"We get it, you're cold," Razon said. "You aren't taking this seriously."

"I am seriously cold," Selma shot back.

Emery huffed out a sigh. "How about what you hear?"

"Razon's balls shriveling up," Leven jested.

Selma let out a snort of laughter, and it was not just her—Emery was trying unsuccessfully to hold back her laugh.

Razon added, "I assure you that everything in that department is just fine. Want to come over here and inspect?"

Leven jumped in quickly. "Sure, do you have a microscope?"

All four of them were smiling and laughing in the grass. Selma's muscles untangled, and she sucked in a breath of air. The chilly current felt healing in her lungs. She focused on the air around her, taking in the sounds of laughter and then letting them dance into the breadth of the courtyard. She focused on the breeze and the slight crunch of spent blades of grass bumping into one another. A hawk called in the distance, and a low, deep, prolonged call of a highland cow added to the cacophony of the countryside.

Taking steady breaths, Selma followed her mind back to her iron gate. She carefully unlatched all the locks she had put in place, feeling her body relax with each one. She pushed the gate open just enough for a sliver of her mind to feel her magic. Sitting in the courtyard, her finger grazed the grass.

"Come on. I can do this. If they are hiding behind my gate, I can do this."

She thought back to all the criticism and harsh words she had heard about her magic over the years. The looks of disappointment. She pictured packing them all into a box and closing it up. Still nothing. She did not know if the others were still with her; she could not hear them. Better to be alone for this anyway, in case she could not make it happen.

She needed something else. Something different. Instead of her aunts and Uma, she thought back to Millie and saw her beautiful inner light. Just then, she felt her fingers tingle. She looked back at her gate to see tiny green threads peeking out, only an inch or so, but they were there. She had them in her. Now, to coax them out.

She thought about the kiss that she and Razon had shared in the yard of her aunts' house. She thought back to the Christmas market she had visited with her father in France. The memory was becoming clearer now, and she could taste the caramel sauce. Feel the snowflakes on her tongue.

With her eyes still closed, she took to her surroundings once more. It was as if her senses were overloaded. She could feel, hear, taste everything around her. Her senses raced around the courtyard, taking in every creature, every blade of grass. It was overwhelming and beautiful.

Her threads were swimming around her. Selma felt her new-found energy and was surprised to see how easily it responded to her. She felt it move toward her core like a current. After a few minutes, she felt a chill once more. She must have been using too much energy, and she panicked.

Opening her eyes, she cut the connection from the energy. But what she saw was not terror on Razon's face, but a smile. A wall of fire had formed around them, the heat from the flames warming their skin but not burning the ground underneath them. Selma wiggled her fingers, and the flames followed her movements. She giggled at her new pet and wondered, if she could make flames, could she conjure up the other elements as well?

With one swipe of her hand, the wall of flames turned into a frozen sanctuary. All the Wargraves were gawking at her, including a new guest. Alister had joined them, and he stood next to Leven and Emery. His face showed no emotion. Selma could not read him, but she did not care. Moving her hands to her sides, the frozen walls fell in waves of water and puddled at their feet. Her body was tired, but she wanted to try harder. She pushed her threads further into the ground, feeding off the energy as trees began sprouting all around them.

"This is unbelievable," Selma said with a smile on her face.

Razon did not take his eyes off her as he spoke. "You have untapped potential. Who knows what you are capable of?"

Selma felt dizzy as her threads flickered. Her skin was flushed with heat. The earth around them began to tremble. She was asking too much. She needed to pull back. The others shifted on their heels, noticing Selma's obvious fatigue. She began to panic, as her threads would not retract. She needed to pull back before she burned out. Sweat dripped from her brow.

"Easy, Selma. Breathe. Trust your threads," said Razon, stepping closer to her.

Selma breathed in through her nose and out through her mouth, the way her therapist had taught her. She focused on Razon's face, his eyes, drinking in his calming demeanor. Her iridescent violet threads cradled him, and she could feel her skin start to cool. Her heart rate slowed, and she felt her threads loosen. They slithered back, returning home, and the earth stopped trembling.

Selma dropped to the cold ground and let her body slump. All four Wargraves raced to her side.

She heard Leven's concerned voice first. "How did you get out? How did you stop the burnout?"

"I don't know," Selma whispered. "I just felt them release."

"You summoned both your Elemental threads and your Spirit threads," said Razon. "You were able to temporally feed off my emotions to gain control over them again."

Selma's eyes filled with tears. "I'm sorry."

Razon pulled her into his arms and ran his hands over her back in small, soothing circles. "Don't be sorry. That was incredible."

Selma closed her eyes and let Razon pull her closer. Eventually, her breaths evened out and her tears dried, but she still held close to his leathers.

Alister, Emery, and Leven went inside to escape the cold, leaving Selma and Razon trapped in each other's embrace.

"The Brocken bark is to be protected at all costs. Only the truest among us will know the awesome power of its destruction."

—An excerpt from the Canon, as translated by Leven Kara, property of the Warriors of Sever

CHAPTER 39

When Selma regained her strength and was able to pull herself from Razon's grasp, they met back up with the others in the library. The room was breathtaking. The shelves of books seemed endless. It smelled of rich leather, not unlike Razon. He must have spent a great deal of time here.

Selma walked past alcove after alcove, mesmerized by the vast collection of works. The massive windows were not windows at all, but enchantments. Views of distant lands encased in magic played out through each framed pane as the illusion of buttery sunshine poured in. Selma assumed that in addition to being awe-inspiring, the enchanted windows were to protect the ancient books from decay.

Leven and Emery dug into their research, looking for anything that would help them translate the Canon. Selma looked for any other books that might offer insight into the Brocken liquid and how to extract it from Millie. If Alister was not going to step in, no matter what the plan for bringing down the Order would be or who would be helping her, she would still need to survive the last trial. Fire. And if they suspected anything at all about the true nature of Selma's magic, then the trial would not be all she had to worry about.

The sun had long tucked itself in, and Selma was swimming ceaselessly in a pool of witch lore. One by one, they all retired for the evening. Leven was first to leave, pointing to his rumbling stomach as the reason for surrender. Realizing she had long since missed dinner, Selma walked to her room. Someone had already lit the fire, and the flames danced in and out of the cherrywood logs, filling the room with a distinct tart fragrance. The fireplace, like this castle, was immense. The joyful warmth of the fire felt good, even if it was at odds with the weight of her thoughts.

She thought back to what Alister had said about meeting Leven and Emery and letting them live here in one of his family homes. How many castles did he have? And did she have any other family? She had been too distracted to ask. The last few weeks had been filled with worry and stress, and the magnitude of her situation felt as if it were about to tumble right out of her. Today, she had accessed magic she had no idea was inside of her. And what of the magic her mother had passed on to her?

Selma smiled at that thought. It was a gift from her biological mother that Selma could carry with her, even if she would never know her mother any other way. She wondered what the woman had been like.

Minutes ticked by. Her muscles ached, and she longed for the warm, sudsy comfort of a bath. Without thinking, she summoned her threads, sending a surge of heat through the logs, lighting them aflame once more. She slowly moved into the bathing room, removing her dirt-and-sweat-soaked pants with what seemed like the last ounce of energy she could muster—only to discover that there was no bathtub. Her eyes widened at the discovery. Her bathing room backed up to the mountain's edge, and on the other side of the vaulted windowpanes was a view of the most incredible waterfall Selma had ever seen. Clear and cream water fell between glistening black rock that looked more like cut glass. Lush greenery grew on either side of the water and opened to a canopy of stars. The room was carved from floor to ceiling with black marble, the same shade as the natural rock framing the waterfall, pausing only briefly to show three large glass skylights. Two raw-edged benches sat in the middle of the room.

Selma was awestruck. The room was large enough to fit twenty people and was fully stocked with plush black towels, oils, and soaps. It smelled incredible. She could not wait another minute to get out of these clothes and experience this shower. But then she looked around and noticed that it did not have any showerheads. Had she been mistaken? Was this just an elaborate sunroom, and would she need to share a bathing room with another guest?

Just then, a knock came at the door. It was light but intentional. Selma groaned. She did not have the energy for whatever was on the other side of that door.

She turned the brass knob only to be met with those familiar blue eyes. Razon's silver specks were brighter than she had ever seen them. One hand leaned on the doorframe, and the other was in the pocket of his black jeans.

Selma's heartbeat quickened as she backed up and turned around. With everything that had happened today, she had almost forgotten about Razon's betrayal and how he had kept so many secrets from her. They had not yet talked about it. Since he walked into her life, his existence had been a mystery, and now more than ever she was not sure what to think of him. Even if her traitorous body did know exactly what it wanted. It ached for him to come further into her room.

"What's going on?" Selma asked, hoping she had come across more nonchalant than she felt. Razon's eyes raked her up and down, hovering at the bottom of her T-shirt. It was just barely covering her underwear, and Selma blushed. She should have put on pants before opening the door.

"I just left Alister and the others," he said. "Alister is reconsidering. You must have made quite the impression."

"What? That is amazing!" said Selma. "I mean, that is good right?" She was smiling and was surprised when he did not return the gesture.

Instead, he asked, "May I come in?"

Selma nodded and gestured for him to enter. "If this is about more training, I'm toast. I really do not have it in me," she said.

Razon quickly responded, "It's not about training."

Selma sensed a heaviness within him as he stood in the middle of the room with his head hanging low. He was always so absolute, so confident. But this Razon was a portrait of defeat. She was starting to worry. Everything they had learned, all the pieces they had put into place…was it all about to fall apart? Had it all been for nothing?

Her thoughts immediately went to Millie.

"What's going on?" Selma asked, her voice breaking as it slipped from her lips.

"I am sorry," said Razon, lifting his eyes to meet Selma's.

"Sorry for what?" asked Selma.

His voice was guttural as he answered, "For keeping everything from you."

The sour taste of betrayal was rising in her throat. Her heart rate remained quick, but not because of Razon's perfect skin or the way his muscles flexed and moaned beneath his black shirt.

"I thought I was keeping you from hurt, but now I see I was doing what everyone else in your life had done—I was keeping you in the dark. I knew you deserved to know, and still..." His words tapered off. "I will not make that mistake again. That night at dinner, I saw your trauma solidify right in front of you. I watched you harden when Alister looked you in the eye and told you that he would do it again, that he would hide the truth from you. I saw it," said Razon with anger in his eyes.

"You don't need to protect me," said Selma. A tremor tickled down her fingers. She could feel her body want to become smaller, but she shoved it off. Razon moved forward toward her.

"I am not sure I can dismiss the urge to protect you, but I can trust you to protect yourself just as much. You are not simply the girl he walked away from. You are strength. You are wit and beauty. I should have told you the moment you walked out of the assembly room that first day," said Razon, holding Selma gently by her elbows and looking into her eyes so intently that she felt like he was looking into her soul.

"Yes, you should have," Selma responded. "But I didn't ask. All this time, I have let others dictate my own power. I have let my circumstances be my excuse, and I cannot keep running or looking the other way. We have come too far, and now I know too much to waste time blaming you. All that matters is what we do moving forward," said Selma. "Fuck the Order and whatever cowards won't stand up to them."

"There's my fierce princess," Razon said, his lips parting in a half smile.

His eyes turned glassy, and she could feel wild heat pulsing off his touch. She breathed him in. Cedar and leather. She stepped closer, straightening her posture and taking up the space between them. Razon's hand moved up her arms. She wanted to reach out with her gift and know what he was thinking, but what if it was not what she wanted to hear? What if he did not want the same things she did? He had been a thorn in her side all these weeks, digging deeper at every turn. But this, now…What he was saying made her thoughts go fuzzy.

He leaned in closer, his forehead just barely touching hers. Her breath quickened. Razon moved his hand up to her cheek and with a featherlight touch graced the edge of her bottom lip with his thumb.

"Go on, look," Razon said in a deep, feral whisper.

Selma's eyes went wide, and she took in deep, nourishing breaths. She had never been asked to explore someone's thoughts. An open invite to delve into someone's innermost private feelings. She was trying to remember why this was a bad idea. She had kept all her thoughts about him at bay these last weeks. Days of intentionally reminding herself to focus on his snide comments and dismissive behavior instead of his intoxicating smell. But the temptation was too strong to fight. She let her shield down and let her magic pour out. His mind was wide open for her to stroll through as his silver-flecked eyes locked on hers.

I'm going to kiss you, and I'm going to mean it.

Her breath hitched as her core went liquid.

He lowered his lips to her neck, and she felt his hair fall around her shoulder. His breath tickled her as his tongue traced a path to her collarbone. He was teasing. Being so gentle. She did not want him to be gentle. She wanted more.

Razon nipped at her skin with his teeth, releasing a delicious ache. Selma flinched and took in a gasp of air. She waited for the urge to pull back, but it never came. That feeling that she should not cross this line fizzled.

Do you want me to stop? Razon was still communicating with her mind to mind. The thought of being so connected to him sent a bolt of electricity down her spine. She did not want him to stop. She wanted more.

Before she could fashion a lie and produce an excuse, she moaned, "No."

Razon picked her up and moved over to the wall. Their bodies were so close she could feel him hard against her. His arms braced the wall on either side of her head, his fingers spread wide, as if he were holding up the wall. As if he were stopping himself from ravaging her. The thought of him wanting her like that sent her need over the edge. She had waited long enough, and it did not matter if it made sense anymore. She needed a distraction. She needed just a moment of relief. She wanted to give in to the way her body felt when he was around.

She leaned in closer to him, her hips grazing the power between his legs. Razon read her movements and trailed his hands under her worn shirt, drawing small circles around her belly button. His lips still tickled her neck, and, like an animal restraining himself, he grazed his teeth along her flesh. He let out a moan, and Selma could not wait any longer. Her breath was wild and wanting. She ran her fingers through his dark, silky hair and urged his lips to rise.

She angled her head up so that their lips teased one another, and with whatever strength she could muster, she offered him a whisper: "I want it."

Razon showed his teeth. His smile was animistic as he growled, "You want what?"

"I want you. All of you," she breathlessly responded.

Razon snarled and finally granted her request, crashing his mouth into hers. His lips parted, letting his tongue explore and play. It swept over her tongue, tasting her. There was no space between them now. Selma could feel his muscles pulsing below his shirt.

Razon reached down and cupped both hands around her backside, picking her up off the floor. In one graceful movement, he walked them both over to the shower. Still biting her lower lip, he reached out and pulled on the brass lion's head. Water poured down, like rain falling from the sky in warm droplets. Selma pulled away long enough to look up at the ceiling and laugh. The entire room had turned into a rain shower. The room became a forest, and they became the storm.

Razon put her down and pulled off his wet shirt, releasing his beautiful skin and tattoos. Selma took in the gorgeous sight. Drank him in. He reached over and peeled off her shirt. Now she was in only her lace bralette and cotton boxer briefs. For a moment, she pulled her arms up to cover the mismatched pieces, but he quickly stepped forward and grabbed her wrists.

"Don't. I want to see all of you. You are beautiful," said Razon in a soft and confident tone. He cupped her face with one hand and leaned in for a kiss. It was gentler than the one from a moment before. His other hand reached back and released the snap on her bralette. Selma pulled her arms through the straps and let it fall to the shower floor.

"I told you that I would kiss you and mean it, and I always

follow through with my promises," he growled with that side smile that made Selma melt.

"Mm…It was a good kiss," she moaned.

"That wasn't the kiss I was talking about," Razon said. He picked her up, resting one arm below her knees and one around her back. He walked over to the bench and laid her down on the smooth wood. Selma let the warm droplets fall around her. They touched every inch of her body and ignited her nerves. Razon never took his eyes off her as he bent down onto his knees and peeled the soaked boxer briefs down her legs, exposing her fully. He ran his callused fingers up her skin, grazing the inside of her upper thigh, trailing soft kisses up near her center and letting his tongue find the way.

He paused for a moment, and Selma's chest rose and fell with a fury, her core molten. She wanted him. Needed him. Just the sight of him between her legs was too much for her to bear. She let out a small, wanting moan as Razon licked up her center. He continued moving up and down, quick and then measured, feasting on her essence. He explored her thighs, his large fingers traversing her skin. Then he paused, and her nerves yearned for more. But before she could protest, one finger slipped inside of her as he placed small kisses below her belly button. Selma breathed heavy with approval as he moved in and out of her, feeling her slickness. He added another finger, only adding to her pleasure as he pumped.

Selma's head fell back, and her back arched. Razon gripped her thigh, strong and possessive. But she was not scared. Her body moved into his touch, and she wanted to open herself up to him completely. She wanted to know every inch of his body. What did he taste like? His fingers moved in and out, each time inflaming her nerves, her body responding to each flick of his fingers.

Razon watched as her body writhed with pleasure. He purred

in a deep, brutish tone, "Now be a good girl and come for me, princess."

Her nerves quaked as white-hot pleasure surged through her core and out toward her limbs, as if her body were going to shatter. Her back arched off the wood, his fingers still inside, caressing her wetness.

Her body went limp with pleasure. Razon stopped and pulled away from her, leaving her still wet and wanting. He could not stop now or she would crack in half from the ache. She opened her eyes and saw the water still falling from above. Razon stood over her, dripping wet. His hair fell into his face, and his eyes had glossed over in a feral haze. His jeans were dark and heavy from the shower, sitting just below his waist and giving her a delicious view of the notches on his hips. A sure sign of a beautifully toned body.

He reached down and began to unbutton his jeans, still staring at her. She could feel his eyes roaming over every inch of her as she lay there. Selma sat up and reached to help him with his pants.

"No," Razon cut in.

His response startled her, but she stopped.

"I want to see you. I have not been able to stop thinking about you since that first day. Your body, your taste, what you would feel like wrapped around my cock. I have imagined your curves, and I want to see all of you before I take you."

Selma laid back down gently, but this time she turned around, exposing her backside. She looked over her shoulder and let him drink her in.

"Then take it. Tonight, it is yours," Selma returned with a wry smile.

Razon growled and unbuttoned the final button, sliding his jeans down and releasing the full length of him. She could see how much he wanted her now. His entire body was hard, his cock pulsing and begging to be touched. Selma took a moment to survey his flesh. He gripped himself base to tip, pre-come spilling out as he watched her. His muscled arm twitched as if he were holding back. And as quickly and gracefully as he had picked her up and brought her here, he pulled her up from the bench and brought her close to him. Her ass was now pushed up to him, and she could feel him hard against her. Razon wrapped his arms around her. His tattoos enveloped her like living art. His thumbs caressed the tips of her breasts as he kissed the back of her neck. There was no space between them now, but still Selma wanted him closer. She needed him closer.

His teeth scraped her skin, followed by his tongue tasting every inch of her. The warm water fell around them, and the droplets formed rivulets down their bodies, flowing and joining together with every movement. His mouth moved to her ear, and his breath tickled, forcing Selma's flesh to prickle with goose bumps.

A deep, hushed command dripped from his lips: "You're mine."

And Selma let out a moan of approval. She bowed her back, pushing her backside harder into him. The touch was delicious, but it was not enough. Even their slick bodies hot against one another could not quell the crackle of energy between them.

"Make sure to breathe when you take me in, princess," Razon snarled. "Are you ready?"

"Yes." Selma could barely get words out. "Fuck me."

In one smooth movement, he sank into her core. Selma sucked in a breath and felt the delicious stretch as he rocked into her. His tongue still tickled the back of her neck as he pushed into her again. Deeper this time. Inch by inch, he filled her. She moaned from the inviting ache of his length. He answered with a growl.

"Fuck. You feel good," he moaned.

With another thrust, he filled her to the hilt. Selma's nerves tingled and threatened to put her over the edge again. But she wanted more. She did not want this to end.

Selma pushed off of the bench and walked away, gesturing for Razon to follow and giving him a full view of her body. His eyes were dark as he watched her every movement. She stopped in front of the bed, water still dripping from her body as Razon's chest rose and fell in long, deep waves. His red threads flowed out from him, cradling Selma's body and gently lifting her into the air above her bed. The heat from his magic evaporated the leftover droplets, leaving her skin warm.

Razon climbed onto the soft mattress and spread her legs. His mouth feasted on her again, his tongue licking delicate swirls and sucking on the small bundle of nerves. Selma felt her body vibrate with pleasure. He set her down on the bed and replaced his tongue with two fingers, trailing kisses up her body until his eyes met hers. She was on the edge. Pulsing need raced through her body as he removed his fingers, her slickness running down her leg. She could feel his throbbing girth at her entrance.

"Look at me when you come," he growled.

He grabbed the back of her hair with one hand and plunged deep, her eyes widening, the two of them locked in a gaze. Razon took her, claiming her body. Again. Again. Again. Selma's nerves erupted, sending sizzling pleasure through her body. Vivid colors lit the room as her threads reacted to her body bursting with pleasure. He held her as he howled, losing control and then releasing her.

Quickened harsh breaths and a prism of threads filled the room as they clung together. Selma wanted to stay just like this. Bound together. But when he pulled away, he trailed soft kisses down her neck until the flames from the fire dwindled, giving way to smoldering logs.

"They are all dead. The Mavens have returned to Sever."

—Recovered correspondence from Warrior Leclerc to Warrior Lourdes, property of the Warriors of Sever

CHAPTER 40

T*hrum thrum thrum.* Razon's steady heartbeat attempted to lull Selma back to sleep. And she might have let it, if it had not been for the rush of memories from the last few days. Her mind did not know how to sort the emotional whiplash of highs and lows.

The sun shone through the seams of the heavy velvet curtains. Morning beckoned her to get up and out of bed, but Razon's warm embrace kept her there in the sheets, and she wished that she could stay like this. Tucked away from the Order and her aunts and family. It would be so much easier to let someone else come up with a plan. They knew more about this world anyway. But something in her had awoken, and knowing what she knew now, continuing to let the Order make people suffer would be unforgivable.

She slowly lifted her head and moved to the side of the bed to push herself off and get dressed without waking Razon. As her feet swung over the side, an arm reached around her waist and pulled her back.

"Where are you going?" Razon spoke into her ear and kissed along her neck.

Selma smiled as he snuggled up to her and started rubbing his finger around her hips and tickling around her thighs. Goddess, it felt good to be held like that. She wanted him to touch her like he had last night, wanted to feel the white-hot pleasure course through her body. Just thinking about it sent goose bumps down her flesh. But last night was different. In the light of day, everything came flooding back, and she remembered their challenges and the people who did not deserve to suffer. She pulled away.

"Last night was..." Selma searched for the right word. She jumped at the sound of a knock on the door. It was hurried and purposeful. She was thankful for the interruption.

"Uh, whoever might be in there, and I'm not saying I know there are, but if there are people in there, then I think you should come out. There is something I think you should see." Leven's voice rang through the door.

Damn it. How could he have known that Razon was here? Leven must have gone to his room first and discovered it was vacant.

Selma was mortified as she rushed around trying to find anything to cover herself up with. She silently prayed to the Goddess that they had not been as loud as she thought. This was bad. Maybe she could play it off like Razon was not here and was off brooding somewhere instead.

Razon got up so quickly that Selma did not even know it was happening. He opened the door. His naked body was exposed except for a single pillow covering below his waist, his perfectly sculpted backside on full display for Selma. She plastered an incredulous smile on her face for Leven. Playing it off like she was alone was no longer an option.

"What is it?" Razon's enunciation was clipped and harsh. Selma knew his grating tone had nothing to do with Leven knocking on the door.

"Uh." Leven looked from Razon to Selma. Amusement tugged at the sides of his mouth. "I think we found something in the Canon."

"I'll be right there," said Razon. And he closed the door without another word from Leven.

Selma waited patiently while Razon gathered his clothing, still wet from the night before, from around the room. She took in the last fleeting glimpses of his chiseled body. She could not take back what happened last night. Not anymore. But did she even want to? Did she want it to happen again?

Selma looked at the now vacant spot on the bed and did not know if it was guilt or longing that filled her chest. Her body could not help but think of last night's delicious details and the scrumptious soreness between her legs.

A strong hand wrapped around her waist, pulling her in. In an instant, his breath was warming her skin, and the tip of his nose was grazing the sensitive part of her neck.

"Last night was incredible," Razon whispered in that low, guttural tone that made her wet. "And if I didn't have to go see what this news was, I would stay here all day and make you scream my name. Now, princess, get that gorgeous ass dressed, and let's go win a war."

✝

Selma desperately wanted breakfast, but there was no time to tame her hunger. After training and her extracurricular activities, she was ravenous. But whatever they had found in the Canon was more important than her stomach turning and barking for sustenance.

She kept walking toward the hum of voices. There in the center of the library, the shelves widened and opened to a, circular atrium. Glass towered over the space, letting in soft light. Water droplets settled on the glass, creating small currents, and her core burned as she thought back to last night.

Selma shook her head, wiping her mind free from the thought. She would not be able to focus if she kept picturing Razon's long length.

Leven, Emery, and Razon were all at the table in the center, poring over the Canon.

Selma nervously spoke up. "What did you find?"

Leven looked up and shot Selma a tight smile. Probably apologizing for whatever he had interrupted this morning.

Razon stood up and walked over to her, grabbing a plate of fruit from a nearby table that was stacked high with breakfast food. Thank the Goddess.

"Thank you. "I'm hungry after skipping dinner." Selma graciously looked at the plate.

"But if I remember correctly, you did get dessert," said Razon, a wide grin taking shape on his face.

"You're vile," Selma snorted.

Razon let out a low laugh that made her body heat. He reached out for the tray of honey biscuits and jam. Selma summoned her threads and released the power she had stored earlier. Suddenly, the silver tray of fluffy pastries was gone, leaving only Razon's open, empty palms and a puzzled look in his eyes.

He appeared more intrigued than angry. "Did you just object summon my biscuits?"

Selma kept her face impassive as she said, "Well, it looks like they are my biscuits now. I have never been a fan of dessert. All sweets and no substance."

Razon's gaze cut into her as he stepped closer, making the space between them vanish. He leaned in close to her ear, and Selma could feel his lips brush against her earlobe as he whispered, "Your moans would say otherwise. I myself could not get enough of that sweet taste."

Selma's core ached with a whole different kind of hunger. She hoped her walls were still intact, because visions of the night before flashed in her mind. His head between her legs as he tasted her.

Razon backed away and put his hands in his pockets. His smile clearly indicated that he had noted her flushed skin.

Emery cleared her throat. "It's mostly traditional witchcraft and stories."

Leven broke in with a high-pitched mocking tone, reading from the book. "'Our Goddesses succeeded in breaking magic apart. Our universe was forever changed when they ripped the tethers and created balance. Our origin of inception, the Brocken, will forever be a holy sector.'"

Leven and Emery laughed, filling the room with some much-needed mirth.

"Can the two of you focus, please? We do not have much time, and, as I was ripped from my bed this morning, I would like to move this along." Razon's look was anything but patient.

"We all know that it was not *your* bed you were ripped from this morning," said Emery with a smirk.

Selma's cheeks flushed, and she cut in quickly, ignoring Emery's comment. "You said you found something. What did you find?"

Leven obliged. "After the Brocken is mentioned, it goes on to say, 'The purest taste of power brings death. For only in death is life anew.'"

Selma leaned her head forward a bit, hoping that there was more, or that he would explain further.

Razon was the first to speak. "And are you sure you've translated correctly?"

"Fairly sure," Leven added. "But I'm a little rusty on Theban runes."

Razon countered, "'Fairly sure' isn't going to cut it."

"If you have a more thorough translation, then by all means, enlighten us," Emery added.

Selma cut in, "I'm sorry, but what does that *mean?*"

Razon turned to her. "It means that the Order is not trying to kill Millie. They are trying to turn her."

"But you said the poison could kill a human without witch blood," Selma said.

"It can. But they must have found a way to prolong it. It makes sense. All her symptoms are similar to the change, but slowed somehow."

"We must stop them. Millie did not consent to this. How did they learn to turn humans into witches? And why?"

Razon became unnaturally quiet and still. Emery and Leven exchanged a look that suggested there was a piece of information they had not yet shared.

Razon turned to Selma and raised his hands to her neck, gently thumbing the pendant. His eyes met hers. "The Brocken bark, once heated at temperatures beyond those that can be reached on the surface of earth, will melt into a serum. It contains the purest form of magic. It changes your DNA and morphs your magic. The change is what we endure to become Wargraves. Not everyone can withstand it. I suspected that your pendant was made from the Brocken bark."

"We suspected as much," Emery added.

Razon's eyes were sharp as blades when he spoke. "The only difference between witches and humans is their soul. If you can figure out a way to alter one's soul, then you can use Brocken to make the change into witch."

"Change a soul? But that is impossible," Selma scoffed.

Alister's voice rang through the room. "It isn't. The Goddess Saint was known to 'experiment' on humans. All evidence of those experiments was collected and locked away in an undisclosed location. If souls can be altered, then instructions are buried with those texts." Alister shared a look with Razon. "Finding those texts is what Razon was tasked with after the war. And if the Order has found them, then we may be too late."

Selma's spine straightened. More secrets.

"It is not too late. They still want Alister and the Canon. The Order thinks he knows where the Brocken is. They could not have taken much from the Wargraves' temple when it was ransacked. They need more," said Razon. "They want an army. That might even be why they tried with the Mavens first. They wanted to transform their treads into something they could control."

"Goddess, but they couldn't control it, and the power flooded the entire faction, causing them to burn out." Leven's face went pale. "An army for what?"

Selma's eyes widened. The inky black fog she saw in Millie. "An army to take out the mortals. They want to create their own army of Wargraves who do not live by a code."

The thought made her stomach turn.

Razon turned to Leven. "Have you found out where the Brocken is located?"

Leven shook his head. "There is nothing about its location. But what if they already have it? I think we should reconsider sending Selma to her third trial. If they know who she is, they will not let her walk away unscathed."

"We don't know that," Emery chimed in.

Leven shot back sarcastically, "Oh, we don't?"

"If I don't go, Millie is dead. They will kill her," said Selma.

Leven raised his voice, pointing at Selma. "And if they have caught on to the fact that she is of Maven blood? What then?"

Silence.

"It's up to you, Selma." Razon's gaze drank her in. He had never called her by her name before.

Every moment brought more questions, and Selma wished that her Aunt Verda were here so that she could ask her about everything. When Verda was alive, she seemed to be the only person in the world who was on Selma's side. But she supposed Verda had lied to her too. Selma would need to make this decision by herself.

"If I don't go, they will kill Millie, or complete the transformation, and I cannot let that happen," said Selma. "I go, but I go alone."

Razon stood all the way up, his shoulders broadening and enveloping Selma in shadow. "Absolutely not," he said sharply. "If you go, I go as well. That way, if anything goes wrong, I can get you out of there."

"No. You cannot risk being found out by the Order, and stopping them is more important than my powers," Selma shot back.

"Not exactly," said Leven. "The two are intrinsically linked. Your unique powers might be what we need to access the Brocken and stop the Order."

"Now is not the time to be a martyr," added Razon. His eyes pleaded with her. Selma knew how important bringing down the Order was to him. She knew he was not willing to risk failure.

"He is right. If you pass the trial, that is one thing, but we put everything at risk if they find out about your threads. Your magic might be what we need to turn the tides against the Order, and putting yourself at risk would change everything," Leven said with resolve in his tone.

"Then we all go," Emery suggested.

Selma looked around the room at the people gathered around her. Warriors who were putting themselves between her and danger. Witches and warlocks she barely knew. She could sense their magic, their threads, and she felt the bonds strengthening between them. They had already lost too much.

"No. I go alone." Selma's tone was resolute.

"Respect the natural order, the innate rights of sentient beings."

—An excerpt from the Canon, as translated by Leven Kara, property of the
Warriors of Sever

CHAPTER 41

Three long weeks had gone by before Razon had heard word from the council. Moving Millie was too risky with so many eyes on her, and they still did not know how to cure her. Nobody knew how far Olivier's power would reach if he were to find out they had tried.

Razon had been going back and forth, feeding Olivier false information about Selma's whereabouts and checking on Millie. Her condition was getting worse. The transformation was taking a sickening toll on her fragile human body. Selma desperately wanted to use her healing powers, but her magic was still too unstable to try. Millie did not have much time. They needed to get the poison out of her before it was too late.

Selma's body ached and moaned after the training she received at Tullamore Castle. While Razon was more powerful, Leven and Emery had not held back. Especially Emery. Her magic was brutal, but helpful. They had spent days wielding and calling on the elements. Selma still could not summon all her threads on command, but she now had much more magic than she was accustomed to.

Selma had no idea she could wield power like this. It was as if something had arisen, stirring a deep, old magic within her. She felt her threads sizzling all the time under her skin. She was not going to have the full force of the Wargraves behind her, but she did have her newfound powers. Plus, she would not necessarily need to access her threads. Ideally, the Order would think nothing of the oddities during her previous trials and release the poison from Millie, buying Selma some time. She still had a few weeks before the council would put her and her family in servitude for not disclosing the location of her father.

Leven and Emery took it upon themselves to find something to release the binding magic on the Order's servants and release them from their hell. They had come close a few times but still had no solution yet. Helping those witches was as important to Selma as saving Millie.

‡

Razon and Selma evanesced back to the island. The silence was deafening. Razon had been distant since this morning, barely uttering a word to her. She could feel tension radiating from him, and it was apparent that he was still uncomfortable with Selma going to the trial alone. But to come along would jeopardize his position in the Order. If Olivier were to find out that Razon had been spying, his life would be in immediate danger. Selma had no doubt that Razon could hold his own against Olivier, but at what cost? She would not risk him or any of them. They needed more time to gather whatever help they could.

Selma shuffled through everything she had learned. "Why did you suspect that my pendant was made from the Brocken?"

"Because it pulses when a Wargrave is near unless we know to shield against it. It calls to us because the serum is in our blood."

Selma considered that for a moment. "Do you think it is summoning you home? Like two magnets?"

"Perhaps," Razon responded.

"Then maybe my pendant could heal Millie. Maybe the bark in the pendant could pull the serum out of her," said Selma.

Razon's eyes swam with thought. "We can try."

She smiled back at him. Feeling hope. But did they have time? The final task was upon her. Soon, as the moon hung at its peak, the familiar orb would appear at the door. A trial by fire. The world she had known before had burned to ash, and yet she still stood, like hardened stone. At least, hardened stone is what her heart felt like. What flames could the Order hold to her flesh to make her quiver?

Without hesitating, Razon grabbed her hand, and they were swirling through gray mist. Their feet landed softly on a familiar hardwood floor. Selma looked around and raced up the stairs, her heart pounding as she took each step two at a time. When she reached Millie's room, David was leaning over the bed, tears running down his cheeks. Millie lay motionless on the bed, her skin pale, her breaths shallow. She was alive.

David turned to look at Selma and shook his head slightly. "She doesn't have much time," he whispered.

"I know," Selma said breathlessly.

She rushed to the side of the bed and gently shoved David aside. She ripped the silver chain from her neck, leaving a red mark. She placed the pendant on Millie's chest and covered it with her own chest. For the first time in her life, she closed her eyes and prayed to Goddess Sever.

They stayed that way for minutes, in silence, but there was no change. Selma wanted to believe she could fix this. For one peaceful moment, she had let herself believe that she could take away Millie's pain and put her out of danger. David quietly sobbed next to her.

Suddenly, Razon's strong hand met her shoulder. "Selma, we need to go."

Selma nodded in understanding. She grabbed Millie's hand and squeezed.

"Hold on a little bit longer. You have to fight. I know you already do so much, but please, just a little longer," said Selma.

The pendant began to thrum. Not the same way it did when Razon was near, but in slower, rhythmic pulses.

They watched as a dark, smokelike substance enveloped Millie, the ominous fog shielding her from sight. Then her body jerked back and forth. The sharp motions mimicked an electric current, and although her eyes remained closed, her limbs shook.

"What is happening? What is it doing?" David's voice cracked.

"I don't know," Selma responded. Panic rose in her throat. She looked to Razon for answers, but his wide eyes offered none.

Millie's screams penetrated the fog, forcing David to spring forward for the pendant.

Selma caught him before he could reach it. "No! Not yet."

"You're hurting her," David pleaded.

Razon jumped up, grasped David, and pulled him back. "Give her some room. We have to trust her."

Selma looked at Razon. *Should* they trust her? She did not know what she was doing, but something in her gut told her to wait. David looked at his wife, tears falling down his cheeks, and Selma knew that if she was not making the right decision, her heart would not be the only one to shatter.

Selma reached her threads out to the men, touching their fear and anger. Soaking in their thoughts of panic. Her magic sizzled under her skin as it fed on the emotions. Memories flashed— she and Millie as girls in the forest, the first time she had shared her magic. Teenagers around a bonfire on the beach. Images of Millie's wedding flowers spilled into her mind. The violet threads curled around Millie, swallowing her screams as they turned to whimpers. Selma's threads pulsed alongside the onyx pendant as they absorbed the black fog.

When Millie's face came into view, her cheeks were flushed, but she took one enduring breath, and Selma sighed with relief. It was working. The pendant was pulling the poison from her body.

Selma secured the pendant around Millie's neck and turned to David, who seemed tired from fighting against Razon's firm grip. "Do not move that pendant until I come back. Do you understand?" Her tone was firm but loving.

David looked down at Millie as color began to come back into her face. Her lips were no longer a watery blue. He nodded, releasing more tears.

She needed to get to the trial. Even if the poison was out of Millie's system, she still needed to complete the final trial and allow Leven and Emery more time to find the Brocken before the Order forcefully placed her and her family in servitude. She leaned down quickly and kissed Millie on the cheek, noticing a bit of warmth there. Thank the Goddess, Millie would be alright. But something had replaced Selma's fear. A much stronger emotion. Rage.

The Order was going to pay for what they had done.

‡

The air was stagnant. An indistinct musty smell wafted through Selma's nostrils as she walked through the trees, careful to navigate the branches, which were barer than they had been before. Autumn had robbed the leaves of their lush emerald color, and winter was on the horizon.

She paired her steps with her breaths. Her lungs stung with crisp air. She must have been getting close now, because the orb was slowing down. She knew what to expect by now, at least in terms of the Order's grand entrance. Goddess, they were arrogant.

The orb grew and dimmed into a warm rust color, the way it had in previous trials before it burst into glittery specks. Anticipating the theatrics, Selma closed her eyes to avoid temporary blindness. When she opened them, all five cloaked men stood side by side.

"This formation is a little stale, don't you think?" scoffed Selma. It was not a great idea to prod them right now, but their arrogance was too much to bear.

Olivier spoke up. "It does not surprise me, child, that you mock our traditions. But I would be careful about spewing such infidelity among our Goddess's chosen."

Selma scoffed. These men had not been chosen by anyone.

They were a collection of self-appointed murderous pricks.

Olivier continued, ignoring Selma's quiet reaction. "I do say that I am surprised you have agreed to participate thus far. Especially given your unique circumstances. How odd that your skin did not want to bear the mark of our Goddess. Perhaps you need more reassurance before sharing yourself?"

Each word was laced with disdain and something else, something that Selma could not put her finger on. She reached out to Olivier's mind, but his walls were firmly in place.

"In fact, we are so thrilled you have made it this far that we have brought an audience for your final trial," Olivier sneered. "Razon, would you like to join us?"

Razon walked out from the trees flanked by two of the largest warlocks Selma had ever seen. Each of them wore an expression that implied that they killed first asked questions later. The skin of their arms looked like it was straining against their bulging muscles. Razon's face was a calm mask, but something was off. His eyes did not focus on any one thing.

"Good," Olivier drawled. "We are all here."

What was happening? Had Razon betrayed her? Had he been shuffling information to the Order all this time? Selma thought back to everything she had learned and how devastating it would be if the Order knew what she now knew. Alister was in danger, and Leven and Emery would be as well. Was it possible that Razon had betrayed all of them?

Olivier turned and walked toward Selma. Razon and his two menacing guards followed. In an instant, Razon was on his knees after one of the guards shoved him to the ground. Dust billowed from the forest floor around him, and his jaw ticked. Selma could not tell much, but he looked paler than usual. Why had he helped her hone her magic if he meant for it to end like this?

Olivier's voice boomed, "As children of our Goddess Saint, we must solidify our commitment to her teachings and embolden ourselves to supply her and her descendants with the power she needs to thrive. Child Selma, are you prepared to commit to Saint? Do you pledge to do whatever is necessary to imbue her and your fellow children with power?"

Selma's hands trembled, and she hoped that Olivier and the other members of the Order would not notice.

"Yes," she lied.

"Excellent," Olivier responded, lifting his hand and signaling the guards. They stepped back, but Razon remained on the ground. His chin was raised high in the air, and his gaze did not falter from Selma.

"Kill him," Olivier sneered.

CHAPTER 42

Selma's eyes narrowed on Olivier. He was smiling back at her.

Olivier continued, "It has come to our attention that Razon has committed treason against the Order—a crime punishable by death. Prove your allegiance and take his life before the Goddess Saint."

Selma clenched her hands into fists. "And if I refuse?"

Olivier clicked his tongue. "Then I will be forced to kill him myself." His eyes grew black and cold as he focused on Selma. "And then I will come for you."

Selma sucked in a sharp breath.

"Of course, we could make a trade," Olivier carried on, making his way closer to her. "Do you think I do not know who you are? Or should I say *what* you are, Selma Lourdes?"

Selma's skin shuddered. Her name felt like oil in her ears as he spat it out.

"They have done a fine job of hiding you all these years, but that magic you so clumsily displayed during your second trial was unmistakable," Olivier snarled. "You would be a fine asset to our cause. All you have to do is tell us where your father is and agree to work with the Order."

Selma was breathing heavily now. Her heart sank. Alister for Razon. They had trapped her, and now she would lose everything she had just barely found. These last few weeks, she had felt more like herself than she ever had.

Her threads were thrumming under her skin. Her magic. She still had her magic. But was it enough to take out Olivier and the rest of the Order? She could not take them all down without a solid plan.

Selma took a fortifying breath. It would have to be enough.

She looked over at Razon. His eyes had changed. There was something there, but she could not place it. Her thoughts frantically wandered her lessons. She needed to stall and produce a plan, so she shouted, "And if I kill him?"

Olivier's smile turned even more sinister as he tilted his head. Selma threw out her threads toward Razon, hoping that Olivier would be too distracted to notice.

"Well, that would be a surprise, wouldn't it?" Olivier said, lost in thought.

Her threads were quicker than usual as they reached for the Wargrave. They wrapped around him in a web of embrace, and Selma could have sworn he leaned into them. She felt the gentle hum of acceptance. Heat radiated off him. She opened a small sliver of her mental gate, small enough to let his thoughts leak through if he could sense it. And in an instant, he touched her mind.

Go, Razon said. *If you don't run, they will kill you. I will be fine. Go and hide, take Millie with you.* His connection was weak. She could barely make out his thoughts.

Selma gasped. He had not been lying; he had not betrayed her. But why was he not fighting back? And then she remembered the servants at the Luminescence Ball. They had drugged him.

Selma's reaction must have caught Olivier's attention, because his face twisted with hatred. He reached his hand out toward Razon, and black threads raced toward the Wargrave, piercing his side. Razon screamed in agony.

"I have had enough of toying with you, you filthy Wargrave. You think you are entitled to more power, and yet you do not even know what to do with it," Olivier bellowed. Razon shrieked in pain, and Selma felt helpless. She must have been yelling at Olivier to stop, but the sound died out among Razon's screams.

She had to do something. Selma reached for her magic. Her threads responded. Desperately seeking power, she quickly drank from the energy around her and then sent her threads throttling forward, forming daggers in the air. Not toward Olivier, but toward his sinuous black threads, severing them in half. Razon's screams faltered, and his body hit the forest floor with a sickening thud. *He cannot be dead*, Selma begged the Goddess.

"Enough!" a familiar voice bellowed. Alister.

Olivier's attention was pulled to the tree line. His feline smirk was a sign of his triumph. "Alister, it has been too long," he sneered. "It looks as though I will get both of you this evening. What a night it will be."

"It's not him you want, Olivier. Let him go," Alister insisted.

Olivier clicked his tongue. "I wish I could, but it is out of my hands. Not only was he found guilty of heresy, but he has now been found guilty of treason against the Order."

This was the distraction that Selma needed. If she could just find a way to get to Razon and make sure he was alright, then maybe she could heal him, draw out the poison so they could escape.

"You said you would let him go if I delivered Alister," Selma shouted.

"Ah, yes, but you see, *you* did not deliver him to us. He arrived of his own accord," Olivier countered.

Without another breath, Olivier sent his inky black threads toward Alister. Alister quickly countered, throwing up a shield of blazing fire, his red threads both drinking up energy and twisting among the flames fortifying the wall. The other members of the Order joined Olivier, sending an attack of blackened, corrupt magic straight for Alister. His shield was holding them, but barely. Each second quelled his flames and tore away at his threads, exposing him.

Just then, Leven and Emery leaped out from behind the trees, each bolting toward a member of the Order. Selma's chest rose and fell with her breaths. Tears fell from her eyes as she ran for Razon, but before she could reach him, she felt the rip of skin on her side, and she fell to the ground. Heat scorched her nerves as she gasped for air. She could not move. Her body was stiff, and she was ablaze in pain. She could just barely make out an ominous black figure stalking toward her. Olivier. He was going to kill her and then the others. She needed to do something. Anything.

Selma willed her body to obey as she strained to crawl away, grasping at the moss on the ground. Meanwhile, Olivier crept closer, hunting her. She needed to get up if she was going to have a chance. Razon might have already been gone, and the others were fighting for their lives.

"I am done with you. It is a shame to waste magic. You were born with such glorious gifts, magic that most only dream of, but so be it," Olivier bit out. He looked down at Selma with disdain as he lifted his arms to release his killing blow. But he was tackled by a dark shadow.

"Razon," Selma breathed, her lungs still burning.

Razon and Olivier tumbled along the ground. All Selma could see through her blurry vision was a cloud of cloak and dust. He was alive.

She managed to pull her arms under her and push up to her knees. She looked around at the others, who were locked in battle. Emery and Alister working together to hold off two members of the Order. One dark cloak lying motionless on the ground nearby. Leven's leathers were covered with dark blood, his threads drinking in energy as icy daggers lashed out at the man who had wanted Selma in servitude. He fought back, tossing Leven to the ground, and his black threads tore into the dirt.

A rumble sounded from the earth. A distraction. The uneasy forest floor swayed below Selma's feet, and the dirt began to split, swallowing up the rocks and trees in its path, along with the member of the Order who Alister had been fighting, but not before landing a devastating blow to Alister's heart.

Leven quickly sprinted from the crevasse. He yelled out for Emery, who was sprinting toward Alister with a pack of wolves that looked like they had been formed from water. Their terrifying figures crashed into one another like waves in a storm. Emery tripped, and her water-wolves disappeared, sending her falling toward the break. Leven grabbed her hand and held on, furiously pulling her back from the void.

Selma reached into the ground, searching for any energy she could find. She tried to block out the chaos and the fighting around her and focus on the nature that surrounded them. But her eyes darted back and forth over the field, searching for Alister. It was hard to see in the dark, but she could just make out his hunched-over figure.

"No!" Selma yelled, her voice cracking.

She reached her mental gate, opening it more, so her threads had an open pathway. The green threads slithered out through her fingertips and into the ground. She could feel their reluctance, but she pushed through, building a berm around the three Wargraves and protecting them from view.

She ran up to Alister, taking in the murky black threads burning into him, a stark contrast to his graying skin. His breaths were shallow in his chest. Leven had gone straight to work trying to untangle the toxic threads. But they were everywhere. Selma tumbled to the ground, her knees scraping broken rocks. But she could not feel anything. She needed to heal her father, but her violet threads were sluggish and weak.

His trembling hands rose to her cheeks. "I never should have left you," Alister whispered. His voice was sluggish, but his eyes burrowed into her like he was seeing a memory. "You are everything she dreamed you would be."

"No, no, no. You cannot go now. I just got you back," Selma pleaded.

Alister's arm fell to the ground, and his eyes went vacant. Leven and Emery were holding back tears. They hovered over Alister's still body in disbelief. He was not even supposed to be here.

"Go!" shouted Emery. "There is nothing you can do for him right now. We will watch over him."

Selma looked down at her father with the eyes he had given her.

"Go!" shouted Emery again. "Razon needs you."

Selma pulled herself from the tear-and-blood-soaked ground and began running in the direction Razon and Olivier had gone, ignoring the searing pain in her gut. She could not make out any member of the Order, but they would likely be skulking nearby unless the earthquake had bested them. She needed a plan.

In the next clearing, Selma halted as Olivier and Razon came into view. Razon was hanging in midair. His hands clutched his throat as his legs dangled. Olivier's hand was raised, keeping black threads tangled around Razon's throat.

"I will enjoy seeing your soul drain from your body," hissed Olivier. His eyes were wild, and the veins in his arms protruded from his skin. He was going to kill Razon.

"Razon!" Selma shouted.

Olivier turned his head. His savage eyes locked on Selma. He raised his other hand and shot his threads directly toward her, each one piercing her skin more painfully than the last and knocking her back into the tree behind her.

Selma felt bone crack as she hit the massive tree trunk. She slunk to the ground, her arms and legs like rubber, bruised and broken. She could not breathe. A sharp pain shot through her lungs as she tried to take in air. Blood dripped down the side of her head as she lay on the cold forest floor. She knew if she turned onto her side, the blood would run into her eyes and hinder her vision. Her ears thrummed, and a high-pitched tone drowned out the shouts coming from the distance. The intensity of Olivier's blow was astronomical. Her shoulder ached with sharp pain. She knew without moving that it was dislocated. This was it. She was going to die here. The Order was going to take and take and take no matter who was trampled down in the process, and she would die here in this field. At least she had saved Millie.

The shouts were getting closer now. She needed to get up, but her body did not seem to want to respond. She could not feel her legs, only the warm blood starting to pool around her. Her entire body was on fire, like her nerves were trying to jump out of her skin. Everything seemed to swirl around her in a gentle motion. She rocked back and forth, feeling the sharp rip of tendons in her arm as she tried to pry herself off the ground. What was she forgetting? There had to be something she could use to at least delay the next hit. But her mind had shattered. All her training was a blank mist. But even as her body turned cold and her blood fell to the ground, she knew she could not give in. She had to have one more play. Her eyes tried to adjust to the small black speck in the distance. Razon.

She reached out for her mental gate, swinging it wide open, allowing a path for her power. She pleaded with her magic. Anything. She needed any of her threads to respond. Razon and the others needed to survive. They were a light in the darkness. They could find a way to overcome the Order. They could save Millie and protect those without magic.

Her body splintered and her mind sluggish, she reached for her threads, but they shuddered. She needed to do this. She needed to release her doubts. She needed to trust herself and her magic. It was a part of her. A gift from her mother and father, who had loved one another. She had seen it in Alister's eyes as he took his last breath.

With that, she closed her eyes and let go. Her threads burst out in every direction, gathering as much power as her body would hold. She called on all her threads. Silver, red, and violet strands vibrated through the air, weaving in and out of one another, creating a rainbow of power. She felt her magic growing stronger with each moment. She had to hurry. Razon did not have much time.

Her threads went farther out and whipped straight back to Selma. She was vibrating with power. Pain emanated from her flesh. Her body thrummed with power, and her skin was aflame with heat. All her threads were reverberating at full force, the burden laying waste to her body. She was burning out. She would not be able to hold them much longer. Her body trembled with each second. Her head throbbed, and her thoughts became blurry. She felt every fiber of herself as her magic burst, releasing thunderous tendrils of magic straight at Olivier, enveloping him in a cloud of red, silver, and violet flame. His eyes went wide as the threads overtook him, drowning him in a sea of color and squeezing until bones cracked. His body went limp on the ground, his black threads withering next to his lifeless body.

Selma turned to Razon. He lay unconscious. She could feel his threads fighting to stay aflame, their red light flickering. She tied her threads to his, cradling them. Letting them latch on to the last bits of power she had.

She slumped to the ground, her breaths shallow and her heartbeat slowing. She could hear someone yell her name in the distance, but she could not see anyone. Her body was weightless, as if she were floating in air. Then everything was quiet.

She was dying.

But maybe she had saved the people who had been willing to risk their lives for her. She had stopped Olivier, and maybe that would be enough. She felt warm threads wrapping around her, but nothing else. All she had to do was let go. She had never thought much about the afterlife, but the calmness beckoned her. This heat did not feel like the heat from before, when Olivier struck her. It felt warm, like the bonds she had touched earlier. Then the familiar threads cradled her, and Razon's perfect silver-specked eyes came into view. At least his face would be the last thing she saw before she left this world.

That thought cut at her. She would never see him again. Sadness tugged at her heart. The threads cradling her burned skin as she flailed. She wanted more time. She pulled at the threads in a desperate attempt to find her way back, all while focusing on Razon's eyes.

And then he was gone, and there was no more pain.

"You will be my salvation and my demise."

—Recovered correspondence from Warrior Razon Leclerc to Selma
Lourdes

CHAPTER 43

Voices trickled in. Her mind could not piece together their meaning or discern who they were coming from. The sounds were muffled under the weight of her eyelids. Her body felt warm and tightly wrapped. As she lay there in the darkness, Selma felt her nerves power on. A wave of electricity moved through her body, traveling from her fingertips down her spine and bringing her flesh to life. The warm wrap swaddling her began to feel too tight, and she attempted to push against it with her arms, but she did not make it far before the restriction stopped her. She still could not open her eyes, but the voices became increasingly clear.

A male and multiple female voices drifted in and out of her ears. Several long moments later, she lifted her lids. They ached. Everything ached. She could feel every inch of her body and the pain that accompanied it. Did that mean she was alive? Selma thought back, trying to recall what happened before she lost consciousness. She remembered Razon crawling toward her. And just then, a wave of panic raced through her. Was Razon still alive? Had the Order managed to kill him?

"You sure do put on a show." The witty, sultry voice of Emery broke through. Her figure was blurry, but Selma could make out her red lipstick. "The whole almost-dying part was a bit dramatic, but you saved our asses, so I'll take it."

Selma blinked, panic racing through her bones. "Leven." Her voice was hoarse.

"I'm fine. Thanks to you," Leven said. Selma could just make out his wide smile.

Tears fell down Selma's cheeks, and she could feel blood rushing to her limbs. Her fingers tingled as they began to regain mobility. She needed to ask, but she could not bring herself to. She needed to know if she had acted in time to save Razon. But her heart ached. It was not the same ache as her muscles, but deeper somehow.

"And him—?" Selma managed to get out before a deep voice interrupted her.

"His pride is bruised, but he will be just fine, princess," said Razon.

He met her grasp and wrapped his fingers around hers. He brought his lips to her palm and kissed it gently.

"We lost you there for a minute," he whispered.

"It was a little more than a minute," Emery added.

"Well, I feel like death, so that tracks," Selma retorted, letting out a hoarse chuckle.

Razon gave her a half smile. "I will never let that happen again."

Leven snorted. "She saved your ass. It looks like *she* will never let that happen again."

"I'm good with that," said Razon, still smiling at Selma.

"Help me up." Selma braced her hands on each side of her, feeling a rigid wooden table. She was in Uma's house, on the dining table. Razon reached one hand for her lower back and kept holding Selma's hand with the other. She slowly sat up, careful to take stock of every part of her that hurt. She looked down at her torn shirt, her chest half exposed except for a bralette.

"So much for propriety," stuttered Selma.

But it was not her almost-bare chest that caught her attention. It was the intricately woven scar that spanned from each of her collarbones and down between her breasts, ending just above her belly button. It was pulsing as if it were alive.

Selma's confusion was evident as she asked, "What is this?"

Emery and Leven stared at each other, and then at Razon. His gaze was more stoic than she had ever seen.

"It's a relic," he said, not taking his eyes off her. "It happens when one life is bonded to another. You were burning out from the release of power, and this was the only way to bring you back."

Selma must have been still fuzzy from her injuries, because she could not seem to find an appropriate follow-up question. Razon unbuttoned his black shirt, revealing the same marking. But his was much larger.

"You mean…?" Selma paused as Razon nodded his head.

"Yes, Selma. Your life is bonded to mine. It was the only thing I could do to save you," he added.

The others left the room to give them privacy. Selma swallowed, trying to think of what that may mean. Razon walked over to her and put his hands on her cheeks.

"This does not mean that your life is not your own. You're welcome to leave at any time and live your life separately from me. I will respect any decision you make," he said.

Selma looked into his silver-speckled eyes and knew he meant it. She did not need to summon her power to know.

"But does it mean that if I die, then you die?" Her question struggled to step off her tongue.

Razon nodded. "And the same for you." He looked weary, as if waiting for her to lash out.

"I thought the Order had drugged you," Selma murmured quietly, recounting the moments just before the battle.

They were both silent for a moment. Razon lowered his head. "They did. We were right about the Brocken. They have harnessed its power and created a toxin. We will need to find it before they do. Do you remember anything after Olivier died?"

"Not much. I reached out to you," Selma responded.

He nodded in agreement. "Your threads fed magic back into me somehow. Not much is known about Mavens, but we think it has something to do with your unique abilities. That's how I was able to summon a relic and bind us."

As life-altering as this information seemed to be, Selma had too many other questions. "What of the Order? The witches in servitude? We need to help them."

Razon dropped his hands and responded, "The Order has weakened since you took Olivier out. Many got away. But this will rally the Wargraves to rise up and help. You did good, princess."

"I think we should establish a new council, one where all the factions are represented. I do not know exactly how, but if the Order has been keeping magic from the people it rightfully belongs to, then it is time we give it back," Selma declared. "I want other witches and warlocks to find their magic."

"I think that sounds perfect. Emery is already calling a meeting of the Wargraves. We can discuss it there," he said. "We will also need to inform them of Alister."

Selma's heart sank. She was so relieved to be alive she had almost forgotten that she had witnessed her father's final moments. But he had given her the most precious gift before he died—she had felt seen and loved.

"He will be missed," Razon added.

Selma nodded in agreement.

A slender figure slid around the corner wearing a wide smile. Millie walked up to Selma and wrapped her arms around her.

Selma's voice cracked through wet tears. "Millie, you are here! How are you feeling?"

"I'm going to be okay, thanks to you and this smoke show," she said. "Are we going to talk about him when he leaves the room?"

Selma laughed, and Razon took that as his cue to leave. Millie had color back in her cheeks, and she was as radiant as Selma remembered. It was all worth it.

Selma looked around the house she grew up in. It no longer felt the same. Nothing did. Her skin hummed with magic, and there were so many people who were intricately tied to her now. There had been so much death, and everything she thought she knew now lay shattered.

She looked down at her relic. It may have been a new life, but it felt freshly broken. She put her palm on her chest. And now she had another life to be responsible for.

GLOSSARY

Common: *com·mon* [kämən] Witches or Warlocks born with magic blood, but do not have control of the elements nor access threads.

Elemental: *el·e·men·tal* /el'əmen(t)l/ A faction of magic made up of Witches or Warlocks born with the ability to feed off of raw energy and wield elements such as water, earth, air or flame.

Wargrave: *war·grave* [wôr'grāvz,gräv] Worshippers of the Goddess Sever. A sub-faction of warriors created by ancient means and gifted with powerful magic by the Goddess to protect all sentient beings. Devoted to honor, life and the safe pursuit of magic.

Maven: *ma·ven* /ˈmāv(ə)n/ Faction of magic made up of Witches or Warlocks born with the ability to feed off raw energy and wield elemental and spirit magic. Thought to be extinct.

Canon: *can·non* /ˈkanən/ A formal ancient doctrine stating the Wargraves guiding principles and laws.

Goddess Saint: god·dess saint /ˈgädəs əv sānt/ Being perfect in power, worshipped, creator and ruler of life, light, Spring and Summer.

Goddess Sever: *god·dess sev·er* /ˈgädəs əv sevər/ Personal supreme spirit, worshipped, creator and ruler of death, dark, Autumn and Winter.

Edicts of Order: *e·dict of or·der*/ˈēdik(t)s əv ˈôrdər/ A testament of fundamental laws or established precedents according to which all factions of magic must be acknowledged to be governed.

Axiom: *ax·i·om*/ˈaksēəm/ Fundamental tenants of the Maven.

Order: or·der /ˈôrdər/ Ruling council of warlocks made up of one member of each of the six founding elemental families appointed to rule over all factions of magic.

ACKΠOWLEDGEMEΠTS

This has been such an amazing process for me, and I have not been on this journey alone. There is a band of people and businesses that have been my cheerleaders along the way for without this book it would not have been possible.

‡

I would like to thank Humble House Cafe in Golden, Colorado for providing a comfortable writing trailer for me and my Portuguese Water Dog to punch out my first draft. It was my first safe space for writing and I'm not sure I would have ever even started without it. The caffeine boost did not hurt either.

‡

My appreciation would not be complete without acknowledging Ms. V. Whose passion for the written word ignited a fire that I was not able to squelch. Your lessons dug deeper than 'I before E' and

I think of you every time I pick up the proverbial quill.

‡

Next, I have to thank my perfect baby boy, Zoidberg for being my writing buddy. He has heard more drafts than anyone. Such a good boy.

‡

This would also not have been possible without my friend, Julia. As a debut author herself, she was such an amazing sounding board, and it has been wonderful to have a partner in crime that also had no idea what they were doing.

‡

I would like to thank STENO Denver for providing a welcoming space for me to hunker down and finish my edits. Again, the caffeine boost did not hurt either.

‡

Megan and Sarah, for whom without I would not have fallen in love with this genre and have both ignited my love of reading and writing again. I truly cherish the time we spend talking about books and your hilarious banter is the unofficial soundtrack to my writing process.

‡

To the Bergs, you are always my cheerleaders, and I am pretty sure that if I told you that I wanted to be a princess that you would be the first ones to jump on board and help me fit my tiara. Thank you, always, for everything.

‡

Cory, my creative hype person. Thank you for saying, 'yes' whenever I bring up another crazy creative journey. You have a unique way of harnessing enthusiasm, while still maintaining credibility in your critiques.

‡

To Jaime, my "dead body in the trunk" friend. No, there is not a dead body in the trunk, but when I call you to tell you I'm going to ignore my successful career and become an author, you are always down with no questions asked. So, I guess in this scenario the dead body in the trunk is my career. You get the picture. Thank you!

‡

And last, but certainly not least, my loving and ever-present husband, Rex. I have already dedicated this book to you, but nothing ever seems enough to express how much joy, love, and support I feel from you. This would not have been possible without you.

ABOUT THE AUTHOR

Zamantha is a life-long lover of art and regularly suffers from an inclination to jump into the deep end without floaties. Or to put in a phrase, "How hard can it be?"

Hard. It will be hard.

An artist stuck in a creative rut is a death sentence. So, Zamantha, author of Threads of Saint and Sever, is also many other things. She is dedicated to creativity and the pursuit of splendor. Rooted in Denver with Mr. Roberts and her fluffy Portuguese water puppy, Zoidberg. She continues to be inspired by the stories that transport us wherever the wind might take us.

www.instagram.com/misszimmie

www.tiktok.com/@zimmiejoeh